Night Games

Arthur Schnitzler

Night Games

AND OTHER STORIES AND NOVELLAS

Translated from the German by Margret Schaefer

With a Foreword by John Simon

IVAN R. DEE

Chicago • 2002

NIGHT GAMES and Other Stories and Novellas, by Arthur Schnitzler. English translation copyright © 2002 by Margret Schaefer. The special contents of this edition copyright © 2002 by Ivan R. Dee, Inc. All rights reserved, including the right to reproduce this book or portions thereof in any form. For information, address: Ivan R. Dee, Publisher, 1332 North Halsted Street, Chicago 60622. Manufactured in the United States of America and printed on acid-free paper.

Library of Congress Cataloging-in-Publication Data:
  Schnitzler, Arthur, 1862–1931.
    [Short stories. English. Selections]
    Night games and other stories and novellas / Arthur Schnitzler ; translated from the German by Margret Schaefer ; with a foreword by John Simon.
      p. cm.
    Contents: A farewell—Blind Geronimo and his brother—The second—Night games—Baron von Leisenbohg's destiny—The widower—The dead are silent—Death of a bachelor—Dream story.
    ISBN 1-56663-386-9 (alk. paper)
    1. Schnitzler, Arthur, 1862–1931—Translations into English. I. Schaefer, Margret. II. Title.

PT2637.N5 A28   2002
833'.8—dc21

                                                        2001028196

Contents

Foreword

TIME WAS when unrecognized geniuses were the order of the day. One almost had to die in relative obscurity before the world discovered one's importance. Today the reverse obtains. In a twinkling, some young hotshot is declared absolutely indispensable; then, in the time it takes for the media to start pumping up the next one, our purported genius is history—albeit not history of art, music, or literature.

There remains, though, to this day the odd undervalued genius, not so much undiscovered as neglected. A prime example of this is the Austrian novelist, short-story writer, and playwright Arthur Schnitzler (1862–1931). Although he thought of himself as of the second rank, and although his fame has faded somewhat even in German-speaking countries (while his popularity in France is considerable), I do not doubt that he will in time be recognized as the master he was, the equal or superior of such other Austrian geniuses—even if they came from Prague or some other part of the far-flung Austro-Hungarian Empire— as Kafka, Musil, Rilke, Hofmannsthal, Horváth, and Roth, to name only the most obvious ones.

For me, Schnitzler belongs in the vicinity of Proust, Joyce, and Chekhov. Like Proust, he can analyze psyches down to their subtlest, most secret tremors and convey this in complex, refined, and chiseled language. Like Joyce, and well before him, he put the stream of consciousness to supremely character-revealing use while also evoking the atmosphere and essence of a big city. And like Chekhov—both in drama and narrative—he brought to pulsating immediacy any number of dashingly histrionic or shadowily marginal lives, bestowing on most of his characters a fine compassion never veering into sentimentality, patronization, or special pleading.

These Schnitzler characters, on page or stage, speak a language that blends near-scientific naturalism with a soaring, but never uncontrolled, poetry (in the fiction, of course, located more often in the descriptions). Schnitzler is the lyricist of mundane existence, the comically or cuttingly ironic observer, the nonbeliever in any transcendence who nevertheless flirts with mysticism and searches in the nooks and crannies of vanity, greed, concupiscence, hypocrisy, and even banality for that which might still deserve the designation Soul.

Although Eros and Thanatos, sexual love and death, were his chief concerns, he was alert to all the strange, irrational, indeed extraordinary vagaries and pitfalls of so-called ordinary life. Grist for his exceedingly fine mill were the transience of love, the mysteries of contempt and hate, the dark forces toying with human behavior, the fragility, brevity, or futility of lives. Though the exercise of any, even the most trivial, kind of power matters greatly to Schnitzler's characters, erotic fulfillment is an equally consuming pursuit, even if—as these stories illustrate—bliss is pitifully short-lived, often lasting no longer than one night or just a single hour.

But this melancholy evanescence and its accompanying frustrations are examined with the scientific rigor of a physician, which Schnitzler for many years was. His eminent laryngologist father coerced Arthur to follow in his footsteps, though the youth's heart was in aesthetic and bohemian pleasures for which the Vienna of that period was ideally suited, and which Arthur did not wholly give up. An empire in its decline is the breeding ground for both a heartbreakingly true art and for epicurean, even convulsively decadent, pursuits. The close proximity of nonchalant wealth and throttling poverty (and the easy fall from one to the other through various kinds of gambling) made for, among other things, the kind of sexual exploitation by idle young gentlemen to which pretty but impecunious young women readily exposed themselves. And not only they: also well-off but underoccupied young housewives, the targets of artists and minor but indulged aristocrats, usually members of the officer class.

It was a snake-filled Eden. As the distinguished historian Golo Mann put it: "Why did Austrian statehood that exhibited so many tolerant traits nevertheless end up becoming so culpable? Alas, there was much hatred in old Austria, and Vienna itself, golden Vienna, spawned it as a marsh does feverish diseases. Hate of the little folks for the Jews (of whom there were numerous and affluent ones in the capital), stirred up by demagogues but extending even to major political parties; hate of the burgers for the Social Democrats; hate of the constituent nationalities, Germans and Slavs, for each other; hate of the unsuccessful for the more prosperous: Hate."

As the literary historian Ernst Alker observed: "If much of [Schnitzler's writing] may now feel like curiosities of an inconceivably idyllic era whose people, despite favorable living conditions, had a knack for being very unhappy, the fact remains that a vanished epoch here achieves its literary expression." Or, to quote another scholar, Reinhart Müller-Freienfels, we have here "the finally vain attempt of [Schnitzler's] characters to escape the comfortless reality of their existence into fantasies and self-deceptions, into art, into the attitude of the distanced spectator, even into suicide; at last also into concentration on the immediate, unmediated moment."

So there was Dr. Schnitzler (even if literary success had made him relinquish medical practice), the cool-eyed diagnostician of the age's excesses—including his own; and Arthur the poet, several of whose plays are indeed in polished verse, and all of whose prose is suffused with a poet's hypersensitive perceptions. In short, a hard-nosed realist and elegiac post-romantic in the same skin. Perhaps the greatest tribute Schnitzler received was from his erstwhile colleague and friend Sigmund Freud, who subsequently stopped associating with him for fear—supreme compliment!—of falling too much under his influence. Even so, Freud wrote Schnitzler in 1906: "I often asked myself in amazement where you could have gotten this or that secret knowledge I had to acquire through painstaking investigation of the subject, and I eventually got to the point of envying the writer whom I otherwise admired." And again in 1922, on Schnitzler's sixtieth birthday, "At the root of your being, you are a psychological depth explorer as honestly unprejudiced and unafraid as anyone ever."

To repeat, then, in no other writer is the febrile polarity Love (or Sex) and Death more powerfully ubiquitous than in Arthur Schnitzler, scion of the dying Habsburg Empire. Why is it that periods that so thrill to sex are also thrall to death? Is it identification with threatening social change? Or is the post-coital *animal triste* in a state of exhaustion and blankness that presages annihilation? Or is the swift waning of ecstasy— the death of passion—the foreshadowing of death itself?

In his bachelor days as *junger Herr,* the handsome Schnitzler was less successful than others with the *süsse Mädel* (sweet young girls). His most enduring affair was with Jeanette (actually Anna) Heger, a needleworker with whom he fell into instant reciprocal love. About a previous girl he had written: "I could not seem to be completely happy with her. I don't think I am wrong in ascribing the blame for this to the hypocritical element in my nature and the capital of mistrust that went with it, which paid dividends in the form of self-torture and the desire to torture others; but I was also irked that I was wasting my time, my thoughts, my finest emotions on a basically insignificant creature."

Eventually the fine passion for Jeanette took a similar turn: "Now we were together evening after evening, yet somehow couldn't be happy. I tormented her incessantly with my jealousy, strangely enough not in connection with the months just gone by but with the more distant past. She wept, kissed my hands humbly, yet couldn't assuage me. Sometimes—and not under the influence of some baseless hypochondriac mood or other—I felt on the verge of despair and filled with dread as I realized the futility and irrevocable passing of the years."

In these passages, as in countless others from Schnitzler's letters and memoirs, you recognize the traits of the typical Schnitzler hero and some of his female companions. It may be that what made the writer such a keen dissector of neurotic relationships was that he was his own best physician as well as neediest patient.

It is no accident that of the nine stories herein included, eight revolve wholly or in large measure around a death. The ninth contains no death and ends on a positive note as a blind beggar realizes that his sighted brother was not stealing from him but for him; yet the realization comes as the two are about to be delivered to the law.

Still, that is as close as we get to a happy ending. But what about *Dream Story,* which owes its recent celebrity to Stanley Kubrick's wretched movie version, *Eyes Wide Shut*? In it, a young married couple become briefly estranged: he through a rather harmless confession of his wife's that piques his jealousy, and through some nocturnal adventures that indirectly turn him even more against her; she through a dream betokening intense latent resentment of her husband. Yet, in the end, they are reconciled and seem to resume normal family life. But did not their strongest sexual fulfillment come after a masked ball at which each of them was aroused by seductive strangers? What does this say for their future happiness?

Schnitzler's focus is admittedly narrow. Dueling, for example, which he execrated, claims one life in these stories and raises its head in a couple of others. The experience of a lover at the deathbed of his adulterous beloved has its counterpart in a scene where a husband discovers at the deathbed of his wife that his best friend, who has come to console him, was sleeping with her. But such similarities hardly matter because what Schnitzler explored so inspiredly was the particular, the individual, the unique, however superficially similar to some other particular and unique. He himself defined his procedure: "To be an artist means to know how to polish the rough surfaces of reality so smooth that it may mirror all of infinity from the heights of heaven to the depths of hell." But what if this mirror is not so huge, merely a pocket mirror handled with surpassing dexterity?

In a typically waspish essay, the brilliant but malicious critic Karl Kraus described Schnitzler as "standing between those who hold a mirror up to the time, and those who hold a bedroom screen up to it; somehow he belongs in the boudoir." What was intended as a dig comes out a compliment. Yes, Schnitzler was, though a reflector of his times—note the pungent details, piquant digressions, apparent irrelevancies with which he enriches his stories, creating a background almost as dense and absorbing as the foreground—even more one of those Chinese or Japanese screens that modestly concealed people's beds. But weren't those very screens witnesses to two supreme human experiences: the making of love and the meeting up with death?

So yes, Schnitzler divided his attention between the often anti-climactic everyday and the dramatic climaxes of love and death. He encompassed great passions, great hatreds, and great losses. Also petty obsessions, ludicrous peeves, and stony detachments. You cannot read him without feeling that this man really *understood.* And, in feeling that, learn from him.

JOHN SIMON

Night Games

Night Games

"LIEUTENANT! . . . LIEUTENANT! . . . LIEUTENANT!" Only after the third call did the young officer move, stretch himself, and turn his head toward the door. Still half asleep, he growled from between the pillows, "What's going on?" Then, having roused himself, and seeing that it was only his orderly standing in the shadow of the half-opened door, he shouted, "What the devil do you want so early in the morning?"

"There is a gentleman below in the courtyard, sir, who wishes to speak with you, sir."

"What do you mean, a gentleman? What time is it? Didn't I tell you not to wake me on Sundays?"

The orderly walked over to the bed and handed Wilhelm a visiting card.

"Do you think I'm an owl, you blockhead? Do you think I can read in the dark? Pull up the shades!"

Even before the command was finished, Joseph had opened the inner shutters of the window and drawn up the dirty white curtain. The lieutenant, half sitting up in bed, could now read the name on the card. He let it fall on the bedcovers, looked at it again, ran his fingers through his blonde, close-cropped, morning-messy hair, and thought quickly: "Send him away? Impossible! I don't really have any reason to. Just because I receive someone, that doesn't imply that I'm close friends with him. Anyway, it was only because of his debts that he had to quit the regiment. Others just have better luck. But what could he want from me?"

He turned back to his orderly: "How does he look, the first lieut—I mean, Herr von Bogner?"

The orderly replied with a broad but somewhat melancholy smile: "If I may be permitted to say so, sir, the first lieutenant looked better in uniform."

Wilhelm was silent for a moment, then sat up more comfortably in the bed. "Well, ask him to come in. And beg the—first lieutenant—to be so good as to excuse me if I'm not quite dressed. And see here—if any of the other officers should ask for me, First Lieutenant Höchster or Lieutenant Wengler, or the captain, or anyone else—I'm not at home. Understand?"

As Joseph closed the door behind him, Wilhelm hurriedly pulled on his shirt, ran a comb through his hair, and, crossing to the window, looked down into the still-deserted courtyard of the barracks. As he saw his former comrade walking up and down with bowed head, a stiff, black hat pressed down over his forehead, in an unbuttoned yellow overcoat and brown, not very clean shoes, he felt a pang of sympathy. He opened the window and was almost at the point of waving to the waiting man and greeting him out loud when he saw his orderly approach him and Wilhelm observed, by the anxious and drawn look on his old friend's face, with how much emotion he was waiting for the answer. Since it was favorable, Bogner's features lightened, and he disappeared with the orderly through the door beneath Wilhelm's window—which Wilhelm now closed, as though he suspected that the coming conversation would call for that kind of precaution. All at once the odor of forest and spring was gone again—that odor which permeated the courtyard of the barracks on such Sunday mornings, but which curiously enough could never be noticed on weekdays. Whatever happens, thought Wilhelm—and what could happen anyway?—I'm going to Baden today, and I'll have dinner at the Stadt Wien—if they don't keep me for dinner at the Kessners as they did the other day.

"Come in!" And with rather exaggerated cordiality, Wilhelm held out his hand. "How are you, Bogner? I'm delighted to see you. Won't you take off your coat? Yes, look around; everything's the same as ever. The place hasn't gotten any larger. But there's room enough in the smallest hut for a happy . . ."

Otto smiled politely, as if he were aware of Wilhelm's embarrassment and wished to help him out of it. "I hope," he said, "that your quote about the 'smallest hut' is usually more apt than it is at the moment."

Wilhelm laughed more loudly than was necessary. "Unfortunately, it isn't often. I live quite simply. I assure you, no female foot has stepped into this room for at least six weeks. Plato was a womanizer compared to me. But do sit down." He took some linen from a chair and threw it on the bed. "And may I offer you a cup of coffee?"

"Thank you, Kasda, don't go to any trouble for me. I've already had breakfast. . . . A cigarette, though, if you don't mind. . . ."

Wilhelm wouldn't permit Otto to use his own cigarette case but pointed to the smoking stand, where an open box of his cigarettes was lying. Wilhelm offered him a light, and Otto silently took a few puffs, glancing at the well-known picture that hung on the wall above the black leather sofa and depicted an old-fashioned officers' steeplechase.

"Well, now tell me about yourself," said Wilhelm. "How've you been? How come no one has heard from you for such a long time? When we parted—two or three years ago now—you did promise that from time to time you—"

Otto interrupted him: "It was better, perhaps, that I let no one see or hear of me, and it would certainly have been better if I hadn't been obliged to come to you today, either." And, to Wilhelm's surprise, he suddenly sat down in a corner of the sofa whose other corner was filled with a clutter of well-thumbed books. "For, as you may well imagine, Willi"—he spoke rapidly and sharply—"my visit today, at this unusual hour—I know you like to sleep in on Sundays—my visit, of course, has a purpose. Otherwise I'd certainly not have allowed myself—to be brief, I've come in the name of our old friendship—unfortunately, I can't say our 'comradeship' any longer. You don't have to turn so pale, Willi; it's nothing dangerous. It's a question of a few gulden, which I simply must have by tomorrow morning, because if I don't, there's nothing left for me to do but"—his voice rose to a military pitch—"well—what I should have done two years ago if I had been wiser."

"Don't talk nonsense!" said Wilhelm in a tone of annoyance tempered by friendly embarrassment.

The orderly brought in breakfast and disappeared. Willi poured the coffee. He became conscious of a bitter taste in his mouth and felt peeved that he had not been able to complete his morning toilet. Fortunately he had planned to take a Turkish bath on his way to the station. He didn't need to be in Baden until around noon anyway. He hadn't made a definite appointment, and if he were to show up late—yes, even if he were not to come at all, no one would think it strange, neither the men in the Café Schopf nor Miss Kessner. Only her mother—who wasn't bad-looking herself—might wonder why he hadn't come.

"Please, do help yourself," he said to Otto, who had not yet put the cup to his lips.

Otto took a quick sip and started at once, "I'll be brief: maybe you know that for the last three months I've had a position as a cashier in the office of an electrical installation company. But why should you know that? You don't even know that I'm married and have a son—a four-year-old boy. You see, I already had him when I was here. No one knew. Well, anyway, things didn't go so well for me. You can imagine. It was especially bad this last winter. The boy was ill—well, the details can't really be of interest to you—and so I was forced to borrow from the cash drawer on a few occasions. I've always paid it back in time. But this time it was a bit more than usual, unfortunately, and"—he paused for a moment while Wilhelm stirred his coffee with his spoon—"and even worse, as luck would have it, I learned just by chance that this time, on Monday, tomorrow morning in other words, we're to be audited by the company headquarters. We're a branch, you understand, and we handle only very small accounts. Really, the amount I owe is trivial—nine hundred and sixty gulden. Let's say a thousand, more or less. But the exact amount is nine hundred and sixty. And that has to be there tomorrow by half past eight, otherwise—well, you get the idea. You really would be doing me a tremendous favor, Willi, if you could—"

Suddenly, he could go no further. Willi was a little embarrassed for him, not so much because of the petty cheating or—well, theft, that's what it really was—which his old comrade was guilty of, but rather because the former First Lieutenant Otto von Bogner—only a few years ago a popular, well-situated, and fashionable young officer—now sat pale and crumpled in a corner of the sofa, unable to go on talking because he was choking back tears.

He placed his hand on Otto's shoulder. "Come on, Otto," he said, "you don't have to take it so tragically." As if in answer to this not very auspicious beginning, Otto looked up at him with a desolate, frightened air, so Wilhelm added, "The trouble is, I'm pretty broke myself just now. My entire fortune at the moment consists of a little over a hundred gulden. A hundred and twenty, to be as exact as you were. Of course it goes without saying that the entire amount is at your disposal, down to the last kreuzer. But if we make an effort, I'm sure we can think of some way out."

Otto interrupted him. "You can be sure that I've already exhausted all the other—ways. So we don't have to waste time racking our brains unnecessarily—especially since I've come with a definite proposal."

Wilhelm looked at him intently.

"Try to imagine, Willi, that you found yourself in just such a difficulty. What would you do?"

"I don't quite understand," Willi replied defensively.

"Naturally, I know that you've never taken money from someone else's cash drawer—that's something that can only happen in civilian life. Okay. But still, if for some—less criminal—reason you desperately needed a certain sum of money, to whom would you turn?"

"I'm sorry, Otto, but I've never thought about something like that, and I hope . . . Of course, I don't deny that I've also sometimes had debts. Just last month Höchster helped me out with fifty gulden, which of course I repaid him on the first. That's why I'm so short right now. But a thousand gulden—a thousand!—I have absolutely no idea how I could get a hold of such a sum!"

"You really don't?" said Otto, looking him squarely in the eye.

"That's what I said."

"What about your uncle?"

"What uncle?"

"Your Uncle Robert."

"What—makes you think of him?"

"Why, it's obvious. He's helped you out on several occasions. And you have a regular allowance from him as well."

"There hasn't been an allowance for a long time now," answered Willi, annoyed by the inappropriate tone his former comrade had taken. "And not only is there no more allowance: Uncle Robert has become an eccentric. The truth is that I haven't set eyes on him for over a year now. And the last time I went to him for a little something—as a very special accommodation—well, he practically threw me out of the house."

"Hmm. Is that so?" Bogner rubbed his forehead. "So you really feel it's totally out of the question?"

"I hope you don't doubt my word," replied Wilhelm sharply.

Suddenly Bogner rose from the corner of the sofa, pushed the table aside, and went over to the window. "We have to try it anyway," he then said with certainty. "Yes, pardon me, but we must. The worst that can happen to you is that he'll say no. And maybe not too politely. But compared to what I'll have to face if I don't succeed in getting the few paltry gulden together by tomorrow morning, that's nothing but a little unpleasantness."

"Maybe," said Wilhelm, "but it would be an unpleasantness that would serve absolutely no purpose. If there were the slightest chance— well, I trust that you don't doubt my good intentions. But damn it, there must be other possibilities. For example—don't get angry, I just thought of it—what about your cousin Guido, the one who has the estate near Amstetten?"

"I assure you, Willi," Bogner replied calmly, "that there's no possibility of getting anything from him. If there were, I certainly wouldn't be here. In short, there's no person on the face of the earth—"

Willi suddenly lifted a finger, as if an idea had just struck him. Bogner looked at him expectantly.

"Rudi Höchster—what if you were to try him! Only a few months ago, as it happens, he received an inheritance. Twenty or twenty-five thousand gulden! He's got to have some of that left!"

Bogner wrinkled his brow, then replied with some hesitation, "Once, three weeks ago, when it wasn't half as urgent as it is now, I wrote to him, asking for much less than a thousand, and he never even answered me. So you see, there is just one possible solution—your uncle." And, as Willi shrugged his shoulders, he added, "After all, I know him, Willi—he's such a likable, charming old gentleman. We were at the theatre together several times, and at Riedhof's—he'll no doubt remember. For God's sake, he can't suddenly have become someone else!"

Willi interrupted him impatiently. "But it seems that he has! I don't know myself what's happened to him. But it's not uncommon for people between fifty and sixty to change in peculiar ways. I can't tell you any more than that—for at least fifteen months or more I haven't been in his house and—in short—I'll never under any circumstances enter it again."

Bogner stared ahead. Then suddenly he looked at Willi absentmindedly and said, "Well, sorry to have troubled you then. Goodbye." And, taking his hat, he turned to go.

"Otto," cried Willi, "wait! I have another idea."

"Another idea? Good!"

"Well, listen to me, Bogner. I'm going out to the country today—to Baden. There, on Sunday afternoons, in the Café Schopf, we sometimes gamble a little: a friendly game of twenty-one, or baccarat, as the case may be. Of course, I only play very modestly, if at all. I've played three or four times, mostly just for the fun of it. The main organizer is Dr. Tugut, the regiment doctor, who incidentally has recently had a fantastic run of good luck. Lieutenant Wimmer is usually there, and Greising, of the 77th. . . . You don't know him. He's in treatment in Baden—on account of an old ailment. A few civilians also participate—a local attorney, the manager of the local theatre, an actor, and an older man, a certain Consul Schnabel. He's having an affair with an operetta singer—well, really a chorus girl—there. Those are the regulars. Two weeks ago, Tugut raked in no less than three thousand gulden from Schnabel in a single sitting. We played on the open veranda until six o'clock in the morning, to the musical accompaniment of the morning birds. The hundred and twenty gulden that I still have today I owe only to my endurance—otherwise I'd be totally broke. Tell you what, Otto—I'll bet a hundred of those hundred and twenty for you today. I know the chances of winning aren't overwhelming, but only a few days ago Tugut sat down with only fifty and got up with three thousand. And there is still another point—in the last few months I haven't had any luck at all in love. Maybe we can rely more on the old saying than on people!"

Bogner said nothing.

"Well—what do you think of my idea?" demanded Willi.

Bogner shrugged his shoulders. "Naturally, I thank you—obviously I'm not going to say no—even though . . ."

"Of course, I can't make any guarantees," Wilhelm interrupted with an exaggerated vivacity, "but in the end it's not risking very much. And if I win—whatever I win—a thousand of it is yours—at least a thousand. And if I should happen to make an extraordinary killing . . ."

"Don't promise too much," said Otto with a melancholy smile. "But I don't want to keep you any longer, for my own sake as well as yours. Tomorrow morning I will permit myself—rather . . . I'll wait for you tomorrow at half past seven, over there, near the Alser Church." With a bitter laugh, he continued, "We could have met there by chance." Silencing an attempt at a reply from Willi with a gesture, he added quickly, "Besides, I'm not going to stay idle in the meantime. I still have seventy gulden left. I'll bet those this afternoon at the races—at the ten-kreuzer window, of course."

He crossed over to the window with quick steps and looked into the courtyard of the barracks. "The coast is clear," he said, his mouth twisted into a bitter and sardonic smile. Pulling up his collar, he shook hands with Willi and left.

Willi sighed softly, pondered for a moment, and then hurried to get ready to leave. He wasn't very happy with the condition of his uniform. If he should win today, he would buy himself a new cape at the very least. He abandoned the idea of a Turkish bath because of the lateness of the hour and decided to take a carriage to the train. Two gulden more or less didn't really matter today, considering.

II

Getting off the train in Baden around noon, Willi found himself in excellent spirits. At the train station in Vienna he had had a very cordial conversation with Lieutenant Colonel Wositzky—an extremely disagreeable person when on duty—and two girls in his compartment had flirted with him so vivaciously that he was almost relieved when they didn't get out with him at his station, because he knew he would have had difficulty in carrying out his plan for the day if they had. Despite his good mood, however, he still felt inclined to reproach his former comrade Bogner, not so much because he had taken money from the cash drawer—since that, given his unlucky circumstances, was to a certain degree excusable—but more because of the stupid gambling scandal by which he had so abruptly cut off his promising career in the service three years ago. An officer, after all, ought to know just how far he could go in that sort of thing. For example, three weeks ago, when he had been dogged by bad luck, he had simply gotten up from the card table, even though Consul Schnabel had offered him access to his wallet in the most charming way. In fact, he had always known how to resist temptation, and he had always succeeded in making ends meet on his small salary and the meager allowances he had received, first from his father, and then, after his father's death as a lieutenant colonel at Emesvar, from his Uncle Robert. And when these small additions to his salary had stopped, he had known how to make do with less: he had stopped going to the cafés as frequently, cut down on new purchases, saved on cigarettes, and determined that women should no longer cost him anything at all. Indeed, just three months ago a little adventure that had begun most auspiciously had failed because Willi had literally not been able to pay for a dinner for two on a certain evening.

It was truly sad, he decided as he thought about it. Never before had he been so aware of the narrowness of his circumstances as he was today—on this beautiful spring day—as he wandered through the fragrant gardens of the country estate in which the Kessner family lived and which they probably owned, wearing a cape that was showing signs of wear, shabby trousers that had begun to shine at the knees, and a cap that sat much lower than the latest officer style demanded. Today he also realized for the first time that his hope for an invitation to dinner—or rather, the fact that such an invitation was something he *needed* to hope for— was shameful.

Nevertheless he was by no means displeased when his hope was fulfilled, not only because the meal was tasty and the wine excellent, but also because Fräulein Emily, who sat at his right, proved to be an exceedingly agreeable table companion with her friendly glances and her familiar touches—which, to be sure, could have been merely accidental. He was not the only guest. There was also a young lawyer whom the head of the household had brought from Vienna and who knew how to lead the conversation into light, gay, and at times ironic channels. The host was polite but somewhat cool toward Willi: in general he didn't seem altogether pleased by the Sunday visits of the lieutenant, who had taken entirely too literally the invitation to stop in sometime for tea which the ladies of the house, to whom he had been presented at a ball during last year's Carnival, had extended to him. And the still attractive lady of the house apparently didn't remember that only two weeks ago, while seated on a secluded bench in the garden, she had withdrawn herself from the lieutenant's unexpectedly bold embrace only when sounds of approaching footsteps on the adjoining gravel path became audible. The first subject of conversation at table, a suit that the lawyer was pursuing for the head of the household in a matter related to the latter's factory, was conducted in terms sometimes barely comprehensible to the lieutenant. But fortunately the conversation then turned to the subject of country life and summer travel, giving Willi the opportunity to jump in. Two years ago he had participated in the imperial maneuvers in the Dolomites, and now he was able to tell of camping under the open sky, of the two dark-haired daughters of a Kastelruth innkeeper who had been called the Two Medusas because of their unapproachability, and of a certain field marshal who, almost before Willi's very eyes, had fallen into disgrace as a result of a bungled cavalry attack. And, as always after his third or fourth glass of wine, he became less and less awkward, more gay, almost witty. He could feel that he was gradually winning the host's favor, that the lawyer's tone was gradually becoming less and less ironic, and that a certain memory was beginning to surface in the lady of the house. The energetic push from Emily's knee no longer took the trouble to appear accidental.

For coffee, a somewhat corpulent, elderly lady appeared with her two daughters. Willi was introduced to them as "our dancer from the Industry Ball." It soon developed that the three ladies had also been in South Tirol two years ago; and wasn't it the lieutenant whom they had seen galloping past their hotel in Seis on a stallion one beautiful summer day? Willi was reluctant to deny this, though he knew very well that he, an obscure lieutenant of the 98th Infantry, could never have been seen charging through any village, in Tirol or anywhere else, on a proud stallion.

The two young ladies were attractively clad in white. Fräulein Kessner, in light pink, was in the middle as all three ran mischievously over the lawn.

"Just like the three Graces, aren't they?" observed the lawyer. Again it sounded like irony, and the lieutenant was tempted to challenge him: just how do you mean that, Herr Doctor? Yet it was all the easier to suppress this remark as Miss Emily, out on the lawn, had just turned around and was beckoning him to join her. She was blonde, slightly taller than he was, and it could be presumed that she had expectations of a rather considerable dowry. But to get to that stage—if one might even dare to dream of such a possibility—would take a long time, a very long time, and meanwhile the thousand gulden that his unlucky comrade needed had to be acquired by tomorrow morning at the latest.

So there was nothing left for him to do, in the interests of former First Lieutenant Bogner, but to make his excuses just as the party was at its best. They acted as though they wanted to keep him, and he voiced his regrets: unfortunately he had made an appointment; and, most especially, he had to visit a comrade who was taking a cure in the nearby military hospital for an old case of rheumatism. The lawyer responded to all this with his usual ironic smile. Would this visit occupy the whole afternoon? Frau Kessner, with a smile full of promise, wanted to know. Willi shrugged his shoulders uncertainly. Well, at any rate, they would all be happy to see him again in the course of the evening if he should manage to get free.

Just as he was leaving the house, two elegant young men rode up in a carriage. This did not please Willi at all. What kind of wonderful things might happen in this house while he had to earn a thousand gulden in a café for the sake of a compromised comrade? Wouldn't it be far wiser just to abandon the whole affair and to return in half an hour or so to the beautiful garden and the Three Graces, pretending to have visited his sick friend? All the wiser, he thought with self-satisfaction, as—if the old saying was to be believed—his chances for winning at cards must just have sunk precipitously with this unexpected good luck with the ladies.

III

A large yellow poster advertising the races stared at him from a kiosk, and it occurred to him that at this hour Bogner must be at the Freudenau races, perhaps at this very minute winning the sum that would save him. Might Bogner not conceal such a lucky win in order to get the thousand gulden that Willi meanwhile would have won at cards from Consul Schnabel or the regiment doctor Tugut? Why certainly—since he had already sunk so low as to take money from a cash drawer that didn't belong to him . . . and in a couple of months or even a few weeks, mightn't Bogner be in exactly the same fix he was in today? And then what?

Willi heard music. It was some Italian overture, in that half-forgotten style in which only resort orchestras played nowadays. But Willi knew it well. Many years ago he had heard his mother in Temesvar play it four handed, with some distant relative. He himself had never gotten so far as to be able to serve his mother as partner in four-handed playing, and since she died eight years ago, there had been no more of the piano lessons that had been a standard feature of his visits home from the military academy on holidays. Softly and somewhat poignantly the music reverberated in the tremulous spring air. He crossed the little bridge over the muddy Schwechat, and after a few more steps he was standing in front of the spacious terrace of Café Schopf, crowded as usual on Sundays. Lieutenant Greising, the alleged patient, looking pale and malicious, was sitting at a little table near the street. With him sat Weiss, the fat theatre manager, in a somewhat rumpled, canary-yellow flannel suit, a flower in his buttonhole as usual. Willi pushed his way toward them between the tables and chairs with some difficulty. "I see there's nobody here today!" he called out, affably, extending his hand toward them. And suddenly he thought with relief that perhaps there would be no card game today. But Greising explained that the two of them, he and the theatre manager, were only sitting outdoors in order to strengthen themselves for the "work" to come indoors. The others were already inside at the card table. Consul Schnabel had arrived too, having, as usual, come from Vienna in a carriage.

Willi ordered an iced lemonade. Greising demanded to know where he had already so overheated himself that he needed a cooling drink, and then, without further preliminaries, remarked that the girls of Baden were decidedly good-looking and lively. Then, in not particularly well-chosen phrases, he told of a small adventure he had begun last evening in the Kurpark and which he had been able to bring to the desired conclusion that very night. Willi drank his lemonade slowly and Greising, who guessed what was going through his head, replied with a brief burst of laughter as though in answer, "Well, that's the way of the world, like it or not!"

Suddenly, First Lieutenant Wimmer, from the Transport Corps (whom the uninformed often mistook for a cavalryman), appeared behind them. "What are you thinking of, gentlemen? Are we supposed to plague ourselves to death with the consul all by ourselves?"

And he gave his hand to Willi, who had already conscientiously saluted his higher-ranking comrade, as was his custom even when off duty.

"How're things going inside?" asked Greising, brusquely and suspiciously.

"Very slowly," answered Wimmer. "The consul is already sitting on his gold like a dragon—on my gold, unfortunately, as well. So—up and into battle, my dear toreadors!"

The others rose. "I'm invited somewhere else," said Willi, lighting his cigarette with studied carelessness. "I'll just watch for a quarter of an hour."

"Ha," laughed Wimmer, "the way to hell is paved with good intentions." "And the way to heaven with bad ones," added Weiss, the theatre manager. "Well said," said Wimmer, and clapped him on the shoulder.

They went inside the café. Willi cast one last glance back over his shoulder out into the open air, over the roofs of the villas toward the hills. And he swore to himself that he would be sitting in the garden with the Kessners in no more than half an hour at the most.

Together with the other men he entered a dark corner of the café, a place where neither the spring air nor the spring light could penetrate. To show that he had absolutely no intention of joining the game, he pulled his chair way back from the table. The consul, a gaunt man of uncertain age, with a mustache trimmed English style and reddish, partly grey, thinning hair, elegantly dressed in a light grey suit, was studying, with the thoroughness that characterized him, a card which Dr. Flegmann, acting as banker, had just dealt him. He won, and Dr. Flegmann drew some brand-new bills from his wallet.

"He doesn't even bat an eyelash," noted Wimmer with ironic appreciation.

"Eyelash-batting doesn't change anything," answered Flegmann coolly, his lids half closed. Regiment Doctor Tugut, division chief of the military hospital in Baden, put down a bank of two hundred gulden.

This is not for me today! thought Willi, and pulled his armchair still farther back.

The actor Elrief, a young man of good family, more famous for his stinginess than for his talent, allowed Willi to see his cards. He bet small sums and shook his head in bewilderment when he lost. Tugut soon doubled his capital. The theatre manager Weiss borrowed some money from Elrief, and Dr. Flegmann took still more money out of his wallet. Tugut was on the point of withdrawing when the consul, without counting, cried, "The whole bank!" He lost, and with a quick reach into his wallet he made good his debt, which amounted to three hundred gulden. "Once more the whole bank!" he said. The regiment doctor declined. Dr. Flegmann took over as banker and dealt the cards. Willi declined to take one, and only for fun, at Elrief's continued urging, he placed a gulden on Elrief's card "to bring him luck"—and won. In the next round Dr. Flegmann tossed Willi a card which he didn't refuse. He won again, lost, won, pulled his chair up to the table between the others, who willingly made room for him, and won—lost—won—lost, as if fate could not quite decide what she had in store for him today. The theatre manager had to return to the theatre and forgot to give Elrief back the money he had borrowed from him, even though he had already won far more. Willi was a little ahead but was still nine hundred and fifty gulden short of the thousand he needed.

"Nothing's happening!" Greising declared, dissatisfied. The consul became the banker again, and at that moment everyone knew that the game was finally about to get serious.

Hardly anything more was known about Consul Schnabel other than that he was a consul, the ambassador of a small free state in South America, and a "wholesale merchant." It had been Weiss who had introduced him into the officers' circle, and the theatre manager's relationship with him came about because the consul had known how to interest him in hiring a minor actress, who, immediately upon her appearance in a small part, had entered into a more intimate relationship with Herr Elrief. The company would have enjoyed engaging in the good old custom of making fun of the deceived lover, but ever since he had casually asked Elrief, while dealing cards and without looking up, a cigar between his teeth, "Well, how's our little mutual lady friend?" it was clear that the consul could not be gotten the better of with jokes and taunts. This impression was substantiated by a remark he once made to Greising, who late one evening, after two glasses of cognac, had allowed himself an offensive remark about consuls of unknown countries. With a piercing look he had said, "Why are you taunting me, Herr Lieutenant? Have you already inquired as to whether I am of sufficient rank to give you satisfaction in a duel?"

A long, contemplative silence had followed this speech, but, as if by tacit agreement, no further consequences were drawn from this statement, and it was decided, without any explicit discussion, but unanimously, that the consul should be treated more gingerly.

The consul lost. No one objected when, against his usual custom, he immediately put down a new bank, and, after losing that one as well, still another. The other players won, especially Willi. He put his original capital, the one hundred and twenty gulden, back into his pocket—nothing would induce him to risk those again. Then he put down a bank himself. Soon he had doubled it. He withdrew, and with a few minor exceptions, his luck held out against the other bankers, who changed in quick succession. Soon he had already exceeded by a few hundred the thousand gulden he had set out to win—for someone else—and since Elrief now rose to go back to the theatre to rehearse a role—about which he would say nothing despite Greising's ironically expressed interest—Willi used the opportunity to leave with him. The others were soon deep in their game again, and when Willi turned around to look at them once more at the door, he saw that only the consul's eyes had left the cards to follow him with a quick, cold glance.

IV

Only now, as he once more stood outdoors with the soft evening air caressing his brow, did Willi fully realize the extent of his good luck, or rather, as he immediately corrected himself, of Bogner's good luck. Still, there was enough left over for him to buy himself a new cape, a new cap, and a new sword belt, just as he had dreamed. And even after that, there was still enough for a few suppers in some pleasant company, which he could easily attract now. Aside from all that—how satisfying to be able to give his old comrade the sum that would save him, tomorrow morning at half past seven in front of Alser Church!—he actually had a thousand gulden; yes, the celebrated thousand-gulden bill which he had only read about in books was in his wallet along with a few hundred-gulden bills. Well, my dear Bogner, here you are. A thousand gulden exactly. I've won them. To be more precise, I've won one thousand and one hundred and twenty-five. Then I stopped. Self-control, right? And I hope, my dear Bogner, from now on you'll also . . . No, no, he couldn't permit himself to preach a moral lesson to his former comrade. Bogner would get the point on his own, and one hoped he would be tactful enough not to feel that this windfall entitled him to enter into a closer relationship with Willi. Maybe it would be better after all, and more correct even, to send his orderly to Alser Church with the money.

On his way to the Kessners, Willi wondered whether they would ask him to stay for the evening meal as well. Well, fortunately the meal itself was no longer important to him! After all, he himself was now rich enough to invite the whole company to dinner! Too bad there was no place to buy flowers. But as he passed an open pastry shop, he decided to buy a box of chocolates; then, turning back again as he reached the door, he bought another, even larger one, and pondered how properly to divide them between mother and daughter.

When he entered the front garden of the Kessners' estate, a housemaid met him with the information that the Kessners had driven to the Helene Valley with everyone, probably to the Krainer Lodge. The Kessners would no doubt also have dinner out, as was their custom on Sunday evenings.

A mild disappointment painted itself on Willi's face, and the housemaid smiled at the two boxes that the lieutenant held in his hand. What should he do with these? "Please give my respects and—here"—he handed the housemaid the two packages—"the larger one is for the lady of the house, and the other one is for the Fräulein. And give them my regrets."

"Perhaps if the lieutenant were to take a carriage—they're probably still at the Krainer Lodge."

Willi looked at his watch ponderously and a little self-importantly.

"Well, I'll see," he remarked carelessly, gave a humorously exaggerated salute, and left.

He was now alone on the evening street. A small, merry band of tourists, ladies and gentlemen with dirty shoes, passed by. In front of a villa an elderly gentleman sat in a wicker chair reading the paper. A little farther up the street an elderly lady sat crocheting on a second-story balcony while speaking with a woman who was leaning out the open window of the house opposite, her arms crossed over the windowsill. It seemed to Willi as though these people were the only ones in the whole town who had not gone somewhere at this hour. The Kessners might have left word for him with the housemaid! Well, he had no intention of forcing himself on them. He really didn't need to do that. But what to do? Return to Vienna right away? That would perhaps be best. How would it be just to leave the decision to fate?

Two carriages stood in front of the casino. "How much to go to the Helene Valley?" One driver was already engaged, and the other demanded a really outrageous price. So Willi decided instead in favor of an evening walk in the park.

The park was still crowded at this hour. There were married couples and pairs of lovers, whom Willi thought he could distinguish with certainty. Many young girls and women walking alone or in twos or in threes lightheartedly passed him by, and he returned many a smiling, even encouraging, glance. But one could never be sure that a father, brother, or fiancé was not walking behind, and as an officer it was his duty to be doubly, even triply, careful. For a while he followed a dark-haired, slim woman who was leading a boy by the hand. She went up the stairs to the terrace of the casino, seemed to be looking for someone, at first unsuccessfully, until someone beckoned to her enthusiastically from a distant table, whereupon, giving Willi a quick, taunting look, she took her place in the middle of a large company. Willi then also pretended to be looking for someone, and went from the terrace into the restaurant, which was almost empty, and from there reached an entrance hall and then a reading room, already lit, where a retired general in uniform, the only guest, sat at a long, green table. Willi saluted and clicked his heels, the general nodded back crustily, and Willi hurried out again. Outside in front of the casino one of the carriages was still there, and the driver, unasked, now declared himself ready to take the lieutenant cheaply to the Helene Valley.

"Thanks, but it's too late now," Willi replied, and rapidly started back to the Café Schopf.

V

The players were still there, in exactly the same positions as before, as if not one minute had passed since Willi's departure. A light gleamed dimly from under a green shade. Willi believed he saw a taunting smile play around the mouth of the consul, who was the first to notice his arrival. No one expressed the slightest surprise when Willi again pulled his chair, which had remained empty, up to the table between the others. Dr. Fleg-mann, who was the banker at the moment, dealt him a card as though it were tacitly understood that he should do so. In his hurry, Willi bet a larger bill than he had intended. He won, and then proceeded more carefully. But his luck had changed, and soon there came a moment when his thousand-gulden bill seemed to be in grave danger. Well, what do I care? thought Willi; I wouldn't have had anything from it anyhow! But then he won again, and he didn't even find it necessary to change the thousand-gulden bill. His luck held, and around nine o'clock, when the game ended, Willi found himself in possession of over two thousand gulden. A thousand for Bogner, a thousand for me, he thought. I'll reserve half of it as a gambling purse for next Sunday. But he didn't feel as exultant as he ought to have under the circumstances.

The entire company adjourned to the Stadt Wien for dinner, sat in the garden beneath a shady oak, and spoke about gambling in general and in particular about famous card games played for high stakes at the Jockey Club. "It is, and always will be, a vice," Dr. Flegmann declared in all seriousness. Everyone laughed, but First Lieutenant Wimmer diverted himself by taking offense at the remark. What was perhaps a vice among lawyers, he said, was far from being one among officers. Dr. Flegmann explained politely that it was possible to have a vice and still be a man of honor, as countless examples showed: Don Juan, for example, or the Duc de Richelieu. The consul expressed the opinion that gambling was a vice only when someone couldn't pay his gambling debts. And in that case, he added, it was really not merely a vice but a fraud, and a fraud of a particularly cowardly kind at that. There was a moment of silence at this. But fortunately Herr Elrief appeared at this moment with a flower in his buttonhole and victory in his eyes. "You tore yourself away from the ovations?" asked Greising. "I don't appear in the fourth act," answered the actor, and carelessly drew off his glove as though rehearsing for an upcoming role as a viscount or marquis. Greising lit a cigar.

"Better if you didn't smoke!" said Dr. Tugut.

"But my dear doctor! There's nothing wrong with my throat any more," answered Greising.

The consul had ordered a few bottles of Hungarian wine. The company toasted one another. Willi looked at his watch. "Oh, I'm so sorry, but I have to go. The last train leaves at 10:40." "Finish your wine," said the consul. "I'll have my carriage bring you to the station." "Oh, Consul, thank you, sir, but I can't. . . ."

"Yes, you can," interrupted First Lieutenant Wimmer.

"Well, what's going on?" Dr. Tugut asked. "Are we going to continue playing tonight?"

No one had doubted that the session would be continued after dinner. The same thing happened every Sunday. "But not for long," the consul said.

"Lucky devils!" thought Willi, and envied them all the prospect of sitting down at the card table once more to try their luck and possibly win thousands. The actor Elrief, whose wine invariably went promptly to his head, conveyed to the consul a greeting from their mutual lady friend Fräulein Rihoscheck, with an inane and yet impudent expression on his face. "Why didn't you bring the young lady with you, Mr. Mime?" asked Greising. "She'll come later to the café to watch—if the consul permits," said Elrief. The consul did not react.

Willi finished his wine and stood up. "Till next Sunday!" said Wimmer. "We'll take a little of that weight off of you then!"

"In that," thought Willi, "you'll be disappointed. It's impossible to lose if one is cautious."

"Would you be so kind, Lieutenant, as to send my coachman immediately back from the station to the café?" asked the consul. And turning to the others, he added, "But, gentlemen, we can't play as late, that is, until as early, as we did last time!"

Willi once more saluted all around and turned to go. Suddenly, to his pleasant surprise, he saw that the Kessner family and the lady with the two daughters were sitting at an adjacent table. Neither the ironical lawyer nor the elegant young men who had driven up to the villa in a carriage were there. They greeted the lieutenant most amiably, and he remained standing at the table, gay and unaffected—a chic young officer in comfortable circumstances, not to mention three glasses of strong Hungarian wine, at this moment without rivals. He was invited to sit down but demurred gracefully with a vague gesture toward the entrance where the carriage was waiting for him. Still, he couldn't refuse to answer a few questions: who was the handsome young man in civilian clothes?—Ah, an actor!—Elrief?—No one had heard of him. The theatre here wasn't much to speak of, maintained Frau Kessner; there was not much more than operetta here. But with a promising glance she intimated that when the lieutenant came the next time, they could perhaps go together to visit the Arena Theatre.

"The nicest thing would be to take two boxes side by side," observed Fräulein Kessner, and smiled in the direction of Elrief, who smiled back enthusiastically.

Willi kissed the hand of all the ladies, once more saluted in the direction of the officer's table, and a minute later was sitting in the consul's carriage.

"Hurry," he said to the coachman. "You'll get a good tip."

In the indifference with which the driver received this promise, Willi thought he detected an annoying lack of respect. Still, the horses maintained a good clip, and in five minutes they were at the station. But at precisely the same moment the train, which had arrived just a minute earlier, began to move from the gate in the station above. Willi leaped from the carriage, started after the brightly lit coaches as they moved slowly and heavily forward across the viaduct, heard the whistle of the locomotive fade into the night air, shook his head, and didn't quite know whether he was angry or pleased. The coachman sat indifferently on his high seat and was stroking one of the horses with the handle of his whip. "There's nothing to be done," Willi finally declared. And, turning to the coachman, he directed, "Back to the Café Schopf."

VI

It was pleasant to whirl through the small town in a carriage, but next time it would be even more pleasant to drive out into the country, either to Rodaun or to the Rote Stadl, on such a mild summer evening as this, in the company of an attractive female creature, and to have supper outdoors. Ah, what bliss not to have to turn every gulden over twice before being able to decide to spend it! Careful, Willi, careful, he told himself, and firmly resolved not to risk all his winnings but only half of them at most. Moreover he would use Flegmann's system: begin with small bets, don't increase them until you have won, and then never risk the whole amount at once but only three-fourths of it, and so on. Dr. Flegmann always began with this system, but he didn't have the discipline to carry it through. So of course he got nowhere with it.

In front of the café, Willi swung himself off the coach before it had even stopped, and gave the coachman a generous tip, so much that he could have hired a carriage himself for the same amount. The coachman's gratitude still left something to be desired, but he was amiable enough.

The card party was still assembled and now included the consul's girlfriend, Fräulein Mitzi Rihoscheck—a stately-looking woman with excessively black eyebrows but otherwise not too highly made up, wearing a light summer dress and a flat-brimmed straw hat with a red band on her brown, well-waved hair. She sat next to the consul, one arm thrown across the back of his chair, watching his cards. He did not look up as Willi approached the table, yet the lieutenant could feel that the consul was at once aware of his arrival.

"Missed the train!" observed Greising.

"By half a minute," answered Willi.

"That's the way it goes," remarked Wimmer, and dealt the cards.

Flegmann was just excusing himself, having lost three times in a row with a small bet against a large one. Elrief was still in, though he had not a kreuzer left. A heap of bills lay in front of the consul.

"Big stakes tonight!" said Willi, and immediately bet ten gulden instead of the five he had intended. His boldness was rewarded: he won and kept winning. On a small side table stood a bottle of cognac. Fräulein Rihoscheck poured the lieutenant a small glass and gave it to him with an engaging smile. Elrief begged him for a loan of fifty gulden to be paid back punctually tomorrow at noon. Willi passed him the bill. A second later it had already wandered over to the consul. Elrief stood up, drops of perspiration on his forehead. At that moment Weiss arrived in his yellow flannel suit, and a whispered conversation resulted in his paying the actor back the money he had borrowed from him that afternoon. Elrief lost this last amount, too, and—quite unlike what the gallant viscount that he hoped to play soon would have done—shoved his chair back in a rage, stood up muttering a curse under his breath, and left the room. When he did not reappear after a certain time, Fräulein Rihoscheck also stood up, stroked the consul's hair with a delicate and abstracted gesture, and disappeared.

Wimmer and Greising, and even Tugut, had become careful as the end of the session approached. Only the theatre manager still displayed some boldness. But the game was gradually taking the form of a contest between Lieutenant Kasda and Consul Schnabel. Willi's luck had shifted; apart from the thousand he had reserved for his old comrade Bogner, he had scarcely a hundred gulden left. If these hundred go, I'm definitely stopping, he swore to himself. But he didn't believe it. What is this Bogner to me after all? he thought. I owe him nothing!

Fräulein Rihoscheck reappeared humming a melody, fixed her hair in front of a large mirror, lit a cigarette, took up a billiard cue, tried a few shots, put the cue back in the corner, and then amused herself by spinning alternately first the white, then the red, balls on the green cloth. A cold glance from the consul called her back to the table, and, humming once more, she took her place by his side again, resting her arm over the back of his chair. A student song, many voices strong, broke into the stillness that had long since settled outside. How are they going to get back to Vienna today? Willi wondered. Then it occurred to him that they could be students from the local gymnasium in Baden. Since Fräulein Rihoscheck had sat opposite him again, his luck was slowly returning. The song became more and more distant, and gradually died out. A bell struck in a church tower.

"A quarter to one," said Greising.

"This'll be the last round," declared the regiment doctor.

"A last round for everyone," suggested First Lieutenant Wimmer.

The consul indicated his agreement with a nod.

Willi didn't say a word. He won, lost, drank a glass of cognac, won, lost, lit a new cigarette, won and lost. Tugut's bank held for a long time. The consul finally relieved him of it with a large bet. Curiously enough,

Elrief reappeared after almost an hour's absence, and, still more curiously, he had money again. With an elegant indifference, as though nothing had happened, he sat down again in the manner of that viscount he would probably never play, and he had even added a new attitude of superior indifference, which he had really copied from Dr. Flegmann: half-closed, weary eyes. He put down a bank of three hundred gulden, as if that were the most commonplace thing to do, and won. The consul lost to him, then to the army doctor, and especially to Willi, who soon found himself in possession of no less than three thousand gulden. That meant a new military cape, a new sword belt, new linen, patent leather shoes, cigarettes, dinners for two and even three, rides in the Vienna Woods, two months' leave of absence with his vacation—and at 2 a.m. he had won four thousand two hundred gulden. There they lay before him, a concrete reality that could not be doubted—four thousand two hundred gulden, more or less. The others had all pulled back and scarcely played anymore.

"That's enough," said Consul Schnabel abruptly.

Willi was of two minds. If they stopped now, nothing more could happen to him, and that was good. At the same time he felt an uncontrollable, truly fiendish urge to continue playing, to conjure a few more, no, all of the remaining crisp thousand-gulden bills out of the consul's wallet into his own. That would be a hoard with which he could make his fortune! It didn't always have to be baccarat—there were also the horse races at Freudenau and the Trabrennplatz, and there were also fine casinos such as the one at Monte Carlo on the seacoast—with beautiful women from Paris. . . . While his thoughts drifted in this direction, the regiment doctor was trying to rouse the consul to one last round. Elrief poured the cognac as though he were the host. He himself was drinking his eighth glass. Fräulein Mitzi Rihoscheck swayed her body and hummed a soundless melody. Tugut gathered the scattered cards and shuffled them. The consul remained silent. Suddenly he called for the waiter and ordered two new, fresh decks of cards. Everyone's eyes lit up. The consul glanced at his watch and said, "Till half past two on the dot, and that's final!"

It was five minutes after two.

VII

The consul put down a bank larger than any this company had ever seen—three thousand gulden. Apart from the players and a single waiter, there was not a soul left in the café. The song of the morning birds was already drifting in through the open door. The consul lost, but for the time being he maintained himself as banker. Elrief had completely recovered his losses and withdrew from the game upon a warning glance from Fräulein Rihoscheck. The others, all somewhat ahead, played on modestly and carefully. Half the bank was still intact.

"The whole bank!" Willi suddenly proposed, and was frightened at his own words—at the very tone of his voice. Have I lost my mind? he wondered. The consul uncovered a nine, and Willi was fifteen hundred gulden the poorer. Remembering Flegmann's system, Willi now put down a ridiculously small sum, fifty gulden—and won. How stupid! he thought. I could have won the whole amount back at once! Why was I so cowardly?

"The bank, again!"

He lost.

"The bank, once more!"

The consul appeared to hesitate.

"What has come over you, Kasda!" cried the regiment doctor.

Willi laughed and felt an intoxication rise into his head. Was it the cognac that was dulling his reason? Evidently. Of course he had made a mistake; not in his wildest dreams had he intended to risk a thousand or two thousand on a single bet.

"Excuse me, Consul, I really meant—"

The consul did not let him finish. In an amiable tone he said, "If you didn't know how much money was in the bank, of course I will take your retraction into consideration."

"What do you mean, retraction into consideration, Consul?" Willi found himself saying. "A bet is a bet."

Was it really he who was speaking? His words? His voice? If he were to lose, it would be all over with the new military cape, the new sword belt, the dinners in attractive female company. He would have left only the thousand earmarked for that swindler Bogner—and he himself would be the same poor devil that he had been two hours ago.

Wordlessly, the consul uncovered his card. Nine. No one uttered the number out loud, yet it resounded loudly throughout the room like the echo of a ghost. Willi felt a strange moisture on his brow. Damn, that was quick! Well, at any rate, he still had a thousand gulden lying in front of him, maybe a few more. He didn't want to count them—that would bring bad luck. In any case, he was still considerably richer than he had been when he had stepped off the train today at noon. Today at noon? And, after all, nothing was forcing him to risk the whole thousand at once. He could begin again with a hundred or two hundred, using Flegmann's system. Only there was so little time left—hardly twenty minutes. There was silence all around.

"Lieutenant?" the consul began inquiringly.

"Ah—yes," Willi laughed, and folded the thousand-gulden bill together.

"Half, Consul," he said.

"Five hundred?"

Willi nodded. The others also placed bets, but merely out of formality. An end-of-the-game atmosphere was already settling over them. First Lieutenant Wimmer was standing up with his coat over his shoulders. Tugut was leaning over the billiard table. The consul uncovered his card.

"Eight." And half of Willi's thousand was gone. He shook his head as though something were amiss.

"The rest," he said, and thought to himself: I'm really quite calm. He uncovered his cards slowly. Eight. The consul had to buy a card. Nine. And the five hundred was gone, the thousand was gone. Everything was gone! Everything? No. He still had the hundred and twenty gulden with which he had come, more or less. Funny, suddenly he was once more the same poor devil he had been before. And outdoors the birds sang . . . as they had before . . . when he could have gone to Monte Carlo. Well, it was a pity, but now he really had to stop. He certainly couldn't risk the few gulden that he still had . . . he had to stop, though there was still a quarter of an hour left to play. What bad luck! In a quarter of an hour he could win five thousand gulden as easily as he had just lost them!

"Lieutenant?" asked the consul.

"I'm very sorry," replied Willi in a high-pitched, grating voice, and pointed to the few miserable bills lying in front of him. His eyes were almost laughing, and almost as a joke he placed ten gulden on a card. He won. Then twenty. And won again. Fifty—and won again. His blood mounted into his head; he could have cried with rage. Now his luck was back—and it was too late. And with a sudden, bold idea he turned to the actor who was standing behind him near Fräulein Rihoscheck.

"Herr von Elrief, would you be so kind as to loan me two hundred gulden?"

"I'm terribly sorry," replied Elrief, shrugging his shoulders aristocratically. "You saw that I lost everything, down to the last kreuzer, Lieutenant." It was a lie, and everyone knew it. But it seemed they found it quite proper that the actor Elrief should lie to the lieutenant. But the consul casually thrust a few bills to him across the table, seemingly without counting them. "Please help yourself," he said. Tugut cleared his throat audibly. Wimmer warned, "I'd stop if I were you, Kasda."

Willi hesitated.

"I don't wish to persuade you in any way, Lieutenant," said Schnabel. He still held his hand spread lightly over the money.

At that Willi hastily grasped the bills, then acted as if he wanted to count them.

"It's fifteen hundred," said the consul. "You can depend upon it, Lieutenant. Do you want a card?"

Willi laughed: "What else?"

"Your bet, Lieutenant?"

"Oh, not all of it!" cried Willi, his head clearing. "The poor have to be economical. One thousand to begin with."

He uncovered, imitating the consul's customary exaggerated slowness. Willi had to buy a card, and added a three of spades to his four of diamonds. The consul also uncovered; he, too, held a seven.

"I'd stop," warned First Lieutenant Wimmer again, and now his words sounded almost like a command. And the regiment doctor added, "Now, when you are just about even."

Just about even! Willi thought. He calls that "just about even!" A quarter of an hour ago I was a well-to-do young man; now I'm a beggar, and he calls that "even"! Should I tell them the story of Bogner? Maybe then they would understand.

New cards lay in front of him. Seven. No, he didn't want to buy a card. But the consul didn't even ask him; he simply uncovered an eight. A thousand lost! buzzed in Willi's brain. But I'll win it back! And if I don't, it won't make any difference. I can no more pay back a thousand than I can pay back two thousand. It's all the same now! Ten minutes is still time enough. I could even win back the four or five thousand I had before.

"Lieutenant?" asked the consul.

The words echoed through the room, for everyone was quiet, absolutely quiet. Will no one now say, "I'd stop if I were you?" No, thought Willi, no one has the audacity. They know it would be stupid for me to stop now. But what should he bet now? He had only a few hundred gulden lying in front of him. Suddenly there were more. The consul had pushed two thousand more his way.

"Help yourself, Lieutenant."

Indeed, he helped himself. He put down fifteen hundred and won. Now he could pay back his debt and still have something left over. He felt a hand on his shoulder. "Kasda," said First Lieutenant Wimmer behind him. "No more!" His voice sounded hard, almost severe. But I'm not on duty now, thought Willi, and I can do what I want with my money and my life! And he bet again, bet only a modest thousand gulden and uncovered the card he had been dealt. Schnabel took his time, playing with deadly slowness, as though they had all the time in the world. There was still time, indeed; no one was going to force them to stop playing at 2:30 a.m. The last time they had played until 5:30. The last time . . . that beautiful, distant time. Why were they all standing around him? It was as if in a dream. Ah, they were all more agitated than he was. Even Fräulein Rihoscheck, who was standing across from him, a straw hat with a red band on her well-waved hair, had curiously shining eyes. He smiled at her. She had a face like a tragic queen, though she was little better than a chorus girl. The consul uncovered his cards. A queen. Ha, Queen Rihoscheck and a nine of spades! That damned spade!—it always brought him bad luck. And the thousand wandered over to the consul. But what did it matter? He still had something left. Or was he already completely ruined? He hadn't the slightest . . . Suddenly there were a few more thousand in front of him. A noble man, that consul. To be sure, he was certain he would get them back. An officer, after all, had to pay his gambling debts. Someone like Elrief remained an Elrief in any case, but an officer, unless he was named Bogner . . .

"Two thousand, Herr Consul!"

"Two thousand?"

"Indeed, Consul!"

He didn't buy a card; he held with his seven. The consul had to buy. This time he didn't bother with ceremony; he was in a hurry, and he added an eight—an eight of spades—to his one, and that made nine. No doubt about it. The eight would have been enough by itself. And the two thousand wandered back to the consul—and then immediately back to Willi. Or was it more? Three or four thousand? Better not to look at all; that would bring bad luck. The consul wouldn't cheat him, and in any case the others were all standing around and watching closely. And since he no longer knew exactly what he already owed, he bet two thousand again. The four of spades. Yes, he was forced to buy at that. Six. The six of spades. So that made one too many! The consul didn't even have to make an effort, and he had only a three . . . and the two thousand wandered over to the consul again—and then immediately back. It was ridiculous! Forward and back, forward and back. The church tower clock struck again—the half-hour. But evidently no one had heard. The consul dealt the cards calmly. Everyone was standing around, all the men; only the regiment doctor had left. Yes, Willi had noticed how, a little while ago, he had shaken his head angrily and had mumbled something between his teeth. Evidently he couldn't bear to see how Lieutenant Kasda was playing for his life. How could a doctor have such weak nerves!

And again new cards lay in front of him. He bet—how much exactly he didn't know. A handful of bills. This was a new way to tempt fate. Eight. Now his luck had to change.

It did not. The consul uncovered a nine, looked around at the group, and then pushed the cards away. Willi opened his eyes wide. "Well, Consul?" But the consul lifted his finger and pointed outdoors, "It has just struck the half hour, Lieutenant."

"What," cried Willi, pretending to be astonished. "Couldn't we give it another quarter of an hour?"

He looked around the circle as though he sought approval. Everyone was silent. Herr Elrief looked away, very aristocratically, and lit a cigarette; Wimmer bit his lips; Greising whistled nervously, almost soundlessly; and the theatre manager remarked somewhat rudely, as though it were trivial, "The lieutenant has really had bad luck today!"

The consul stood up and called for the waiter—as though it had been a night like any other. Only two bottles of cognac were on his own account, but to simplify things he wished to take care of the entire bill. Greising refused and paid for his coffee and cigarettes personally. The others accepted the consul's hospitality indifferently. Then the consul turned to Willi, who was still sitting, and again pointing outdoors with his right arm as he had before when he had called attention to the striking of the church clock, he said, "If you like, Lieutenant, I'll take you back to Vienna in my carriage."

"Very kind of you," replied Willi. And at this moment it seemed to him as though the last quarter of an hour, in fact the whole night and everything that had happened, were canceled out. The consul no doubt regarded it in the same light. Otherwise how could he have invited him into his carriage?

"Your debt, Lieutenant," the consul added in a friendly manner, "amounts to eleven thousand gulden net."

"Correct, Consul," replied Willi in a military tone.

"Do you want it in writing?" asked the consul, "or is that not necessary?"

"Not necessary," remarked First Lieutenant Wimmer gruffly. "We're all witnesses."

The consul paid no attention either to him or to the tone of his voice. Willi was still sitting at the table. His legs felt as heavy as lead. Eleven thousand gulden—not bad! About three or four years' salary, including bonuses. Wimmer and Greising were speaking together in low and agitated tones. Elrief was evidently saying something very funny to the theatre manager, as the latter burst into laughter. Fräulein Rihoscheck stood next to the consul and addressed a question to him, which he answered in the negative with a shake of his head. The waiter helped the consul into his cape, a wide, black, armless cape with a velvet collar which had recently impressed Willi as very elegant, though somewhat eccentric. The actor Elrief quickly poured himself a last glass of cognac from the almost empty bottle. It seemed to Willi that they were all avoiding having to trouble themselves with him, even to look at him. He now rose abruptly. Suddenly Tugut, who, to Willi's surprise, had returned, stood near him, seemed to grope for words, and finally said, "You can find the money by tomorrow morning, I hope?"

"But of course, Doctor," replied Willi, with a broad and empty smile. Then he walked over to Wimmer and Greising and shook hands with them. "Till next Sunday," he said lightly. They didn't answer, didn't even nod.

"Are you ready, Lieutenant?" asked the consul.

"At your service!"

Willi now took his leave in a very cordial and animated manner, and quite gallantly kissed Fräulein Rihoscheck's hand—it couldn't do him any harm!

Everyone left. On the terrace the tables and chairs glowed a ghostly white. Night still covered the city and the fields, though not a star remained to be seen. In the neighborhood of the train station the horizon was beginning to lighten. The consul's carriage was waiting outside; the coachman was sleeping with his feet on the dashboard. Schnabel touched him on the shoulder and he awoke, lifted his hat, went to the horses, and took off their blankets. The officers touched their caps once more, then sauntered away. The manager, Elrief, and Fräulein Rihoscheck waited until the driver was ready. Willi mused: why doesn't the consul stay in Baden with Fräulein Rihoscheck? Why does he keep her if he doesn't stay with her? It occurred to him that he had once heard of an older man who had suffered a stroke in the bed of his mistress, and he glanced obliquely at the consul. The latter, however, seemed very fresh and cheerful, not in the least ready for death, and—evidently to annoy Elrief—he was just saying goodbye to Fräulein Rihoscheck with a delicate caress that didn't seem in keeping with his usual manner. Then he invited the lieutenant into the carriage, offered him the seat on the right, and at the same time spread a light yellow blanket lined with brown fur over his own and Willi's knees. Thus they drove off. Elrief lifted his hat once more in a wide, sweeping gesture that was not without humor, in the Spanish manner that he intended to use in the role of grandee that he hoped to play in the course of the next season in some small, subsidized, provincial theatre. As the carriage wheeled around to cross over the bridge, the consul turned and waved a farewell to the three who were just now strolling away arm in arm with Fräulein Rihoscheck in the middle. Engrossed in lively conversation, they did not notice.

VIII

As they drove through the sleeping town, no sound could be heard except the clattering of the horses' hoofs.

"It's a bit cool," remarked the consul.

Willi had little desire for conversation, but he recognized the need to make some sort of reply, if only to keep the consul in a friendly mood. So he said, "Yes, it's always refreshing in the early hours of the morning. We soldiers learn that from maneuvers."

"About the twenty-four hours," began the consul after a short pause, "we don't need to take that literally."

Willi breathed more easily and took the opportunity to say, "I was just about to ask your indulgence, Consul, as I don't have the whole sum at hand at this moment, as you can well understand."

"Of course," interrupted the consul. The hoofbeats clattered on, echoing now as they drove under a viaduct out into open country. "If I were to insist on the usual twenty-four hours," he continued, "you would have to pay your debt tomorrow evening at half past two in the morning, and that would be inconvenient for both of us. So let's set the hour"—he appeared to be considering the matter—"on Tuesday at 12 o'clock noon, if that suits you."

He took a visiting card from his wallet and gave it to Willi, who scrutinized it. Dawn had progressed enough that he could read the address—Helfersdorferstrasse 5. Not more than five minutes from the military barracks, he mused.

"Tomorrow, then, Consul, at twelve noon?" he said, and he could feel his heart beat faster.

"Yes, Lieutenant, that's what I had in mind. Tuesday at twelve o'clock sharp. I'll be in my office from nine o'clock in the morning on."

"And if I were not able to pay at that hour, Consul—if, for example, I could not satisfy you before that afternoon or on Wednesday . . ."

The consul interrupted him. "You'll be in a position to pay, Lieutenant, I have no doubt. Since you sat down to play, you must naturally also have been prepared to lose, just as I had to be, and if you don't have a private fortune, you can, at any rate, expect that your parents will not let you down."

"I have no parents anymore," answered Willi quickly, and as Schnabel allowed a sympathetic noise to escape him, he added, "my mother has been dead for eight years, and my father died five years ago, as a lieutenant colonel in Hungary."

"So, your father was also an officer?" The consul's tone sounded sympathetic, almost warmhearted.

"Yes, Consul. Who knows if I would have chosen a military career under other circumstances!"

"It's remarkable," the consul agreed, "when you think about it, how some people's entire life is, so to speak, all planned out in advance, while others change theirs from one year, sometimes even from one day, to the next. . . ." He paused, shaking his head. Somehow this altogether general, not quite finished sentence struck Willi as reassuring. And in order, if possible, to cement this new relationship with the consul still further, he too searched for a general, somewhat philosophical observation; without thinking it through enough, as he immediately realized, he remarked that there were sometimes officers, too, who were obliged to change their careers.

"Yes," replied the consul, "that's true, but it's mostly not by their own free choice. They are, or rather, they feel themselves to be, embarrassingly compromised, and it's usually not possible for them to go back to their former profession. On the other hand, people such as myself—I mean, people who through no privilege of birth or rank or—something else—are prevented—I myself, for example, have been down and up half a dozen times at least. And how low—ah, if you and your comrades knew how low I've been, you would probably not have sat down with me at a gaming table! That's probably why you and your comrades preferred not to inquire too carefully about me before sitting down with me!"

Willi remained silent. He was most painfully touched and uncertain as to how he should react. Of course, if Wimmer or Greising had been in his place, they would have found the right thing to say. But he, Willi, had to keep quiet. He didn't dare ask, "What do you mean, Consul, by 'far down,' and what do you mean by 'inquire'?" Oh, he could imagine what was meant. He himself was just now as low, as low as it was possible to be, lower than he could ever have imagined a couple of hours ago.

He now depended on the mood, on the good graces, on the mercy of this man, however low he might once have been. Would he be merciful? That was the question. Would he agree to be paid in installments over a year's time—or over a period of five years—or to a revenge match next Sunday? It didn't look likely—no, at the moment it didn't look very likely at all. And—if he were not to be merciful—hmm, then there would be nothing left for him to do but to go begging to Uncle Robert. Still— Uncle Robert! It would be a most painful, a truly frightening endeavor, but nonetheless he would have to do it. Absolutely . . . and it was really unthinkable that his uncle would refuse to help him when his career, his existence, his very life—yes, truly, the very life of his nephew, the only son of his deceased sister, stood in the balance. A man who lived on his income, lived quite modestly, to be sure, but was nevertheless a capitalist who had merely to take the money out of the bank! Eleven thousand gulden—that certainly wasn't even a tenth, not even a twentieth, of his fortune! Actually, he might just as well ask him for twelve as for eleven thousand gulden—what did it matter? If he did, Bogner would also be saved. This thought immediately made Willi feel more hopeful, as

though Providence had the obligation to reward him for his noble intentions. In any case, he wouldn't have to resort to any of that unless the
consul remained obstinate. And that wasn't certain yet. Willi threw a
quick sideways glance at his companion. He seemed to be lost in memories. His hat was lying on the blanket, his lips were half open, as though
about to break into a smile, and he looked older and less severe than before. Wasn't this the right moment? But how to begin? Should he confess
that he just wasn't in a position—that he had thoughtlessly let himself get
into a situation—that he had lost his head; that indeed, for a quarter of an
hour he had not been capable of thinking at all? And also—would he
have gone as far, would he have forgot himself so completely, if the consul—yes, he could mention this—if the consul had not, unasked, indeed
without the slightest hint from him, placed the money at his disposal—
pushed it over to him, in a certain sense forced it on him, though in the
most amiable way possible?

"A ride like this in the early morning is quite wonderful, don't you
think?" observed the consul.

"Splendid," replied the lieutenant conversationally.

"It's a pity that the price for such a ride seems to be staying up all
night, whether at a gaming table or at something even more stupid."

"Well, in my case," observed the lieutenant quickly, "it frequently
happens that I'm up and about outdoors at this early hour of the morning,
even without staying up all night. Day before yesterday, for example, I
was already standing in the courtyard of the barracks with my companions at half past three in the morning. We were drilling in the Prater. But
of course I wasn't riding in a carriage then."

The consul laughed heartily, which raised Willi's hopes, even
though the laughter sounded somewhat forced.

"Yes, I've occasionally experienced something like that myself,"
said the consul, "of course not as an officer, not even as an enlisted
man—I never got even that far. Just think, Lieutenant, I did my three
years' service in my time and never made it beyond the rank of corporal.
I'm such an uneducated person—or at least I was. Well, I've caught up a
little during the passage of time. Travel brings opportunities to do that."

"You've seen much of the world," remarked Willi ingratiatingly.

"Indeed I have!" replied the consul. "I've been almost every-where—except in the country that I represent as consul, Ecuador. But I've decided to give up my title of consul in the near future and to travel there." He laughed, and Willi joined in, though a little wearily.

They were driving through a flat and wretched area, among uniformly grey and drab dilapidated houses. In a little front yard an old man in shirtsleeves was watering the bushes while a young woman in a rather shabby dress was just coming out into the street with a full canister of milk from the door of a shop that had opened early. Willi felt a certain envy of these two, of the old man who was watering his garden and the woman who was bringing milk home for her husband and her children. He knew that these two were happier than he was. The carriage passed a high, bleak building in front of which a soldier walked back and forth. He saluted the lieutenant, who reciprocated more politely than he usually did men of lower rank. The way the consul looked at this building, at once contemptuous and full of memories, made Willi think. Yet how could it help him at this moment that the consul's past in all likelihood was not exactly free from stain? Gambling debts were gambling debts, and even a convicted criminal had the right to insist on payment. Time was passing and the horses trotted faster and faster; in an hour, in half an hour they would be in Vienna—and what then?

"And creatures such as this Lieutenant Greising," said the consul, as though to end an inner conversation, "are allowed to run around free."

So I was right, thought Willi. This man has been in prison. But at this moment that did not matter—the consul's remark constituted an incontrovertible insult of an absent comrade. Could he just let it pass as though he had barely overheard it, or as though he tacitly agreed?

"I must beg you, Consul, to leave my comrade Greising out of this discussion!"

To this the consul only answered with a deprecatory gesture. "It's really remarkable," he said, "how these gentlemen who stand so strictly on their professional honor tolerate a person in their midst who, with complete consciousness of what he does, endangers the health of another, a silly, inexperienced girl, for example, and makes such a creature ill, possibly kills her—"

"We have no knowledge of anything like that," answered Willi, somewhat hoarse by now. "At least I don't know about anything like that."

"But Lieutenant, I have absolutely no interest in reproaching you. You personally are not responsible for these things, and it's absolutely not in your power to change them."

Willi sought vainly for a reply. He reflected whether he was duty bound to bring the consul's remarks to his comrade's attention—perhaps he should first talk this over unofficially with the regiment doctor, Tugut? Or should he perhaps ask First Lieutenant Wimmer for advice? But what did all this have to do with him? His main concern right now was for himself, for his particular problem—his career—his life! There in the first sunbeams stood the monument of the Weaver at the Cross. And still he hadn't spoken the words that might have served to gain him an extension, a little extension. Suddenly he felt his neighbor touch his arm lightly.

"Excuse me, Lieutenant, but let's drop the subject. It's at bottom no concern of mine whether Lieutenant Greising or anyone else—all the more so since I will hardly have the pleasure of sitting down at a table with these gentlemen again."

Willi started.

"What do you mean, Herr Consul?"

"I'm leaving the country," the consul answered coolly.

"So soon?"

"Yes. The day after tomorrow—more precisely: tomorrow, Tuesday."

"For a long time, Consul?"

"Rather—for three—to thirty years."

The highway was now filled with trucks and market wagons. Willi, looking down, saw the golden buttons of his military cape gleam in the rays of the rising sun.

"A sudden decision, Consul, this departure?"

"Oh, not at all, Lieutenant. A long-standing decision. I am leaving for America, not for Ecuador at the moment but for Baltimore, where my family lives and where I also have a business. Of course, I've not been able to supervise either of these personally for the eight years I've been gone."

So he has a family, thought Willi. And what about Fräulein Rihoscheck? Does she even know that he's leaving? But what concern of mine is that? It's high time. I'm choking. And involuntarily he put his hand to his throat.

"Well, it's very unfortunate," he said helplessly, "that you intend to leave tomorrow. For I was expecting, yes, I was expecting with some confidence"—he took on a light, somewhat jocular tone—"that you would give me the opportunity for a little revenge next Sunday."

The consul shrugged his shoulders, as though this had long been beyond the realm of possibility.

What am I going to do? thought Willi. What'll I do? Just—beg him? What can a few thousand gulden mean to him? He has a family in America—and Fräulein Rihoscheck—he has a business over there—what can a few thousand gulden mean to him? But for me they're a matter of life or death!

They drove under the viaduct into the city. A train was just pulling out of the South Station. Here are people going to Baden, thought Willi, and further, to Klagenfurth, to Trieste—and from there perhaps across the ocean to another hemisphere. . . . And he envied them all.

"Where can I drop you, Lieutenant?"

"Oh, please," answered Willi, "anywhere you want. I live in the Alser Barracks."

"I'll bring you to your door, Lieutenant." He gave the coachman the necessary directions.

"Thanks a lot, sir, it really isn't necessary. . . ."

The houses were all still asleep. The streetcar tracks, still untouched by the traffic of the day, ran smooth and gleaming alongside. The consul looked at his watch.

"He drove well—an hour and ten minutes. Do you have a maneuver today, Lieutenant?"

"No," answered Willi, "today I'm to teach a class."

"Well, then you can still lie down for a while."

"So I will, consul, but I believe I'll take the day off—I'll report myself sick."

The consul nodded and said nothing.

"So you are leaving on Wednesday, sir?"

"No, Lieutenant," answered the consul, emphasizing every word, "tomorrow. Tuesday evening."

"Consul—I'll frankly confess to you—it's extremely embarrassing to me, but I fear that it'll be totally impossible for me in such a short time—before tomorrow at 12 o'clock noon . . ."

The consul remained silent. He seemed hardly to be listening.

"If, sir, you would be so kind as to give me a respite?"

The consul shook his head.

"Oh, not a very long one. I could perhaps give you a promissory note or a confirmation, and would give you my word of honor that within fourteen days I could find a way . . ." The consul kept shaking his head, mechanically, without any emotion.

"Consul," began Willi again, and against his will it sounded like pleading, "Consul, my uncle, Robert Wilram—maybe you know the name?" But the other continued to shake his head firmly. "I am not absolutely certain that my uncle, on whom I can otherwise positively rely, has such a sum at hand. But of course, within a few days . . . he is a wealthy man, my mother's only brother, retired, living on his income." And suddenly, with a queer catch in his voice which sounded like a laugh: "It's really disastrous that you're going as far away as America so soon!"

"Where I travel, Lieutenant," answered the consul calmly, "is of absolutely no concern to you. It's common knowledge that debts of honor are to be paid within twenty-four hours!"

"I know, Consul, I know. But still it sometimes happens—I personally know some among my comrades who, in a similar position . . . It depends entirely upon you, Consul, whether you are willing to content yourself with a promissory note or my word of honor for the moment until—until next Sunday at least."

"I am not willing to be satisfied that way, Lieutenant. Tomorrow,

Tuesday at noon, that's the latest—or—notification to the commander of your regiment!"

The carriage crossed over the Ring and passed by the Volksgarten, whose treetops hung down in rich, green foliage over the gilded fence. It was a glorious spring morning. Hardly a person was yet to be seen on the street. Only a young, very elegant woman in a high-collared, tailored coat was walking rapidly along the gilded fence with a small dog, as if in fulfillment of a duty, and threw an indifferent glance toward the consul, who turned around after her, despite the wife in America and Fräulein Rihoscheck in Baden, who, admittedly, really belonged more to the actor Elrief. What business of mine is Elrief, thought Willi, and why should I worry about Fräulein Rihoscheck? Who knows, had I been nicer to her, perhaps she would have put in a good word for me. And for a moment he considered seriously whether he shouldn't ride back to Baden at once in order to beg for her intercession. Intercession with the consul? She would laugh in his face. She knew him well, after all, the consul, it was evident that she knew him. . . . And the only possibility of salvation was Uncle Robert. That was certain. Otherwise there was nothing left for him except a bullet in the head. That was clear.

A steady sound like that of the approaching steps of a marching column of men struck his ear. Wasn't the 98th having a drill today? On the Bisamberg? It would be embarrassing for him to meet his comrades at the head of the company now while he was in a carriage. But it was not a military troop that was marching toward him; it was only a group of boys, evidently schoolboys, on an outing with their teacher. The teacher, a pale young man, looked with instinctive respect at the two gentlemen in a carriage driving past him at such an early hour. Willi had never expected there would come a moment in which even a poor schoolteacher would seem to him a creature worthy of envy. Then the carriage overtook the first streetcar, whose only passengers were a man in work clothes and an old woman. A street-cleaning wagon came toward them with a wild-looking fellow in rolled-up shirtsleeves on top who was swinging a hose like a rubber band to and fro, spraying the street. Two nuns with lowered eyes crossed the tracks in the direction of the Votiv Church, whose slim light grey steeples pointed toward the sky. On a bench beneath a tree covered with white blossoms sat a young creature with dirty shoes, her straw hat in her lap, smiling as if after a pleasant experience. A closed carriage with drawn curtains whizzed past. A fat old woman was polishing the high windowpane of a café with a brush and cloth. All these people and things, which Willi normally would not have noticed, now assumed an almost painfully sharp clarity in his overalert gaze. The man beside him in the carriage had almost vanished in his mind. Now he looked at him again with a shy glance. The consul sat leaning back with closed eyes, his hat in front of him on the blanket. How gentle, how kindhearted he looked! And he—was driving him to his death! Was he really sleeping—or only pretending? Don't worry, Consul, I won't bother you any more. You'll have your money Tuesday at twelve. Or maybe not! But in no case . . . The carriage stopped in front of the barrack gates, and the consul awoke at once—or at least he pretended to have just awakened, even going so far as to rub his eyes, a somewhat exaggerated gesture after a two-and-a-half-minute nap. The guard at the gate saluted. Willi leapt deftly from the carriage without touching the running board and smiled at the consul. He even gave the coachman a tip, not too much, not too little, like a cavalier to whom gaming losses or winnings meant nothing.

"Thank you very much, Consul—until later."

The consul reached out his hand toward Willi from the carriage and pulled him a little closer, as if he wanted to say something that he didn't want anyone else to hear.

"I advise you, Lieutenant," he said in an almost fatherly tone, "don't take this situation too lightly, if you place any value . . . on remaining an officer. Tomorrow, Tuesday, at twelve o'clock." Then aloud, "Well, until later, Lieutenant."

Willi smiled politely and raised his hand to his cap, and the carriage turned around and drove off.

IX

The Alser Church clock struck a quarter to five. The big gate swung open and a company of the 98th, eyes right, marched past Willi. Willi gratefully raised his hand to his cap several times.

"Where are you going, Wieseltier?" he offhandedly asked the last cadet.

"Rifle practice, Lieutenant."

Willi nodded as though in approval and remained for a while watching the 98th pass by, though not really seeing them. The guard remained saluting as Willi walked through the gate, which now closed behind him.

Sharp commands from the end of the courtyard assaulted his ear. A troop of recruits was practicing weapon handling under the direction of a corporal. The courtyard lay in the glare of the sun, bare except for a few trees scattered here and there. Willi walked along the wall. He looked up to his room when his orderly suddenly appeared at the window, looked down, stood stock still for a moment, and then disappeared. Willi hurried up the steps and began to remove his collar and his military cape as he stepped into the parlor, where the orderly was just now lighting the fire.

"At your service, Lieutenant! Coffee will be ready soon!"

"Good," said Willi, and stepped into the room, closing the door behind him as he took off his coat and threw himself on his bed with his trousers and shoes still on.

I can't possibly go to Uncle Robert before nine o'clock, he mused. In any case, I'll ask him at once for twelve thousand—Bogner might as well get his thousand too, if he hasn't already shot himself in the meantime. Anyway, who knows? Perhaps he won at the races after all and is even in a position to rescue me! Ha! Eleven thousand, twelve thousand—that's not so easily won at the races!

His eyes closed. Nine of spades—ace of diamonds—king of hearts—eight of spades—ace of spades—jack of clubs—four of diamonds—the cards danced before him. The orderly brought the coffee, moved the table closer to the bed, and poured; Willi propped himself up on his arm and drank.

"Shall I pull off your boots, sir?"

Willi shook his head. "It's no longer worth the trouble."

"Shall I wake you up later, sir?"—and, as Willi looked at him blankly—"At your service, Lieutenant! You were to report to the academy at seven."

Willi shook his head again. "I'm ill; I must go to the doctor. Report me to the captain . . . ill, you understand? I'll send a slip in later. I have an appointment with an eye specialist, a professor, because of my eyes, at nine. Please ask the cadet substitute Mr. Brill, to hold class for me. Go—wait."

"Lieutenant?"

"At 7:15 go over to Alser Church—the gentleman who was here yesterday, First Lieutenant Bogner, will be waiting there. Beg him to excuse me—tell him that unfortunately I was unable to do anything. Do you understand?"

"Yes, Lieutenant."

"Repeat it."

"The lieutenant wishes to be excused—he was unable to do anything."

"Unfortunately was unable to do anything. Wait. If there were still a little more time, until this evening or tomorrow morning"—he suddenly paused. "No, nothing more! Tell him that I was unfortunately unable to do anything, and that's all. Do you understand?"

"Yes, Lieutenant."

"And when you come back from Alser Church, be sure to knock. And now, close the window."

The orderly did as he was instructed, abruptly breaking off a piercing command from the courtyard in the middle. When Joseph had closed the door behind him, Willi lay down again, and his eyes fell shut. Ace of diamonds—seven of clubs—king of hearts—eight of diamonds—nine of spades—ten of spades—queen of hearts—damned Canaille! thought Willi. For the queen of hearts was really Fräulein Kessner. If I hadn't stopped at that table, this whole disaster wouldn't have happened. Nine of clubs—six of spades—five of spades—king of spades—king of hearts—king of clubs—"Don't take it lightly, Lieutenant!" The devil take him! He'll get his money, but then I'll send him two seconds!—can't be done—he isn't even of a high enough rank to duel with! King of hearts—knave of spades—queen of diamonds—nine of diamonds—ace of spades—thus they danced by—ace of diamonds—ace of hearts—meaninglessly, incessantly, until his eyes burned underneath his eyelids. There could not be as many packs of cards in the whole world as flew by in his vision at this hour.

There was a knock, and he awoke with a jerk, the cards still racing by his now open eyes. His orderly stood before him.

"Lieutenant, I beg to report that the First Lieutenant thanks you very much for your trouble and sends his respects."

"So. And aside from that—he didn't say anything else?"

"No, Lieutenant, the First Lieutenant turned around and left immediately."

"So—he immediately turned around . . . and did you report me ill?"

"Yes, sir."

And, as Willi saw that the orderly was smirking, he asked, "Why are you grinning so stupidly?"

"Excuse me, sir—because of the captain."

"Why? What did the captain say?"

Still grinning, the orderly explained, "The captain said that if the lieutenant has to go to an eye doctor—it's probably because he's ruined his eyesight looking at some girl!"

And when Willi did not smile at that, the orderly added, somewhat alarmed, "That's what the captain said, sir. At your service, sir."

"You may go," said Willi.

While he readied himself for his visit to his uncle, he contemplated the phrases and practiced the tone of voice with which he hoped to move his uncle's heart. It had been two years since he had seen him. At the moment he was barely able to picture Wilram at all, or even to remember his features. Only streams of different Wilrams appeared before him, each with a different face, different habits, and different ways of speaking, and he couldn't predict which Wilram he would chance to meet today.

From childhood he remembered his uncle as a slim, always fastidiously dressed but still youthful man, though even then the man who was twenty-five years older had seemed to him to be rather old. Robert Wilram's visits to the Hungarian town where his brother-in-law, at that time still Major Kasda, was on garrison duty, had always been for only a few days. Father and uncle did not get along particularly well, and Willi even had a vague and disquieting memory of a quarrel between his parents about his uncle, which had ended with his mother leaving the room crying. His uncle's profession had never been a topic of conversation, but Willi thought he remembered that Robert Wilram had once held a civil position of some sort, which he had given up when he was widowed at an early age. He had inherited a modest fortune from his deceased wife, and since then he had lived on his income, traveling a good deal about the world. The news of his sister's death had reached him in Italy, and he had not arrived until after the burial; but the image of his uncle standing at the grave with him, dry eyed but with a desolate and earnest expression, looking down into the still unfaded wreaths, had remained forever imprinted in Willi's memory. Soon afterward they had both left the small town, Robert Wilram to return to Vienna and Willi back to his cadet school in Vienna-Neustadt. Thereafter he would visit his uncle sometimes on Sundays and holidays, and was from time to time invited to accompany him to the theatre or to a restaurant. Later, after his father's sudden death, after Willi had been assigned a position as lieutenant in a Viennese regiment, his uncle on his own initiative had given him a monthly allowance, which was paid to the young officer punctually at regular intervals through a bank, even when Wilram was away on a trip. On one of these trips, Wilram had fallen dangerously ill and had returned a noticeably aged man. Even though the monthly allowance still arrived regularly at Willi's address, the personal relationship between the uncle and the nephew had then suffered many interruptions, just as Robert Wilram's life itself seemed to change in peculiar ways. There were times when he appeared to live a gay, sociable life and would, as in former times, take his nephew to various restaurants and theatres and even to nightclubs of somewhat questionable character, to which he would be accompanied by a lively young lady whom Willi would meet on these occasions for the first and indeed for the last time. Then there would be weeks in which the uncle seemed to withdraw completely from the world and from everyone, and if Willi did succeed in being admitted to his presence at such times, he found himself facing a serious, laconic, prematurely aged man, who, wrapped in a dark brown dressing gown that resembled a monk's cassock, was either pacing up and down his dimly lit, high-ceilinged room with the expression of a soured actor, or else was sitting reading or working at his desk beneath an artificial light. At such times the conversation would be strained and halting, as though the two were total strangers. Only once, when the conversation had happened to turn to a comrade of Willi's who had just committed suicide over an unhappy love affair, Robert Wilram had opened a desk drawer and, to Willi's amazement, had taken out a number of handwritten pages and read his nephew some philosophical observations about death and immortality and some unpleasant and melancholy remarks about women, in the course of which he seemed completely to forget the presence of the younger man, who was listening to all this not without embarrassment and with more than a little boredom. Just as Willi had attempted to stifle a little yawn without success, his uncle had happened to glance up from the manuscript. His lips had curled into an empty smile; he had folded his papers together, put them back into the drawer, and had spoken abruptly of other matters that might lie closer to the interests of a young officer. But even after this rather unfortunate meeting a number of light-hearted evenings in the old manner still followed, and there were also a few small walks together, especially on fine holiday afternoons. One day, however, when Willi was supposed to pick up his uncle at the latter's home, he had received an abrupt cancellation and shortly thereafter a letter from Wilram saying that he was now so exceedingly busy that he had to ask Willi to stop his visits for the time being. Soon thereafter the allowance also stopped. A polite written reminder was not answered, and a second one met the same fate; the third received the reply that Robert Wilram was very sorry to be forced, "because of a fundamental change in his circumstances," to curtail any further financial assistance "even to near relatives." Willi had tried to speak to his uncle in person. Twice he was not received, and the third time he had seen his uncle, who had given out that he was not at home, disappear quickly through a door. So he had to admit to himself the uselessness of further effort, and nothing remained for him but to make do. He had just exhausted the small inheritance from his mother on which he had lived until now, but, true to his manner, he had not given serious thought to his future until suddenly, from one day—indeed, from one hour—to the next, his difficulties assumed threatening proportions.

In a depressed but not totally hopeless mood, Willi finally walked down the spiral staircase of the officer's quarters, and in the perpetual half-darkness of the stairs he didn't immediately recognize the man who was barring his way with outstretched arms.

"Willi!" It was Bogner who addressed him.

"It's you?" What could he want? "Don't you know? Didn't Joseph tell you?"

"I know, I know, I just wanted to tell you—in any case—that the audit has been postponed until tomorrow."

Willi shrugged his shoulders. It really didn't interest him very much!

"Postponed, do you understand!"

"It isn't difficult to understand," he said and took another step down.

Bogner would not let him pass. "But that's an omen!" he cried. "It could mean that I'll be saved after all! Don't be angry, Kasda, that I once more—I know that you didn't have any luck yesterday—"

"You can say that again!" Willi exploded. "I certainly didn't have any luck!" And with a short laugh, he added, "I've lost everything—and a little more." And now unable to control himself, as though Bogner were the one and only cause of his misfortune, "Eleven thousand gulden, man! Eleven thousand gulden!"

"Good God, well that is certainly . . . what are you . . ." He interrupted himself. Their eyes met, and Bogner's face suddenly lit up. "You're going to have to go to your uncle after all!"

Willi bit his lips. The nerve! Shameless! he said to himself, and he was not far from saying it out loud.

"Pardon me—it's none of my business, I know—I mean, I don't want to interfere—all the more as I am, so to speak, partly responsible . . . oh well, but if you are going to try, Kasda—whether it's eleven thousand or twelve thousand can't make much difference to your uncle."

"You're crazy, Bogner. I have as little chance of getting eleven thousand as I would twelve thousand!"

"But you're going there anyway, Kasda!"

"I don't know . . ."

"Willi—"

"I don't know," he repeated impatiently. "Maybe—but maybe not. . . . Goodbye." He thrust him aside and dashed down the stairs.

Twelve or eleven—that wasn't at all the same! It could be that single thousand that would make the difference! And it buzzed in his head: eleven, twelve—eleven, twelve—eleven, twelve! Well, he didn't have to decide before he was actually in his uncle's presence. The moment would decide. In any case, it was stupid of him to have mentioned the sum to Bogner, to have even let himself be detained on the staircase. What concern of his was this man? They had been comrades, yes, but never really friends! And now his fate was suddenly to be linked inextricably to Bogner's? Nonsense. Eleven, twelve—eleven, twelve. Maybe twelve did sound better than eleven; maybe it would bring him luck . . . maybe a miracle would occur—if he asked for exactly twelve. And on the entire journey from the Alser barracks through the city to the ancient house in the narrow street behind the Stefansdom he tried to decide whether he should beg his uncle for eleven or for twelve thousand gulden—as though success, and ultimately his life, depended on it.

An elderly person that he didn't know opened the door when he rang. Willi gave his name. His uncle—yes, he really was Mr. Wilram's nephew—his uncle should excuse him, but it was a matter of great urgency, and he wouldn't disturb him very long. The woman, at first undecided, withdrew, and then came back surprisingly quickly, in a much friendlier manner, and Willi—he took a deep breath of relief—was admitted at once.

X

His uncle was standing near one of two high windows. He was not wearing the monkish dressing gown in which Willi had expected to find him, but a well-cut, though somewhat worn, light summer suit and patent leather shoes that had lost some of their luster. With a broad but tired gesture he motioned his nephew to approach. "Hello, Willi. Nice of you to think of visiting your old uncle again. I thought you had completely forgotten me!"

Willi was on the point of replying that he had not been admitted on his last few visits and that his letters had not been answered, but he thought it better to express himself more circumspectly. "You live such a secluded existence," he said, "that I had no way of knowing whether you would welcome a visit from me."

The room was unchanged. Books and papers were lying on the desk; the green curtain over the bookcase was half drawn so that a few old leather volumes were visible; the same Persian rug was spread out over the sofa, and the same embroidered cushion lay on it. On the wall hung two yellowed engravings of Italian landscapes, and family portraits in matte gold frames. The sister's picture stood in its place, as before, on the desk. Willi recognized it from the rear by its shape and frame.

"Won't you sit down?" Robert Wilram asked.

Willi was standing with his cap in his hand, his sword strapped to his side, stiffly, as though on an official visit. In a tone that didn't quite match his posture, he began, "To tell the truth, dear Uncle, I probably wouldn't have come today either, if I didn't—well, in a word, if it didn't concern a very, very serious matter."

"You don't say," remarked Robert Wilram in a friendly manner, though without any particular sympathy.

"At least it's very serious for me. In short, without beating about the bush, I've committed a stupidity, a great stupidity. I—I gambled and lost more money than I have."

"Hmm, that's a bit more than just a stupidity," said the uncle.

"It was thoughtless," Willi agreed, "criminally thoughtless! I don't want to put a good face on it. But the fact of the matter unfortunately is: if I don't pay my debt by this evening at seven, I'm—I'm—" He shrugged his shoulders and paused like a stubborn child.

Robert Wilram shook his head regretfully but made no reply. The silence in the room became at once so unbearable that Willi immediately began to speak again. Quickly he reported his experiences of the day before: he had gone to Baden to visit a sick comrade, had met other officers, good old friends, there, and had let himself be seduced into a card game, which had started innocently enough but had changed, without his having had anything to do with it, into a wild gambling spree. He would rather not reveal the names of the participants with the exception of the one who had become his creditor, a wholesale merchant, a South American consul, a certain Herr Schnabel, who was unfortunately leaving for America tomorrow morning and had threatened to report him to the commander of his regiment if the debt were not paid by this evening. "You know what that means, Uncle!" Willi concluded, and suddenly sank exhausted onto the sofa.

The uncle, looking over Willi's head at the wall, but still in a friendly manner, asked, "How large is the sum in question?"

Willi hesitated again. First he thought he would add the thousand for Bogner as well, but then he was suddenly convinced that precisely this extra amount would jeopardize the outcome, and so he named only the amount that he owed.

"Eleven thousand gulden," repeated Robert Wilram, shaking his head, and it sounded almost as if there were a tone of admiration in his voice.

"I know," Willi interjected quickly, "it's a small fortune. I won't even try to justify myself. It was an act of unspeakable thoughtlessness, I think the first—certainly the last of my life. And I can't do anything but swear to you, Uncle, that I'll never touch another card in my whole life, that I'll make an effort to show you my eternal gratitude by leading a most strict and solid life. I'm even prepared—I declare it formally—to forever forswear whatever claims our family relationship might entitle me to later, if you could just this time, this one time—Uncle—"

Until now Robert Wilram had shown no emotion, but he seemed

gradually to feel some agitation. He had already raised one hand in a dismissive gesture, but now he raised the other one as well, as though with this highly dramatic gesture he hoped to silence his nephew, and in an unaccustomedly high, almost shrill voice, he interrupted: "I'm very sorry, really very sorry, but with the best intentions in the world, I can't help you!" And when Willi opened his mouth to reply, he added, "I absolutely can't help you; it's useless to say anything else, so spare yourself the effort." And he turned toward the window.

Willi, who felt at first as though struck on the head, collected himself and considered that he could not actually have expected to win over his uncle on the first try. And so he began anew: "I'm not trying to deceive myself, Uncle. I know that my request is an effrontery, an unspeakable effrontery. And I should certainly never have dared to approach you, if I had the slightest chance of getting the money in some other way. Only put yourself in my place, Uncle! Everything, everything is at stake, not only my position as an officer. What else should I, can I, do? I haven't studied anything else, I don't know anything else. And as a dismissed officer I just couldn't—just yesterday I chanced to meet a former comrade, who also—no, no, better a bullet in the head. Don't be angry, Uncle. Just imagine it! Remember, my father was an officer, my grandfather died as a lieutenant field marshal! For God's sake, I can't end up this way. That would be too hard a punishment for a thoughtless prank. I'm not a compulsive gambler, you know I've never let myself be tempted, even though I was often encouraged. True, it's so much money that I don't believe I could ever get such an amount, even from a usurer. And what would happen if I could? In half a year I would owe twice as much, in a year ten times—and—"

"Enough, Willi," Wilram finally interrupted him, in a still shriller voice. "Enough, I can't help you—I'd like to, to be sure, but I can't. Don't you understand? I don't have anything myself; I don't even have a hundred gulden to my name as I am standing before you! Here, here. . . ." He opened one drawer after another, the desk drawers, the dressing table drawers, as if it were proof of the truth of his words that there were neither bills nor coins there but only papers, boxes, linen, and all sorts of other items. Then he threw his wallet on the table, "Look for yourself, Willi, and if you find more than a hundred gulden, you can judge me—for what you will." And suddenly he sank into his desk chair and let his arms fall heavily on the surface of the table, so heavily that a few sheets of paper fluttered to the floor.

Willi picked them up quickly, then looked around the room as if searching for some changes here and there that would testify to his uncle's so incomprehensibly altered circumstances. But everything looked just as it had two or three years ago. And he asked himself whether what his uncle said could really be true. Wasn't the peculiar old man who had so suddenly and so unexpectedly left him stranded two years ago also capable of trying to protect himself from his nephew's continuing pleas with a lie which he sought to make more believable by acting a role? How could it be that someone who lived in such a well-ordered house in the central part of the city with a housekeeper, and had, as before, beautiful leather volumes in his bookcase and matte-gilt-framed pictures hanging on all the walls—how could the owner of such things have become a pauper? What could have happened to his fortune in the last two or three years? Willi didn't believe him. He had not the slightest reason to believe him, and still less reason to give up and acknowledge himself beaten, since he had nothing to lose in any case. So he determined to make one last attempt, which, however, was not as bold as he had intended, for suddenly, to his own surprise and to his shame, he found himself standing before his Uncle Robert with clasped hands and pleading, "It's a matter of life and death, Uncle. Believe me, it's about my life. I beg you, I—" His voice failed him, but, following a sudden impulse, he seized the photograph of his mother and held it up to his uncle, as though he were conjuring him on her behalf. His uncle, however, merely wrinkled his brow lightly, and, gently grasping the picture, calmly put it back in its place, and softly, not angrily, he remarked, "Your mother has nothing to do with this. She can't help you—any more than she can help me. If I didn't want to help you, Willi, I wouldn't need to think up an excuse. I don't recognize any duties, especially in such a situation. And, in my opinion, it's possible to be an honorable man—or become one—even in civilian life. Honor is lost in other ways. But you can't understand that at this point in your life. And therefore I'll tell you again: if I had the money, you can be certain I would give it to you. But I don't have it. I have nothing! I don't have my fortune anymore. I only have an annuity now. Yes, on the first and on the fifteenth I get so and so much, and today"—he pointed to his wallet with a sad smile—"today is the twenty-seventh." And since he saw in Willi's eyes a sudden gleam of hope, he immediately added, "Oh, you think I could make a loan on the strength of my annuity? Well, my dear Willi, that depends on how and under what circumstances the annuity was obtained!"

"Maybe, Uncle, maybe it would be possible after all, maybe together we could—"

But Robert Wilram interrupted him vehemently. "Nothing is possible, absolutely nothing!" And as though in deep contemplation, "I can't help you, believe me, I can't." And he turned away.

"Well," answered Willi after short reflection. "Then nothing remains for me other than to beg your forgiveness that I—goodbye, Uncle." He was already at the door when Robert's voice stopped him cold. "Willi, come back, I don't want you to think that—I might as well tell you that, to be blunt about it, that I have made what fortune I had—it wasn't so much anymore anyway—over to my wife."

"You're married?" cried Willi in astonishment, and a new hope gleamed in his eyes. "Well, if your wife has the money, then there should be a way—I mean, if you said to your wife that it's—"

Robert Wilram interrupted him with an impatient wave of his hand. "I won't tell her anything. Don't urge me any further. It would be useless." He stopped.

But Willi, unwilling to relinquish this last hope so quickly, attempted to press the subject again and began, "Your—wife—evidently doesn't live in Vienna?"

"Oh yes, she lives in Vienna, but not with me, as you see." He paced up and down the room a few times, and then, with a bitter laugh, he said, "Yes, I've lost more than a sword belt, and I'm still alive. Yes, Willi—" He suddenly interrupted himself but immediately began again, "A year and half ago I made over my entire fortune to her—of my own free will. And I did it really more for my sake than for hers. . . . For I'm not very economical, and she—she is very frugal, I have to admit, and also very good at business, and she's managed the money much better than I would have. She's invested it in some kinds of enterprises—I haven't been kept informed of the exact circumstances—I wouldn't understand anyway. And the income which I receive amounts to twelve and a half percent. That isn't so small, so that I really haven't the right to complain . . . twelve and a half percent. But not a kreuzer more! Every attempt that I made at the beginning to get an occasional advance was useless. After the second attempt I wisely gave up trying. For after that I didn't get to see her for six weeks, and she swore under oath that I would never see her again if I were ever to come to her with such a request again. And that—I didn't want to risk that. For I need her, Willi, I can't exist without her. Every week I see her, she comes to me once a week. Yes, she keeps our agreement; she's really the most dependable creature in the world. She's never failed to come, and the money has always arrived promptly on the first and the fifteenth of every month. And in the summer, every year, we go away together to the country for two whole weeks. That's in our contract, too. But the rest of the time is her own."

"And you yourself, Uncle, you never visit her?" asked Willi, a little embarrassed.

"But of course, Willi. On the first day of Christmas, on Easter Sunday, and every Whitmonday. That comes on the eighth of June this year."

"And if you—excuse me, Uncle—if you should happen to want to visit her on some other day—why, you're her husband, after all, Uncle, and who knows if she wouldn't even be flattered if you sometimes—"

"Can't risk it!" interrupted Robert Wilram. "Once—since I've already told you everything—well, one evening I walked up and down the street near her house for two hours—"

"And?"

"I didn't see her. But the next day I received a letter from her which contained only the message that I would never see her again in my entire life if I ever had the notion of promenading up and down in front of her house again. Yes, Willi, that's the way it is. And I know that even if my own life depended upon it, she'd rather let me die than give me even a tenth of what you're now asking me for before it was due. You stand a much better chance of persuading the consul to be lenient than I do of ever softening my wife's heart!"

"And—was she always that way?" asked Willi.

"What does it matter?" answered Robert Wilram impatiently. "Even if I had foreseen everything, it wouldn't have helped me. I was doomed from the moment I first laid eyes on her, or at least from our first night on, and that was our wedding night!"

"Of course," said Willi, as if to himself.

Robert Wilram burst into laughter. "Oh, you imagine she was a respectable young woman from a good bourgeois family? Far from it, my dear Willi! She was a whore! And who knows if she isn't one still—for others!"

Willi felt obliged to indicate doubt through some gesture, and he really did have doubts, because, after his uncle's story, he couldn't imagine his uncle's wife as a young and charming creature. Throughout his uncle's story he had had an image of a thin, yellowed, tastelessly dressed, elderly person with a sharp nose, and he fleetingly wondered whether his uncle wasn't trying to vent his anger at the humiliation he suffered at her hands through a deliberately false and unjust portrayal. But Robert Wilram cut his every word short and continued immediately, "Well, maybe whore is a little too harsh—in those days she was really a flower girl. I saw her for the first time at the Hornig four or five years ago. In fact, you saw her there too. Yes, maybe you remember her." And at Willi's questioning look, he explained, "We were there together at a large party—it was a banquet for the folksinger Kriebaum. She wore a bright red dress and had tousled blonde hair, and a blue ribbon around her neck." And with a kind of embittered joy he added, "She looked pretty vulgar then. Next year, at Ronacher's, she already looked quite different; at that time she could have had her pick of men. Unfortunately I never had any luck with her then. In other words, I wasn't wealthy enough for her in relation to my years—well, then it happened, what sometimes happens when an old fool loses his head over some young female. Two and a half years ago I married Fräulein Leopoldine Lebus."

So Lebus was her last name, thought Willi. That the girl in question could be none other than Leopoldine—even if he had long since forgotten her name—had become clear to him the moment his uncle mentioned the Hornig, the red dress, and the tousled blonde hair. Of course he took great care not to reveal that he knew her, because even though his uncle did not seem to entertain any illusions about what kind of life Fräulein Leopoldine Lebus had previously led, it undoubtedly would still have pained him to surmise how that evening at the Hornig had continued, and even more to learn that on that night at three in the morning, Willi, after dropping his uncle at his house, had secretly met Leopoldine again and had stayed with her until the next morning. So he pretended that he didn't quite remember that evening, and, as though it were important to console his uncle, he remarked that oftentimes it was exactly those kinds of tousled blondes who became the best wives and housekeepers, whereas girls from good families with spotless reputations gave their husbands the most awful disappointments. He knew for example of a baroness who had married one of his comrades, a young lady from the best aristocratic family, who after just two years of marriage had been presented to another comrade of his in a "salon" where "respectable ladies" were to be had for a fixed price. The unmarried comrade had felt obliged to report this to the husband, and the result had been a court of honor, a duel, the severe wounding of the husband, and the suicide of the wife—his uncle must have read about it in the newspapers! The affair had aroused great publicity. Willi spoke very animatedly, as though this whole affair suddenly interested him more than his own, and there came a moment in which Robert Wilram looked at him rather strangely. Willi collected himself, and even though he was sure that his uncle could not in any way suspect the plan he had suddenly conceived and developed, he thought it wiser to lower his voice and to abandon the subject, which after all didn't really belong here. So abruptly he declared that now, after the revelations that his uncle had made, he would certainly not importune him any further, and he even allowed his uncle to think that he agreed with the idea that an appeal to Consul Schnabel would be more likely to be successful than an appeal to the former Fräulein Leopoldine Lebus. He intimated further that it was not unthinkable that perhaps First Lieutenant Höchster, who had just received a small inheritance, or even a certain regiment doctor who had participated in the gambling yesterday, would cooperate to help him out of his dreadful situation. Yes, he would search out Höchster at once; he was on barracks duty today.

He was itching to leave, looked at his watch, suddenly acted as though he were in even more of a rush than he actually was, shook hands with his uncle, tightened his sword belt, and left.

XI

Now the most important thing was to find Leopoldine's address, and so Willi went directly to the registry office. That she would refuse his request once he had convinced her that his life was at stake he could not at the moment believe. Her image, which had not surfaced in his mind in all these years, was suddenly newly vivid, together with the memory of that evening. Once more he saw the tousled blonde head lying on the rough linen pillowcase, tinged with the red of the pillow beneath, and the pale, touchingly childlike face, on which the faint light of the summer morning had fallen through the cracks of the dilapidated wooden shutters on the windows. He saw the little gold ring with the semi-precious stone on the ring finger of her right hand, which was lying on top of the red bedspread, and the slender, silver bracelet that encircled the wrist of the left hand that she had stretched out toward him in waving him farewell from the bed as he was leaving. She had pleased him so much that when he left he was firmly determined to see her again. It happened, however, that just at this time another woman had prior claims on him, a woman who, since she was being kept by a banker, didn't cost him a kreuzer—a consideration given his circumstances. And so it happened that he had never gone to Hornig's again, and had never made use of her married sister's address, with whom she lived, and where he could have written her. Thus he had never seen her again after that one night. But however much might have changed in her life since then, she herself couldn't have changed so much that she would calmly stand by and let happen—that which had to happen if she rejected his plea.

He had to wait an hour at the registry office before he held the slip of paper with Leopoldine's address in his hand. Then he took a closed carriage to the corner of the street where Leopoldine lived, and climbed down.

The house was fairly new, four stories high, not prepossessing to look at, and situated opposite a fenced-in lumber yard. On the second floor, a neatly dressed maid opened the door. At his question of whether Frau Wilram was at home, she looked at him hesitatingly, whereupon he handed her his visiting card—Wilhelm Kasda, Lieutenant of the 98th Infantry Regiment, Alser Barracks. The maid came back at once with the answer that Frau Wilram was very busy—what did the lieutenant want? And only then did it occur to him that Leopoldine probably didn't know his last name. As he was pondering whether he should present himself simply as an old friend or facetiously as a cousin of Herr von Hornig, the door opened and an elderly, poorly dressed man with a black briefcase emerged and walked toward the outer door. Then a female voice called, "Herr Krassny," which the latter, already on the staircase, did not seem to hear. Then the woman who had called out came into the reception room herself and called to Herr Krassny again, so that this time he turned around. But Leopoldine had already noticed the lieutenant and had immediately recognized him, as her glance and her smile disclosed. She did not look at all like the creature he remembered. She was now stately and fuller of figure; yes, she even seemed to have become taller, and she wore her hair in a simple and flat, almost severe style. But the oddest thing of all was that on her nose she wore a golden pince-nez whose cord she had wound around her ear.

"How do you do, Lieutenant?" she said. And now he noticed that her features were really quite unchanged. "Please go right in, I'll be ready in a moment." She pointed to the door from which she had just come, turned to Herr Krassny, and seemed to be admonishing him sharply with regard to some commission, but in a voice so low that Willi could not understand what she was saying. Meanwhile Willi entered a large, light-filled room, in the middle of which stood a long table with pens and ink, a ruler, pencils, and ledgers. On the walls to the right and the left stood two tall filing cabinets, and on the rear wall, over a table covered with newspapers and business prospectuses, hung a huge map of

Europe. Willi was inadvertently reminded of the travel agency of a provincial town in which he had once had some business. But a moment later he saw the rundown hotel room with its dilapidated shutters and the shabby pillowcase—and he felt very strange, almost as if he were in a dream.

Leopoldine entered, closed the door behind her, and, playing with the pince-nez that she had now removed, extended her hand to the lieutenant in a friendly manner but without any noticeable emotion. He bent over the hand as though he were about to kiss it, but she withdrew it at once.

"Do sit down, Lieutenant. To what do I owe this pleasure?" She offered him a comfortable chair while she herself took her apparently customary place on a straight-backed chair behind the long table with the business ledgers opposite him. Willi felt as though he were in a lawyer's or a doctor's office. "What can I do for you?" she asked now in an almost impatient tone which did not sound very encouraging.

"Madame," Willi began, after slightly clearing his throat, "I must begin by telling you that it was definitely not my uncle who gave me your address."

She looked up at him in astonishment. "Your uncle?"

"My uncle Robert Wilram," Willi replied, with emphasis.

"Oh, of course," she smiled and looked down.

"He knows absolutely nothing of this visit," Willi continued more rapidly. "I want to emphasize that." And at her astonished glance, he added, "I really haven't seen him for a long time, but that wasn't my fault. Only today, in the course of conversation, he told me that he—had married in the meantime."

Leopoldine nodded her head in a friendly manner. "A cigarette, Lieutenant?" She indicated an open box. He helped himself, and she lit it for him and then lit one for herself as well. "Well! So may I finally know to what I owe the pleasure of—"

"Madame, my visit to you has to do with the same circumstance that led me—to my uncle. A rather—embarrassing matter, as I'm sorry to have to admit at once"—and since her expression immediately darkened noticeably, he hastily added, "I don't want to take too much of your time, madam. So, without further preliminaries: I would like to request that you—advance me a certain sum for three months."

Strangely enough, her demeanor immediately became more amiable. "Your confidence in me is extremely flattering, Lieutenant," she said as she tapped the ashes off the end of her cigarette, "though I really don't know to what I owe this honor. But may I ask what the amount in question is?" She drummed her pince-nez lightly on the table.

"Eleven thousand gulden, madam." He immediately regretted that he hadn't said twelve. He was just about to correct himself when it occurred to him that the consul might be satisfied with ten thousand, and so he left it at eleven.

"So," said Leopoldine, "eleven thousand. Hmm, that really is 'a certain sum.'" Her tongue played against her teeth. "And what security can you offer me, Lieutenant?"

"I'm an officer, madam!"

She smiled—almost benevolently. "I beg your pardon, Lieutenant, but in business matters that doesn't suffice as security. Who would be willing to answer for you?"

Willi remained silent and looked at the floor. A curt refusal would not have embarrassed him more than this cool politeness. "I beg your pardon, madam," he said. "It's true that I haven't thought enough about the formal aspect of the matter. As it happens, I find myself in a truly desperate position. It concerns a debt of honor, which has to be paid tomorrow by eight o'clock in the morning. Otherwise my honor is lost and—everything that is lost along with that among us officers." And, imagining that he now saw a glimmer of sympathy in her eyes, he told her, just as he had told his uncle an hour before, though in more elegant and moving phrases, the story of the previous night. She listened with ever increasing evidence of sympathy, even of pity. And as he finished, she asked with a promising lift of her eyes, "And I—I, Willi, am the only person on earth to whom you can go in this emergency?"

These words, and even more her use of the intimate form of "you," encouraged him. He already believed himself saved. "Would I be here otherwise?" he said. "I really have no one else!"

She shook her head sympathetically. "That makes it all the more painful for me," she answered, slowly extinguishing her still glowing cigarette, "that I am unfortunately not in a position to help you. My money is invested in various enterprises. I never have access to large sums of cash. I'm really very sorry!" And she rose from her chair, as though the interview were at an end. Willi, deeply in shock, remained seated. And hesitantly, clumsily, almost stuttering, he asked her to consider if it were not possible for her, given the evidently very advantageous condition of her enterprises, to secure a loan from some bank, or perhaps a line of credit. Her lips curved upward ironically, and smiling indulgently at his business naiveté, she said, "You imagine these things to be a little simpler than they are, and apparently you take it for granted that I should enter into some sort of financial transaction on your account which I would never undertake for myself. And that without any sort of security!—How did I achieve this honor?" These last words again sounded so friendly, even coquettish, as if she were really prepared to yield and were only waiting for a last plea from him. Believing he had found the right word, he said "Madame, Leopoldine—my existence—my very life—is at stake!"

She started a little, and, fearing that he had gone too far, he added softly, "I beg your pardon."

Her look became impenetrable, and after a short silence she remarked dryly, "In any case, I can't make any such decision without consulting my lawyer." And since she saw that his eyes began to gleam with new hope, she added with a dismissive gesture, "I'm having a consultation with him anyway—today, at five o'clock, in his office. I'll see what can be done. However, I advise you, don't depend on it, not in the least. For naturally I won't make a cabinet-level question out of it." And, with a sudden hardness, she added, "I really don't know why I should." But then she smiled again and gave him her hand. This time she permitted him to press a kiss on it.

"And when can I come for my answer?"

She appeared to consider for a while. "Where do you live?"

"In the Alser Barracks," he answered promptly. "The officer's wing, third floor, room four."

She smiled vaguely. Then she said slowly, "Around seven or seven thirty I will at least know whether I'm in a position to help or not—" She reflected again for a moment and then finished decisively, "I'll send you my answer between seven and eight through a person I can trust." She opened the door for him and accompanied him into the waiting room. "Goodbye, Lieutenant."

"Until then," he replied, taken aback. Her expression was cold and distant. And by the time the maid had opened the door to the staircase for the lieutenant, Frau Leopoldine Wilram had already disappeared back into her room.

XII

During the short time that Willi had been with Leopoldine, he had gone through so many different moods, of encouragement, hope, security, and renewed disappointment, that he descended the stairs in a daze. Only when he was outdoors once more did his mind clear, and then his situation did not seem to him so unfavorable. He was sure that Leopoldine could get him the money if she wished. Her very attitude was evidence enough that it was within her power to influence her attorney as she pleased. And the feeling that her heart must finally have spoken for him became so powerful in Willi that, mentally jumping a long distance, he suddenly saw himself as the husband of the now widowed Frau Leopoldine Wilram, now Frau Major Kasda.

But this daydream soon faded as he walked rather aimlessly toward the Ring in the midday heat through not overcrowded streets. He remembered again the disagreeable office room in which she had received him, and her image, which for a while now had been suffused with a certain feminine grace, once more took on the hard, almost severe expression that had intimidated him from time to time during his visit. In any case, come what may, there were still many hours of uncertainty to go, and these had to be passed in some manner. It occurred to him to have a "good time," as the expression went, even—yes, especially even!—if it were to turn out to be his last. He decided to have lunch in an elegant hotel restaurant where he had occasionally dined with his uncle. He selected a table in a cool, quiet corner, ordered an excellent meal, drank a bottle of half-dry Hungarian wine, and soon found himself in such a contented state that not even the thought of his predicament could disturb him. He sat for a long time with a good cigar in the corner of the velvet couch, the sole remaining guest, feeling woozy and half giddy, and when the waiter offered him authentic imported Egyptian cigarettes, he bought a whole box at once. What did it matter anyway? At the worst his orderly would inherit them.

As he stepped into the street again, he felt as though a somewhat somber, but in essence still mostly interesting, adventure, awaited him—as if he were anticipating a duel, for example. And he remembered an evening, actually half an entire night, that he had spent two years earlier with a comrade who was to fight with pistols the next morning. The first part of the evening had been spent with him in the company of a couple of young ladies; then, when they were alone, they had entered into serious, somewhat philosophical discussion. Yes, his comrade must have been in a similar mood then as he was now, and the fact that the affair at that time had turned out well seemed to Willi a good omen.

He sauntered through the Ring—a young, not too elegant officer, but of a tall and slender build, passably handsome and not unpleasing to the young ladies of all classes who passed by, as he could tell from the many who batted their eyelashes at him. In front of a café, at an outdoor table, he drank a mocha, smoked cigarettes, turned the pages of a few illustrated magazines, and surveyed the passersby without really seeing them. Only gradually, without wanting to but out of necessity, did he awake to a clear consciousness of reality. It was five o'clock. Inexorably, even if too slowly, the afternoon was passing; and now it would be wisest to go home and get a little rest, if possible. He took a horse-drawn bus, got out in front of the barracks, and, without encountering any unwelcome acquaintance, reached his quarters on the far side of the courtyard. Joseph was busy in the reception room bringing order to the lieutenant's wardrobe, and reported politely that nothing had happened, except—Herr von Bogner had been there in the morning and had left his calling card. "What do I need his card for?" Willi said crossly. The card was lying on the table; Bogner had written his private address on it: Piaristengasse 20. Not even far from here, thought Willi. But what does it matter whether he lives near or far, the fool! He follows me as though I were his savior, the pushy fellow! Willi was just about to tear up the card when he changed his mind and threw it casually on the dresser. He turned to his orderly: In the evening, between seven and eight, someone would inquire after him, Lieutenant Kasda, perhaps a gentleman with a lady, perhaps an unaccompanied lady. "Understand?"

"Yes, sir, Lieutenant."

Willi closed the door behind him and threw himself on the sofa that was a little too short for him, so that his feet dangled over the lower arm, and he sank into sleep as though into an abyss.

XIII

It was already growing dark when an indistinct noise awakened him. He opened his eyes to see a young lady in a blue and white polka-dot dress standing in front of him. Still heavy with sleep, he rose and saw his orderly standing behind the young lady, looking anxious and guilty. At the same time he heard Leopoldine's voice say, "I must apologize, Lieutenant, for not allowing your—orderly to announce me, but I preferred to wait here until you woke up on your own account."

How long could she have been standing there, thought Willi, and what can I infer from her voice? How different she looks! This was someone completely different from the person he had seen that morning. Surely she's brought the money! He waved away his orderly, who disappeared at once. And turning to Leopoldine, he said, "Well, madam, make yourself comfortable—I'm very happy to see you—please, madam"— and he invited her to sit down.

She glanced around the room with a bright, almost gay look and seemed to like what she saw. In her hand she held a white-and-blue-striped umbrella, which went perfectly with her blue and white polka-dot foulard dress. She wore a straw hat that wasn't quite in the latest fashion but rather was broad-brimmed, in Florentine fashion, with hanging artificial cherries. "Your place is quite attractive, Lieutenant," she said, and the cherries swung to and fro against her ear. "I never imagined that a room in an army barracks could be so comfortable and attractive."

"They're not all the same," remarked Willi with some self-satisfaction. To which she added with a smile, "I suppose it depends on the occupant."

Willi, awkward yet pleasurably aroused, set the books on the table in order, closed the door of a small cabinet that was ajar, and abruptly offered Leopoldine a cigarette from the box he had bought in the hotel. She declined but let herself sink lightly into the corner of the sofa. She looks marvelous! Willi thought. She actually looks like a lady from good, bourgeois circles. She reminded him as little of the business woman of this morning as she did of the tousled blonde of former times. But where could she have the eleven thousand? As though she guessed his thoughts, she looked at him smilingly, almost mischievously, and then asked, apparently harmlessly, "And how do you normally live, Lieutenant?"

Since Willi hesitated to answer her entirely too general question, she began to inquire in detail as to whether his service was easy or difficult, whether he would soon be promoted, what his relations with his superiors were, and whether he often made excursions into the surrounding countryside such as he had the preceding Sunday, for example. Willi answered that his service was variable, sometimes easy and sometimes difficult; that he had no complaints against his superiors; that Lieutenant Colonel Wositzky was especially pleasant to him; that he couldn't expect a promotion for at least three years; that he didn't have very much time for excursions, as madam could well imagine, except on Sundays—whereupon he let a sigh escape. Leopoldine, glancing up at him in a most friendly way—for he was still standing on the far side of the table from her—responded that she hoped he knew of better ways to spend his evenings than at the card table. At this point she could easily have added, "Yes, Lieutenant, so I won't forget, here, the little matter about which you spoke to me this morning." But no, there was no word, no gesture that could be interpreted in that way. She just kept looking up at him in the same smiling, approving way, and there was nothing for him to do but carry on the conversation with her as well as he could. So he told her about the appealing Kessner family and the beautiful villa in which they lived, about the stupid actor Elrief, about the painted Fräulein Rihoscheck, and about the nighttime carriage ride to Vienna.

"In pleasant company, I hope," she said.

Oh, not at all. He had ridden home with one of his card-game companions. Then she asked him in a teasing voice whether Fräulein Kessner was blonde- or brown- or black-haired. He really couldn't say for sure, he answered. And his tone intentionally revealed that there were no affairs of the heart of any meaningful sort in his life. "I think, madam, that you imagine my life to be quite different from what it actually is!"

Sympathetically, her lips half open, she looked up at him.

"If one were not so utterly alone," he added, "such dire events wouldn't happen."

She glanced up at him with an innocent, questioning look, as though she didn't quite understand, but then she nodded gravely. But even at this point she did not take the opportunity, and instead of talking about the money, which of course she had brought with her, or, still more directly, simply putting the bills on the table, she remarked, "To stand alone and to be alone—those are two different things."

"That's true," he said.

But since her only response to that was to nod understandingly, and as he grew ever more anxious as the conversation began to falter, he decided to ask her how things had gone with her all this time, and whether she had had many good experiences. He avoided mentioning the elderly gentleman to whom she was married and who was his uncle, just as he avoided mentioning Hornig's, and, above all, a certain hotel room with dilapidated shutters and a worn pillow with a ruddy shine. It was a conversation between a not particularly adroit lieutenant and a pretty young woman from a good bourgeois family, who both knew all sorts of things about each other—quite incriminating things—but who both had reasons not to speak of these things, if only not to spoil the mood, which was not without its charm and even its promise. Leopoldine had taken off her Florentine hat and had put it on the table in front of her. She was still wearing the smooth and flat coiffure of the morning but had allowed a few locks to escape and fall in curls over her temples—which reminded him, very remotely, of a former tousled blonde head.

The darkness outdoors deepened. Willi was just considering whether he should light the lamp that stood in the niche of the white tile stove when Leopoldine reached for her hat. At first it looked as though this had no further meaning, as she had meanwhile begun to tell him about an excursion that she had made the previous year by way of Mödling, Lilienfeld, and Heiligenkreuz to precisely that same Baden. But suddenly she put her Florentine hat on, pinned it onto her hair, and remarked with a polite smile that it was time for her to leave. Willi smiled too, but it was an uncertain, almost frightened smile that trembled on his lips. Was she making fun of him? Or did she merely want to amuse herself with his anxiety, his fear, in order to make him all the happier at the very last moment with the news that she had brought the money? Or had she only come to excuse herself, to tell him that it had not been possible for her to get the desired amount in cash, but she simply couldn't find the words to tell him? In any case, it was obvious that she was in earnest about leaving, and in his helplessness he could do nothing but keep on acting the part of the gallant young man who had received a pleasant visit from a young and beautiful woman, and now simply could not bear to let her go in the middle of the most enjoyable conversation.

"Why do you want to leave so soon?" he asked in the voice of a disappointed lover. And then, more urgently, "You don't really mean to leave so soon, do you, Leopoldine?"

"It's late," she answered. And she added in a light, teasing tone, "And you undoubtedly have something better planned on such a beautiful summer evening."

He breathed more easily, as she had suddenly spoken to him again in the intimate form of "you," and it was difficult for him not to betray a new hope. No, he had no plans, he said, and seldom had he been able to speak so truthfully. She hesitated a little, kept her hat on, went to the open window, and looked down into the courtyard of the barracks with a seeming sudden interest. There was not much to be seen there, granted: opposite, in front of the canteen, a few soldiers sat around a long table;

an officer's orderly was rushing diagonally across the courtyard with a wrapped package under his arm; another was pushing a small wheelbarrow with a barrel of beer toward the canteen; two officers were walking toward the gate, engrossed in conversation. Willi stood next to Leopoldine, a little behind her; her blue and while polka-dotted foulard dress swished softly, her left arm hung down limply, and her hand did not move as his touched hers. Gradually her fingers slowly slipped lightly between his. Through the open window the melancholy sounds of someone practicing a trumpet from the barracks across the way wafted into the room. Silence.

"It's rather melancholy in here," said Leopoldine finally.

"Do you think so?"

And, since she nodded, he said, "But there's no need for it to be sad at all."

Slowly she turned her head back toward him. He had expected to see a smile on her lips, but he noticed instead a tender, almost melancholy look. Abruptly she stretched herself and said, "Now it's really high time for me to go! My Marie will be waiting with supper for me."

"Has madam never let Marie wait before?"

And as she looked smilingly at him in answer, he became bolder and asked her if she would not give him the pleasure of dining with him this evening. He would send his orderly over to Riedhof's, and she could still easily be home by ten. Her protestations sounded so little authentic that Willi rushed into the anteroom without further ado, quickly gave his orderly the necessary commands, and in a flash was back with Leopoldine, who, still standing at the window, was just flinging her Florentine hat across the table where it dropped upon the bed. And from that moment on she seemed to become someone else. Laughingly she now stroked Willi's smooth hair, and he responded by seizing her around the waist and drawing her down next to him to the sofa. But when he drew nearer to kiss her, she turned away so abruptly that he ceased any further attempts and instead asked her how she usually spent her evenings. She looked him earnestly in the eye.

"I have so much to do the whole day long," she said, "that I'm only too glad to have my peace in the evenings and not see anyone."

He confessed that he didn't really understand what kind of business she was involved in, and that it puzzled him how she had come to have this kind of life at all. She evaded his questions. He wouldn't understand such matters. He didn't desist from his questions immediately—she must at least tell him something about the course of her life, not everything, naturally, he wouldn't expect that, but he really would like to know in a general way what had happened to her since the day when—when they had last seen each other. More questions rose to his lips, and the name of his uncle too, but something held him back from saying it out loud. And so he only asked her abruptly, too hastily, if she were happy.

She looked down. "I think so," she answered softly. "Above all, I'm a free person. That's what I always wanted to be most. I'm not dependent on anyone, just like—a man."

"Fortunately, that's the only thing that's like a man about you," said Willi. He moved closer to her and began to caress her. She allowed him to continue, yet almost as though she didn't notice. And when the outside door opened, she drew away from him quickly, and, standing up, took the lamp out of the niche of the porcelain oven and lit it. Joseph entered with the meal. Leopoldine glanced at what he had brought and nodded in approval. "The Lieutenant obviously has had some experience," she remarked, smiling. Then she and Joseph together set the table. She didn't permit Willi to help, and so he remained sitting on the sofa, "like a pasha," as he put it, smoking a cigarette. When everything was ready and the first course was set out on the table, Joseph was dismissed for the day. Before he went, Leopoldine pressed such a generous tip into his hand that he was quite taken aback with surprise, and saluted her with as much awe as if she were a general.

"Your health," said Willi, and clicked his glass with Leopoldine's. Both emptied their glasses, and she put hers down with a clink and suddenly pressed her lips passionately against Willi's mouth. But as he became more passionate in return, she again pushed him away and said, "First, let's eat," and changed the plates.

She ate as healthy creatures do who have ended their day's work successfully and can afford to enjoy themselves. She ate with strong white teeth but very delicately and correctly, in the manner of ladies who have now and then dined in elegant restaurants with fine gentlemen. The bottle of wine was soon emptied, and it was good that the lieutenant remembered in time that he still had half a bottle of French cognac left over from God knows what occasion standing in his cabinet. After the second glass, Leopoldine seemed to become a little drowsy. She leaned back into the corner of the sofa, and as Willi bent over her, kissing her eyes, her lips, her neck, she, yielding, whispered his name, as though in a dream.

XIV

It was dawn when Willi awoke, and a cool morning breeze was blowing in through the window. But Leopoldine was already standing in the middle of the room, completely dressed, the Florentine hat on her head, her parasol in her hand. Good God, how soundly I must have slept! was Willi's first thought, and his second, Where is the money? There she stood with hat and parasol, evidently prepared to leave the room the next moment. She nodded a morning greeting toward him. He stretched out his arms toward her, as if in longing. She stepped closer and sat down on the bed next to him with a friendly but serious expression. But as he wanted to put his arms around her and pull her toward him, she pointed to her hat and to her parasol, which she held in her hand almost like a weapon, and shook her head, "No more nonsense," she said, and attempted to get up. But he restrained her. "You don't intend to go, do you?" he asked in an almost tearful voice.

"I certainly do!" she said, and stroked his hair in a sisterly fashion. "I want to get a few hours of real rest; I have an important conference at nine."

It occurred to him that this might be a conference—how that word sounded—to discuss his affair—the consultation with the lawyer for which she evidently didn't have time yesterday. And in his impatience he asked her outright, "A conference with your lawyer?"

"No," she replied with ease. "I'm expecting a business friend from Prague."

She bent down to him, pushed his little mustache away from his lips, and kissed him fleetingly. "Goodbye," she whispered, and rose to go. In the next second she might be out the door. Willi's heart stood still. She wanted to go? Just like that?! But then a new hope awoke within him. Maybe she—out of discretion perhaps—had put the money somewhere? Anxiously, restlessly, his eyes wandered over the room—across the table, to the niche of the oven. Or maybe she had put it under the pillow while he was sleeping? Instinctively his hand reached for the place. Nothing. Or maybe she had put it in his wallet, which was lying near his watch? If only he could look there! And all the while he felt, he knew, he could see that she was following his every move, his every glance, with derision if not malice. Their eyes met for only the merest fraction of a second. He turned his away as though he had been found out—and then she was already at the door and had the door handle in her hand. He wanted to call out her name, but his voice gave out as if in a nightmare. He had an impulse to leap out of bed, to throw himself at her, to hold her back; yes, he was ready to run down the stairs after her, in his nightshirt—exactly—he saw the image clearly in his mind—as he had once seen a prostitute run after a man who had not paid her in a provincial bordello many years ago. . . . But Leopoldine, as if she had already heard her name, though he had not yet spoken it aloud, without letting go of the door handle, reached with her other hand into the neckline of her dress.

"I almost forgot," she said casually, and, stepping closer, she let a bill flutter onto the table—"There!" she said—and was already back at the door.

With a start, Willi sat upright at the edge of his bed and stared at the bill. It was only a single bill, a thousand gulden note. There were no higher denominations, so it could not be more than a thousand.

"Leopoldine," he cried, in a strange, unnatural voice. But when she turned around, her hand still on the door handle, and looked at him with an ice-cold and somewhat questioning look, shame overcame him, a shame deeper and more humiliating than any he had ever felt before in his life. But now it was already too late; he had to go on, no matter where it led him, no matter how deep his humiliation. Uncontrollably the words tumbled from his lips:

"But that's too little, Leopoldine! I didn't ask you for a thousand, I

asked you for eleven thousand—you must have misunderstood me yesterday." And instinctively, under her ever more icy stare, he pulled the
covers over his naked legs.

She stared at him as though she didn't quite understand. Then she
nodded a couple of times, as though everything were now finally clear to
her. "Oh, yes," she said, "you thought . . ." and with her head she ges-
tured contemptuously toward the bill—"that has nothing to do with your
request. The thousand gulden are not a loan; they are yours—for last
night." And between her half-opened lips, her moist tongue played between her sparkling teeth.

The covers slipped off of Willi's feet. He stood erect and his blood
mounted, burning into his temples and his eyes. She looked at him unmoved, as though curious. And as he was unable to utter a single word,
she asked, "It isn't too little, is it? What exactly did you expect? A thousand gulden! I only received ten from you that time. Don't you remember?" He took a few steps toward her. Leopoldine remained calmly
standing at the door. With a sudden movement he now seized the bill and
crumpled it, his fingers trembling, as though he were about to throw it at
her feet. At that she let go of the door handle, walked over to him, and
looked straight into his eyes. "That wasn't a reproach," she said, "I had
no right to expect more at that time. Ten gulden—was enough then, too
much even." And, looking deeper into his eyes, she added, "To speak
more accurately, it was exactly ten gulden too much!"

He stared at her, then looked away, beginning to understand. "I
couldn't have known that," he said tonelessly. "Yes, you could have," she
answered. "It wasn't so difficult to see."

Slowly he raised his eyes again, and now, in the depths of her eyes,
he became aware of a strange radiance: it was the same innocent and tender radiance that had shone in her eyes on that night so very long ago.
And suddenly vivid memories came back to him—and he recalled not
only the voluptuous pleasure she had given him, as had many others before and after her—and not only the affectionate, caressing words she
had spoken, the same ones he had heard from others, too—but also the
wonderful surrender with which she had clasped him around the neck

with her slight, childlike arms, a surrender that he had never experienced before or since, and long-forgotten words also resurfaced in his memory—words and the tone in which she had uttered them, such as he had never heard from anyone else: "Don't leave me! I love you." All these long forgotten things—suddenly he remembered them again. And just as she was doing now—he now knew this, too—he, undisturbed, thoughtlessly, while she still seemed to slumber in sweet exhaustion, had risen from her side, and, after a hasty consideration of whether a smaller bill would do as well, had nobly put a ten gulden note on her night table. Then feeling the still drowsy and yet already anxious look of the slowly awakening girl on him when he was already at the door, he had run away quickly in order to snatch a few hours of rest in his bed at the barracks. In the morning, even before the start of his duties, he had already forgotten the little flower girl from Hornig's.

Meanwhile, however, as that long forgotten night became so incomprehensibly vivid to him, the innocent and tender radiance in Leopoldine's eyes gradually faded. Now cold, grey, and distant, they stared into his, and to the same degree that the image of that night was now fading within him, anger, aversion, and bitterness arose instead. What did she think she was doing? What did she allow herself in regard to him? How dare she act as though she really believed that he had offered himself to her for money! How dare she treat him like a gigolo who wanted to be paid for his favors? And she had the effrontery to add to this outrageous insult by bargaining for a lower price than had been set, like a lover disappointed by the erotic skills of a prostitute? As if she could have any doubt that he would have thrown the whole eleven thousand back at her feet if she had dared to offer them as payment for his services!

But even as the abusive word that she deserved was finding its way to his lips, as he was raising his fist against her as though he wanted to crush her into the ground, the word dissolved unspoken on his tongue, and his hand sank slowly to his side. Because suddenly he realized—and hadn't he suspected it before?—that he had been prepared to sell himself. And not only to her but to any other, to anyone at all, anyone who would have offered him the sum that could save him. And thus—despite the cruel and malicious injustice that a spiteful woman had done him—in the depth of his soul, though he fought against it, he began to feel the hidden and yet inescapable justice that had trapped him not only in this sorry adventure but in the essential core of his life.

He looked up and looked around the room; he felt as though he were awakening from a confused dream. Leopoldine had gone. He hadn't yet opened his mouth—and she was already gone. He couldn't understand how she had contrived to disappear from his room so suddenly—without his noticing it. He felt the crumpled bill in his still cramped hand, dashed to the window, and threw it wide open as though he wanted to fling the thousand gulden after her. There she was! He wanted to call out to her, but she was already too far away. She was walking along the wall with a lilting and joyous step, the parasol in her hand and the Florentine hat whipping on her head. She walked as though she had just come from some night of love, as no doubt she had come from a hundred others. She was at the gate. The guard saluted her as though she were a person of rank, and she disappeared.

Willi shut the window and stepped back into the room. His glance fell on the rumpled bed and on the table with the remainders of the meal, the emptied glasses, and the bottles. Involuntarily his hand opened, and the bill fell onto the plate. In the mirror above the dresser he caught a glimpse of himself—of his tousled hair, the dark rings under his eyes— and he shuddered. It disgusted him deeply that he was still in his nightshirt. He reached for his coat, which was hanging on a hook, pulled it on, buttoned it up, and turned up the collar. He paced aimlessly up and down the small room several times. Finally he stopped in front of his dresser, as if rooted to the spot. In the middle drawer, between the handkerchiefs, he knew, lay his revolver. Yes, he was at that point. At the same point as the other man, who had perhaps already gone beyond it. Or was he still waiting for a miracle? Well, in any case, he, Willi, had done his duty, and even more. And at this moment it really seemed to him as though he had sat down at the card table only for Bogner's sake, had tempted fate so long that he himself had become a victim, only for Bogner's sake.

The bill still lay on the plate with the half-consumed piece of cake, just where it had fallen a moment ago out of his hand, and it didn't even look markedly crumpled anymore. It had begun to unroll—it wouldn't be very long until it was smooth again, as smooth as any piece of pure paper, and no one would be able to tell that it was nothing more than what one used to call the wages of sin—shame money. Well, in any case, it now belonged to him, to his estate, so to speak. A bitter smile played on his lips. He could leave it to anyone he wished—and he would leave it to the one who had a right to it. That was Bogner, more than any other! Involuntarily he burst into laughter. Excellent! Yes, he would take care of that matter, in any case! He hoped Bogner had not killed himself already. The miracle had actually happened for him! All he had to do was wait for it.

But where was Joseph? He knew that there was a maneuver scheduled today. Willi was supposed to have been ready precisely at three o'clock in the morning, and it was already half past four. By now the regiment was long gone. He hadn't heard a thing; he had slept so deeply. He opened the door to the anteroom. There he sat, the orderly, on a stool next to the little iron stove, and immediately stood at attention. "I beg to report, sir, that I have reported the lieutenant ill."

"Ill? Who told you to do that? . . . Oh, yes. . . ." Leopoldine—! She might just as well have given the order to report him dead—that would have been simpler. "Very well. Make me a cup of coffee," he said, and closed the door.

Where could that calling card be? He searched—searched in all the drawers, on the floor, in every corner—searched as though his own life depended upon it. In vain! He couldn't find it. Well, it wasn't meant to be. So Bogner was unlucky too; their fates were indeed inextricably intertwined. Then suddenly he saw something white gleam in the oven niche. There was the card with his address on it: Piaristengasse 20. Quite nearby. What if it had been farther? So he was lucky after all, this Bogner. What if he hadn't been able to find the card—?

He took the bill, looked at it for a long time without really seeing it, folded it, inserted it into a sheet of white paper, considered whether he should write a few explanatory words, then shrugged his shoulders.

"What for?" and he put only the address on the envelope: First Lieutenant Otto von Bogner. First Lieutenant!—yes—he was giving the man his commission again, upon his own authority. Once an officer, always an officer—no matter what one did—or one became an officer again—when one had paid one's debts.

He called the orderly and gave him the letter to deliver. "See to it that you go quickly."

"Do you wish an answer, Lieutenant?"

"No. But give it to him personally and—no answer. And whatever happens, don't wake me when you get back. Let me sleep. Until I wake by myself."

"Very good, sir!" He clicked his heels, turned around, and hurried off. From the steps he could hear the key turning in the door behind him.

XV

Three hours later there was a ring at the hall door. Joseph, who had returned long ago and had fallen asleep, awoke with a start and opened it. It was Bogner—the man to whom he had delivered the letter three hours ago as ordered.

"Is the lieutenant at home?"

"I'm sorry, the lieutenant is still sleeping."

Bogner looked at his watch. Right after the accountants had examined his books and found them in order, he had taken an hour off in his anxiety to thank his savior, and it was important to him not to be gone any longer than he had to be. Impatiently he paced up and down in the small anteroom. "Doesn't the lieutenant have any duties today?"

"The lieutenant is ill."

The door to the hall was still open, and suddenly regiment doctor Tugut entered. "Is this where Lieutenant Kasda lives?"

"Yes, sir."

"May I speak with him?"

"Sir, I beg to report, the lieutenant is ill. He's sleeping now."

"Announce me to him, please. Regiment doctor Tugut."

"I beg to report that the lieutenant gave orders not to be awakened."

"It's urgent. Wakè the lieutenant up. I'll be responsible."

While Joseph, after a slight, hardly noticeable hesitation, was knocking on the door, Tugut threw a suspicious glance at the civilian who was standing in the anteroom. Bogner introduced himself. The regiment doctor, who was not unfamiliar with the name of the officer who had been dismissed under awkward circumstances, didn't let on that he knew, and introduced himself in turn. They did not shake hands.

In Lieutenant Kasda's room everything remained quiet. Joseph knocked more loudly, put his ear to the door, shrugged his shoulders, and said, as if to calm his own fear, "The lieutenant always sleeps very soundly."

Bogner and Tugut looked at one another, and a barrier fell between them. Then the regiment doctor stepped up to the door and called out Kasda's name. No answer. "Strange," muttered Tugut, wrinkling his brow, and pushed the door handle down—in vain.

Joseph stood with pale face and wide eyes.

"Fetch the regiment locksmith, and be quick about it!" ordered Tugut.

"Yes, sir!"

Bogner and Tugut were alone.

"Incomprehensible," said Bogner.

"You know something about it Herr—von Bogner?" asked Tugut.

"You mean about his gambling loss, doctor?" And, as Tugut nodded in answer, "Unfortunately I do."

"I wanted to see how the affair stood," began Tugut hesitatingly. "Whether he was successful in getting the sum—do you know anything about it, Herr von Bogner?"

"I know nothing," Bogner replied.

Again Tugut went over to the door, shook it, and called out Kasda's name. No answer.

Bogner, from the window now, announced, "There is Joseph with the locksmith."

"You were his comrade?" asked Tugut.

Bogner, with a slight tightening of the corner of his mouth, answered, "I'm the one you were thinking of."

Tugut paid no attention to the remark. "Sometimes it happens that, after great excitement," he began again—"I suspect that he didn't sleep last night, either."

"Yesterday morning," said Bogner in a factual tone, "he certainly hadn't yet gotten the money together."

Tugut looked at Bogner questioningly, as though he considered it possible that Bogner was perhaps bringing a part of the money. As though in answer, Bogner said, "Unfortunately, I didn't succeed either— in getting the money."

Joseph appeared, accompanied by the locksmith, a well-nourished, red-cheeked, very young man in the uniform of the regiment, carrying the necessary tools. Tugut knocked violently on the door once more—a last attempt. They all stood by for a few seconds, holding their breaths. There was no sound.

"Very well, then," Tugut turned to the locksmith with a gesture of command, and the latter set to work immediately. It didn't require much effort. After a few seconds the door stood open.

Lieutenant Willi Kasda, in his overcoat, with his collar raised, was leaning in the corner of the black leather sofa facing the window, his lids half shut, his head on his breast, his right arm hanging limply over the side of the sofa. The revolver was lying on the floor. From his temple a narrow stream of dark red blood trickled over his cheek, disappearing between his neck and his coat collar. Even though they had all been prepared for the worst, they were nevertheless deeply shocked. The regiment doctor was the first to step closer. He lifted the drooping arm, let it go, and it immediately dropped limply over the side of the sofa as before. Then Tugut, quite unnecessarily, unbuttoned Kasda's coat, under which the rumpled nightshirt stood wide open. Bogner stooped to pick up the revolver. "Stop," cried Tugut, his ear on the naked breast of the dead man. "Everything must remain as it is!" Joseph and the locksmith still stood motionless in the open door. The locksmith shrugged his shoulders and threw a half-embarrassed, half-fearful glance at Joseph, as though he felt some responsibility for the frightful sight that was hidden behind the door he had sprung open.

Steps approached from below, at first slowly then ever more

rapidly, until they ceased. Bogner's glance turned to the door. An elderly man appeared in the opened door, dressed in a light, somewhat worn summer suit, with something of the attitude of a soured actor, and looked uncertainly around the room.

"Herr Wilram," exclaimed Bogner. "His uncle!" he whispered to the regiment doctor, who was just straightening up from his examination of the body.

But Robert Wilram did not immediately grasp what had happened. He saw his nephew leaning in the corner of the sofa with his limp arm hanging down, and wanted to approach him—no doubt he suspected that something terrible had happened but refused to believe it. The regiment doctor held him back, and laid his hand on his arm: "Unfortunately, a terrible accident has happened. But there is nothing that can be done now." And as the other stared at him uncomprehendingly, he added, "I'm the regiment doctor, Dr. Tugut. Death must have occurred several hours ago."

Robert Wilram—and his behavior struck everyone as extremely peculiar—suddenly pulled an envelope from his breast pocket with his right hand and waved it in the air. "But I've brought it, Willi!" he cried. And, as though he really believed he could thus bring him back to life, he shouted, "Here's the money, Willi! She gave it to me this morning. The whole eleven thousand, Willi! Here it is!" And he turned around to the others as though imploring them to bear witness. "That's the entire amount, gentlemen! Eleven thousand gulden!"—as though, now that the money was here, they should at least make some effort to revive the dead man.

"It's too late, unfortunately," said the regiment doctor. He turned to Bogner, "I'm going to make the report." Then he commanded, "The body is to remain in the position that it was found." And glancing at the orderly, he added severely, "You'll be responsible that everything remains as it is." And before he left, he turned around again and shook hands with Bogner.

Bogner wondered—so where did he get the thousand—for me? His glance now fell on the table that had been moved away from the sofa. He noticed the plates, the glasses, the empty bottle. Two glasses . . . ?! Did he bring in a woman for his last night?

Joseph crossed over to the sofa to the side of his dead master. He stood stiffly erect, like a guard. Nevertheless he did not attempt to interfere as Robert Wilram suddenly went up to the the dead man with raised, imploring hands, in one of which he still held the envelope with the money. "Willi!" he pleaded. He shook his head in despair. Then he sank to his knees in front of his dead nephew, and was now so near him that he became aware of a strangely familiar perfume wafting toward him from the naked breast and the rumpled nightshirt. He inhaled it deeply and looked up into the dead man's eyes, as though he were tempted to ask him a question.

The regular, rhythmic marching beat of the returning regiment echoed from the courtyard below. Bogner was anxious to leave before some of his former comrades came into the room, as could be expected. In any case, his presence here was superfluous. He cast a farewell glance at the body, which was still reclining motionless in the corner of the sofa, and, followed by the locksmith, hurried down the steps. He waited in the entrance to the gate until the regiment had passed, and then crept away, pressing close to the wall.

Robert Wilram, still on his knees in front of his dead nephew, looked around the room. Only now did he notice the table with the remains of the meal, the plates, the bottles, and the glasses. On the bottom of one of them there was still a moist golden yellow shimmer. He asked the orderly, "Did the lieutenant have a visitor here last night?"

There were steps outside. A babble of voices. Robert Wilram stood up.

"Yes," answered Joseph, still standing erect, like a guard. "Until late into the night—a gentleman, a comrade."

And the desperate suspicion that had come fleetingly into the old man's head vanished into nothingness.

The voices, the steps came nearer.

Joseph stood more stiffly erect than before. The committee entered the room.

The Dead Are Silent

HE COULDN'T BEAR to sit quietly in the carriage any longer; he jumped down and paced back and forth. It was already dark. The light from the few street lanterns on this quiet, deserted side street flickered as they swayed back and forth in the wind. It had stopped raining. The sidewalks were almost dry, but the unpaved streets were still wet, and in a few places small puddles had formed.

It's strange, thought Franz, how it's possible here, just a hundred steps from the Praterstrasse, to feel transplanted into a small Hungarian town. In any case, at least it's safe here: she won't bump into any of her dreaded acquaintances.

He glanced at his watch . . . seven . . . and already totally dark. An early fall this year! And this damned storm!

He turned up his collar and paced back and forth more rapidly. The glass sides of the lanterns jangled. "Another half an hour," he told himself, "then I can go. Ah, I almost wish it were already time." He stopped at the corner: here he had a view of both the streets from which she might be coming.

Yes, she'll come today, he thought, while he held on to his hat, which was threatening to fly away. Friday—the faculty meeting—she'll dare to come today and will even be able to stay longer than usual. . . . He heard the jangle of the bells of the horse-drawn tram; and now the bell in nearby Nepomuk Church began to ring as well. The street became livelier. More people passed: most of them seemed to be employees of the shops that closed at seven. They were all hurrying and seemed to be engaged in a kind of battle with the storm that made it difficult for them to walk. No one paid any attention to him; only a couple of shop girls glanced at him with mild curiosity. Suddenly he saw a familiar figure approaching quickly. He rushed toward her. Not in a carriage? he thought. Is it she?

It was. When she caught sight of him, she quickened her footsteps.

"You're walking?" he asked.

"I had the carriage let me out at the Karl Theatre. I think I've had this coachman once before."

A man walked by and glanced casually at the young woman. The young man fixed him with a sharp, almost threatening look; the man passed by quickly. The woman followed him with her eyes. "Who was that?" she asked anxiously.

"I don't know him. Nobody knows us here; don't worry—but now hurry up. Let's get in."

"Is this your carriage?"

"Yes."

"An open one?"

"An hour ago it was still nice weather."

They hurried over to it; the young woman climbed in.

"Driver!" called the young man.

"Where on earth is he?" asked the young woman.

Franz looked around. "This is incredible," he cried, "the fellow is nowhere to be seen."

"For God's sake!" she exclaimed under her breath.

"Wait a minute, dear. He's got to be around somewhere."

The young man opened the door to a small tavern. The driver was sitting at a table with a few other people; now he rose hurriedly.

"Coming, sir," he said and finished his glass of wine standing up.

"What do you think you're doing?"

"Beg your pardon, sir. I'll be there right away."

He hurried to the horses a little unsteadily. "Where to, sir?"

"To the Prater—the Pleasure Pavilion."

The young man climbed into the carriage. The young woman was leaning in the corner under the raised top, almost cowering, and quite hidden.

Franz took both her hands into his. She remained motionless. "Don't you at least want to say hello to me?"

"Please, I beg you, give me a minute. I'm still breathless."

The young man leaned back into his own corner. They were both silent for a while. The carriage had turned into the Praterstrasse, passed by the Tegetthoff Monument, and in a few minutes was flying down the broad, dark Prater Boulevard. Then Emma suddenly threw her arms around her lover. Tenderly he pushed back the veil that still separated him from her lips and kissed her.

"Finally, I'm with you!" she said.

"Do you know how long it's been since we've seen each other?" he exclaimed.

"Since Sunday."

"Yes, but that was only from a distance."

"What do you mean? You were at our place."

"Well, yes . . . at your place. No, it can't go on this way. I'll never come to your house again. But what's the matter now?"

"A carriage just passed us."

"My dear child, the people out riding in the Prater today certainly aren't worrying about us."

"You're right. But someone might accidentally look in."

"It's impossible to recognize anyone."

"Please, I beg you, let's drive somewhere else."

"As you wish."

He called out to the driver, who didn't seem to hear him. He leaned forward and touched him with his hand. The driver turned around.

"I want you to turn around. And why are you beating the horses like that? We're not in any hurry, do you hear! We'll drive to the . . . you know, the boulevard that goes to the Reichsbridge?"

"The Reichstrasse?"

"Yes, but don't go on racing like this. It's senseless."

"Please, sir, it's the storm that's making the horses so wild."

"Oh, of course, the storm." Franz sat down again.

The driver turned the horses around. They drove back.

"Why didn't I see you yesterday?" she asked.

"How could I have?"

"I thought you were invited to my sister's, too."

"Oh, that."

"Why weren't you there?"

"Because I can't stand to be with you when there are other people around. No, never again."

She shrugged her shoulders.

"Where are we?" she asked then.

They were driving under the railroad bridge into the Reichstrasse.

"That's the way to the Danube," said Franz. "We're on the way to the Reichsbridge. You won't run into any of your friends here!" he added teasingly.

"The carriage is shaking horribly."

"Yes, we're driving over cobblestones again."

"Why does he keep zigzagging across the road?"

"It just seems that way to you."

But he himself felt that the carriage was tossing them back and forth more violently than usual. He didn't want to say anything about it for fear of making her even more afraid.

"I have a lot of important things to talk to you about, Emma."

"Then you have to start soon, because I have to be home at nine."

"Everything can be settled in two words."

"My God, what was that?" The carriage had been running in a horse tram track and now, as the driver was trying to get out of it, swerved so sharply that it almost turned over. Franz grabbed the driver by his coat. "Stop!" he shouted at him, "Why, you're drunk!"

The driver stopped the horses with great effort. "But, sir . . ."

"Come on, Emma, let's get out of here."

"Where are we?"

"We're already on the bridge. It's not quite so stormy now. Let's walk a bit. We can't really talk while driving." Emma pulled her veil over her face and followed.

"You call that 'not stormy'?" she exclaimed as a gust of wind blew against her just as she was climbing down.

He took her arm. "Follow us," he shouted to the driver.

They walked on ahead. All the while they walked up the gradual incline of the bridge, they said nothing, and when they heard the water rushing underneath them, they stopped. It was pitch-dark. The broad stream below them was a boundless expanse of grey. In the distance they saw red lights that appeared to float above the water and were mirrored in it. Quivering streams of light from the bank they had just left were sinking into the water; and on the other shore it seemed as if the stream lost itself in black pastures. A faint and distant thunder seemed to come closer and closer, and without meaning to, they both looked in the direction where the red lights gleamed. Trains with lighted windows rolled between iron arches that rose up suddenly out of the night and then sank down again as suddenly as they had appeared. The thunder gradually lost itself in the distance, and it grew quiet. Only the wind blew in sudden gusts.

After a long silence Franz said, "We should go away."

"Of course," said Emma softly.

"We should go away," Franz said animatedly, "really go away, I mean."

"But that's impossible."

"Because we're cowards, Emma, that's why it's impossible."

"And my son?"

"I'm sure he'd let you have him."

"And how would we do it?" she asked softly. "Just run away in the dead of night?"

"No, not at all. All you have to do is tell him that you can no longer live with him because you belong to another."

"Are you crazy, Franz?"

"If you want, I'll spare you that too—I'll tell him myself."

"You won't do that, Franz."

He tried to look at her, but in the darkness he could only see that she had lifted her head and turned it toward him.

He was silent for a while. Then he said calmly, "Don't worry, I won't do it."

They approached the other shore.

"Don't you hear something?" she said. "What's that?"

"It's coming from over there," he said.

Slowly something came rattling out of the dark. A small red light floated toward them. Soon they saw that it came from a small red lantern that was attached to the front of a peasant's wagon. But they couldn't see whether the wagon was loaded with goods or whether anyone accompanied it. Right behind it came two similar wagons. On the second one they could make out a man in peasant clothes who was just lighting his pipe. The wagons passed. Then they again heard nothing but the muffled noise of the carriage which was slowly rolling twenty paces behind them. At this point the bridge began to slope gently toward the other shore. They saw the road in front of them disappear between the trees into the darkness. To their right and their left in the depths below lay meadows. It was as if they were looking into deep abysses.

After a long silence Franz suddenly said, "Well then, this is the last time . . ."

"What?" asked Emma in a worried tone.

"—that we'll be together. Stay with him. I'll say goodbye to you."

"Are you serious?"

"Absolutely."

"You see, it's always you who spoils the few hours that we have together, not me!"

"Yes, yes, you're right," said Franz. "Come on, let's drive back."

She grasped his arm more tightly. "No," she said tenderly, "Not now. I don't want to. I'm not going to let you send me away like that."

She pulled him down toward her and gave him a long kiss. "Where would we end up," she said, "if we continued on this street?"

"This goes directly to Prague, sweetheart."

"We won't go that far," she said smilingly, "but let's go on a little farther, if you don't mind." She pointed into the darkness.

"Hey, driver," Franz called. But the driver didn't hear.

Franz shouted, "For heaven's sake, stop!"

The carriage kept on rolling. Franz ran after it. Then he saw that the driver had fallen asleep. Franz finally succeeded in waking him up by yelling loudly. "We want to drive a little farther—along this straight street—do you understand?"

"Yes, sir, all right, sir. . . ."

Emma climbed back in; Franz followed. The coachman whipped the horses and they flew across the muddy street as if mad. But the two in the carriage held each other in a tight embrace while the carriage tossed them from side to side.

"Isn't this beautiful, too?" Emma whispered, her lips close to his.

At that very moment it seemed to her as if the carriage was suddenly flying up into the air—she felt herself hurled out; she wanted to grab hold of something but grasped only empty air. It seemed to her that she was spinning round and round in a circle at such a dizzying speed that she had to close her eyes—and suddenly she felt herself lying on the ground as an enormous, heavy silence broke over her, as if she were far away from the whole world and all alone. Soon she heard a jumble of noises: the sound of horse's hoofs pawing the ground nearby and a soft moaning, but she could see nothing. Then a wild fear gripped her and she screamed; and her terror became even greater when she realized that she couldn't hear her own screams. All of a sudden she knew exactly what had happened: the carriage had struck something, probably one of the milestones, had overturned, and they had been thrown out. Where is he? was her next thought. She called his name. And she heard her voice, very weakly to be sure, but she heard it. There was no answer. She tried to get up. She succeeded to the extent that she was able to sit up on the ground, and as she groped around with her hands she felt a human body near her. And now she could see more clearly in the darkness. Franz was lying next to her, completely motionless. She touched his face with her outstretched hand and felt something warm and moist flowing over it. She gasped. Blood? . . . What had happened? Franz was injured and unconscious. And the driver—where on earth was he? She called out to him. No answer. She was still sitting on the ground. Nothing's happened to me, she thought, although she felt pains all over her body. What should I do, what should I do . . . it isn't possible that nothing's happened to me. "Franz," she called. A voice nearby answered, "Where are ye, miss, where's the gentleman? Nothing's happened, has it? Wait a minute, miss, I'm just going to light the lantern so we can see somethin'. I don't know what's got into them nags today. It ain't my fault, by God . . . they went into a rut, the damned nags."

By this time Emma had stood up completely despite her pain, and, realizing that nothing had happened to the driver, she calmed down a bit. She heard the man open the lantern cover and strike a match. Anxiously she waited for the light. She didn't dare touch Franz again. He was lying stretched out on the ground next to her. She thought: everything seems worse when you can't see. He'll have his eyes open . . . nothing's really happened.

A beam of light came from the side. She suddenly saw the carriage, which to her surprise had not turned over but was only leaning crookedly against the ditch in the street, as though a wheel had broken. The horses were standing completely still. The light was coming closer. She saw it creep over the milestone and over the gravel heap; then it crawled over Franz's feet, glided over his body, and lit up his face, where it remained. The coachman had set the lantern on the ground next to the head of the outstretched man. Emma sank to her knees, and when she saw his face she felt as if her heart had stopped beating. He was pale, and his eyes were half open so that she could only see the whites. A stream of blood was slowly trickling down from his right temple over his cheek, losing itself under his collar. His teeth had bitten into his lower lip. "It's just not possible," Emma murmured to herself.

The driver was also kneeling down and staring at the face. Then he grabbed the head with both hands and lifted it up. "What are you doing?" screamed Emma in a muffled voice, and recoiled from this head that seemed to lift up of its own accord.

"Ma'am, I think an awful accident has happened."

"No, no," said Emma, "it can't be. It isn't true. Has anything happened to you? Or to me? . . ."

The coachman let the head of the motionless man slowly sink—into

Emma's lap. She was trembling. "If only somebody came . . . if only those peasants had come a quarter of an hour later. . . ."

"What shall we do?" said Emma with trembling lips.

"Well, miss, if that there carriage weren't broke . . . but as it looks like now . . . we've just got to wait till somebody comes." He continued talking, though Emma didn't take in his words, but meanwhile she regained control of her senses and suddenly knew what to do.

"How far is it to the nearest houses?" she asked.

"Not very far, miss, we're almost in the Franz Josef Quarter. . . . We'd see the houses if it was light. It's only about five minutes away."

"You go there, then, and get help. I'll stay."

"Yes, miss, but I think it'd be better if I stayed with you—it won't be long before somebody comes. It's the Reichsstrasse after all, and—"

"Then it'll be too late. It might be too late. We need a doctor."

The driver looked at the face of the motionless man, and then at Emma, shaking his head.

"You can't know that," cried Emma, "and I can't either."

"Yes, miss, . . . but where do I find a doctor in the Franz Josef Quarter?"

"Someone should go into the city center from there and . . ."

"Miss, d'ye know what? I think they'll have a telephone there. And we could call an ambulance then."

"Yes, that's the best thing to do! Go already, hurry up, run fast, for heaven's sake! And bring help. . . . And . . . please, just go. What are you still doing here?"

The driver was looking at the pale face now resting in Emma's lap. "Ambulance—doctor—they can't help much any more."

"Oh please, go! For God's sake! Go!"

"I'm going—just don't go getting scared here in the dark, miss." And he hurried off down the street. "It's not my fault, by God," he was murmuring to himself. "What an idea anyway, to go down the Reichsstrasse in the middle of the night. . . ."

Emma was left alone on the dark street with the motionless body. "What now?" she wondered. "It just isn't possible". . . the thought kept going through her head again and again . . . it just isn't possible. Suddenly she thought she heard breathing next to her. She bent down to the pale lips. No, there was not even the faintest breath coming from them. The blood on the temple and the cheeks appeared to have dried. She stared into the eyes, the broken eyes, and her whole body shook. Well, why don't I believe it?—it's a certainty . . . this is death! A horror seized her whole body. Her only thought now was: there's a dead man here. Just me and a dead man. There's a dead man in my lap! And with trembling hands she moved the head away and placed it back on the ground. Only then did a terrifying feeling of abandonment come over her. Why had she sent the coachman away? What stupidity! What should she do with a dead man on a main thoroughfare? If anyone came . . . yes, what on earth was she to do when someone came along? How long would she have to wait here? And she looked at the dead man again. I'm not alone with him after all, it suddenly occurred to her. The light is here. And it seemed to her as if the light of the lamp was something kind and friendly, for which she ought to be thankful. There was more life in this small flame than in the entire immense darkness around her. Yes, it almost seemed to her as if this light were a protection against this pale, horrifying man who lay next to her on the ground. . . . And she gazed into the light for so long that her eyes swam and everything began to dance. Suddenly she felt as though she were waking up. She jumped up. I can't do this, this is impossible, I can't be found here with him! . . . It seemed to her that she saw herself standing on the street, the dead man and the light at her feet, and that she loomed tremendously tall into the darkness. What am I waiting for? she thought, and her thoughts raced on. . . . What am I waiting for? Other people? What do they need me for? They'll come and ask . . . and I . . . what am I doing here? They'll all ask who I am. What should I tell them? Nothing. I won't say a word when they come; I'll say nothing. Not a word . . . they can't force me to, after all.

Voices came from afar.

Already? she thought. She listened anxiously. The voices were coming from the direction of the bridge. These couldn't be the people that the coachman had gone to get. But whoever they were, they would certainly notice the light—and that shouldn't happen, for then she would be discovered.

She kicked the lantern over with her foot. It went out. Now she was standing in total darkness. She saw nothing. Not even him. Only the white gravel heap gleamed a little. The voices came closer. Her whole body began to tremble. Only not to be discovered here! For God's sake, that was the only important thing, the only thing that counted—she would be lost if anyone discovered that she was the lover of . . . Now she folds her hands desperately. She prays that the people on the other side of the street will pass by without noticing her. She listens. Yes, over there. . . . What are they saying?. . . It's two or three women. They've discovered the carriage, because they're saying something about it; she can distinguish the words. A carriage . . . turned over . . . what else are they saying? She can't quite understand it. They're walking on . . . they're gone . . . thank God! And now, what now? On, why isn't she dead like him? He's to be envied; everything's over for him. For him there is no more danger and no more fear. But she's afraid of many, many things. She's afraid they will find her here, ask her who she is . . . that she'll have to go to the police, that everyone will find out that her husband . . . that her son . . .

And she doesn't understand why she's standing here for so long as though rooted to the spot. . . . She can leave, after all. She can't be of use to anyone here anymore, and she's only courting tragedy. She takes a step . . . carefully . . . she has to go over the ditch . . . across . . . one step up—oh, it's so muddy!—and two more steps, to the middle of the street . . . and then she stands still for a moment, looks ahead, and can see the dim outline of the road into the darkness. There—there is the city. She can't see anything in front of her . . . but she knows the right direction. Once more she turns around. It isn't so dark after all. She can now see the carriage pretty well, and the horses, too . . . and if she really tries she can make out something like the outline of a human body lying on the ground. She opens her eyes wide; she feels as if something is holding her back . . . the dead man wants to keep her there! She is terrified of his power . . . but she tears herself away with all her might, and now she notices what it is: the ground is muddy, she is standing on the slippery street, and the wet mud will not let her go. But now she is walking . . . walking faster . . . running . . . away from there . . . back . . . into the light, into the noise, toward others! She runs along the street and holds her dress up high in order not to fall. The wind is at her back; it's as if it is pushing her forward. She no longer knows exactly why she's fleeing. It seems to her that she has to flee from that pale man lying there far behind her next to the ditch . . . then she realizes that she is fleeing the living ones who will soon be there looking for her. What will they think? Won't they come after her? But they can't catch up with her anymore; she's almost at the bridge; she has a considerable head start, and now the danger is over. No one can possibly guess who she is; no one can know who that woman was who was driving over the Reichstrasse with that man. The driver doesn't know her and won't recognize her even if he should chance to see her someday. No one will bother about who she is, either. Whose business is it anyway? It was very wise of her not to stay, and not contemptible either. Franz himself would have said she was right to do what she did. She has to get home, after all. She has a son, she has a husband, she would be lost if they had found her there with her dead lover. There's the bridge; the street seems brighter . . . yes, she already hears the water rushing beneath her as it did before. She is now at the same place where she walked with him arm in arm—when—when? How many hours ago? It can't have been very long ago. Not long? Maybe it was! Maybe she had been unconscious for a long time, maybe it's already after midnight, maybe it's near morning and she is being missed at home. No, no, that just isn't possible; she knows that she wasn't unconscious at all. She remembers it now more clearly than she did at that first moment when she fell out of the carriage and realized what had happened. She runs over the bridge and hears her steps echo. She looks neither left nor right. Now she notices a figure coming toward her. She slows down. Who can be coming toward her? It's someone in uniform. She walks very slowly. She mustn't attract attention. She believes the man has his eyes fixed on her. What if he asks her? She's now near him and recognizes the uniform; it's a policeman, and she passes him. She hears him pausing behind her. With effort she stops herself from running again; that would be suspicious. She walks on as slowly as she did before. She hears the jangle of the horse-drawn tram. It can't be anywhere near midnight yet. She walks a little faster now; she hurries toward the city whose lights she can now see gleaming in the distance from where she is under the railroad viaduct at the end of the street, toward the city whose muted tumult she thinks she already hears. Just this one lonely side street and then she's safe. Now she hears shrill whistles in the distance, coming ever louder and nearer. A carriage races past her. Instinctively she stands still and follows it with her gaze. It's the ambulance carriage. She knows where it's going. How fast it's going! she thinks. . . . It's like magic. For a moment she feels as though she must call out to the ambulance, as though she must go with it, go back to where she's just come from—and for a moment the most enormous shame she has ever experienced overcomes her, and she knows that she's been cowardly and bad. But as she hears the sound of the wheels and the whistles receding in the distance, a wild joy comes over her, and she hurries forward like one saved. People are coming toward her; she is not afraid of them anymore—the worst is over. The tumult of the city becomes more audible; there's more and more light around her. Already she sees the rows of houses on the Praterstrasse, and she feels as though a flood of people into which she could disappear without a trace awaits her. As she comes to a street lantern she has the presence of mind to look at her watch. It's ten minutes before nine. She holds the watch to her ear—it hasn't stopped. And she thinks: I'm alive and healthy . . . even my watch is still running . . . and he . . . he . . . dead . . . fate. . . . She feels as though everything is forgiven her . . . as though she has never been guilty of any wrongdoing. That's clear to her now, yes, that's clear. She hears herself saying these words out loud. And what if fate had decreed otherwise?— what if she were the one now lying in the ditch and he were still alive? He would not have fled, no . . . not he. Well, he's a man. She's a woman—and has a child and a husband. She was right to act the way she did—it was her duty—yes, her duty. But she knows very well that she didn't act as she did out of a sense of duty. . . . But still she did the right thing. Instinctively . . . as . . . decent people always do. By now she would already have been discovered. Now the doctors would be asking her: and your husband, madam? O God! . . . and the newspaper tomorrow—and the family—she would have been destroyed for all time and still she wouldn't have been able to bring him back to life. Yes, that was the main thing; she would have destroyed herself for nothing. Now she's under the railroad bridge. Keep going . . . keep going. . . . Here is the Tegetthoff Monument, where many streets come together. Today, on this rainy, windy autumn evening, there are few people outdoors at this hour, but she feels as though the life of the city is surging around her, because where she came from there was only the most awful silence. She still has time. She knows that her husband won't get home today until around ten—she can even still change her clothes. Now it occurs to her to look at her dress. To her horror she notices that it's filthy. What will she tell the chambermaid? It occurs to her that tomorrow the story of the accident will be in all the newspapers. Everyone will read about a woman who had been in the carriage but could not be found afterward. At this thought she starts to tremble all over again—one careless move and all her cowardice will have been in vain. But she has her house key with her; she will open the door herself—she'll be careful not to be heard. She quickly catches a carriage. She is about to give the driver her address when it occurs to her that that might not be the best thing, and instead she gives him the name of the first street that happens to occur to her. As she is driving through the Praterstrasse, she wants to feel something, anything, but she can't. She has only one wish: to be at home, to be safe. Nothing else matters. The moment she decided to leave the dead man lying on the street, everything in her that wanted to mourn and lament him had to be suppressed. She can feel nothing but concern for herself. She's not heartless . . . oh no! . . . she's sure that in days to come she will feel despair. Maybe it will destroy her in the end, but now there is nothing in her except the desire to sit calmly, with dry eyes, at home at the table with her husband and her son. She looks through the window. The carriage is driving through the inner city; here everything is well lit, and quite a few people are hurrying by. Then it suddenly seems to her that everything that's happened in the last few hours could not be real. It was like a bad dream . . . completely incomprehensible. She bids the carriage to stop in a side street off the Ring, climbs out, hurries around the corner, and then gets into another one, giving the driver her address. She feels that she can't think anymore. Where is he now? she wonders. She closes her eyes and sees him in front of her, lying on a stretcher in the ambulance—and suddenly she feels as though she were sitting next to him and riding with him. And the carriage begins to sway, and she fears that she'll be thrown out as before—and she screams. The carriage stops. She's startled; she's already in front of her house. Quickly she steps out and hurries through the hallway with such light steps that the porter behind his window doesn't even look up. She races up the stairs, opens the door so quietly that no one hears . . . through the hall into her bedroom—she's made it! She turns on the light, tears off her clothes, and hides them in the armoire. They will dry overnight—tomorrow she'll brush and clean them herself. Then she washes her face and hands and puts on a dressing gown.

Then the doorbell rings. She hears the chambermaid go to the front door and open it. She hears her husband's voice; she hears how he puts down his cane. She feels that she must be strong now or everything will have been in vain. She hurries into the dining room so that she enters at the same time as her husband does.

"Ah, you're home already?" he says.

"Certainly," she answered, "I've been here for quite a while."

"Evidently no one saw you come in." She smiles without having to force herself. It just makes her very tired, having to smile. He kisses her on the forehead.

The little boy is already sitting at the table; he has had to wait a long time and has fallen asleep. He had put a book on the plate, and his head now rests on the open book. She sits next to him; her husband sits across from her, picks up a newspaper, and fleetingly glances at it. Then he puts it down and says, "The others are still at the meeting and continuing the discussion."

"What about?" she asks.

And he begins to talk about today's meeting, in great detail and for a very long time. Emma pretends that she's listening and nods from time to time.

But she hears nothing. She doesn't know what he's talking about, and she feels like someone who has magically escaped horrible dangers . . . she feels nothing except: I'm home! And while her husband keeps on talking, she moves her chair closer to her son, takes his head,

and presses him to her breast. An enormous weariness overcomes her—
she can't control herself; she suddenly feels sleep overpower her, and she
closes her eyes.

Suddenly a possibility that she had not thought about since the moment she had climbed out of the ditch comes to her. What if he isn't really dead after all? If he . . . no, it couldn't be . . . those eyes . . . that
mouth—and then . . . no breath from his lips. But there's such a thing as
a death trance—instances when someone was only apparently dead, and
even practiced eyes had erred. And she herself certainly didn't have a
practiced eye. If he were still alive, if he had regained consciousness, if
he had suddenly found himself all alone in the middle of the night on the
highway . . . if he were calling out to her . . . her name . . . if in the end
he were to worry that she herself was injured . . . if he were to tell the
doctors that there was a woman, too, a woman who must have been
thrown farther still? And . . . and . . . yes, what then? They would search
for her. The coachman would come back from the Franz Josef Quarter
with others . . . he would explain . . . there was a woman here when I
left—and Franz would guess. Franz would know . . . he knew her so
well . . . he would know that she had run away, and a terrible fury would
seize him, and he would speak her name in order to revenge himself. Because he is lost . . . and he would be so devastated that she had left him in
his final hour that he would say ruthlessly: it was Frau Emma, my
lover . . . a coward, and also stupid, because isn't it true, my dear doctors,
you certainly would not have asked her name if you had been asked to be
discreet. You would have let her go, and I, too, oh, yes—only she should
have stayed here until you came. But since she acted so badly, I'm telling
you who she is . . . it's . . . Oh!

"What's the matter with you," the professor asked in a serious tone
of voice, standing up.

"What . . . how . . . what is it?"

"What's wrong with you?"

"Nothing." She presses the boy closer to her.

The professor looks at her for a long time. "Do you know that you
began to doze and . . ."

"And?"

"You suddenly screamed."

". . . Really?"

"As if you were having a nightmare. Were you dreaming?"

"I don't know. I don't know anything."

And in the wall mirror opposite her she sees a face, a face with a dreadful smile and distorted features. She knows it's her own face, but still she's afraid of it. . . . And she notices that it's becoming frozen. She can't move her mouth now; she knows: this dreadful smile will play around her lips for the rest of her life. She tries to scream. Then she feels two hands on her shoulders and sees how the face of her husband is forcing itself between her own face and the face in the mirror. His eyes, questioning and threatening, are sinking into hers. She knows: if she doesn't pass this last test, everything is lost. And she feels herself becoming stronger again; once again she has control over her expressions and her limbs. At this moment she can do with them what she wants, but she has to use this moment, otherwise everything is over. With both her hands she reaches for her husband's hand, still lying on her shoulders, and draws him down to her and smiles at him cheerfully and tenderly.

And as she feels her husband's lips on her brow, she thinks: of course . . . a bad dream. He wouldn't tell anyone, would never take revenge, never . . . he's dead . . . he's most certainly dead . . . and the dead are silent.

"Why are you saying that?" she suddenly hears her husband's voice say.

She's struck with terror. "What did I say?" And it seems to her that she had suddenly said everything out loud . . . that she had told the whole story of the evening here at table . . . and once more she asks, collapsing under his horrified gaze, "What did I say?"

"The dead are silent," her husband repeats, very slowly.

"Yes . . ." she says, "yes . . ."

And, looking him in the eyes, she realizes that she can no longer hide anything from him, and they look at each other for a long time. "Put the boy to bed," he then says to her. "I think you have something more to tell me. . . ."

"Yes," she says.

And she knows that in the next moment she'll tell this man, whom she has deceived for many years, the whole truth.

And as she slowly goes through the door with her boy, her husband's eyes on her, a great calm comes over her, as though everything, everything will be all right again. . . .

Blind Geronimo and
His Brother

BLIND GERONIMO got up off the bench and picked up the guitar lying ready on the table next to the wine glass. He had just heard the distant, faint rumble of the first carriages. Now he felt his way along the familiar path to the open door and began to descend the narrow, freestanding wooden steps that led into the covered courtyard below. His brother followed him, and the two positioned themselves next to the staircase with their backs against the wall, in order to protect themselves against the cold, damp wind that whipped over the muddy floor through the open gates.

All the carriages taking the road over the Stilfser Pass had to pass beneath the gloomy arch of the old inn. For travelers going from Italy to the Austrian Tirol, it was the last stop before the climb to the summit began. The inn did not encourage a long stay, however, for its position between two bare cliffs blocked the mountain view. But the blind Italian and his brother Carlo had more or less made it their home during the summer months.

The mail coach arrived, and other carriages came shortly after. Most of the travelers stayed seated in their places, well wrapped in their blankets and coats. The few who climbed out paced impatiently up and down between the arches. The weather continued to grow worse, and a cold rain splattered on the ground. After a series of beautiful days, fall seemed to have arrived suddenly and much too early.

The blind man sang and accompanied himself on the guitar. He sang with an uneven and sometimes suddenly shrill voice, as always when he had been drinking. Now and then he turned his head upward with what seemed to be an expression of futile pleading. Yet the features of the face with the black stubble and the bluish lips remained totally immobile. The older man, his brother, stood almost motionless next to him. Whenever someone dropped a coin into his hat, he nodded his thanks and glanced at the donor's face with a quick unfocused look. But immediately, almost fearfully, he turned away again and, like his brother, stared into space. It was as though his eyes were ashamed of the gift of light that had been granted them and which he could not share with his blind brother.

"Bring me some wine," said Geronimo, and Carlo went, obedient as always. As he walked up the stairs, Geronimo began to sing again. He hadn't listened to his own voice for a long time, and therefore could pay attention to what was happening around him. He heard two whispering voices very close to him, those of a young man and a young woman. He wondered how often these two might already have traveled this same road back and forth, for in his blindness and his intoxication it seemed to him sometimes as though the same people wandered over the pass daily, sometimes from north to south, sometimes from south to north. And so he felt that this young couple, too, were old acquaintances of his.

Carlo came down and handed Geronimo a glass of wine. The blind man raised it toward the young couple and said, "To your health, ladies and gentlemen!"

"Thanks," said the young man, but the young woman pulled him away, for she felt uneasy near the blind man.

At that moment a carriage containing a rather boisterous crowd pulled in: it was a father, a mother, three children, and a nursemaid.

"A German family," Geronimo whispered to Carlo.

The father gave each of the children a coin to toss into the beggar's hat. Every time one fell in, Geronimo nodded a thank you. The oldest boy looked the blind man in the face with an anxious curiosity. Carlo observed him. The sight of the boy forced him to remember, as he always did when he saw children of that age, that Geronimo had been that very age when the misfortune through which he had lost his eyesight had occurred. Even today, almost twenty years later, he still remembered that day with total clarity. The shrill, piercing outcry with which little Geronimo had collapsed on the lawn still rang in his ears today; he still saw the sunlight playing and dancing on the white garden wall, and he still heard the Sunday church bells which had begun to peal at that very moment. He had been shooting at the ash tree in front of the garden wall with his peashooter, as he had often done before, and he knew as soon as he heard the scream that he must have injured his little brother, who had run by just then. He let the peashooter fall from his hands, jumped through the window into the garden, and dashed over to his little brother who was lying on the grass screaming with his hands clutched tightly over his face. Blood was dripping down his right cheek and his neck. At that very moment their father had returned home from the fields through the small garden gate, and both of them had knelt down helplessly next to the wailing child.

Neighbors had rushed over; the old Vanetti woman was the first who was able finally to remove the child's hands from his face. Then the blacksmith to whom Carlo had been apprenticed at the time and who knew a little bit about first aid arrived and saw immediately that the right eye was lost. The doctor who had come that evening from Poschiavo couldn't help either. On the contrary, he had warned that the other eye was in danger, too. And he had been right. A year later Geronimo's world had sunk into darkness.

At first everyone had tried to persuade him that he would recover later on, and he seemed to believe it. But Carlo, who knew the truth, had roamed the country road between the vineyards and the forest for many days and nights, and had come close to committing suicide. But the priest in whom he had confided had explained to him that it was his duty to live and to dedicate his life to his brother. Carlo was convinced. A terrible pity seized him. Only when he was with the blind boy, when he could stroke his hair and was allowed to kiss his forehead, tell him stories, and take him for walks in the fields behind the house and between the grapevines, did his agony cease. Ever since the accident he had neglected his apprenticeship in the blacksmith's shop because he could not bear to be separated from his brother, and later he was unable to commit himself again to his trade, despite his father's warnings and admonitions. One day it suddenly struck Carlo that Geronimo had entirely stopped talking about his misfortune. Soon he knew why: the blind boy had come to realize that he would never again see the sky, the hills, the roads, other people, or any light at all. Now Carlo suffered more than ever, even though he tried to calm himself with the thought that he had caused the accident quite unintentionally. And sometimes, when he watched his brother sleeping next to him early in the morning, he was seized by such a fear of seeing him awaken that he ran out into the garden so as not to have to be there when those lifeless eyes once again tried to find the light that had forever vanished for them. It was at that time that Carlo thought of having Geronimo, who had a pleasant voice, take music lessons. The school teacher from Tola, who sometimes came over to their village on Sundays, taught him to play the guitar. Of course at that time the blind boy had no idea that his newly learned art would one day become his livelihood.

With that miserable summer's day, misfortune seemed to have moved permanently into the house of old Lagardi. The harvest failed year after year, and a relative cheated the old man out of the small amount of money he had managed to save. When he was felled by a stroke while out in the fields on a sweltering August day and died, he left nothing but debts. The small estate was sold, and the two brothers, now homeless and poor, left the village.

Carlo was twenty, Geronimo fifteen years old. It was then that they began their life of begging and wandering which they led to this day. At first Carlo had thought about looking for some sort of work that would support the two of them, but nothing had worked out. Besides, Geronimo was restless and always wanted to be on the road.

For twenty years now they had been wandering up and down the roads and mountain passes of northern Italy and the southern Tirol, placing themselves wherever the heaviest stream of travelers flowed by.

And even if Carlo now, after so many years, no longer felt the burning torment with which every gleam of the sun, every view of a pleasant landscape, had earlier filled him, an ever-present, gnawing pity of which he was scarcely aware was always with him, like the beating of his heart and the heaving of his breath. And he was glad when Geronimo got drunk.

The carriage with the German family had driven off. Carlo sat down on the bottom step of the stairs, as he liked to do, but Geronimo remained standing, letting his arms hang limply down and tilting his head skyward.

Maria, the maid, came out of the inn above.

"Did you make a lot of money today?" she called down.

Carlo didn't even turn around. The blind man bent over toward his glass, picked it up off the ground, and drank to Maria. In the evening she would sometimes sit with him in the inn, and he knew that she was good-looking.

Carlo leaned forward and looked down the road. The wind was blowing, and the rain clattered so loudly on the stones that the rumbling of the oncoming carriage was lost in the violent noise. Carlo stood up again and once more took his place at his brother's side.

Geronimo began to sing while the carriage with only one passenger was pulling in. The driver hurriedly unhitched the horses and then rushed up to the inn. The traveler remained seated in his corner, completely enveloped in his grey raincoat. He did not seem to hear the singing at all. But after a while he jumped out of the carriage and paced up and down near it in great haste. He kept rubbing his hands together to warm himself. Only then did he seem to notice the beggars. He placed himself opposite them and looked them over for a long time. Carlo nodded his head slightly, as though to greet him. The traveler was a very young man with a handsome, beardless face and restless eyes. After he had stood watching the beggars for a long time, he once more hurried over to the gate through which he would continue his travels, and shook his head in annoyance at the bleak view of the rain and the fog that presented itself to him.

"Well?" asked Geronimo.

"Nothing yet," answered Carlo, "He'll probably give us something when he leaves."

The traveler came back and leaned against the side of the carriage. The blind man began to sing. Now the young man seemed suddenly to listen with great interest. The stable boy appeared and hitched up the horses again. And only then, as if it were just now occurring to him, did the young man reach into his pocket and give Carlo a franc.

"Oh thank you, thank you," said Carlo.

The traveler seated himself in the carriage and wrapped himself in his coat again. Carlo picked up the glass from the ground and went up the wooden stairs. Geronimo continued to sing. The traveler leaned out of the carriage and shook his head with a simultaneous expression of superiority and sadness. Suddenly an idea seemed to strike him, and he smiled. He turned to the blind man who was standing barely two steps away from him, and asked, "What's your name?"

"Geronimo."

"Well, Geronimo, look out, don't let yourself be cheated!" At that moment the coachman appeared at the top of the stairs.

"What do you mean, 'cheated,' sir?"

"I just gave your companion a twenty-franc piece."

"Oh, sir, thank you, thank you."

"Yes. Well, watch out."

"He's my brother, sir; he doesn't cheat me."

The young man was taken aback for a moment, but while he was still deliberating on this, the coachman climbed into his seat and began to drive the horses forward. The young man leaned back with a toss of his head as though to say: destiny, take your course! And the carriage drove away.

The blind man sent lively gestures of gratitude in his direction, with both hands. Then he heard Carlo, who had just come out of the inn, call down to him, "Come on up, Geronimo, it's warm up here. Maria's made a fire."

Geronimo nodded, tucked his guitar under his arm, and groped his way up the stair rail. While still on the stairs, he began to shout, "Let me feel it! how long it's been since I last felt a gold piece!"

"What?" asked Carlo. "What are you talking about?"

Geronimo arrived at the top and reached for his brother's head with both hands, a gesture he always used to express joy or tenderness. "Carlo, my dear brother, there are good people in the world after all!"

"Of course," said Carlo. "Up to now we've made two lire and thirty centimes, and there's also some Austrian money, maybe half a lire."

"And twenty francs—and twenty francs!" shouted Geronimo. "I know about it!" He staggered into the room and plopped heavily down on the bench.

"You know about what?" asked Carlo.

"Stop joking around already! Put it in my hand! How long it's been since I've had a gold piece in my hand!"

"What are you talking about? Where would I get a gold piece? There are two or three lire here."

The blind man pounded on the table. "That's enough now, enough! Are you trying to hide it from me?"

Carlo looked at his brother with apprehension and astonishment. He sat down next to him, moved up close, and grasped his arm soothingly. "I'm not trying to hide anything from you. How can you think that? It didn't occur to anyone to give me a gold coin, I can assure you!"

"But he told me he did!"

"Who?"

"The young man who was pacing up and down."

"What? I don't understand."

"Well, he said to me, 'What's your name?' and then, 'Watch out, watch out, don't let yourself be cheated!'"

"You must have been dreaming, Geronimo—this is nonsense."

"Nonsense? I heard him say it, and I hear well. 'Don't let yourself be cheated, I gave him a gold piece.' No, actually he said, 'I gave him a twenty-franc piece.'"

The innkeeper came in. "What's the matter with you two? Have you given up your business? A four-horse carriage just drove up."

"Come on," shouted Carlo, "come on!"

Geronimo remained seated. "Why? Why should I come? What good does it do me? You stand there and—"

Carlo touched him on his arm. "Calm down; come on down now!"

Geronimo fell silent and obeyed his brother. But on the steps he said, "We'll talk about this later, we'll talk about this later!"

Carlo could not comprehend what had happened. Had Geronimo

suddenly lost his mind? For even though Geronimo was easily provoked to rage, he had never spoken to him in this way before.

In the carriage that had just arrived sat two Englishmen. Carlo tipped his hat to them, and the blind man sang. One of the Englishmen climbed down and threw a couple of coins into Carlo's hat. "Thank you," said Carlo, and then, as though to himself, "Twenty centimes." Geronimo's face remained motionless, and he began a new song. The carriage with the two Englishmen drove off.

The brothers went silently back up the stairs. Geronimo seated himself on the bench, and Carlo remained standing by the stove.

"Why don't you say something?" asked Geronimo.

"Well," replied Carlo, "it's exactly the way I told you." His voice shook a little.

"What did you say?" asked Geronimo.

"Maybe he was crazy."

"Crazy? Wouldn't that be wonderful! When someone says, 'I gave your brother twenty francs,' he must be crazy, huh! And why did he say, 'Don't let yourself be cheated'—huh?"

"Okay, maybe he wasn't crazy . . . but there are people who like to play jokes on us poor folk. . . ."

"Hah," shouted Geronimo. "Jokes? Yes, you would say that—I was waiting for that!" He drank the glass of wine standing in front of him.

"But Geronimo!" protested Carlo, and noticed that in his dismay he could hardly speak, "why should I . . . how could you believe . . . ?"

"Why is your voice quivering . . . hah? . . . why?"

"Geronimo, I assure you, I . . ."

"Hah—and I don't believe you! Now you're laughing . . . I know you're laughing!"

The stable boy called from below, "Hey, blind man, some more people just arrived!"

The two brothers stood up mechanically and went down the stairs. Two carriages had arrived simultaneously, one carrying three men, the other an old married couple. Geronimo sang and Carlo stood next to him, perplexed. What should he do now? His brother didn't believe him! How was that possible? With a sidelong glance he anxiously observed Geronimo, who was singing his songs with a broken voice. It seemed to him that in Geronimo's face he could see the shadow of thoughts that he had never suspected before.

The carriages were already gone, but Geronimo kept on singing. Carlo didn't dare to interrupt him. He didn't know what to say, and he worried that his voice would quiver again. Then he heard laughter from above, and Maria called down, "Why are you still singing? You're not going to get anything from me!"

Geronimo stopped suddenly in the middle of a song. It sounded as though his voice and the guitar string had both snapped at the same time. Then he went up the stairs, and Carlo followed him. He sat down next to his brother in the inn. What should he do? He had no choice: he had to try once more to clear this up with his brother.

"Geronimo," he said, "I swear to you . . . think it through, Geronimo, how can you believe that I . . ."

Geronimo remained silent; his lifeless eyes seemed to be looking at the grey fog outside the window. Carlo kept talking. "Well, maybe the man wasn't crazy, maybe he just made a mistake . . . yes, he just made a mistake. . . ." But he sensed that he didn't believe what he was saying himself.

Geronimo moved away from him impatiently. But Carlo kept on talking, with a sudden intensity: "Why should I . . . you know that I don't eat or drink any more than you do, and if I buy something new to wear, you know it. . . . Why would I need so much money? What would I do with it?"

At that Geronimo hissed through his teeth, "Stop lying! I hear how you're lying!"

"I'm not lying, Geronimo, I'm not lying!" gasped Carlo, now frightened.

"Hah! Did you give it to her already then? Or is she going to get it afterward?" shouted Geronimo.

"Who, Maria?"

"Who else! Maria of course! Hah, you liar, you thief!" And as if he no longer wanted even to sit next to him at the same table, he elbowed his brother roughly in the ribs.

Carlo stood up. First he stared at his brother, then he left the room and went down the stairs into the courtyard. With wide eyes he stared out into the road that was sinking into a brownish fog in front of him. The rain had let up. Carlo stuck his hands in his pockets and went outside. He felt as though his brother had chased him away. What on earth had happened? . . . He still couldn't understand it. What kind of a man could he have been? To give a franc and say he had given twenty! He must have had some reason for saying so? . . . And Carlo tried to remember whether he had made an enemy somewhere who might have sent someone to get back at him. . . . But as hard as he tried, he couldn't remember ever insulting anyone, or having had a single serious argument with anyone. For twenty years he had done nothing but stand in courtyards or on the edge of roads with his hat in his hand. . . . Did someone have it in for him because of a woman? . . . But it had been so long since he had had anything to do with a woman! . . . the waitress in La Rosa had been the last one, and that was last spring . . . and no one could have envied her . . . it was incomprehensible! . . . What kind of people existed in that world out there that he didn't know? . . . they came from everywhere . . . what did he know about them? . . . This stranger must have had a reason for saying to Geronimo, 'I gave your brother a twenty-franc piece.'. . . Well, then . . . but what to do? . . . Suddenly it was clear to him that Geronimo didn't trust him! . . . he couldn't stand that! He had to do something to fight back. . . . And he hurried back.

When he came back into the inn, Geronimo was stretched out on the bench and didn't seem to notice Carlo's entrance. Maria brought both of them food and drink. They didn't speak a single word during the entire meal. As Maria was clearing the dishes, Geronimo suddenly laughed out loud and said to her, "What are you going to buy with it?"

"With what?"

"Well, what are you going to buy? A new dress or earrings?"

"What does he want from me?" she turned and asked Carlo.

Meanwhile the sound of heavily loaded wagons and loud voices rose from the courtyard below, and Maria rushed downstairs. After a few minutes three drivers came up and took a table; the innkeeper came over and greeted them. They complained about the bad weather.

"You're going to get snow tonight," said one of them.

The second driver recounted how ten years ago he had been snowed in in the middle of the pass in mid-August and had almost frozen to death. Maria sat down and joined them. The stable boy also joined them and asked for news of his parents who lived down below in Bormio.

Just then yet another carriage filled with travelers arrived. Geronimo and Carlo went downstairs, Geronimo sang, Carlo held out his hat, and the travelers gave their alms. Geronimo now seemed quite peaceful. Sometimes he asked, "How much?" and lightly nodded his assent to Carlo's answers. Meanwhile Carlo tried to gather his thoughts. But he couldn't get rid of the nagging, awful feeling that something terrible—something that he could not defend himself against—had happened.

As the brothers went back up the stairs, they heard the boisterous talk and laughter of the drivers upstairs. The youngest one called out to Geronimo, "Sing for us too! We'll pay you! Won't we?" he turned to the others.

Maria, who was just walking in with a bottle of red wine, said, "Don't start anything with him today, he's in a bad mood."

Instead of giving an answer, Geronimo stood up in the middle of the room and began to sing. When he finished, the drivers applauded.

"Come here, Carlo," one of them shouted. "We want to throw money in your hat just like the people downstairs do!" And he took a small coin and lifted his hand as if he wanted to drop it into the hat that Carlo was stretching out toward him. At that the blind man grasped the driver's arm and said, "Give it to me, give it to me instead! It could miss the mark and fall to the side!"

"Where would it fall?"

"Well, between Maria's legs!"

Everyone laughed, including the innkeeper and Maria; only Carlo stood there motionless. Never had Geronimo joked in this way! . . .

"Sit down with us! You're a funny guy!" shouted the drivers. And they squeezed closer together to make room for Geronimo. Their talk became ever louder and wilder, and Geronimo joined in, louder and more animated than usual, drinking without stopping. When Maria came in once more, he wanted to pull her toward him. One of the drivers said to him, laughing, "What, maybe you think she's beautiful? She's an old, ugly woman!"

But the blind man pulled Maria into his lap. "You're all stupid idiots," he said. "Do you think I need my eyes in order to see? I even know where Carlo is now—yes—he's standing over there at the stove with his hands in his pockets, and he's laughing."

Everyone looked at Carlo, who was leaning open-mouthed against the stove and was now twisting his mouth into a grin, as though he didn't wish to prove his brother a liar.

The stable boy came in to tell the drivers that if they still wanted to get to Bormio before dark, they had to hurry. They stood up and noisily said their goodbyes. The two brothers were once again alone in the restaurant. It was the hour when ordinarily they slept. The entire inn always sank into a peaceful calm at this time in the early hours of the afternoon. Geronimo, his head on the table, seemed to sleep. At first Carlo paced up and down, and then he too sat down on the bench. He was very tired. It seemed to him as though he were caught up in a terrible dream. He thought about all sorts of things, about yesterday and the day before yesterday, and all the days before that, and especially of the warm summer days and the white roads over which he was accustomed to wander with his brother, and all of that now seemed so remote and incomprehensible, as if it could never be the same again.

Late in the afternoon the mail carriage came from Tirol, and soon thereafter, at intervals, other carriages that were taking the same route south arrived. The brothers had to go down into the courtyard four more times. When they came back up for the last time, twilight had fallen and the oil lamp hanging from the wooden ceiling hissed. Workers from a nearby quarry who had set up their wooden huts a hundred paces below the inn came up. Geronimo sat down with them; Carlo remained alone at his table. It seemed to him that his loneliness had been with him for a very long time. He heard Geronimo speaking loudly, almost shouting, about his childhood, saying that he still remembered clearly everything he had seen before he went blind—the people and the things he knew: his father as he worked in the fields, the small garden with the ash tree near the wall, the little low house that belonged to them, the shoemaker's two small daughters, the vineyard behind the church; yes, even his own face as he had seen it in a mirror as a child. How often Carlo had heard him tell all this! Today he couldn't bear it. It all sounded so different: every word that Geronimo said had a new meaning and seemed to be directed against him. He slipped out and walked toward the main road, now lying in total darkness. The rain had stopped, the air was quite cold, and he was almost tempted by the thought of going farther and farther, deeper into the blackness, and finally lying down at the end somewhere in a ditch by the side of the road, falling asleep, and not awakening again. Suddenly he heard the rumbling of a carriage and caught sight of two beams of light from two lanterns coming closer and closer. In the carriage that drove past sat two men. The one with a narrow and beardless face started when he saw Carlo's figure appear out of the darkness in the light of the lanterns. Carlo, who had stood still, lifted his hat. The carriage and the lights disappeared. Carlo was once more standing in complete darkness. Suddenly he started in fear. For the first time in his life he was afraid of the dark. He felt he couldn't stand it a minute longer. In his dulled senses, his dread in a strange way mixed with the tormenting pity for his brother and chased him back home.

When he entered the inn he saw the two travelers who had driven past him a moment ago, sitting at a table with a bottle of red wine, talking earnestly to each other. They hardly looked up when he entered.

At the other table Geronimo was sitting with the workers as before.

"Where have you been hiding, Carlo?" the innkeeper said to him when he entered. "Why did you leave your brother all alone?"

"Why, what's wrong?" Carlo asked anxiously.

"Geronimo's treating everyone. It isn't any of my business, but you two should remember that bad times will come again soon enough."

Carlo quickly walked over to his brother and grabbed him by the arm. "Come on!" he urged.

"What do you want?" shouted Geronimo.

"Come to bed," said Carlo.

"Leave me alone, leave me alone! I earn the money, I can do with it what I want—hey, you can't pocket everything! You all probably think he gives me everything! Oh no! I'm a blind man, after all! But there are people who—there are good people who tell me, 'I gave your brother twenty francs!'"

The workers burst out laughing.

"That's enough," said Carlo. "Come on!" And he pulled his brother along, almost dragged him, up the stairs to the bare attic room where they slept. The whole way Geronimo screamed, "Yeah, now it's come out, yeah, now I know it for sure! Oh, just wait. Where is she? Where's Maria? Or are you putting it in her savings account? Hah, I sing for you, I play the guitar, you live off of me—and you're a thief!" And he fell down on the straw bed.

A dim light streamed in from the hallway; across the hall, the door to the only guest room of the inn stood open, and Maria was turning down the beds for the night. Carlo stood before his brother and saw him lying there with a bloated face and bluish lips, his damp hair sticking to his forehead, looking many years older than he was. And slowly he began to understand. His blind brother's mistrust could not have begun today; it must have been brewing in him for a long time, and only the opportunity, or perhaps the courage, to express it had been missing. So everything that Carlo had done for him so far had been in vain: in vain his remorse, in vain the offering of his whole life. What should he do now? Should he keep on leading him through his eternal night day after day, for who knows how long, keep on caring for him, begging for him, and have no other reward except mistrust and complaints? If his brother thought him a thief, any stranger would do as well or better. Truly, the best thing to do would be to leave him alone, to part from him forever. Then Geronimo would have to see that he was unjust; then would he find out what it means to be cheated and robbed, alone and miserable. And he, what should he do? Well, he wasn't old yet, after all; if he were all alone, he could begin to do a number of things. At the very least he could make a living as a hired hand somewhere. But while these thoughts were running through his head, his eyes all the while remained fixed on his brother. And he suddenly saw him in his mind's eye, alone and sitting on a rock at the edge of a sunlit road, staring with wide white eyes at a sky which could not blind him, his hands grasping into the eternal night that was always around him. And he realized that, just as the blind man had no one in the world except him, so he too had no one except this brother. He understood that his love for his brother was the whole meaning of his life, and he knew for the first time with total clarity that only the belief that the blind man returned his love and had forgiven him had let him bear all this misery so patiently. He could not give up this hope all at once. He felt that he needed his brother just as much as his brother needed him. He couldn't, he didn't want, to leave him. He had either to bear the mistrust or find a way to convince the blind man that his suspicion had no basis in reality. . . . Yes, if he could only get hold of that gold coin somehow! If he could say to his brother tomorrow morning, "I only kept it so that you wouldn't drink it away with the workers, so that these people wouldn't steal it from you" . . . or something like that.

He heard footsteps on the stairs coming closer; the travelers were going to bed. Suddenly the idea of knocking on their door and telling them truthfully what had happened and asking them for twenty francs flashed into his mind. But he knew immediately that it was totally pointless. They wouldn't even believe the story. And now he remembered how the one pale traveler had recoiled when he, Carlo, had suddenly appeared in the dark in front of his carriage.

He stretched himself out on the straw bed. It was pitch black in the room. Then he heard the workers walking heavily down the wooden steps, talking loudly. Soon after that both doors were closed. The stable boy went up and down the steps once more, but then it was completely quiet. The only thing Carlo now heard was Geronimo's snoring. Soon his thoughts became entangled with the beginning of a dream. When he awoke, it was still pitch dark. He looked in the direction of the window; if he strained his eyes, he could perceive a deep grey square in the middle of the impenetrable black. Geronimo was still sleeping the heavy sleep of the drunkard. And Carlo thought of the coming day, and shuddered. He thought about the night after this day, about the day after this night, about the future that lay before him, and he was filled with horror at the loneliness that awaited him. Why hadn't he been more courageous that evening? Why hadn't he gone up to the strangers and asked them for the twenty francs? Maybe they would have sympathized after all. And still—maybe it was better that he hadn't asked them. Well, why was it better? . . . He suddenly sat up straight and felt his heart beating. He knew why it was better: if they had turned him down, he would have been the one they suspected—but this way . . . He stared at the grey spot, which began to gleam faintly. . . . The idea now going through his mind, totally against his will, was impossible, totally impossible! . . . The door across the way was locked . . . and anyway, they could wake up. . . . Yes, over there . . . the grey spot outside in the middle of the darkness was the new day. . . .

Carlo stood up as though pulled by some force, and touched his forehead to the cold windowpane. Why had he gotten up? To think about it? . . . To try it? . . . What then? . . . It was just impossible—and besides that, it was a crime. A crime? What did twenty francs mean to such people, people who traveled a thousand miles just for pleasure? They wouldn't even notice that it was missing. . . . He went over to the door and carefully opened it. Right opposite, just two steps away, was the other one, closed. On a nail in the doorpost hung some clothes. Carlo felt the clothes with his hands. . . . Yes, if people left their wallets in their pockets, then life would be very simple, then soon no one would have to go begging anymore . . . but the pockets were empty. Well, now what? Go back to the room, to the straw bed. Maybe there was a better way of getting the twenty francs—a less dangerous and more legitimate way. If he really did hold back a few centimes from the handouts each time until he had saved twenty francs, and then bought the gold coin? . . . But how long would that take? Months, perhaps a year. Oh, if only he had the courage! He was still standing in the hallway. He glanced toward the door. What was this stream of light slanting vertically from the top of the door down to the floor? Was it possible? Was the door only ajar, not locked? . . . Why was he so astonished at that? For months now that door didn't close. Why should it, really? He remembered: people had slept here only three times this summer; twice it was traveling journeymen, and once a tourist who had injured his foot. The door isn't closed—he only needs courage now—yes, and luck! Courage? The worst that can happen is that both men will wake up, but if they do, he can always find some excuse. He peers through the crack into the room. It's still so dark that he can only make out the outlines of two sleeping figures on the bed.

He listens closely: they are both breathing calmly and regularly. Carlo opens the door quietly and enters the room noiselessly in his bare feet. The two beds are standing lengthwise on the same wall opposite the window. In the middle of the room there is a table; Carlo sneaks over to it. He runs his hand over the surface and feels a key ring, a penknife, a little book—and nothing else. . . . Well, of course! That he could have thought they would leave their money out on the table! Now he could leave again right away! . . . And yet, maybe it would take only a good grasp and he would succeed. . . . Now he nears the bed near the door; here, on the armchair, there is something—he feels for it—it's a revolver! . . . Carlo recoils. . . . Should he just go ahead and take it? Why did this man have a revolver ready, anyway? What if he should wake up and notice him? . . . But no, he would just say: it's three o'clock, sir, time to get up! . . . And he leaves the revolver lying there.

He creeps farther into the room. Here on another armchair underneath some underwear . . . Good God! here it is . . . here is a wallet—he has it in his hand! . . . At that moment he hears a soft creaking. With a sudden movement he drops lengthwise at the foot of the bed . . . there is another creak—and heavy breathing—a clearing of a throat—then silence again, deep silence. Carlo remains lying on the floor, the wallet in his hand, and waits. There is no other movement. The pale light of dawn is already breaking into the room. Carlo doesn't dare stand up again but crawls along the floor toward the door, which is open wide enough to let him through; he crawls farther out into the hallway, and only there does he stand up slowly, with a deep sigh. He opens the wallet, which has three compartments; to the right and the left there are only small silver pieces. Now Carlo opens the middle section, which is closed with another latch, and he feels three twenty-franc pieces. For a moment he thinks about taking two of them but quickly resists the temptation, takes only one gold piece, and closes the wallet. Then he kneels down, looks through the crack into the room, which is completely still again, and then he gives the wallet a shove so that it glides underneath the second bed. When the stranger wakes up, he'll think it fell from the armchair. Carlo gets up slowly. Then the floor creaks softly, and at the same moment he hears a voice inside the room say, "What's that? What's going on?" Carlo quickly takes a few steps backward with bated breath, and slips into his own room. Now he is safe and listens hard. . . . Once more the bed across the way creaks, and then there is silence. Between his fingers he has the gold piece. He did it—he did it! He has the twenty francs, and he can tell his brother, "You see now, I'm not a thief!" They'll start off on their journey today—southward to Bormio, and then through the Veltlin Valley . . . to Triano . . . to Edole . . . to Brena . . . to the Lake of Iseo, just as they did last year. . . . That won't look suspicious at all, since the day before yesterday he had told the innkeeper, "We'll be going down the mountain in a couple of days."

It gets lighter and lighter; the whole room is now lit by the grey of dawn. Oh, if only Geronimo would wake up soon! It was so good to walk early in the morning! They could still leave before sunrise. They'd wish the innkeeper, the stable boy, and Maria a good morning and then be on their way. . . . And only when they're two hours away, already near the valley, will he tell Geronimo.

Geronimo stretches himself in bed. Carlo calls to him, "Geronimo!"

"Well, what is it?" Geronimo props himself up with both hands and sits up.

"Geronimo, let's get up."

"Why?" He turns his lifeless eyes toward his brother. Carlo knows Geronimo is now remembering yesterday's incident, but he also knows that he won't say a word about it until he's drunk again.

"It's cold already, Geronimo. Let's leave. It's not going to get better. I think we should go. We can be in Boladore by noon."

Geronimo got up. The sounds of the awakening house became audible. Down in the courtyard the innkeeper was speaking with the stable boy. Carlo stood up and went downstairs. He was usually awake early and often went into the street right at daybreak. He went up to the innkeeper and said, "We're going to say our goodbye."

"Oh, you're going today already?" asked the innkeeper.

"Yeah, it's already really cold when you stand in the yard and the wind cuts through it."

"Well, say hello to Baldetti when you get down to Bormio. Tell him not to forget to send me the oil."

"All right, I'll tell him. By the way—last night's lodging." He reached into his sack.

"That's okay, Carlo," said the innkeeper. "I'll make the twenty centimes a gift for your brother. I heard what he said, too. Good morning."

"Thanks," said Carlo. "Besides, we're not in that much of a hurry. We'll see you again when you come back from your cottages; Bormio isn't going anywhere, is it?" He laughed and went up the wooden stairs.

Geronimo was standing in the middle of the room and said, "Well, I'm ready to go now."

"I'm coming," said Carlo.

From an old chest which was standing in a corner of the room he took their few possessions and packed them in a bundle. Then he said, "It's a beautiful day, but very cold."

"I know," said Geronimo. The two left the room.

"Walk quietly," said Carlo, "the two who came last night are sleeping here." They walked down carefully. "The innkeeper says hello," said Carlo. "He gave us the twenty centimes for last night. He's out at the cottages now and won't be back for two hours. We'll see him again next year."

Geronimo didn't answer. He walked to the main road, which lay before them in the light of dawn. Carlo took his brother's left arm and the two walked silently down to the valley. After a short walk they were already at the spot where the road began to descend in long hairpin turns. Fog rose up toward them, and the peaks above them seemed enveloped by clouds. Now, Carlo thought, now I'll tell him.

But Carlo didn't say a word; he simply took the gold piece from his pocket and gave it to his brother, who took it between the fingers of his right hand, then pressed it on his cheek and on his forehead. Finally he nodded. "I knew it," he said.

"Well, yes," said Carlo, and looked at Geronimo with surprise.

"Even if the stranger hadn't told me anything, I still would have known it."

"Well, yes," said Carlo, at a loss. "But you do understand why, because of the other people up there—I was afraid that you'd take the whole amount and—and look, Geronimo, I thought to myself that it's about time you bought yourself a new coat, and a shirt and some shoes, I think. That's why I've . . ."

The blind man shook his head vigorously. "What for?" And he stroked his hand over his coat. "It's good enough, plenty warm enough, and we're heading south anyway."

Carlo didn't understand why Geronimo didn't seem at all happy, why he didn't apologize. And he continued talking, "Geronimo, didn't I do the right thing? Aren't you glad? This way we have the whole amount left. If I had told you up there, who knows. . . . Oh, it's a good thing I didn't tell you—a good thing!"

At this Geronimo screamed at him, "Stop lying, Carlo! I've had enough of that!"

Carlo stopped and let go of his brother's arm. "I'm not lying."

"I know you're lying! . . . You're always lying! . . . You've already lied a hundred times! . . . You wanted to keep this for yourself, too, but you got worried, that's all!"

Carlo dropped his head and said nothing. He took the blind man's arm again and kept walking with him. He was hurt that Geronimo spoke this way, but actually he was surprised that he didn't feel sadder.

The fog began to break up. After a long silence Geronimo said, "It's getting warm." He said it indifferently, as a matter of course, just as he had said it a hundred times before, and Carlo knew: nothing has changed for Geronimo. I've always been a thief for Geronimo.

"Are you hungry yet?" he asked.

Geronimo nodded and at the same moment took a piece of cheese and a piece of bread from his coat and ate some of it. And they continued on.

They met the mail carriage from Bormio; the driver called to them, "Going down already?" Then other carriages, all of them going up the mountain, came by.

"The air from the valley," said Geronimo, and after one more quick turn, the Veltlin Valley lay at their feet.

Truly, nothing has changed, thought Carlo. . . . Now I've even stolen for him—and even that's been in vain.

The fog below them became thinner and thinner as the rays of the sun tore holes in it. And Carlo thought, "Maybe it wasn't so smart after all to leave the inn so quickly. . . . The wallet is lying underneath the bed, that's bound to be suspicious." But what did all that matter? Could anything worse happen to him now? His brother, whose eyesight he had destroyed, believed that he stole from him and has believed it for years and will always believe it—could anything worse happen to him?

Below them stood the big white hotel as though bathed in the gleam of the morning sun, and farther below, where the valley was beginning to broaden, the village stretched out lengthwise. The two continued on and Carlo kept his hand on the blind man's arm. They went past the hotel park, and Carlo saw guests on the terrace having breakfast in light summer clothes. "Where do you want to stay?" asked Carlo.

"Well, at the Adler, as usual."

When they finally arrived at the small inn at the other end of the village, they went in. They sat down in the tavern and ordered some wine.

"What are you doing here so early this year?" asked the innkeeper.

Carlo started a little at this question. "Is it so early? It's the tenth or eleventh of September, isn't it?"

"Last year when you came down it was much later."

"It's really cold up there already," said Carlo. "We froze last night. And oh yes, I'm supposed to tell you not to forget to send up some oil."

The air in the pub was heavy and humid. A strange restlessness came over Carlo; he wanted to be outside again, on the main street that went to Tirano, to Edole, to Lake Iseo, to anywhere, so long as it was far away! Suddenly he stood up.

"Are we leaving already?" asked Geronimo.

"We wanted to be in Boladore by noon, remember? The carriages stop at the Hirschen for the midday break, so that's a good place for us."

And they left. The barber Benozzi stood in front of his shop smoking. "Good morning!" he called. "Well, how is it up there? Probably snowed last night, right?"

"Yes, yes," said Carlo, and quickened his steps.

The village lay behind them, and the road stretched white through the meadows and the vineyards, alongside a rushing stream. The sky was blue and calm. "Why did I do it?" Carlo asked himself. He cast a sideways glance at the blind man. "Does his face look any different than usual? He's always believed it—and I've always been alone—he's always hated me!" And he felt as though he were walking along with a heavy load that he could never get off his shoulders, as though he could see the night through which Geronimo walked at his side while the sun lay bright on all the roads.

And they kept walking, walking, walking for hours. From time to time Geronimo sat on a milestone, or they both leaned against the railing of a bridge in order to rest. Again they passed through a village. In front of the inn there were carriages standing; a few travelers had gotten out and were walking up and down, but the two beggars didn't stay. Once more into the open road. The sun rose higher and higher; it must be getting near noon. It was a day like a thousand others.

"The tower of Boladore," said Geronimo. Carlo looked up. He was amazed at how exactly Geronimo could calculate distances: the tower of Boladore had actually appeared on the horizon. From rather far away someone came toward them. It seemed to Carlo as though he had been sitting in the road and had suddenly stood up. The figure came closer. Now Carlo saw it was a gendarme, one like they often encountered on the country road. Despite that, Carlo became a little anxious. But when the man came closer, he recognized him and calmed down. It was Pietro Tenelli; just last May the two beggars had sat with him at Raggazzi's inn in Morignone, where he had told them a terrifying story of how he had almost been stabbed to death by a vagrant.

"Somebody has stopped," said Geronimo.

"Tenelli, the gendarme."

Now they had come up to him.

"Good morning, Tenelli," said Carlo, and stopped in front of him.

"It's like this," said the gendarme, "for the time being I've got to take you to the station in Boladore."

"What!" exclaimed the blind man.

Carlo turned pale. How is this possible? he thought. It can't be about that. They certainly can't know about it down here yet.

"You seem to be going that way anyway," said the gendarme, laughing. "It can't make much difference to you if you come with me."

"Why don't you say something, Carlo?" asked Geronimo.

"Oh yes, well, I beg you, Tenelli, how is it possible . . . what are we supposed to . . . or rather, what am I supposed to . . . really, I don't know. . . ."

"It's like this. Maybe you're not guilty. I don't know. In any case, we received a telegram at the station that we should detain the two of you because you are suspected, are the prime suspects, of having stolen money from people up there. Now, it's also possible that you're innocent. So let's go!"

"Why don't you say something, Carlo?" asked Geronimo.

"I am, yes, I am. . . ."

"Come on! What's the sense of standing here on the road? The sun is burning. In an hour we'll be there. Let's go!"

Carlo took Geronimo's arm as usual, and the two moved slowly along, followed by the gendarme.

"Carlo, why don't you say something?" Geronimo asked again.

"But what do you want me to say, Geronimo—what should I say? Everything will be okay, I don't know myself. . . ."

And the thought went through his mind: should I tell him everything, before we stand before the judge? . . . I can't. The gendarme is listening. . . . Well, what's the difference? I'll tell the truth in court. "Your honor," I'll say, "this is not a theft like any other. It was like this. . . ." And now he made an effort to find the right words to present the matter before the court clearly and understandably. "Yesterday a man drove over the pass . . . he may have been a madman—or maybe he just made a mistake—and this man . . ."

But what nonsense! Who would believe it? . . . They wouldn't even let him talk that long. No one could believe this stupid story . . . not even Geronimo believes it. . . . And he cast a sideways glance at him. The blind man's head moved back and forth in rhythm with his steps as it usually did, but his face was motionless and his empty eyes stared into the air. And Carlo suddenly knew what thoughts were running through Geronimo's mind. . . . "So this is the way things are," Geronimo was probably thinking, "Carlo steals not only from me but from other people, too . . . well, he has it good, he has eyes that can see and he uses them. . . ." Yes, that's what Geronimo was thinking, most certainly. . . . And even the fact that they won't find any money on me won't help me . . . not in front of the judge, not in front of Geronimo. They'll lock me up and him . . . yes, they'll lock him up, too, because he has the gold piece. . . . And he couldn't think any more, he felt so confused. It seemed to him that he didn't understand anything at all, and he only knew one thing: that he would gladly sit in jail for a year—or for ten—if only Geronimo knew that he had stolen only for him.

And suddenly Geronimo stopped, so that Carlo also had to stop.

"Well, what is it?" said the gendarme, annoyed. "Go on, get going!" But then he saw with amazement that the blind man had let his guitar fall on the ground, raised his arms, and felt with both hands for his brother's cheeks. Then he moved his lips close to Carlo's mouth, who at first didn't know what was happening, and kissed him.

"Are you crazy?" asked the policeman. "Go on, go on already! I have no desire to roast."

Geronimo picked up his guitar from the ground without saying a word. Carlo breathed deeply and put his hand on the blind man's arm again. Was it possible? His brother wasn't angry with him anymore? He finally understood—? And, doubtfully, he looked at him from the side.

"Go on!" shouted the policeman. "Do you want a . . ." And he gave Carlo a jab between the ribs.

And Carlo, leading the blind man with a firm grasp, moved forward again. He walked at a much faster pace than before. For he saw Geronimo smile in the mild, blissful way that he had not seen him do since childhood. And Carlo also smiled. He felt as if nothing bad could happen to him now—neither before the judge, nor anywhere else in the world—for he had his brother again. . . . No, he had him for the first time. . . .

A Farewell

HE HAD ALREADY BEEN WAITING for an hour. His heart was beating fast, and sometimes it seemed to him that he had forgotten to breathe; he took deep breaths, but that didn't make him feel any better. He really should have been used to it by now, for it was always the same: invariably he had to wait, one, two, even three hours. How often altogether in vain! And he couldn't even reproach her, since she didn't dare leave her house if her husband happened to stay home longer than usual. Only after he had left would she come running in, in despair, press a kiss on his lips, and then immediately leave again, flying down the stairs and leaving him alone once more. Then, when she had gone, he would lie down on the sofa, completely exhausted from the tension of all these terrible hours of waiting, hours that made it impossible for him to work and that were slowly ruining him. This had been going on now for three months, ever since the end of spring. Every afternoon, from three o'clock on, he was in his room with the shades drawn, unable to do anything. He didn't have the patience to read a book or even a newspaper, was incapable of writing a letter, and did nothing but chain-smoke cigarettes until the room was thick with a blue-grey haze. The door to the reception room was always open, and he was always completely alone, as he couldn't have his valet there when she came. And then, when the doorbell suddenly rang, he always started. But when it was *her*, when it really was her, then everything was all right again. Then he felt as though freed from a spell, as if suddenly he were human again, and sometimes he would cry from pure joy that she was at last with him again and that he didn't have to wait any longer. Then he would quickly draw her into his room, close the door, and they would be blissfully happy.

They had agreed that he would stay at home every day until exactly seven o'clock, and that after that she *couldn't* come—he had explicitly told her that he would leave precisely at seven every day because waiting for her made him so nervous. Yet still he would stay at home longer, and often wouldn't leave until eight. Then he would think of all the wasted hours of waiting with a shudder and longingly remember the previous summer when his time had been his own and he had often driven out to the country on beautiful summer afternoons, had gone to the seashore in August, and had been healthy and happy—and he longed for this freedom, for the ability to travel, for distant places, for the privilege of being alone. But he couldn't leave her, for he adored her.

Today seemed to him the worst day of all. She hadn't come at all yesterday, and he had received no word from her. It was almost seven, but that didn't calm him today. He didn't know what to do. The worst thing was that he had absolutely no way of getting in touch with her. He couldn't do anything beyond walk up and down in front of her house and look at her windows, couldn't go to her, couldn't send anyone to her, couldn't ask anyone about her. For no one suspected that they knew each other. They existed in a restless, anxious, and intense tenderness toward one another and were always afraid of being found out. He was glad their relationship was kept secret, but days such as today were all the more painful because of that.

It was already eight—she had not come. He had been standing at his door constantly for the whole of the last hour and had kept looking into the hallway through the little view window in the door. The gas lights on the staircase had just been lit. He went back into his room and threw himself on his sofa, completely exhausted. It was pitch-dark in the room and he fell asleep. After half an hour he got up and decided to go out. He had a headache, and his legs ached as though he had been walking for hours.

He went in the direction of her house. It calmed him to see that all the shades of her windows had been drawn. He could see light gleaming through the shades of the dining room and her bedroom. He walked up and down on the sidewalk across the street from her house for half an hour, gazing up at her windows. There were few people on the street. Only when a few maids and the housekeeper came out of the gate to her house did he leave so as not to be noticed. That night he slept soundly and well.

The next morning he stayed in bed for a long time; he had left a note in the reception room saying that he did not wish to be awakened. At ten o'clock he rang his valet for breakfast. The day's mail lay on the plate, but there was no letter from her. He told himself this was a sign that she would definitely come in person in the afternoon, and thus he remained reasonably calm until three o'clock.

At exactly three, and not a minute before, he returned home from his lunch. He sat down in an armchair in the reception room so that he wouldn't have to run back and forth each time he heard a noise on the staircase. But he was glad whenever he heard any footsteps at all in the downstairs entry, for they always brought new hope. But none of the footsteps proved to be hers. The clock struck four—five—six—seven—and still she hadn't come. He paced up and down in his room, groaned softly, became dizzy, and threw himself on his bed. He was in total despair; he couldn't stand this any longer—the best thing was to go away—he was paying too high a price for this happiness! . . . Or he would have to change their agreement—for example, he would wait only an hour—or two—but things just couldn't go on this way. It would totally ruin him, destroy his ability to work, his health, and in the end even his love for her. He noticed that he wasn't thinking about *her* any more at all; his thoughts whirled about as if in a confused dream. He jumped up from his bed. He tore the window open and looked down at the street in the twilight . . . ah . . . there . . . there at the corner . . . he thought he recognized her in every woman that approached. He drew back from the window; she wouldn't be coming now anymore, for it was already too late. And suddenly it seemed absurd to him that he had set aside so few hours to wait for her. Perhaps only now did she have the opportunity to come—perhaps she could have come early this morning—and he already knew just what he would say to her at their next meeting. He whispered it to himself now: "From now on I'll stay home and wait for you all day, from early in the morning until late at night." But as soon as he had said it, he began to laugh out loud and whispered to himself: "But I'll go crazy!—crazy, completely crazy!"—And again he rushed to her house.—All was the same as on the previous day. Lights gleamed through the drawn shades. Again he walked up and down on the sidewalk opposite the house for half an hour—and again he left when the housekeeper and a few maids came out of the gate. It seemed to him that they had noticed him today, and he was convinced that they were talking about him and saying: that's the same man who was walking up and down the street at just this time last night. He walked around the neighboring streets, but when the church towers struck ten o'clock and the gates were locked, he went back to her house and stared up at her windows again. Now the only visible light came from the bedroom. He looked up at it as though in a spell. There he stood, helpless, and could neither do anything nor ask anything. He shuddered when he thought of the hours that lay before him. Another night, another morning, another day until three o'clock. Yes, until three—and then . . . what if again she didn't come? . . . An empty carriage passed by, and he beckoned the driver and had himself driven slowly up and down the evening streets. . . . He remembered their last meeting—no, no, she hadn't stopped loving him—no, definitely not! . . . Perhaps her husband had suspected something? . . . No, that wasn't possible either . . . they hadn't left a trace—and she was so careful. There could be only one reason: she was ill and was confined to bed. That's why she couldn't send him a message. . . . And tomorrow she would be well and be able to get out of bed and she would immediately send him a few lines to calm him. . . . Yes, but what if she couldn't leave her bed for a couple of days . . . what if she were seriously ill? . . . Good God! . . . what if she were seriously ill? . . . no, no, no . . . why should she be seriously ill? . . .

Suddenly he had what struck him as a brilliant idea. Since she was almost certainly ill, he could send and ask how she was. The messenger would not even have to know just who sent him—he could just not quite have caught his name. . . . Yes, yes, that's what he would do! He was pleased with this idea.

So he was less anxious that night and the next day, though he had not received any news from her. He even stayed calm that next after-noon—for he knew that in the evening, this evening, the uncertainty would be ended. He longed for her more intensely and more tenderly than he had these last few days.

He left his house that evening at eight o'clock. At a street corner some distance away from his, he engaged a messenger who didn't know him and beckoned the man to follow him. Not far from her house he stopped with him. He sent him with urgent and exact instructions.

He looked at his watch by the light of the street lamp and began to walk up and down. But the thought immediately occurred to him: what if the husband suspected something after all, took the messenger into his confidence, and had him lead him here? He started after the messenger; but then he walked more slowly and stayed a short distance behind him. At last he saw him disappear into the house. Albert stood very far back; he had to strain his eyes so as not to lose sight of the gate. . . . After only three minutes he saw the man reappear. . . . He waited a few seconds to make sure he was not being followed. No one came out after him. Then he rushed up to the man. "Well," he asked, "what's happened?" "The gentleman thanks you for your concern," answered the man, "and says that his wife is not yet better, and won't be up and about for a couple of days."

"Whom did you speak to?"

"With a chambermaid. She went into the room and came right out again. I think the doctor was there at the moment. . . ."

"What did she say?" He had the message repeated several times and finally realized that he knew little more than he had before. She had to be very ill; evidently everyone was making inquiries—that's why no one had noticed the messenger. . . . And for that very reason he could risk more. He engaged the messenger for tomorrow at the same time.

She would not be up for a few days—and that was all he knew. . . . Did she think about him, could she imagine how much he was suffering on her account?—he knew nothing.

Did she perhaps guess that it was he who had sent the last messen-ger to ask about her? . . . "The gentleman thanks you for your concern." Not she, he. Maybe they couldn't even give her the message. . . . Yes, and what was wrong with her? The names of a hundred diseases went through his head at the same time. Well, in a few days she would be up and about again—so it couldn't be anything really serious. . . . But that's what they always said. When his own father was on his deathbed, they had told everyone the same thing. . . . He noticed that he had begun to run, and now that he had arrived in a more crowded street, people were getting in his way. He knew that the time until tomorrow evening would seem like an eternity.

The hours went by and he wondered why he just couldn't believe that his beloved was seriously ill. At the same time it seemed to him to be a sin that he was so calm. . . . And in the afternoon—how long since this had happened!—he read a book for hours as though there were nothing to fear or to wish for. . . .

The messenger was already waiting for him at the corner when Albert arrived in the evening. Today he gave the man an additional assignment: besides asking the same question as yesterday, he should try to begin a conversation with the chambermaid and find out exactly what was wrong with her mistress. This time it took longer for the man to reappear, and Albert began to feel anxious. Almost a quarter of an hour passed before he finally saw the man come out of the house. Albert ran toward him—

"They say the lady of the house is doing very badly. . . ."

"What?" shrieked Albert.

"They say the lady of the house is doing very badly," the man repeated.

"To whom did you speak? What did they tell you?"

"The chambermaid told me that it was very dangerous. . . . There were already three doctors there today, and they say the gentleman is desperate."

"Go on . . . go on . . . what's wrong with her? Didn't you ask? I told you—"

"Of course! . . . It's said to be typhoid fever, and the lady has been unconscious for two days."

Albert stood still and stared at the man as though he weren't there. Then he asked: "That's all you know?"

The man repeated his story from the beginning, and Albert listened as though each word brought him something new. Then he paid the man and went straight back to the street in front of his beloved's house. Well, of course he could now stand there without being noticed—who would bother about him? And he stared up at her bedroom and wanted to penetrate both the windows and the curtains with his eyes. The sickroom—yes—it was obvious that a very sick person must be lying behind all these still windows!—how could he not have known it the very first night? Today he realized that it couldn't have been anything else. A carriage drove up. Albert rushed over, saw a man who could only be a doctor get out and disappear behind the gate. Albert remained standing very close in order to wait for the doctor to come out, in the undefined hope that he could read something in his expression. . . . For a few minutes he stood stock still, and then the ground in front of him seemed slowly to go up and down. Then he noticed that his eyes had closed, and when he opened them again it seemed to him as if he had been dreaming for hours and was now waking up refreshed. He could believe that she was very ill, yes, but dangerously ill, no . . . she was so young, so beautiful, and so beloved. . . . And suddenly the words "typhoid fever" flew through his mind again. . . . He didn't know exactly what that was. He did remember having read it in obituaries as a cause of death. Then he pictured her name and her age in print, along with "died on the 20th of August of typhoid fever.". . . But that was impossible, totally impossible . . . now that he had imagined it, it had to be totally impossible . . . it would be too odd if he should actually see it in print in a few days! . . . He believed he had conquered fate. The doctor came out of the house door. Albert had almost forgotten him—but now he caught his breath. The doctor's expression was emotionless and serious. He gave the driver an address, climbed in the carriage, and drove off. Why didn't I ask him, thought Albert . . . but then was glad that he hadn't. In the end he might have heard very bad news. This way he could go on hoping. . . . He slowly walked away from the door and firmly made up his mind not to return for at least an hour. . . . And suddenly he fantasized how she would come to him the first time after her recovery. . . . The picture was so vivid that he was astonished. He even knew there would be a fine grey mist that day. She would wear a coat that would slip from her shoulders in the reception room, would rush into his arms and would only be able to cry and cry. Now you have me again . . . she would whisper . . . here I am! Suddenly Albert started. . . . He knew that it would never, never happen! . . . Fate had conquered him! . . . Never again would she come to him—she had been with him five days ago for the last time, and he had let her go for good, and he had not known it. . . .

And once more he rushed through the streets, his thoughts whirling through his mind. He longed to lose consciousness. Now he was in front of her house again . . . the gate was still open, and lights were on in the dining room and the bedroom. . . . Albert ran away. He knew: if he had stayed another minute he would have had to rush upstairs, to her—to her bed—to his beloved. And, as was his manner, he was forced to think that through to the end as well. He saw how her husband, suddenly understanding everything, would run to the patient who was lying there motionless, would shake her and scream in her ear, "Your lover is here, your lover is here!" But she would already be dead. . . .

Bad dreams spoiled his night, a dull fatigue the next day. Already at eleven o'clock in the morning he sent a messenger to find out what was happening. At this point it obviously didn't matter who inquired. Who would worry about who came to ask about her condition? The report he received was: unchanged. . . . He lay on his sofa the whole afternoon and didn't understand why he was doing it. Everything was already a matter of indifference to him, and he thought: it's wonderful to be so tired. . . . He slept a lot. But as it grew dark he suddenly jumped up in a kind of astonishment, as if only now, for the first time in all this, everything was clear to him. And an intense desire for certainty overcame him—he had to speak to the doctor himself today. He hurried over to her house. The housekeeper was standing in front. He walked up to her and, wondering at his remarkable calmness, he asked innocently, "How is Frau . . ." The housekeeper answered, "Oh, she's very sick; she'll never recover. . . ."

"Ah," Albert answered very politely, and added, "that's really sad."

"Of course," said the other, "it's very sad—such a beautiful young woman!" And with that she disappeared into the doorway.

Albert watched her go. . . . She didn't notice anything, he thought, and at the same moment the question of whether he couldn't risk going right into the house, since he was such a good actor, occurred to him. At that moment the doctor's carriage drove up. Albert greeted him as he climbed down, and received a cordial answer in return. That pleased him—for now he had made his acquaintance, in a manner of speaking, and so could all the more easily question him when he came out again. . . .

He stood stock still, and it made him feel good to think that the doctor was with her. He was gone a long time. . . . That must mean there was a possibility of saving her, else he wouldn't stay up there so long. Or maybe she was already in her death agony . . . or . . . Ah, no, no, no! He wanted to banish all thought—it was useless anyway—anything was possible—suddenly it seemed to him that he heard the doctor speak—he even understood the words: this is the crisis. And instinctively he looked up at the closed window. He wondered whether under certain circumstances, when one's senses were at an edge and therefore keener, it was possible to hear someone's words even through closed windows. Yes, of course he had heard the words, heard them not in his imagination but really heard— but at this same moment the doctor came out of the gate. Albert took a step toward him. The doctor probably took him to be a relative, and, reading the unspoken question in his eyes, shook his head. But Albert didn't want to understand him. He began to talk, "May I ask, professor, how . . ." The doctor, who already had one foot in the carriage, shook his head again. . . . "Very bad," he said, and looked at the young man. . . . "You're her brother, aren't you?" . . . "Yes," said Albert. . . . The doctor looked at him compassionately. Then he stepped into his carriage, nodded to the young man, and drove off.

Albert watched the carriage drive off as though his last hope were disappearing with it. Then he left. He talked softly to himself, said things that made no sense, and his teeth chattered all the while. Well, what am I going to do today? . . . It's too late to go out to the country, too late to go out to the country. It's too late, too late. . . . Yes, I'm sad. Am I sad? Am I terribly sad? No, I'm walking around, I'm not feeling anything. I feel nothing. I could go to the theatre now, or drive out to the country. . . . Oh no, I just think that! . . . It's all nonsense, because I'm so deeply shaken. . . . Yes . . . I'm deeply shaken, I'm shattered! This is a profound moment. I must hold on to it. To understand something clearly and not to feel anything . . . nothing . . . nothing. . . . He shivered. . . . Home, home. I've got to have experienced something like this before . . . but when, when? . . . Maybe in a dream? . . . Or is this a dream? . . . Yes, I'm going home now as on every other evening, as though nothing's happened, as if nothing at all's happened. But what kind of nonsense am I talking! I'll not be able to stay home. I'll go to her house again in the middle of the night, to the house of my dying beloved. . . . And his teeth chattered.

Suddenly he found himself in his room and couldn't for the life of him remember how he had gotten there. He lit a lamp and sat down on his sofa. I know how it is, he said to himself: pain is knocking at the door and I won't let it in. But I know that it's out there—I can see it through the little window in my door. How stupid, how stupid! . . . So my beloved is going to die . . . yes she is, she is! Or am I still hoping she'll recover, and is that why I'm so calm? No, I'm sure of it. Hah, and the doctor took me for her brother! What if I'd answered him: no, I'm her lover, or I'm her Celadon, her brokenhearted Celadon. . . .

My God! he suddenly shrieked, sprang up, and ran up and down in his room. . . . I've opened the door! Pain is here! . . . Anna, Anna, my sweet, my only, my beloved Anna! . . . And I can't be with you! I, the only one who really belongs to you! . . . Perhaps she isn't unconscious at all! What do we know about it, after all? And maybe she's yearning for me—and I can't go to her—can't go to her. Or maybe, in her last moment, when she is beyond all earthly constraints, she will say, will whisper: Tell him to come—I want to see him once more . . . and what would he do then?

After a while the whole scene unfolded in front of his eyes. He saw himself hurry up the stairs. Her husband received him, led him to the bed of the dying woman. She smiled at him with broken eyes—he leaned over her, she embraced him, and as he raised himself up again, she breathed her last breath—and then the husband joined them and said to him, "And now please leave, sir, we'll have more to say to one another later. . . . But life wasn't like that, no . . . that would be the most wonderful thing, the most wonderful thing of all, to see her once more, to feel that she loved him! He had to see her again somehow, some way . . . how in God's name could he let her die without having seen her once more? That would be too terrible. He hadn't thought the whole thing out properly. Yes, but what to do? It was almost midnight! What excuse could I use to see her this time? he asked himself. Do I even need an excuse . . . now that death . . . but even if she—dies—do I have the right to betray her secret, to stain her memory for her husband and her family—? But . . . I could pretend to be mad. Ah—I can act very well. . . . Oh God!—what an idea! . . . what if one plays the role too well and is put into an insane asylum for the rest of one's life? . . . Or what if she should get well again and then declare me a madman whom she had never known, had never seen—! Oh, my head, my head! He threw himself onto his bed. Now he was conscious of the night and of the stillness around him. Well, he said to himself, I'll think things through quietly. I want to see her once more—yes, of course . . . that's certain.

And his thoughts ran on: he saw himself running up the stairs to her flat in a hundred disguises: as the doctor's assistant, as a drugstore clerk, as a servant, as an employee of a funeral home, even as a beggar; and finally he saw himself sitting next to her—whom he dared not recognize—as undertaker, wrapping her in a white shroud and laying her in her coffin. . . .

He awoke at dawn. His window had been open, and even though he had gone to bed fully clothed, he shivered, as a light rain had begun to fall and the wind had blown a few drops into his room.

So autumn is here, thought Albert. . . . Then he got up and looked at the clock. So I slept five hours after all! In that time . . . much could have happened. He trembled. Odd, now I suddenly know exactly what I have to do. I'll go there to her door, with my collar turned up and . . . will ask . . . myself. . . .

He poured himself a glass of cognac and downed it quickly. Then he went to the window. God, how awful the streets look. It's still very early. . . . These are all people who have to be at work at seven o'clock. . . . Yes, today I'm also someone who has work to do at seven o'clock. "Very badly," the doctor had said yesterday. But no one has died from that. . . . And yesterday I had the feeling all day that she . . . let's go, let's go. . . . He pulled on his overcoat, took an umbrella, and went into the reception room. His valet looked at him in astonishment. "I'll be back soon," he said, and left.

He took small, slow steps. It was really quite embarrassing for him to go in person. What on earth would he say? He was getting nearer and nearer her house. Already he was on her street and saw her house from afar. It seemed strange to him. Of course he had never seen it at such an hour. How strange the wan light that the rainy morning was spreading over the street seemed! Yes, on days like this people died. If Anna had broken off with him when she was with him the last time, he might perhaps already have forgotten her. Yes, for sure—for it was very strange how long it seemed since he had last seen her. What kind of strange thoughts a rainy morning such as this could induce! . . . Oh God . . . Albert was very tired, very distracted. . . . He almost passed her house without noticing it.

The gate was open and a man carrying milk canisters was just now coming out. Albert walked the few steps through the gate very calmly—but suddenly, just as he was about to step up the first stairs, the full consciousness of what had happened, what was happening now, and what he would learn went through him. He felt as though he had walked the distance from his house to this point half asleep and was just now suddenly jolted awake. He clutched both hands to his heart before he went on. So these were the stairs . . . he had never seen them before. They were still half in darkness; small gas lamps burned on the wall. . . . The flat was on the second floor. What was that? . . . Both sides of the door were open—he could see the reception room—but there was no one there. He opened a small door which led into the kitchen. No one was there either. For a while he remained standing, undecided. Then the door that led to the living quarters opened and a maid came out quietly without noticing him. Albert walked up to her.

"How's your mistress?" he asked.

The girl looked at him distractedly. "She died half an hour ago," she said. Then she turned and went into the kitchen.

Albert felt as though the world around him had suddenly become deathly quiet. He was sure that at this moment all hearts had stopped beating, all carriages had stopped in the streets, and all clocks had stopped ticking. He felt that the whole living and moving world had stopped living and moving. So that is death, he thought . . . I didn't understand it, even yesterday. . . .

"I beg your pardon," said a voice next to him. It was a man dressed all in black who wanted to go from the stairway into the reception room and whose way Albert was blocking. Albert took another step into the reception room and let the man pass. The man paid no attention to him but rushed into the flat and left the door half open. Now Albert could see into the next room. It was almost dark, as if all the shades had been drawn. He saw a few figures who had been sitting around a table and who now stood up to greet the newcomer. He heard them whisper. . . . Then they disappeared into an adjoining room. Albert remained standing at the door and thought: she's lying in there . . . it's less than a week since I held her in my arms . . . and I can't go in. He heard voices on the staircase. Two women came in and went past him. One of them, the younger one, had eyes red from crying. She looked like his beloved. It must be her sister, of whom she had sometimes spoken to him. An elderly lady came to meet the two women, embraced them, and sobbed softly. "A half an hour ago," said the old lady—"quite suddenly." . . . Tears choked her voice and prevented her from continuing. The three of them disappeared through the half-dark room into the adjoining one. No one paid any attention to him.

I can't keep on standing here, thought Albert. I'll go downstairs and return in an hour. He left and was in the street a few minutes later. The bustle of the morning had begun; many people rushed past him, and carriages were rolling down the street.

In an hour there will be more people up there and I'll be able easily to lose myself among them. How certainty consoles! . . . I feel better than I did yesterday, even though she has died. . . . A half an hour ago. . . . In a thousand years she won't be farther from life than she is now . . . and yet, the knowledge that she was still breathing just an hour ago makes me think that maybe she still has some awareness of existence, something that it's impossible to understand as long as one is still breathing . . . perhaps that incomprehensible moment in which we pass from life to death is our poor eternity. . . . Yes, and now there will be no more waiting in the afternoon. . . . I'll never stand at the little window in the door again— never, never. . . . And now all these hours appeared to him as unspeakably beautiful. Only a few days ago he had been so happy—yes, happy. It had been a deep, sultry bliss. Oh, when her feet hurried over the last few steps . . . when she fell into his arms . . . and when they were lying wordlessly and utterly motionless on the white pillows at twilight in the room filled with the scent of flowers and cigarettes. . . . Gone, gone! . . .

I'll go away, that's the only thing left for me to do. Will I even be able to go into my room at all now? I'll have to cry, cry for days and days, cry and cry, always, always. . . .

He passed a café. He realized that he hadn't eaten a thing since yesterday noon, so he went in and breakfasted. As he left the place it was already past nine. Now I can go back—I've got to see her once more—but what will I do there? . . . Will I be able to see her? . . . I've got to see her . . . yes, I've got to see my, yes my, my beloved, dead Anna once more. But will they let me into the death chamber? . . . Of course. There will be many people there, and all the doors will be open.

He hurried there. The housekeeper was standing at the gate and greeted him as he went past. He ran ahead of two men who were also going up the steps. There were already some people in the reception room, and the door was wide open. Albert went in. The curtain of one of the windows had been drawn back and a little light was falling into the room. There were about a dozen people around, sitting or standing, and speaking very softly. The old lady he had seen before was sitting crumpled up in the corner of a dark red sofa. When Albert went past her she looked at him; he stood still and gave her his hand. She nodded her head and began to cry again. Albert looked around; the second door, which led to the adjoining room, was closed. He turned to a man who was standing at the window and absentmindedly looking through the opening in the curtains. . . . "Where is she?" he said. The man pointed to the right. Albert opened the door softly. He was suddenly blinded by a strong light that flowed toward him. He found himself in a very light, small room with white and gold tapestries and light-blue furniture. No one was there. The door to the next room was ajar. He went in. It was the bedroom—

The window shutters were closed; a lamp was burning. The body was lying stretched out on the bed. The covers had been pulled to her lips, and at her head, on a small side table, a candle was burning and throwing its glare on the ashen-grey features. He wouldn't have recognized her if he hadn't known it was she. Only gradually did he see a resemblance—only gradually did it become Anna, his Anna, who was lying there, and for the first time since the beginning of these terrible days he felt tears come to his eyes. A hot and burning pain was in his breast. He wanted to cry out, to sink down next to her, to kiss her hands. . . . Only now he noticed that he wasn't alone with her. Someone was kneeling at the foot of her bed, had buried his face in the sheets, and was holding the dead woman's hand in both of his. At the moment that Albert was tempted to go a step closer to her, the man raised his head. What am I going to say to him? But suddenly he felt the man grasp his right hand and press it, and he heard him say in a sobbing voice, thank you, thank you. . . . And then the crying man turned away again and let his head sink sobbing into the bedcovers. Albert remained standing for a while and looked at the dead woman's face with a kind of cold interest. Tears once more failed to come to him. His pain suddenly became thin and insubstantial. He knew that some day this meeting would seem to him horrible and comical at the same time. He would have felt very ridiculous had he stayed to cry together with this man.

He turned to go. At the door he stopped once more and looked back. The flickering of the candle made it seem to him as if a smile were playing around Anna's lips. He nodded to her as if he were saying goodbye and she could see him. Then he turned to go, but suddenly it seemed to him as though she were holding him there with this smile. And suddenly it became a contemptuous, strange smile, which seemed to speak to him and which he could understand. And the smile said: I loved you, and now you stand there like a stranger and deny me. Tell him that I was yours, that it is *your* right to kneel in front of this bed and to kiss my hands. Tell him! Why don't you tell him?

But he didn't dare. He held his hands before his eyes so that he would no longer see her smile. . . . He turned around on tiptoe, left the room, and closed the door behind him. Trembling, he went through the light salon and crept past all the people who were whispering to one another in the half-dark room and among whom he was not entitled to stay. Then he rushed through the reception room and down the stairs. After he passed through the gate, he crept along the wall of the house, and his steps became ever faster as he felt something driving him away from the house; and, deeply ashamed, he hurried through the streets, for it seemed to him as if he was not entitled to mourn her like the others, as if his dead beloved were chasing him away because he had denied her.

The Second

I WAS TWENTY-THREE YEARS OLD at that time, and it was my seventh duel—not my own, but the seventh in which I participated as a second. You can smirk if you want. I know it's become fashionable these days to make fun of such events. But I don't think that does them justice, and I assure you, life was more beautiful and certainly had a more elevated air in those days—among other reasons, precisely because one sometimes had to put one's life on the line for something that in a higher or at least in a different sense possibly did not exist or which at least—measured by today's standards—was not worth it. For honor, for example, or the virtue of a beloved woman, or the good reputation of a sister, or for some other such triviality. Nevertheless it's important to remember that in the course of the last decades people were required to sacrifice their lives for even more insignificant things, completely needlessly and at the command or wish of others. True, one's own discretion always played a role in a duel, even when it apparently was a matter of compulsion, convention, or snobbishness. That one at least had to come to terms with the possibility or even the unavoidability of duels within social circles—that alone, believe me, gave social life a certain dignity or at least a certain style. And it gave the people in these social circles, even the most worthless or the most ridiculous of them, a certain attitude—yes, the appearance of being constantly ready to die—even if this phrasing should appear to you altogether too grandiose in this context.

But I digress even before I've begun. I want to tell you the story of my seventh duel, and you are smirking as you did before, because I'm talking about my duel again, even though, as appeared to be my fate, I was once again merely a witness and not a dueler. At eighteen, when I was a volunteer in the cavalry, for the first time I was a second in an affair of honor between a comrade and an attaché of the French embassy. Soon after that the famous rider Vulkovicz chose me to be his second in a duel with the Prince of Luginsfeld, and after that, even though I was neither a nobleman nor a professional officer, and was even of Jewish descent, people turned to me, especially for the more difficult cases when a second was required. I won't deny that I sometimes regretted participating in these affairs only as a secondary figure. Just once I would have liked to have stood opposite a dangerous opponent. I don't even know what I would have preferred—to win or to die. But it never came to that, even though there wasn't really any lack of opportunities and, as you may imagine, there was never the slightest doubt about my willingness to duel. Maybe that's why I never received a challenge or why in those cases when I was forced to issue a challenge, the matter was settled in a gentlemanly fashion. In any case, I was a second in body and soul. The consciousness of being put in the midst of destiny, or, more accurately, at the periphery of a destiny, has for me always had something moving, exciting, and grand about it.

But this seventh duel that I want to tell you about today was different from all my other ones either before and after, because in this case I moved from the periphery right into the middle of everything and changed from a secondary to a central figure—and also because till today no one has ever heard this strange story. I wouldn't have told you anything about it either, you with your eternal smirk—but since you don't actually exist, I'll continue to do you the honor of talking to you, a young man who in any case has enough tact to remain silent.

It really doesn't matter how and where I begin. I'm going to tell you the story as it occurs to me, and I'll begin with the moment when I boarded the train in the company of Dr. Muelling. As it was, in order not to raise suspicion of any sort, especially in Eduard's young wife, we had left the villa on the lake on a Monday morning. Yes, we went so far as to get tickets to Vienna, but naturally we got off at the train station in the small town where the duel was to take place the next morning.

Dr. Muelling was a longtime friend of Loiberger's, almost the same age as he was, about thirty-five. I owed the honor of being chosen as the other witness, aside from my already mentioned suitability for it, to the circumstance that I used to spend my vacations in the same fresh summer air as Loiberger and had often been a guest at his villa. I never really developed a particular liking for him, but his house was convivial; many pleasant people came and went; there were music, tennis, joint outings, and rowing parties, and after all I was only twenty-three years old. An exchange of words between Eduard Loiberger and his opponent, the Ulan cavalry captain Urpadinsky, was given me as reason for the duel. I hardly knew the latter. He had been at the lake on Sunday, on a visit from his garrison, evidently only for the sake of the exchange of words which served as the excuse for the duel, but last year he had spent the whole summer there with his wife.

Both men were apparently very anxious to resolve the matter. The meeting of the seconds had taken place in Ischl on Sunday evening, only a few hours after the exchange of words in question. Muelling and I had been instructed by Loiberger to accept the conditions of the opposing seconds without objection. They were difficult ones.

And so on Monday, Muelling and I arrived in the small town.

First we examined the location that had been chosen as the rendezvous spot for the next day. During the little pleasure ride that followed, Muelling spoke of his travels, his long-finished university studies, student duels, professors, villas, rowing championships, and all sorts of acquaintances whom we both happened to know. I was just facing my last state examinations. Muelling was already a well-known lawyer. We didn't speak a word about what was to take place the next day, as if we had agreed not to do so. Dr. Muelling undoubtedly knew more about the reasons for the duel than he felt it wise to confide to me.

Eduard Loiberger arrived in the evening. He had interrupted his summer stay under the pretense of a scheduled mountain-climbing excursion in the Dolomites, a pretext to which the current wonderful August weather lent plausible support. We greeted him matter-of-factly and took him to the venerable old inn on the market square, where we had reserved the best room for him. We had dinner together at the inn, enjoyed some animated conversation, drank, smoked, and in no way attracted attention, not even that of the few officers who were sitting at a table in the opposite corner. Dr. Muelling routinely reported on the location where the duel was to take place the next day. It was the usual forest clearing, as if chosen by fate for just such things—a little inn was nearby, an inn in which, as Muelling remarked gaily, many a reconciliation had taken place over breakfast. But this was the only hint of the purpose of our presence here; otherwise we spoke about the sailing regatta scheduled for next Sunday, in which Loiberger, last year's victor, was supposed to take part—about a planned addition to his villa for which he, by profession a manufacturer but a dilettante in many other fields, had drawn the blueprints himself—about the completion of a cable-car line to a nearby peak, with whose position Loiberger found fault—about a legal case that Dr. Muelling was conducting for him, in which considerable assets seemed to hang in the balance—and about a lot of other things, until Dr. Muelling, with a lukewarm smile, remarked around eleven o'clock, "It's perhaps time to go to bed; it never hurts to be fully rested for such occasions, even for the seconds." We took our leave of Loiberger and sent him to bed, but the two of us walked around the town for another hour in the beautiful, warm summer night. I can't remember anything about this nighttime walk except the deep black shadows that the houses around the market square threw on the moonlit cobblestones, and nothing of what we talked about. I only know that we didn't talk at all about the next day's duel.

But I do remember very clearly the carriage ride the next morning; yes, even now I can still hear the clattering of the horses' hoofs that were bringing us over the dusty road to the forest clearing. Loiberger talked with exaggerated importance about a certain Japanese shrub recently introduced to Central Europe that he planned to plant in his garden, and jumped out of the carriage with an agility that was at the time often mentioned in the newspapers as a special attribute of reigning princes. I thought of that and smiled involuntarily. Loiberger happened to glance at me at that moment, and I felt a little ashamed.

I remember the duel itself almost as if it had been a marionette the-

atre play: like a marionette Eduard Loiberger lay there after his opponent's bullet had felled him, and the regiment physician, a haggard, elderly man with a Polish mustache, who pronounced him dead, was also a
marionette. The sky above us was cloudless but had a strange dull blue
color. I looked at my watch—it was ten minutes before eight. The proto-
col and the other customary formalities were taken care of quickly. Actually I was happy that we still had the chance to make the nine o'clock
express train—it would have been unbearable to have to stay even an
hour longer in this unhappy town.

We paced back and forth on the platform almost unnoticed—two elegant tourists on a summer trip. Then, as I was having a cup of coffee,
Muelling saw in the newspaper that the King of England and his prime
minister would be visiting our emperor in Ischl in the next few days. We
got into a political discussion—actually, it was more like a lecture by Dr.
Muelling, whom I interrupted unnecessarily through rather insubstantial
objections. As the train from Vienna arrived, I breathed more easily, almost as if everything that had happened would now be undone and
Loiberger would return to life. We were alone in our compartment. Only
after a long silence did Dr. Muelling, as though in apology, note that he
had not spoken earlier. "It's impossible to grasp it right away, however
much one has been prepared for it." Then we both talked of all sorts of
other duels in which we had taken part as seconds, harmless ones and
less fortunate ones—but neither of us had previously taken part in a fatal
duel. At first we dealt with today's duel, which had ended so tragically,
without sentiment, from an aesthetic and athletic perspective. Loiberger,
as was to be expected, had conducted himself composedly; the captain
had been far less calm and much paler; yes, we had both clearly noticed
that his hand had been trembling before the first exchange of shots. Both
of them had fired at the same time; both bullets had missed. On the second round the captain's bullet had grazed Loiberger's temple, and
Loiberger had instinctively reached for the spot and then smiled. At the
third round, right after the signal, Loiberger collapsed before he had even
fired.

Only now, as if he had been freed from the obligation of silence, did

Dr. Muelling remark, "To tell the truth, I saw it coming; actually, I expected it last year already. Both of them, our friend Loiberger as well as Urpadinsky's wife—you've never seen the captain's wife, too bad—behaved as indiscreetly as possible. Everyone in town knew about it. Only the captain himself, even though he often came from his garrison for a visit to St. Gilgen, had no idea. Only last winter did he supposedly receive anonymous letters and then investigate the matter. Evidently, under the constant stress of his questioning, his wife finally confessed. Everything ran its course from then on."

"Incomprehensible," I said.

"How incomprehensible?" Muelling asked.

"When someone has a wife like Loiberger's—I thought it was the happiest marriage." I pictured Agatha, who looked like a young girl, like a bride, really, in front of me. When one saw the two of them, Eduard and Agatha, one could have taken them for a pair of lovers rather than a married couple—and that after four or five years of marriage. At that excursion to the Eichberg two weeks earlier, when we were basking in the noontime sun—there were seven or eight of us—actually, I hate group outings and had joined only because of Mademoiselle Coulin—Agatha seemed to have fallen asleep or else she had shut her eyes because the sun was blinding her, and Eduard had stroked her hair and her forehead with his fingers, and they had smiled and whispered like a young couple in love.

"And do you think," I said to Muelling, "that Agatha suspected anything at all?"

Muelling shrugged his shoulders. "I don't think so. In any case she certainly had no idea about the coming duel and doesn't know that her husband is dead right now."

Only now did I realize with a kind of shock that the moving train was bringing us closer and closer to the unfortunate woman. "Who should tell her?" I asked.

"There's nothing to do but for both of us—"

"We can't appear like members of a committee bringing an invitation to a ball," I thought, and said out loud, "We should immediately have telegraphed from there."

"Such a telegram," said Muelling, "could only have served as a kind of announcement. We can't avoid informing her in person."

"I'll do it," I said.

A lengthy discussion of the matter followed. It was still not over as our train pulled into the station in Ischl. It was a gorgeous summer day; there was a crowd of visitors, travelers, and people waiting on the platform—some of our acquaintances were among them, and it wasn't easy to get from the station into the street without being stopped. But finally we were sitting in a carriage without anyone's having come near us, and rushed off. The dust whirled behind us, the sun burned brightly, and we were glad as the town disappeared behind us and we turned into the country road and then into the forest.

Even before we caught sight of the first farmhouses of the village from the last bend in the road, Dr. Muelling had declared his agreement that I, as the more removed, should bring Frau Agatha Loiberger the sad news.

The lake glistened with the reflection of a thousand tiny suns. From the opposite bank, hidden in the bright haze, a droll steamship that looked like a toy was approaching. Its waves were joyfully anticipated by the many young swimmers. Soon we stopped in front of the inn that, undeservedly, called itself the "Grand Hotel"; I climbed down, Dr. Muelling shook my hand, declared that he would call on me at four o'clock in the afternoon, and drove on to the villa in which he had rented a room.

I exchanged my traveling clothes, which hardly seemed appropriate for my mission, for a dark grey suit and carefully chose a black striped tie. In the end I had to rely on my own taste, on my intuition in fact, since for such a visit as stood before me there were understandably no commonly accepted guidelines. With a heavy heart I made my way.

From behind the inn on one side, a shortcut with occasional glimpses of the lake led past small farmhouses to the white and, for my taste, rather too grand villa that Loiberger had designed himself and built to his own specifications. I walked at an exaggeratedly slow pace so that I wouldn't give myself away immediately by breathing too rapidly, but on the whole I felt rather calm or at least composed. I said to myself that

I merely had to fulfill my duty—and I wanted to be able to do that in a reasonable manner. I couldn't allow any more of my feelings to show than good social etiquette demanded and allowed.

The garden gate stood open; the artfully arranged flower beds gleamed colorfully; the sun lay on the white benches to the right and left, and the red-and-white-striped awning extended over the broad veranda with its bright-red wicker chairs. Above the awning in the second story the windows were open, and the small balcony in front of the mansard roof lay bathed with slanting sunbeams. No one could be seen anywhere. Everything was quiet; only the gravel underneath my feet crunched too loudly, it seemed to me. It was near the lunch hour; perhaps everyone was already sitting down to the meal, or perhaps Agatha was sitting down alone, since Eduard was on a trip to the Dolomites. Yes, that was my first thought, before I was shocked into remembering that at this very hour he was laid out in the morgue of a small garrison town. And suddenly I felt the task that stood before me in the next few minutes was so grotesque, so unbearable, so impossible that I felt seriously tempted to turn around right then, before anyone had caught sight of me; yes, just to run away, to get Dr. Muelling and explain to him that it was impossible for me to give Frau Agatha the gruesome news all by myself.

At that moment a servant stepped out of the darkness of the inner rooms and greeted me. Evidently he had heard my footsteps from within. He was a blonde young man in a blue-and-white-striped linen jacket; he came down a few steps toward me and said,

"There's no one at home. Herr Loiberger left yesterday, and Frau Loiberger is still at the lake." But since I made no move to leave, he said to me, "But if you would like to wait, Herr von Eissler—Frau Loiberger should be back any minute."

"I'll wait."

The servant seemed a little disconcerted; perhaps he was struck by the rigidity, the somber seriousness of my demeanor. And so, with a hastily contrived lightness, I looked at my watch and said, "I have something to tell your mistress," and repeated, "I'll wait."

The servant nodded, went on ahead of me, and pushed aside a chair that was blocking the way through the middle door into the salon. With an indefinite gesture he pointed to the various places to sit in the room and disappeared into the adjoining room, where a table sparkling with two place settings could be seen, closed the door behind him, and left me alone.

Like a prisoner about to undergo a difficult interrogation, I stood in the summer room kept cool by shadows. Dominating the room with its ebony black stood a piano, which awakened the memory of the last music evening I had spend here not very long ago. Agatha had accompanied her friend Aline in a Schubert song. I saw her slender fingers glide over the keys and almost thought I heard Aline's voice. "Flowers and wreaths for you, Sylvia. . . ." Later, while the rest of the company was still in the salon, I had sat outdoors in the garden, alone, a little dazed, even enchanted, by the warm night air, the music, and probably also the champagne, which was seldom missing from one of Loiberger's parties. Perhaps I even dozed off; and as if in a dream Agatha walked past me with a man. I sat in the dark, so at first they didn't notice me at all. But suddenly Agatha discovered me, and as she passed by me she slipped her hand through my hair, as if in jest, ruffled it, and was gone again. I didn't think any more about it. For she often behaved in this way. Rather uninhibited, but always with wonderful grace—just as, for example, she seldom called most of their friends by their name or title, but by a nickname that did not always fit the person's personality or manner but often expressed quite the opposite or nothing at all. Me, for example—and it made a certain sense, since at that time I looked even younger than my twenty-three years—she called "the child." I remained sitting quietly on my bench in the dark and waited for them both to pass me again—which happened sooner than I actually expected. And then Agatha nodded to me even though she was hardly in a position to recognize my features clearly. She often did that: nod a few times quickly in succession. I had often seen her greet others in this way when, wrapped in a blue bathrobe, she leaned on the balustrades at the town swimming pool, as she often did. She did the same on walks when she met an acquaintance, but she also greeted flowers the same way before she picked them, and a mountain cottage before she entered it. It seemed to be an innate characteristic, more than just a habit, for her thus to have a personal connection with every person and every thing she encountered, no matter how fleetingly. I became clearly aware of this characteristic of hers only now as I awaited her return in the shady, summer salon, my fingers playing aimlessly with the fringes of the Indian shawl that served as a piano cover.

Suddenly I heard female voices, footsteps on the cobblestones, coming ever closer, then a woman's laugh, then footsteps on the stairs—and my heart stood still.

"Who's here?" called Agatha, in an almost frightened voice. But when she recognized me, she immediately added cheerfully, "The child!" and gave me her hand. I bowed lower than I usually did, and kissed her hand. She immediately turned to Aline, who was standing a little behind her, and said, "You might as well both stay for lunch." And, turning to me, "For I'm all alone. Eduard's been on a mountain tour since yesterday." And with a not quite cheerful laugh, she added, "If you believe that!"

Meanwhile I had also kissed Aline's hand, and as I now looked up again, I saw her eyes look at me with a kind of consent I didn't want. There the two of them stood, the dark-haired Aline dressed all in gleaming yellow, the blonde Agatha in a soft light blue, and despite the contrast between them, they looked like sisters. Both wore the broad-brimmed Florentine hats that were fashionable at the time. Agatha took hers off and placed it on the piano.

"No, dearest," said Aline, "unfortunately I can't stay. I'm expected at home for lunch."

Agatha tried to persuade her a little longer, but she wasn't very convincing. And as she was speaking to her, she gave me such a questioning, such a promising—yes, such a seductive look that I almost became dizzy. And suddenly I knew that it was by no means the first look of that kind she had directed toward me. Aline took her leave. "Goodbye, madam," I said, and was conscious that these were the first words I had spoken, and so I heard them echo in the room with exaggerated brightness and force. Agatha accompanied her friend across the veranda and down the stairs into the garden.

Why didn't I speak when Aline was still here? I thought. Wouldn't it have been a thousand times easier? In the next moment Agatha already stood in front of me again. "Madam," I began, "I have awful news to bring you." No, I didn't say these words. Anyone capable of reading thoughts would have clearly heard me say these words, but no sound came from my lips. Agatha stood in front of me, her light-blue dress shining through the deep shadows of the room, but she wasn't smiling—yes, it seemed to me as though I had never seen her face so serious. Now that she was alone with me I felt clearly that anything that smacked of superficiality, of coquetry, yes, of anything purely sociable, should be banished.

"I'm so happy that you're here," she said.

I didn't reply, because I couldn't find the right words. All sorts of dim experiences in the past few days suddenly lit up in my soul. It occurred to me how she had recently hung on my arm on that last excursion and had walked down the forest trail with me. Then I remembered once again how she had run her slender fingers through my hair that night in the garden, and her name for me resounded tenderly in my mind: "Child." I hadn't understood any of that—I hadn't dared to understand it. Remember how young I was! It was the first time that a beautiful young woman, a woman that I took to be a loving and beloved wife, seemed to be offering me the gift of her heart. How could I have expected that? And when she now expressed her pleasure over my coming so unabashedly, it could mean nothing but that she considered me impatient and lovesick enough to consciously use the absence of her husband for this unexpected and bold visit.

"Lunch is served, madam."

A slight movement by Agatha. I turned around. We stepped into the adjoining room. It was Agatha's boudoir. The window stood open, white curtains separated us from the outdoors, and the garden shone through them with blurred colors.

We sat across from one another, Agatha and I. The servant, now dressed in a dark blue shiny jacket with gold buttons came in and out and served us. Everything was extremely elegantly prepared. It was a simple meal, and there was nothing but champagne to drink. Our lunch conversation was completely innocuous and had to be so, but it was at the same time completely unforced, not only on her side but also on mine. Yet while we talked about everyday matters and the little events in country life, about past and future outings, about the coming regatta on Sunday, about Loiberger's probable participation and chances—although I never forgot for a moment that Eduard was dead, and that I had come only to inform his wife of it—I perceived my presence, this tête-à-tête with Agatha, the gentle fluttering of the curtain, the silent appearance and disappearance of the servant, not at all as dreamlike but rather as another, lesser kind of reality. It was from this other reality that the shrill whistle of the small steamer pierced toward us, in this reality that the lake was lying in the midday sun; into this reality Aline had gone, and there also lay the man whom I had seen felled this morning at the edge of the forest. More real than any of that was what floated back and forth between Agatha and me—not what she said but the tone of her voice, her look, her desire—our longing.

The meal was finished. The servant didn't come back. We were alone.

Agatha got up from the table, walked over to me, took my head in both her hands, and kissed me on the lips. It was not a passionate kiss, but rather a gentle one. More tenderness than passion was in it; it was sisterly and yet intoxicating, ceremonious and passionate at the same time.

And later, wrapped in her arms, I slipped into a thousand dreams.

We lay outstretched on a grassy slope. It's the same slope as the one where she had recently lain at Eduard's side. I am amazed that she's so calm, without the slightest fear that anything terrible has happened—I don't know anything, and also don't think about anything, but I know that we have to get away, as far as possible. Then we are sitting in a train compartment; the window is open, the curtains, not fastened down, are fluttering back and forth; disjointed pictures of rapidly changing landscapes race by—forests, meadows, fences, rocks, churches, and solitary trees, all incomprehensibly fast and without any connection to each other, quickly enough so that no one can come after us, not even the people traveling in the same train; it's impossible to understand, but it's so. Suddenly I hear her name called from outdoors; I know it's a telegraph messenger looking for her. In me is only the fear that she'll hear it. But the sound of her name grows ever softer and finally fades entirely, and the train races on. We are traveling, yes, we are traveling—we are continuously traveling. Now we are in a casino room—it's probably Monte Carlo. How can I doubt it? Of course it's Monte Carlo. Agatha is sitting at the gaming table among others; she is beautiful, she is calm, she plays, she loses, she wins; and I look all around to see if there's anyone who recognizes her and who could perhaps tell her that her husband is dead. But there are only strangers—brown and yellow faces. There is even an Indian sitting at the gaming table with a huge red feathered headdress. Aline stands in the doorway. What, has she come after us? To tell her about it? Away, away! I touch Agatha's shoulder, and she turns toward me with a look full of love. And again the train races off with us. Someone is looking in through the open window—how is that possible? Evidently he is clinging to the windowsill from outside. He has a piece of paper in his hand: the telegram, of course! I push the man, he rolls off, I don't know where—I can't see him. What luck that Agatha hasn't noticed anything! Of course not. She has a large English magazine in her hand . . . and she is leafing through it, looking at the pictures. How strange, there's a picture of the gambling room which shows me with her among the gamblers. How quickly news travels! If her husband sees this picture—what will happen to us? Will he kill me as he killed the captain?

All of a sudden I am back in the villa, in the room, on the sofa, where I really am. It's reality and at the same time still a dream. I dream that I'm awake, I dream that my eyes are open and are staring wide at the fluttering curtains. And I hear footsteps, slow footsteps, the footsteps of six or twelve men. I know they are now bringing the stretcher with the body and I flee. I'm on the terrace outdoors. I have to go down the stairs. Where are the men, where is the stretcher? I don't see it. I only know that it's coming toward me and that it's impossible for me to avoid it. Suddenly I'm standing alone in the garden, but it's not a real garden, it's like a garden from a toy box, exactly like the garden I was once given for my birthday many years ago. I hadn't known until now that one could go walking in it. It even has little birds sitting in the trees. I hadn't noticed them then. And now they're all flying away, to punish me for having noticed them. And by the garden door there stands the servant, who bows very deeply. Because Loiberger himself is just now entering. He has no idea that he's dead, and moreover he is wearing a white raincoat. I have to accompany him into the house so that no one else can tell him that he is dead; he wouldn't survive it, I think—and laugh at the same time. And already the two of us are sitting down to dinner, and the servant is waiting on us. I'm surprised that Eduard is taking something to eat on his plate—he doesn't need it anymore. Agatha sits across from him; I'm not there anymore at all. But I'm sitting on the window ledge, and any minute the curtains will close over my forehead. I so very much want to see how they're looking at each other. Suddenly I hear his voice—oh God, if only I could see—and I hear him say very clearly. "So you're having breakfast with the man who shot me." It doesn't amaze me that he's saying that, because I really did it. I only find it strange that he should make such a stupid remark. He surely knows that it's customary to have breakfast together after a duel.

Again, footsteps in the garden—the stretcher—how strange, first the dead person and then the stretcher—what a snob he is!—and funereal music. A military band? Of course, because he shot a cavalry captain. And applause? Naturally—he won the regatta. I quickly jump out of the window and run, as fast as I can, down to the lake. Why are so few people there—and no boats at all? Only a very small rowboat, and in this rowboat are Agatha and me. Agatha rows. She suddenly knows how. She had said just recently that she can't row. But now she has even won the regatta. Suddenly I feel a hand on my throat, Eduard's hand. The oars slip away from Agatha. Our rowboat is just drifting. She crosses her arms. She is curious to see if Eduard will succeed in throwing me into the water. We try to push each other underwater. Agatha is no longer curious at all. She is drifting away on the boat. It's a motorboat after all, I think. I sink deeper and deeper into the water. Why, why, I ask myself, and I want to say to Loiberger: It's not worth the effort for us to kill each other over such a woman. But I don't say it. He might believe that I'm scared. And I surface again. The sky is infinitely larger than I have ever seen it. And again I sink down into the water, this time even deeper than before. I wouldn't have to, I'm alone after all, the whole lake belongs to me. And the sky too. And again I surface from the waves and from death and from dream. Yes, the deeper I sink down, the more forcefully I am catapulted to the surface, and suddenly I'm awake—completely awake, more awake than I've ever been. But Agatha was sleeping; at least she was lying there with her eyelids shut. The curtains were blowing more strongly now in the summer wind that always blew from the lake at this hour in the afternoon. It couldn't be late yet. By the position of the sun it was no later than four o'clock—the hour when Muelling had wanted to meet me at the hotel. Was this still a dream? Was all of it perhaps a dream? Even the duel? And Loiberger's death? Was it maybe morning and was I sleeping—in my room at the hotel? But this was, so to speak, my last attempt to flee. I couldn't doubt that I was awake and that Agatha was lying here sleeping and knew nothing. Now the only choice I had left was to get up and flee immediately, this very second—or to speak without hesitating a second longer, to wake Agatha up and to tell her. The news could arrive here any minute. Hadn't I heard footsteps in the garden already? Wasn't it almost a miracle that we hadn't been disturbed up to now? And in any case, even if no one in this house or here in town knew anything yet, wasn't it incomprehensibly stupid to stay any longer in this room, which was accessible to everyone, now that the hour of the customary afternoon rest had passed? I myself had gotten up hurriedly—and now, just as I was getting ready to tap Agatha on the shoulder, she blinked as if my glance had awakened her, rubbed her hand over her forehead and her hair, and looked like a small girl rubbing the sleep out of her eyes. She looked at me for all the world as if I were a vanishing dream image. But then she heard my voice, for I had involuntarily whispered her name, and her face darkened; she sprang up, fixed her dress, smoothed the pillows, and hastily put them in order. Then she turned quickly to me and said only, "Go!" But I stayed there as if rooted to the spot, completely incapable of telling her what I had to tell her, yes, incapable of saying anything at all. What a coward I was! Kill myself—there was nothing else for me to do. But I couldn't even take a step. I could only utter her name louder, more pleadingly than before. She grasped my hand tenderly and said, "I love you very much. I didn't know how much I love you. You don't have to believe it. But why should I say it if it weren't true? I just wanted you to know it before you leave."

"When am I going to see you again?" I asked. I didn't say: Eduard is dead. I didn't say: forgive me. I didn't say: I was too much of a coward to tell you right away. No, I asked, "When am I going to see you again?" as though there were no other questions to be answered, as though there were nothing else to say.

"You'll never see me again," she said. "If you care for me, you'll be grateful for this hour just as I am. If you don't want this hour to turn from a wonderful, unforgettable dream into a sad reality, a lie, a hundred lies, a chain of deception and ugliness, then go, go immediately, leave, and never try to see me again."

Inside my head I murmured: Eduard is dead—your husband is dead. Everything you're saying is nonsense, and you haven't the slightest idea. There is no lie, no deception, no ugliness anymore—you're free. But I didn't say any of that. Everything suddenly became clearer to me than I could have thought possible a minute ago. And I said, "It's no deception, no lie. It would be a lie and a deception if after this hour you were to stay in this house any longer and once more belong to another." It seemed to me that the travel dream from before had gained control of me, or as if I were getting control of it.

Agatha turned pale. She looked at me, and I felt that my face had become totally rigid. She touched my arm as if to calm me. "Let's be reasonable," she said, "Or let's at least try to be reasonable again. I do love you, yes, but I don't belong to you, any more than you belong to me. We both know that. It was only a dream, a miracle, a joy; unforgettable, yes, but over."

I shook my head violently. "Everything that happened before this hour is over, this hour has changed everything. You can never belong to him again, you belong to me alone."

She was still holding my arm, and now she grasped it and held it firmly. Yes, she moved it back and forth gently, as though she hoped to awaken me out of an incomprehensible disturbance, out of insanity. But my eyes remained fixed. I knew that there was hardly any love in them, only determination, almost a threat. And I noticed that her anxiety grew, and so she attempted a jocular tone: "Child," she said, "wasn't I right? I've always known why I called you Child. Do I now have to be reasonable for both of us? It isn't easy. Not even for me. But we must, we must be sensible."

"Why must we?" I asked stubbornly, and hated myself at the same time.

"We must," she said, and in her growing anxiety she immediately brought up the strongest, the most irrefutable argument: "We have to be sensible and can't betray ourselves, because you would be lost if he suspected. . . ."

I smiled. I couldn't do anything else. But her opposition, her warning, her attempt to instill fear of a dead man in me, affected me not only as gruesome but as unaccountably comic. At this moment I was not very far from saying something devilish, to put an end to the intolerability and the horror of the conversation with a destructive and yet a saving word. But I didn't do it. I felt my powerlessness precisely at this moment. I felt that the dead man was stronger than me, and I was unable to formulate any other reply than the silly phrase, "And what if in the end fate should decide for me?"

She grasped me by the shoulder. There was fear in her eyes. "What are you saying? What kind of foolishness is this? What are you getting at?"

And at this moment I felt that she was afraid for him—for him, and not in the least for me—that he was everything, and that I was nothing to her. . . . And at this moment we heard footsteps on the garden gravel. I had only a few seconds left. It was impossible, in these few seconds, to tell her what had happened and at the same time to justify why I had been silent up to now. A few minutes ago she would still have understood, might perhaps have been forgiving. Yes, perhaps I could have claimed an actual, permanent victory over the dead man. But now it was I who was the soldier fallen in action, the dead man; yes, at this moment I felt like a ghost, and the footsteps outside in the garden—though I knew that anyone but he could enter at any moment—announced Loiberger's arrival to me in an unfathomable way. Just as he had done in my dream, he walked through the garden and up the steps to the terrace. But whoever it might be, in the few seconds that remained to me it was impossible for me to tell Agatha what had happened and at the same time to justify my silence up to now. It was still more impossible to let what was coming come without preparing her at all. But only one phrase forced its way to my lips: "Don't be afraid." And when I spoke these words I truly felt that her dead husband would arrive the next moment. At first she looked at me with an uncertain smile, as if she wanted to let me know that I needn't worry, that no one would be able to tell from looking at her what had happened in the last hour. But she evidently immediately read in the despairing seriousness of my look that my warning must have some other meaning than the petty concern that she might somehow betray herself. She just had enough time to ask: "What's happened?" But I no longer had the chance to answer.

Footsteps were already echoing in the adjoining room. Agatha walked into the salon without again turning toward me, and I followed her. Aline was standing in the doorway between the salon and the terrace. She glanced at me with a puzzled and astonished look, took the hands of her now pallid friend, and, breaking down in tears, embraced her. Agatha's eyes, however, stared past Aline's into mine with such a relentlessly questioning look that it seemed she wanted to read the answer on my forehead. I put my finger to my lips and realized that this pitiable gesture was meant to beg Agatha to betray me rather than herself. But in her look there was more than I have ever seen in a person's look: presentiment, even knowledge, as well as indignation, understanding, and forgiveness, yes, perhaps even something like gratitude.

Now Muelling was also standing in the door between the salon and the terrace, between shadow and light. He glanced at me questioningly. My presence here declared to him without further notice that I had not been able to bring myself to leave the unfortunate woman after bringing her the awful news. He walked up to her and squeezed her hand without a word. Again she sought my eyes past Muelling's. No one spoke, not she, not Aline, and not Muelling, but it seemed to me that my silence was deeper than that of the others. The summer stillness of the garden echoed into the room. Finally Agatha said—and my heart stood still as she moved her lips—"Now I want," she said, "to hear the whole truth"—and since she noticed the look of estrangement in the expression of the others, and in mine a look of shock, she turned to me and added, in admirable calm: "You didn't want to hide anything from me, but perhaps subconsciously you were trying to protect me. I thank you. But believe me, I'm now composed enough to hear it all. Tell me everything, Dr. Muelling, from beginning to end. I won't ask any questions, I won't interrupt you," and with her voice dying, she added, "Tell me!"

She leaned on the piano and her fingers played with the fringes of the shawl. She didn't betray either herself or me with the slightest quiver of her lips while Muelling spoke. Aline had let herself sink onto the piano stool, and propped her head in her hands. Despite his inner turmoil, Muelling was able to muster the professional habit of speaking fluently in public. He reported the course of events, from the moment that he and I had waited for Eduard at the train station of the small town to the minute that Eduard had fallen dead at the edge of the forest, and it was clear to me that he had already told the story once or twice since we had separated at the gate of his inn. He spoke on the whole as if he were pleading a case for someone atoning all too much for a long-forgotten, trivial offense, whose memory was to be acquitted of every guilt. Agatha actually managed not to interrupt him with a single word. And only when Muelling had finished did she turn to him with a question, to ask whether any arrangements had been made on the spot. And when Muelling replied that the body was to be released by the authorities by the next morning at the very latest, she said, "I'll go to him this evening." Muelling advised her against it, saying that today's night train would not arrive in the small garrison town until after midnight, but she said only, "I want to see him tonight." It was clear to all of us that she meant to get into the morgue tonight. Muelling offered to accompany her, for there were all sorts of things to care for and arrange, which Agatha could not possibly do by herself. But she declined with a decisiveness that allowed for no contradiction. "All this is my affair," she said. "We'll speak again only when everything is over, Dr. Muelling." I was filled with admiration and horror at the same time. She didn't direct a single word to me. She now wanted to be alone; only Aline should come back again later to help her with her travel preparations and to receive instructions as to what to do during her absence.

She shook hands with all of us. With me no differently than with Aline and Muelling. She didn't even avoid looking me in the eye as we parted.

She did actually leave that same night—alone—and brought her husband's body to Vienna the next morning. The next day was the funeral; naturally I took part. Agatha saw no one that day. She never again returned to the lake.

Many years later we met again at a party. She had remarried in the meantime. No one who saw us speaking together could have suspected that a strange, profound, and secret experience joined us together. Did it really join us? I myself could have remembered that uncanny and yet so blissful summer hour as a dream I had dreamed alone, so clearly, so emptily, so innocently did her eyes meet mine.

Baron von Leisenbohg's Destiny

IT WAS A MILD EVENING in May when Clara Hell once again performed as the "Queen of the Night" after a long absence. The reason that had kept the singer away from the opera for almost two months was well known. On March 15, Prince Richard Bedenbruck had had an accident in which he had been thrown from his horse and had died in Clara's arms only a few hours afterward, during which time Clara did not leave his side. Clara's despair had been so great that at first there had been concern for her life, then for her mind, and most recently for her voice. This last fear had proved just as unfounded as the former ones. When she again appeared before the public, she was greeted warmly and expectantly; and as early as the end of the very first great aria, her intimate friends were able to accept the congratulations of her more distant ones. In the fourth gallery the rubicund face of Miss Fanny Ringeiser beamed with happiness, and the regulars in the upper galleries smiled at their comrade. They all knew that Fanny, even though she was nothing more than the daughter of a Mariahilferstrasse shopkeeper, belonged to the intimate circle of the beloved singer; that she was sometimes invited to her house for tea; and that she had also secretly loved the late prince. During the intermission Fanny told her friends that it was Baron von Leisenbohg who had given Clara the idea of choosing the "Queen of the Night" for her first performance, suggesting that the dark costume would most nearly match her mood.

The baron himself took his orchestra seat in the middle section, first row, corner, as usual, and thanked those who greeted him with a gracious but almost pained smile. Many memories flooded his mind today. He had met Clara ten years ago. At that time he was sponsoring the artistic education of a young, slender, red-haired woman and had gone to a performance at the Eisenstein singing academy where his protégé was appearing in public as Mignon for the very first time. On that same evening he saw and heard Clara, who was singing the role of Philine in the same scene. He was then twenty-five years old, independent and inconsiderate. He abandoned Mignon on the spot. Mrs. Natalie Eisenstein introduced him to Philine, and he declared to her that his heart, his fortune, and his connections to theatre managers were at her disposal. At that time Clara was living with her mother, the widow of a higher-ranking post office official, and was in love with a young medical student to whose room in the suburb of Alser she sometimes went for tea and conversation. She rejected the baron's passionate courtship, but, warmed by Leisenbohg's wooing, became the mistress of the medical student. The baron, from whom she did not conceal this relationship, returned to his red-haired protégé but maintained a friendship with Clara. He sent her flowers and chocolates on any holiday that could serve as an excuse, and once in a while appeared for a polite visit in the house of the post office official's widow.

That fall Clara began her first engagement in Detmold. Baron von Leisenbohg—then still a ministry official—used the first Christmas vacation to visit Clara in her new locale. He knew that the medical student had become a physician and had married in September, and so had new hopes. But Clara, honest as usual, informed the baron immediately upon his arrival that she had in the meantime begun an intimate relationship with the tenor at the Court Theatre. And so it happened that Leisenbohg could take from Detmold no other memories than a platonic ride through the city park and a supper in the theatre's restaurant in the company of a few of Clara's colleagues. In spite of this he repeated his visit to Detmold several times, admired Clara's considerable artistic progress while there, and had hopes for the next season, since the tenor had already signed a contract with the Hamburg Opera. But even in that next year he was disappointed, as Clara saw fit to succumb to the courtship of a Dutch whole-sale merchant named Louis Verhajen.

When Clara was called to the Dresden Court Theatre in the third season, the baron, despite his youth, gave up a very promising career in the state service and moved to Dresden. There he spent every evening with Clara and her mother—who knew how to keep a convenient oblivi-ousness in regard to her daughter's relationships—and entertained new hopes. Unfortunately the Dutchman had the inconvenient habit of writ-ing letters announcing his imminent arrival the next day, and of indicat-ing to his beloved that she was surrounded by a network of spies, threatening her with various painful manners of death if she were un-faithful to him. But since he never actually came, and Clara slowly be-came more and more apprehensive, Leisenbohg decided to bring an end to the affair no matter what the price; and he traveled to Detmold so that he could handle it personally. To his great surprise, the Dutchman de-clared that he had written his threatening love letters only out of chivalry, and that actually he would welcome nothing more than to be relieved of any further obligations to Clara. Blissfully happy, Leisenbohg returned to Dresden and informed Clara of the agreeable outcome of his visit. She thanked him heartily but rejected his very first attempt at a closer inti-macy with a vehemence that shocked him. After a few short and urgent questions she finally admitted to him that during his absence no less a personage than Prince Kajetan had been seized with a passion for her and had sworn to inflict harm on himself if she did not accept him. It was nat-ural that in the end she had had to give in to him in order not to plunge the ruling house and the country into deepest despair.

With a broken heart Leisenbohg left town and returned to Vienna. Here he began to cultivate his connections again, and it was not in the least due to his continual efforts on her behalf that Clara received an offer from the Vienna Opera for the coming year. After a successful guest performance, she began her regular engagement that October, and the gorgeous basket of flowers from the baron that Clara found in her wardrobe on the evening of her first performance seemed to express a plea and a hope simultaneously. But the enthusiastic sponsor who waited for her after the performance was destined to find that he had once again come too late. The blonde singing coach—who also had a reputation as a composer of songs—with whom she had studied in the last few weeks had been given rights by her that she was unable to retract for anything in the world.

Since that time, seven years had passed. The singing coach had been followed by Herr Klemens von Rhodewyl, the bold jockey; Herr von Rhodewyl by the choir director Vincenz Klaudi, who sometimes sang along with the operas that he directed so loudly that one couldn't hear the singers; the choir director by Count von Alban-Rattony, a man who had gambled away his Hungarian properties in a card game but later won a castle in Lower Austria; the count by Herr Edgar Wilhelm, composer of ballet scores that he paid dearly for, of tragedies for which he rented the Jantschtheatre, and of poems which were printed in the most beautiful script in the silliest aristocratic paper of the Residenz; Herr Edgar Wilhelm by a man named Amandus Meier, who was only nineteen years old and very handsome—and owned nothing except a fox terrier who could stand on his head; and Herr Meier by the most elegant man in the monarchy: Prince Richard Bedenbruck.

Clara never tried to hide her affairs. At all times she kept a simple bourgeois home in which only the man of the house changed from time to time. She was extraordinarily beloved by the public. Higher circles were pleased that she went to mass every Sunday and to confession twice a month, wore a picture of the Madonna that had been blessed by the pope as an amulet on her breast, and never went to sleep without saying her prayers. There was seldom a charity event in which she did not participate as a sales girl, and aristocratic ladies as well as ladies from Jewish financial circles were happy to be able to offer their wares under the same tent as Clara. She always had a charming smile for the youthful fans who waited for her at the stage door. She divided the flowers that she received among the patient crowd and once, when the flowers had accidently been left behind in the wardrobe, she said in the charming Viennese dialect that suited her so well, "My goodness, I forgot the salad up in my little room! Please come again tomorrow afternoon if you want some of it." Then she climbed up into the carriage, and putting her head out of the window while driving away, called out, "You'll get coffee too!"

Fanny Ringeiser was one of the few who had found the courage to accept this invitation. Clara got into a lighthearted conversation with her, asked about her family affairs as affably as an archduchess, and liked the refreshing and enthusiastic girl so much that she asked her to come back soon. Fanny accepted the invitation, and soon she succeeded in establishing herself as an important part of the artist's household, a position she knew how to keep, for despite all the intimacies that Clara revealed to her, she never allowed herself equal intimacies in return. During the course of the years Fanny received many marriage proposals, mostly from the circle of the young sons of Mariahilfer industrialists with whom she usually danced at balls. But she rejected them, since she regularly fell in love with Clara's current lover.

Clara loved Prince Bedenbruck for more than three years with the same faithfulness but with deeper passion than his forerunners, and Leisenbohg, who despite his numerous disappointments had never given up hope, began seriously to fear that the happiness he had yearned for for ten years would never be his. Always, whenever he saw someone fall from her graces, he broke off with his current lover in order to be ready for her at any moment. He did the same thing after the sudden death of Prince Richard, but for the first time more out of habit than conviction. Clara's pain seemed so limitless that everyone was forced to believe she had given up the joys of life forever. Every day she drove to the cemetery and placed flowers on the grave of the deceased. She had her light-colored clothes put into the attic and locked up her jewelry in the hardest-to-reach drawer of her desk. It took much persuasion to convince her to abandon the idea of leaving the stage forever.

After her first successful reappearance on the opera stage, her life—at least on the surface—resumed its usual course. The circle of her former acquaintances reassembled. The music critic Bernhard Feuerstein appeared again with spinach or tomato stains on his jacket, depending on the menu of previous dinners, and to Clara's open delight complained about colleagues and directors. Once more she allowed herself to be courted by Prince Richard's two nephews, Lucius and Christian, Beden-brucks from the other line, in a way that did not obligate her; a French ambassador and a young Czech pianist were introduced into her circle; and on the 10th of June she once again went to the races. But as Prince Lucius, who was not without poetic talent, expressed it at the time: only her spirit had awakened, but her heart was still asleep. Yes, whenever any of her younger or older friends dared to intimate that there was such a thing as tenderness or passion in the world, every smile disappeared from her face, her eyes darkened, and sometimes she lifted her hand in a pecu-liar gesture of dismissal meant to apply to everyone for all time.

Then in the second half of June it happened that a singer from the North named Sigurd Olse sang Tristan at the opera. His voice was bright and strong, if not completely noble; his figure was almost superhumanly tall, though inclined to fullness; and though his face while not singing lacked expressiveness, as soon as he sang his steel-grey eyes lit up as though from a secret inner fire; and through his voice and his intense look he seemed to hold everyone spellbound, especially the women.

Clara sat with her other currently unoccupied colleagues in the box of the theatre. She seemed to be the only one who was not moved by his singing. The next morning Sigurd Olse was introduced to her in the di-rector's office. She said a few kind but almost cool words about his per-formance of the day before. He visited her that same afternoon, without her having invited him. Baron Leisenbohg and Fanny Ringeiser were there. Sigurd had tea with them. He talked about his parents, who were fishermen living in a small Norwegian city; of the wonderful discovery of his singing talents by a traveling Englishman who had landed on the remote fjord in a white yacht; of his wife, an Italian woman who had died on their honeymoon while on the Atlantic and who was buried at sea. After he took his leave, the others remained silent for a long time. Fanny scrutinized her empty teacup, Clara went to the piano and propped her el-bows up on the closed lid, and the baron brooded silently and anxiously about why Clara, during the story of Sigurd's honeymoon, had not made that peculiar gesture with which she had dismissed all intimations of the continued existence of passionate or tender relationships on earth since the death of the prince.

In his further guest engagements, Sigurd Olse sang Siegfried and Lohengrin. Each time Clara sat unmoved in the loge. But the singer, who otherwise did not associate with anyone except members of the Norwegian delegation, appeared at Clara's every afternoon, seldom without meeting Miss Fanny Ringeiser, and never without meeting the Baron von Leisenbohg.

On the twenty-seventh of June he appeared as Tristan for the last time. Clara sat unmoved in the loge of the theatre. The morning afterward she drove with Fanny to the cemetery and laid a huge wreath on the grave of the prince. That evening she gave a party in honor of the singer, who was scheduled to leave Vienna the next day.

Her entire circle of friends was there. The passion that Sigurd had conceived for Clara was a secret to no one. As usual, he spoke a lot and excitedly. Among other things, he told of how, during his journey by ship to Vienna, an Arabian woman married to a Russian prince regent had read the lines of his hand and had prophesied that he would soon enter the most fateful epoch of his life. He believed in this prophecy strongly, as indeed superstition was stronger in him than the ability to make himself interesting. He also spoke of the well-known fact that the last year, just after landing in New York, where he was supposed to make a guest appearance, he had—despite the large penalty he had to pay—immediately reboarded the ship to return to Europe, merely because a black cat had walked between his legs on the landing pier. Of course he had grounds to believe in such mysterious connections between incomprehensible signs and the fate of men. One evening in London's Covent Garden Opera House, his voice had failed because he had neglected to say a certain magic formula he had learned from his grandmother. One night in a dream a winged genius in a rose-colored leotard had appeared to him and had foretold the death of his favorite barber, and indeed, the unlucky man was found hanging the next morning. In addition, he always carried with him a short but content-rich letter which had been handed to him by the spirit of the late singer Cornelia Lujan in a spiritual séance in Brussels, a letter which in perfect Portuguese contained the prophecy that he was destined to be the greatest singer in the Old and the New World. He recounted all these things now; and as the spiritual letter, written on the rose-colored paper of the Glienwood firm was passed from hand to hand, the whole company was deeply moved. Only Clara was not affected, and simply nodded indifferently from time to time. Despite that, Leisenbohg's anxiety reached new heights. To his sharpened eye the signs of coming danger were ever more clear. Most of all Sigurd, like all of Clara's former lovers, conceived a noticeable liking for him at supper, invited him to his property on the Fjord of Molde, and finally offered him the intimate form of "you." Furthermore, Fanny Ringeiser's entire body trembled whenever Sigurd addressed a word to her; she alternately paled and blushed when he looked at her with his large, steel-grey eyes; and when he began to talk about his coming departure, she began to cry out loud. But Clara remained calm and serious even now. She scarcely responded to the flaming looks that Sigurd directed at her; she did not speak to him more animatedly than to the others; and when he finally kissed her hand and looked up at her with eyes that seemed to beg, to promise, to despair, her own remained veiled and her features impassive. Leisenbohg watched all this with mistrust and fear. But as the party was nearing its end and everyone took his leave, the baron experienced something totally unexpected. As the last one to leave, he gave his hand to Clara in farewell, like the others, and turned to go. But she held his hand tightly and whispered to him, "Please return." He believed he hadn't heard correctly. But she pressed his hand once again, and, with her lips right next to his ear, repeated, "Please return; I'll expect you in an hour."

Almost giddy, he left with the others. He accompanied Sigurd to the hotel with Fanny and heard him sing Clara's praises as though from far away. Then he took Fanny Ringeiser to Mariahilferstrasse through quiet streets in the pleasant night coolness, and as if in a fog he saw silly tears run down her ruddy cheeks. Then he took a carriage and drove to Clara's house. He saw light shine through the curtains of her bedroom; he saw her shadow pass by, and then her head appeared in the opening next to the curtain and she nodded to him. He had not been dreaming; she was awaiting him.

The next morning Baron von Leisenbohg went for a pleasure ride in the Prater. He felt happy and young. In the late fulfillment of his desire there seemed to him to be a deeper meaning. What he had experienced that night was the most wonderful surprise—and yet nothing but the intensification and obvious conclusion of his previous relationship with Clara. He now felt that nothing else could have happened, and made plans for the immediate and distant future. "How long is she going to remain on the stage?" he thought. . . . "Maybe four, maybe five years. Then, but not before, I'll marry her. We'll live together in the country, very near Vienna, maybe in St.Veit or in Lainz. There I'll buy a small house or have one built to her taste. We'll live quite secluded but will often make major trips . . . to Spain, Egypt, India. . . ." He daydreamed all this while he let his horse trot faster and faster over the meadows of Heustadtl. Then he trotted back to the Hauptallee, and at the Praterstern he entered his carriage. He had the carriage stop at Fossati's and sent Clara a bouquet of gorgeous dark roses. He breakfasted in his home at the Schwarzenbergplatz, alone as usual, and after he had eaten, lay down on the sofa. He was filled with intense desire for Clara. What did all the other women mean to him? . . . They had been a distraction—nothing more. And he felt the day would come when Clara too would say to him, "What did all the others mean to me? You are the only and the first one that I ever loved!". . . . And as he was lying on the sofa with his eyes closed, all the other men paraded in front of him . . . certainly she had loved none of them; perhaps she had loved only him always and in everyone! . . .

The baron dressed and walked slowly along the familiar route to Clara's house so that he could have a few more seconds of the pleasurable anticipation of his reunion with her. Many people were out walking on the Ring, but it was still noticeable that the season was reaching its end. Leisenbohg was glad that it was already summer so that he could travel with Clara to the sea or the mountains, and he had to control himself in order not to cry out loud in delight.

He stood in front of her house and looked up toward her windows. The light of the afternoon sun was reflected back from the windows and almost blinded him. He walked up the two steps to her door and rang. No one came. He rang the bell again. No one opened. Now Leisenbohg noticed that a lock had been attached to the door. What did that mean? Had he come to the wrong place? There was no sign on the door, but opposite it he read as usual: "First Lieutenant von Jeleskowits. . . ." There was no doubt: he stood in front of her flat and her flat was locked up. . . . He ran down the stairs and tore open the caretaker's door. The caretaker's wife was sitting on a bed in the half-darkened room; a child was looking through the small basement window up to the street, and another child was whistling an incomprehensible melody on a comb. "Is Miss Hell not at home?" the baron asked. The woman stood up. . . ."No, Herr Baron, Miss Hell has moved out. . . ."

"What?" the baron exclaimed. "Yes, of course," he added immediately . . . "around three o'clock, no?"

"No, Herr Baron, the Fräulein left at eight o'clock in the morning."

"And where to? . . . I mean, did she go directly to—" he just guessed, "did she go directly to Dresden?"

"No, Herr Baron; she didn't leave an address. She did say that she would write and tell us where she is."

"So—yes . . . yes . . . so . . . naturally. . . . Thank you." He turned around and stepped onto the street again. Instinctively he looked back at the house. The late afternoon sun now appeared very different from before. What a dull, melancholy, and oppressive summer evening heat was now lying over the city! Clara was gone? . . . Why? . . . Had she flown from him? . . . What did that mean? . . . His first thought was to drive to the opera. But then he remembered that the summer recess began the day after tomorrow and that Clara didn't have to be there the last two days.

So instead he drove to Mariahilferstrasse 76, where the Ringeisers lived. An old cook opened the door and looked at the elegant visitor with some mistrust. He asked to see Mrs. Ringeiser. "Is Miss Fanny at home?" he asked in an agitation that he could no longer control.

"What do you mean?" Mrs. Ringeiser replied sharply.

The baron introduced himself.

"Oh, yes," said Mrs. Ringeiser. "Does the Herr Baron not want to come in?"

He stood still in the foyer and asked again, "Is Miss Fanny at home?"

"Please do follow me." Leisenbohg had to follow her and soon found himself in a low, dimly lit room with blue velvet furniture and corduroy curtains of the same color on the windows. "No," said Mrs. Ringeiser, "Fanny isn't at home. Miss Hell took her along on vacation."

"Where to?" asked the baron, and stared at a photograph of Clara that was standing on the piano in a slim gold frame.

"Where to? I have no idea," said Mrs. Ringeiser. "At eight in the morning Miss Hell herself came and asked me to let Fanny go with her. Well, and she begged so charmingly—I couldn't say no."

"But where to . . . where to?" asked Leisenbohg urgently.

"Well, that I don't know. Fanny is going to telegraph me as soon as Miss Hell decides where she's going to stay. Maybe as soon as tomorrow or the day after tomorrow."

"So," said Leisenbohg, and sank into a small bamboo chair in front of the piano. He remained silent for a few seconds, then suddenly stood up, gave Mrs. Ringeiser his hand, asked her to excuse him for bothering her, and slowly went down the dark staircase of the old house.

He shook his head. She had been very careful—truly! More careful than necessary . . . she should have known that he wouldn't press himself on her.

"Where're we going, Herr Baron?" the coachman asked him, and Leisenbohg realized that he had been sitting in the open carriage staring straight ahead for a long time. And, following a sudden impulse, he answered, "To the Hotel Bristol."

Sigurd Olse had not yet left. He asked the baron up to his room, greeted him with enthusiasm, and begged him to spend the last evening of his stay in Vienna with him. Leisenbohg was already surprised to find that Sigurd Olse was still in Vienna, but this kindness now moved him almost to tears. Sigurd immediately began to talk about Clara. He asked Leisenbohg to tell him as much about her as he could, since he knew that the baron was her oldest and most faithful friend. And Leisenbohg sat down on a suitcase and talked about Clara. It was good for him to be able to talk about Clara. He told the singer almost everything—with the exception of those things that he felt he had to conceal out of chivalry. Sigurd listened and seemed to be delighted.

At supper the singer invited his friend to leave Vienna with him that very night and to accompany him to his estate in Molde. The baron felt himself wonderfully calmed. He declined but promised to visit Olse in the course of the summer.

They drove to the train station together. "You'll think I'm a fool," said Sigurd, "but I want to drive past her windows once more." Leisenbohg looked at him sideways. Was this perhaps an attempt to deceive him? Or was it the last proof of the singer's trustworthiness? As they stood in front of Clara's house, Sigurd threw a kiss up to the closed windows. Then he said, "Give her my greetings one more time."

Leisenbohg nodded, "I'll tell her when she returns." Sigurd looked at him in amazement.

"She's already gone," added Leisenbohg. "She left this morning . . . without saying goodbye . . . in her usual manner," he lied.

"She left?" repeated Sigurd and fell silent. Then they were both silent.

Before the train left they embraced each other like old friends.

That night the baron cried in his bed in a way he had not done since childhood. The one hour of voluptuous joy he had experienced with Clara now seemed to him to be surrounded by spine-chilling horror. It seemed to him that her eyes last night had glowed as though mad. Now he understood everything. He had accepted her invitation too early. The shadow of Prince Bedenbruck still held power over her, and Leisenbohg felt that he had only possessed Clara in order to lose her forever.

He hung around Vienna for a few days without knowing what to do with his days and his nights. Everything that he used to do—reading the newspapers, playing whist, taking pleasure rides—held no interest for him. He realized that his whole existence had meaning only in relationship to Clara, that even his relationships with other women were mere reflections of his passion for her. The city seemed to be enveloped in an eternal grey mist; the people with whom he talked seemed to have muffled voices and to stare at him peculiarly, almost treacherously. One evening he drove to the train station and almost mechanically bought himself a ticket for Ischl. There he ran into acquaintances who innocently asked about Clara, and he answered them impolitely, with irritation, with the result that he had to fight a duel with someone who didn't interest him in the least. He went to the duel without emotion, heard the bullet whistle past his ear, shot into the air, and left Ischl half an hour afterward. He traveled to Tirol, to the Engadin, to the Bernese Highland, and to Lake Geneva; he rowed, hiked up and down mountains and passes, slept in a dairy hut, and remembered no more of the day before than he knew of the day to come.

One day he received a telegram from Vienna. He opened it with feverish fingers. He read, "If you are my friend, keep your word and rush to me, as I need a friend. Sigurd Olse." Leisenbohg had no doubt that this telegram had some connection with Clara. He packed as rapidly as he could and left Aix—where he happened to be—as soon as he could. He traveled to Hamburg by way of Munich without stopping and there took a boat that brought him via Stavanger to Molde, where he arrived on a bright summer evening. The trip seemed endless to him. His soul was unmoved by the charms of the landscapes he passed. He could hardly remember Clara's singing or even her features. He felt as though he had been away from Vienna for years, even decades. But as he saw Sigurd standing on the shore in a white flannel suit with a white cap, it was as though he had just seen him last night. And despite his confused state, he answered Sigurd's welcome with a smile from the dock, and walked upright down the staircase of the ship.

"I thank you a thousand times for answering my call," said Sigurd. And then he added simply, "It's all over with me."

The baron looked at him. Sigurd was looking very pale, and the hair on his temples had turned noticeably grey. He carried a worn green blanket over his arm.

"What's wrong? What happened?" asked Leisenbohg with a rigid smile.

"You'll soon know everything," said Sigurd Olse. The baron noticed that Sigurd's voice was not as full as it had been before. They drove in a small, narrow carriage through the lovely boulevard along the blue ocean. They were both silent. Leisenbohg didn't dare to ask. He fixed his gaze on water that was moving imperceptibly. He had the peculiar, and, as it turned out, impossible idea of counting the waves; then he looked into the air, and he felt as though the stars were slowly dripping down. Finally he remembered that there was a singer by the name of Clara Hell who was somewhere in this wide world—but that fact was rather unimportant. Suddenly there was a start, and the carriage stood in front of a simple white house entirely surrounded by greenery. They ate supper on a veranda with a view of the ocean. A servant with a severe—and in those moments in which he poured the wine, almost threatening—manner was serving. The bright northern night rested on the horizon.

"Well?" asked Leisenbohg, who was suddenly flooded with impatience.

"I'm a lost man," said Sigurd Olse, and looked down.

"What do you mean?" asked Leisenbohg tonelessly. "And what can I do for you?" he added mechanically.

"Not much. I don't know yet." And Sigurd Olse looked across the tablecloth, the railing, the front garden, the fence, the street, and the ocean into the distance.

Leisenbohg was unable to feel anything . . . all sorts of ideas went through his mind at the same time. . . . What could have happened? . . . was Clara dead—? had Sigurd killed her—? thrown her into the sea—? . . . or was Sigurd dead—? . . . But no, that was impossible . . . he was sitting right in front of him. . . . But why didn't he speak? . . . And suddenly, seized by an enormous terror, he managed to ask, "Where is Clara?"

At that the singer turned slowly toward him. His somewhat fat face began to glow from the inside, and he seemed to smile—though it might have been only moonshine that was playing over his face. In any case at this moment it seemed to Leisenbohg that the man who was sitting next to him with a veiled look, both hands in his pants pockets, his legs stretched out underneath the table, resembled nothing in the world more than a Pierrot. The green blanket hung over the railing of the terrace and seemed to the baron like a good old friend . . . but why should this ridiculous blanket concern him? . . . Was he dreaming? . . . He was in Molde. That was strange enough. . . . If he had had any sense, he could of course have telegraphed the singer from Aix and asked, "What's the matter? What do you want from me, Pierrot?" And suddenly he repeated his earlier question, only much more calmly and politely: "Where is Clara?"

The singer nodded several times. "Yes, it's about her. Are you my friend?"

Leisenbohg nodded. He felt a slight shiver. A warm wind was coming from the sea. "I'm your friend. What do you want from me?"

"Do you remember the evening that we parted, baron, after we had dinner together at the Bristol and you accompanied me to the railroad station?"

Leisenbohg nodded again.

"I'll wager you had no idea that Clara was leaving Vienna with me on the same train."

Leisenbohg let his head fall heavily on his chest.

"Nor did I." Sigurd continued. "I only saw Clara the next morning in the breakfast carriage. She was sitting with Fanny Ringeiser in the dining room, drinking coffee. Her behavior led me to believe that I owed this meeting to chance. But it wasn't chance."

"Go on," said the baron, and looked at the green plaid blanket swaying lightly to and fro.

"Afterward she confessed to me that it had not been by chance. From that morning on we stayed together, Clara, Fanny, and I. We stopped at one of your delightful small Austrian lakes. We lived there in a charming house between the water and the forest, far from other people. We were very happy."

He spoke so slowly that Leisenbohg thought he would go out of his mind.

Why did he call me here? he wondered. What does he want from me? . . . Did she confess to him? . . . What business is it of his? . . . Why is he staring at me so fixedly? . . . Why am I sitting here in Molde on a veranda with a Pierrot? . . . Maybe in the end it's a dream after all? . . . Am I perhaps resting in Clara's arms? . . . Is it still the same night after all? . . . And instinctively he opened his eyes wide.

"Will you revenge me?" Sigurd suddenly asked.

"Revenge? . . . Why? what's happened?" asked the baron, and heard his own words as though from afar.

"Because she has ruined me; because I'm lost."

"Tell me already," said Leisenbohg in a hard, dry voice.

"Fanny Ringeiser was with us," continued Sigurd. "She's an honest girl, don't you think?"

"Yes, she's an honest girl," answered Leisenbohg, and all at once he remembered the dimly lit room with the blue velvet furniture and corduroy drapes where he had spoken with Fanny's mother several hundred years ago.

"But she's a rather stupid girl, don't you think?"

"I believe so," replied the baron.

"I know it for sure," said Sigurd. "She had no idea how happy we were." And he was silent for a long time.

"Go on," said Leisenbohg, and waited.

"One morning Clara was sleeping late," Sigurd began anew. "She always slept late into the morning. But I went for a walk in the forest. Suddenly Fanny came running after me. 'Flee, Herr Olse, before it is too late; leave town, because you're in grave danger!' Strangely enough, she didn't want to tell me anything more at the beginning. But I insisted and finally found out what kind of danger she thought was threatening me. Ah, she believed that I could still be saved, otherwise she certainly wouldn't have told me anything."

The green blanket on the railing blew upward like a sail, and the lamplight on the table flickered a little.

"What did Fanny tell you?" asked Leisenbohg sternly.

"Do you remember the evening," asked Sigurd, "when we were all guests in Clara's house? On the morning of that day Clara had gone with Fanny to the cemetery, and on the grave of the prince she had revealed the horror to her friend."

"The horror?" The baron trembled.

"Yes. You know how the prince died? He was thrown from his horse and lived only an hour afterward."

"I know."

"No one was with him except Clara."

"I know."

"He wanted to see no one except her. And on his deathbed he uttered a curse."

"A curse?"

"A curse. 'Clara,' the prince said, 'don't forget me. I will have no rest in the grave if you forget me.' 'I won't ever forget you,' answered Clara. 'Will you swear that you'll never forget me?' 'I swear.' 'Clara, I love you, and I have to die.' "

"Who's speaking?" cried the baron.

"I'm speaking," said Sigurd, "and I speak for Fanny, and Fanny speaks for Clara, and Clara speaks for the prince. Don't you understand me?"

Leisenbohg listened with effort. He felt as if he heard the voice of the dead prince resound in the night through the triple-sealed casket.

" 'Clara, I love you, and I have to die! You are so young, and I have to die. . . . And there will be someone else after me. . . . I know it; it will happen. . . . Another will hold you in his arms and will be happy with you. . . . He shall not—he cannot! I curse him. Do you hear, Clara? I curse him! . . . The first one that kisses these lips, that embraces this body after me, shall go to hell! . . . Clara, heaven hears the curse of the dying . . . beware! . . . beware! . . . To hell with him! in madness, misery, and death! Beware! Beware! Beware!' "

Sigurd, from whose mouth the voice of the dead prince sounded, had gotten up and now stood tall and strong in his white flannel suit, looking into the bright night. The green plaid blanket fell from the railing into the garden. The baron was freezing. He felt as though his whole body were turning to stone. He wanted to scream but only opened his mouth wide. . . . He found himself at this moment back in the small room of the singing teacher Eisenstein where he had seen Clara for the first time. A Pierrot stood on the stage and declaimed, "With this curse on his lips Prince Bedenbruck died, and . . . hear . . . the unhappy one, in whose arms she lay, the miserable one that will fulfill the curse, am I! . . . I! . . . I!"

Then the stage collapsed with a loud noise and sank into the sea under Leisenbohg's eyes. But he himself fell noiselessly backward with his chair, like a marionette.

Sigurd sprang up and called for help. Two servants came and lifted the unconscious man up and put him in an easy chair near the table; one of them ran for a doctor, the other brought water and vinegar. Sigurd rubbed the baron's forehead and temples, but he did not move. Then the doctor came and examined him. It didn't take long. At the end he said, "This man is dead."

Sigurd Olse was overwhelmed, asked the doctor to do what was necessary, and left the terrace. He went through the salon, walked upstairs to another floor, went into his bedroom, turned on a light, and hurriedly wrote the following words: "Clara! I received your message in Molde, to where I fled without stopping. I'll admit to you that I didn't believe you; I thought you wanted to calm me with a lie. Forgive me. I don't doubt you anymore. Baron von Leisenbohg was with me. I asked him to come. But I didn't ask him about anything, since as a man of honor he would have had to lie to me. I had an ingenious idea. I told him about the curse of the dying prince. The effect on him was surprising: the baron fell backward with his chair and died on the spot."

Sigurd paused, turned very serious, and seemed to reflect. Then he placed himself in the middle of the room and lifted his voice in song. First his voice was unsure and veiled, then slowly it brightened and resounded strong and beautiful through the night, in the end so powerfully that it seemed as though it were echoing from the waves. A calm smile played over Sigurd's features. He breathed in deeply. He went back to the desk and to his letter added the following words:

"Dear Clara! Forgive me—everything is all right again. In three days I'll be with you again. . . ."

The Widower

HE STILL DOESN'T QUITE UNDERSTAND IT; it all happened so fast.

For two summer days she lay sick in bed at the villa, two summer days so beautiful that the bedroom windows looking out into the blossoming garden could be left open all day, and then on the evening of the second day she had died, almost abruptly, without anyone's being prepared for it. And today she had been carried out, over there, up the gradually rising street that he can now follow from his easy chair on the balcony all the way to the end, to where the low white walls encircle the small cemetery where she was laid to rest.

It is evening now. The street on which the sun had burned down only a few hours ago as the black carriages had rolled slowly upward now lies in shadow, and the white cemetery walls no longer gleam.

They had left him alone; he had asked them to. The mourners had all driven back to town; and the grandparents, upon his request, had taken the child along with them for the first few days that he wanted to be alone. In the garden it is now very quiet, too; only now and then does he hear a whispering from below: the servants are standing under the balcony, speaking quietly with one another. He feels more tired now than he has ever felt before, and as his eyelids close again and again, he once more sees, though his eyes are closed, the street in the haze of the afternoon sun, the carriages rolling slowly upward, the people milling around him—even the voices resound in his ears once more.

Almost everyone who had not gone too far away for the summer had been there. Everyone was very moved by the young woman's premature and sudden death, and had uttered kind words of comfort to him. Some had come quite a distance, people that he had never even thought of, and many whose names he hardly knew had grasped his hand. Only the one he most longed to see, his best friend, had not been there. True, he was far away—at a beach resort on the North Sea, and he must have received the news of her death too late for him to leave so as to arrive in time. He wouldn't be there until tomorrow.

Richard opens his eyes again. The street is now completely in shadow; only the white walls still shimmer in the darkness, and that makes him shudder. He stands up, leaves the balcony, and walks into the adjacent room. It is—was—his wife's. He hadn't realized that it was her room when he walked in quickly; and even now he can't make out anything in the darkness; only a familiar fragrance wafts toward him. He lights the blue candle standing on the desk, and, now able to see the whole room in all its brightness and friendliness, he sinks down onto the sofa and cries.

He cries for a long time—wild and empty tears, and when he stands up again his head is dull and heavy. There is a flickering before his eyes; the flame of the candle burns dimly. He wants more light; he dries his eyes and lights all seven candles of the candelabrum standing on the small pedestal next to the piano. And now a brightness floods the room and illuminates every corner; the delicate gold background of the tapestry glistens, and it looks as it did on many an evening when he would come in and find *her* bent over a book or some letters. She would look up, turn toward him with a smile, and await his kiss. But now the indifference of the objects around him, glittering as they had before, as though they didn't know that they had become sad and eerie, wounds him. Before now he had not felt as keenly how lonely he had become; and never before had he longed for his friend so powerfully. But now as he pictures him coming and saying comforting words, he feels that there might still be some consolation for him. If only he were here already! . . . He will come for sure; early tomorrow morning he will be here. And of course he'll stay with him a long time, many weeks; he won't let him go until he has to. They'll walk together in the garden and talk about profound and unusual things *beyond* the realm of the ordinary, just as they used to. And in the evenings they'll sit on the balcony just as they used to, the dark sky above them, so still and so enormous, and they'll talk together late into the night, just as they had so often done long after *she*, whose fresh and lively personality had found little pleasure in serious conversation, had smilingly bid them good night and gone up to her room. How often had these conversations lifted him above the worries and pettiness of everyday life!—but now they would mean even more; they would be a blessing, even a salvation for him.

Richard continues to pace back and forth in the room until finally the monotonous tone of his own steps begins to disturb him. Then he sits down in front of the small desk with the blue candle and scrutinizes the pretty and dainty objects on it with a kind of curiosity. He never actually noticed them before, had seen them only as a part of the background. The ivory penholders, the narrow letter opener, the slender seal with the onyx handle, the small keys held together by a gold string—one by one he takes them in his hands, turns them around and around, and then gently puts them back in their place again as if they were valuable and fragile. Then he opens the middle drawer of the desk, and there in an open box he sees the pale grey stationery on which *she* used to write, the small envelopes with *her* monogram, the slender, oblong calling cards with *her* name. Then he mechanically reaches for the small side drawer. At first he doesn't even notice that it is locked but keeps tugging on it repeatedly without thinking. Gradually he becomes aware of his absentminded rattling, and he makes an effort and now he *will* get it open. He picks up the small keys lying on the desktop. The very first one he tries fits; the drawer is open. And now he sees letters lying there, carefully tied together with blue ribbons, the very letters that he himself wrote to her. He recognizes the very first one lying on top. It is his first letter to her, from the time of their engagement. And as he reads the loving words, words that once more conjure up an illusion of life in the desolate room, he sighs deeply and then says quietly to himself, over and over, the same thing: a confused and horrified: No . . . no . . . no. . . .

And he loosens the silk ribbon and lets the letters slip between his fingers. Random words torn out of their context fly by him; he hardly has the courage to read any of the letters in its entirety. Only the last, which has just a few short sentences—that he wouldn't be returning home from the city until very late—that he'd be enormously happy to see her dear, sweet face again—he reads carefully, syllable by syllable—and he is astounded because it seems to him that he had written these caressing words many years ago—not just last week, and yet it really is no longer than that.

He pulls the drawer out still farther to see whether there is anything else.

There are a few other packets lying there, all of them bound with blue silk ribbons, and instinctively he smiles sadly. There are letters from her sister in Paris—he had always had to read them with her right away; there are also letters from her mother in that peculiarly masculine handwriting he had always wondered about. And there are letters in a handwriting that he doesn't immediately recognize; he loosens the silk ribbon and looks for the signature—they are from one of her friends, one of those who was there today looking very pale, with eyes red from weeping. And behind them, very far in the back, he sees still another packet, which he takes out like the others and examines. Whose handwriting is this? An unfamiliar one.—No, it isn't an unfamiliar one. . . . It is Hugo's. And the first word that Richard reads, even before he has torn off the blue silk ribbon, strikes him numb for a moment. . . . With wide-open eyes he looks around to see if everything in the room is still the same, and then he looks up at the ceiling, and then again at the letters that are now lying silent in front of him and yet in the next minute will tell him everything that the first word intimated. . . . He wants to remove the ribbon—it seems to resist him; his hands shake and finally he rips it apart forcefully. Then he stands up. He takes the packet in both hands and goes to the piano, on whose shining black top the light of the seven candles of the candelabrum is falling. And with both hands braced on the piano he reads them, the many short letters with the small, hard-to-read handwriting, one after the other, greedy for each one as though it were the first. And he reads them all, down to the last one, which had come from that place on the North Sea—a few days ago. He throws it down among all the others and rummages through the letters again as if he were still looking for something, as if something could float up to him from among these pages that he has not yet discovered, something that would negate the content of all the other letters and turn the truth he has suddenly discovered into a delusion. . . . And when his hands finally stop, it seems to him as though everything has suddenly become perfectly quiet after a monstrous noise. He remembers all the sounds: how the dainty objects on the desk sounded . . . how the drawer squeaked . . . how the lock clicked . . . how the paper crumpled and rustled . . . he hears the sound of his hurrying steps . . . his quick, moaning breathing—but now there is not a sound to be heard in the room. And he is astounded at how at one stroke he now suddenly understands everything, though he had never suspected it in the least. He would have liked to understand it as little as he understands death; he yearns for the tremulous hot pain that the incomprehensible brings, but has only the sensation of utter clarity which seems to flow into all his senses so that the objects in the room have a sharper outline than they did before, and he believes he hears the deep stillness that now encircles him. And slowly he walks over to the sofa, sits down, and thinks. . . .

What has happened?

Once more that which happens every day had happened, and he has become one of those whom other men laugh about. And he'll certainly feel—tomorrow or even in a few hours perhaps—all the anguish that every person must feel under such circumstances . . . he suspects that it will come over him, the nameless rage that this woman has died too soon for him to take his revenge; and when the other one returns, he will strike him down like a dog with these hands. Oh, how he yearns for these wild and honorable feelings—and how much better he would feel then than he does now, when his thoughts are dragging themselves dully and heavily through his mind. . . .

Now he knows only that he has suddenly lost everything, that he must begin his life anew, like a child, for he can no longer make use of any of his memories. He would first have to tear from each of them the mask with which she had made a fool of him. For he had seen nothing, nothing at all, had believed and trusted, and his best friend had betrayed him, as in a comedy. . . . If only it weren't him, only not him! He knows from his own experience that there are passions in the blood which do not go deeply into the soul, and it seems to him as though he could forgive his dead wife everything that *she* would have forgotten soon, anyone whom *he* didn't know, anyone who didn't *mean* anything to him—only not him, whom he loved as he loved no other and to whom he was closer even than to his own wife who had never followed him down the darker paths of his own mind as he did; she had given him pleasure and comfort, yes, but never the deep joy of understanding. And hadn't he always known that women are empty and deceitful creatures, and why had it never occurred to him that his wife was a woman like all the others, empty and deceitful, with the desire to seduce? And why had it never occurred to him that his friend, as high-minded as he was, was a man like other men and could fall prey to the intoxication of a moment? And don't many of the hesitant words in these ardent and quivering letters reveal that he had at first struggled with himself, that he had tried to tear himself away, that he had finally adored this woman, and that he had suffered because of it? . . . It seems almost uncanny to him that everything is so clear to him now—as if a stranger were standing there before him and telling him about it. He can't rant and rave, much as he wants to; he simply *understands* it, as he had always understood it when it had happened to others. And as he now remembers that his wife is lying out there in that quiet cemetery, he knows that he will never be able to hate her, that all the childish anger, even if it could fly over those white walls, would sink down onto the grave with lame wings. And he suddenly realizes how many a phrase that is today a cliché reveals its eternal truth in a blinding flash because all at once he understands the deep meaning of a phrase that had always appeared shallow to him before: Death reconciles. And he knows too that if he were now all of a sudden standing opposite his friend, he would not search for powerful and punishing words, for they now seem to him a ridiculous exaggeration of earthly pettiness compared with the dignity of death—no, he would calmly tell him, "Go, I don't hate you."

He *can't* hate him; he sees everything all too clearly. He can see so deeply into other souls that it almost estranges him. It is as if it weren't his own experience anymore—he feels it as merely accidental that this should have happened to him. There is just one thing that he can't understand—that he hadn't always known right from the beginning and—understood it. Everything was so simple, so self-evident, and it had happened for the same reasons as it had in a thousand other cases. He remembers his wife as he knew her in the first and second years of their marriage, that loving, almost wild creature who was then more of a lover to him than a wife. Had he really believed that this blossoming and yearning creature had turned into someone else because the mechanical routines of marriage had overcome *him*? Did he think those flames were extinguished because *he* no longer felt any desire for them? And that it was just exactly *him* to whom she had been attracted—was that so astounding? How often, when he had sat across from his younger friend, who despite his thirty years still had the freshness and the softness of youth in his manner and his voice—how often had the thought run through his mind: he must be really attractive to women. . . . And now he remembers as well how last year just at the time that it—must have begun, Hugo had come to visit him much less frequently than before . . . and he, the proper husband, had said to him then: "Why don't you come to visit us anymore?" And he had personally picked him up from the office, brought him along with them out to the country, and when he had wanted to leave had held him back with friendly, scolding words. And never had he noticed anything, never had he had the slightest suspicion. Hadn't he seen their passionate and melting glances? Hadn't he heard the trembling of their voices as they talked to each other? Didn't he know how to interpret the anxious silence that had overcome them from time to time as they walked in the garden? And didn't he notice how distracted, moody, and unhappy Hugo had often been—since that summer day last year when—it had begun? Yes, he had noticed it and occasionally had thought to himself: it's some affair with a woman that's tormenting him—and he had been happy when he had been able to draw his friend into serious conversation and so raise him above those petty sufferings. . . . And now, as he lets the entire last year glide quickly by, doesn't he realize all at once that his friend's previous cheerfulness had never really entirely returned, that he had gradually accustomed himself to it, as to everything that comes gradually and doesn't disappear? . . .

And a strange feeling now arises in his soul, a feeling that he scarcely wants to trust at first—a deep gentleness, a great pity for this man whom a terrible passion had overcome, like fate; who at this moment, perhaps—no, certainly—is suffering even more than he is; for this man has after all lost a woman whom he loved and now must appear before the friend he deceived.

And he can't hate him because he still loves him. He knows that everything would be different if—*she* were still alive. Then this guilt, too, would be something that would gain the illusion of importance from *her* being and *her* smile. But now the inexorable finality of her death has swallowed up everything that seems important about that wretched adventure.

A soft quiver penetrates the deep stillness of the room . . . footsteps on the stairs—he listens with bated breath; he hears the beating of his pulse.

The outside door opens.

For a moment it seems to him that everything he has built up in his soul will come crashing down; but in the next moment it is secure again. And he knows what he will say to him when he enters: I understand everything—stay!

A voice outside, the voice of his friend.

And suddenly it occurs to him that this man will enter unsuspectingly, that he himself will first have to tell him. . . .

And he feels like getting up from the sofa and locking the door—because he feels that he won't be able to utter a single word. But he can't even move; he feels rooted to the spot. He won't say anything to him, won't say a single word to him today, not until tomorrow . . . tomorrow.

There is whispering outside. Richard can understand the softly spoken question, "Is he alone?"

He won't say anything, won't say a single word to him today, not until tomorrow—or later. . . .

The door opens and his friend is there. He is very pale and remains standing a while as if he must collect himself, then he hurries toward Richard and sits down next to him on the sofa, takes both of his hands, and presses them hard—he wants to speak, but his voice fails him.

Richard only looks at him rigidly; he lets him take his hands. They sit there silently for a long time.

"My poor friend," Hugo finally says softly.

Richard only nods; he can't speak. If he were able to utter a word, he would only be able to say, "I know. . . ."

After a few minutes Hugo begins again: "I wanted to be here early this morning. But I didn't receive your telegram until late in the evening after I came home."

"I thought so," replies Richard and is amazed at how strongly and calmly he speaks. He looks deeply into his friend's eyes. . . . And then it suddenly occurs to him that over there on the piano the letters are lying. Hugo has only to stand up and take a few steps . . . and he will see them . . . and know everything. Instinctively, Richard grasps his friend's hands—that can't happen; it is *he* who is afraid of the discovery.

And then Hugo begins to speak again. With soft, tender words, in which he avoids mentioning the name of the deceased, he asks about her illness, about her death. And Richard replies. At first he is surprised that he can do this, that he finds the repugnant and commonplace words for all the sorrow of the last days. And now and then he steals a glance at his friend's face, which looks pale, with trembling lips.

As Richard pauses, the other shakes his head as though he has heard something incomprehensible, something altogether impossible. Then he says: "It was terrible for me not to be able to be with you today. It was as though fated."

Richard looks at him questioningly.

"On that very same day . . . in that very hour, we were out on the ocean . . ."

"Yes, yes . . ."

"There is no such thing as premonition! We were sailing, and the wind was good and we were so happy . . . horrible, horrible!"

Richard remains silent.

"You're not going to stay here alone now, are you?"

Richard looks up. "Why?"

"No, no, you can't."

"Where should I go then? . . . I hope you'll stay with me a

while?" . . . And the fear that Hugo will leave again without knowing that he knows what has happened overwhelms him.

"No," answers his friend, "I'm taking you with me; you're coming along with me."

"Me, with you?"

"Yes . . ." And he says it with a tender smile.

"Where do you want to go?"

"Back!"

"To the North Sea?"

"Yes, and with you. It will do you good. I'm not going to let you stay here alone, no!" . . . and he pulls Richard toward him as if to embrace him. . . . "You must come to us!"

"To us?"

"Yes."

"What does that mean, 'to us'? Aren't you alone?"

Hugo smiles embarrassedly: "Certainly, I'm alone. . . ."

"You said, 'to us.' "

Hugo hesitates a while. Then he says, "I didn't want to tell you right away."

"What?"

"Life is so strange—you see, I've gotten engaged. . . ."

Richard looks at him rigidly. . . .

"That's why I said 'to us' . . . that's why I'm going back to the North Sea, and you should come with me . . . yes?" And he looks at him with innocent eyes.

Richard smiles. "Dangerous climate on the North Sea."

"What do you mean?"

"So quickly, so quickly!" . . . and he shakes his head.

"No, my friend," the other answers. "It's not so quickly at all. Actually, it's an old affair."

Richard is still smiling. "What? . . . an old affair?"

"Yes."

"You've known your fiancée for a while?" . . .

"Yes, since last winter."

"And you love her? . . ."

"Ever since I met her," answers Hugo and stares out into space, as though retrieving fond memories.

Then Richard stands up suddenly, with such a brusque movement that Hugo starts and looks up at him. And then Hugo sees two large, alien eyes peering at him, and sees a pale, trembling face that he can scarcely recognize looming over him. And as he gets up fearfully, he hears, as if from an alien, distant voice, curt words hissed between Richard's teeth: "I know about it." And he feels himself seized by both hands and dragged over to the piano so violently that the candelabrum shakes on its pedestal. And then Richard lets go of his arms and digs underneath the letters lying on the black piano top with both hands, rummages through them, and lets them fly all over. . . .

"You bastard!" he screams, and throws the pages in his face.

Death of a Bachelor

SOMEONE WAS KNOCKING at the door, very softly, but the doctor awakened immediately, turned on the light, and got out of bed. He glanced at his wife, who was still sleeping quietly, put on his robe, and went out into the hall. He didn't immediately recognize the old woman who was standing there with a grey scarf around her head.

"Our master is feeling very ill," she said. "Would the doctor be so kind as to come right away?"

The doctor recognized the voice. It was his bachelor friend's house-keeper. The doctor's first thought was: my friend is fifty-five, he's already had heart trouble for two years; it could be something really serious.

He said, "I'll come immediately. Do you want to wait?"

"Please excuse me, Doctor, but I have to go to two other gentlemen right away." And she named the businessman and the writer.

"Why are you going to them?"

"My master wants to see them once more."

"Once—more—see them?"

"Yes, Doctor."

He's asking for his friends, thought the doctor; he must feel he's near death. . . . And he said, "Is anyone with your master?"

The old woman replied, "Of course, Doctor. Johann won't leave his side." And she left.

The doctor returned to the bedroom, and while he dressed himself as quickly and as quietly as possible, a bitterness crept into his heart. It was not so much pain at the thought that he might soon lose one of his good old friends, as the painful feeling that they were all now at this stage, all of them, who were still young just a few years ago.

The doctor drove in an open carriage through the warm, heavy spring night into the nearby suburb where the bachelor lived. He looked up to the wide-open window from which a dim gleam of light flickered out into the night.

The doctor went up the stairs; a servant opened the door and greeted him with a serious expression, letting his left hand fall sadly.

"What is it?" the doctor asked, catching his breath. "Am I too late?"

"Yes, Doctor," answered the servant, "our master died a quarter of an hour ago."

The doctor took a deep breath and went into the room. His dead friend was lying there with narrow, bluish, half-opened lips, his arms stretched over the white comforter; his thin beard was disheveled, and a few strands of his grey hair had fallen onto his pale and moist forehead. The silk shade of the lamp on his night table cast a reddish shadow over the pillows. The doctor looked at the dead man. When was he last at our house? he asked himself. I remember it snowed that evening. So it must have been the past winter. We didn't see each other very much lately.

The noise of horse's hoofs came from outdoors. The doctor moved away from the body and saw thin branches waving in the night air across the street.

The servant entered, and the doctor asked him how it had all happened.

The servant told the doctor the familiar story of sudden nausea, difficulty in breathing, jumping out of bed, pacing back and forth in the room, running to the desk and unsteadily returning to the bed, of thirst and moaning, of a last sudden sitting up in bed and a collapse into the pillows. The doctor nodded and rested his right hand on the dead man's forehead.

He heard a carriage pull up. The doctor stepped over to the window. He saw the businessman get out and look up at him questioningly. The doctor instinctively dropped his hand just as the servant who received him had done. The businessman threw his head back as though he didn't want to believe it; the doctor shrugged his shoulders, left the window, and, suddenly exhausted, sat down in a chair at the foot of the dead man.

The businessman entered in an open yellow overcoat, put his hat down on a small table near the door, and shook hands with the doctor. "This is horrible," he said. "How did it happen?" And he stared at the dead man with suspicious eyes.

The doctor told what he knew and added, "Even if I had come in time, I couldn't have helped him."

"Just think," the businessman said, "only a week ago today I spoke to him at the theatre. I was going to have dinner with him afterward, but he had one of his mysterious assignations again."

"Did he still have those?" asked the doctor with a melancholy smile.

Another carriage pulled up. The businessman stepped over to the window. When he saw the writer get out, he drew back because he didn't want to be the one to reveal the unhappy news even through a gesture. The doctor had taken a cigarette from his cigarette case and was idly twirling it around. "It's a habit from my hospital residency," he remarked apologetically. "The first thing I used to do after leaving a sick bed at night was to light a cigarette, whether I had just given a morphine injection or had examined a dead body."

"Do you know how long it's been since I've seen a dead body?" asked the businessman. "Fourteen years—since the time my father was lying on the stretcher."

"And—your wife?"

"I did see my wife in her last moments, but—not later."

The writer appeared and shook hands with the others while casting an uncertain glance in the direction of the bed. Finally he stepped closer and looked earnestly at the body, though not without a contemptuous twitch of his lips. So it was he, he thought, since he had often toyed with the question of which of his closest friends would be fated to be the first to go.

The housekeeper entered. With tears in her eyes she sank in front of the bed, sobbed, and folded her hands. The writer put his hand on her shoulder lightly and comfortingly.

The businessman and the doctor stood at the window feeling the dark spring air on their foreheads.

"It's really strange," began the businessman, "that he sent for all of us. Did he want to see us assembled around his deathbed? Did he want to tell us something important?"

"As far as I'm concerned," said the doctor, with a pained smile, "it's not so strange, since I'm a doctor, after all. And you," he turned to the businessman, "were at times his business adviser. Perhaps he wanted to inform you in person of some last-minute arrangements."

"That could be," said the businessman.

The housekeeper had left the room, and the friends could hear her talking with the servant in the hallway. The writer was still standing at the bed and conducting a dialogue with the dead man. "He," the businessman said to the doctor in a low voice, "he, I believe, was more often with him lately. Maybe he can give us an explanation."

The writer was standing motionless; his eyes were boring into the dead man's closed eyes. He had crossed his hands, in which he was holding his broad-brimmed grey hat, behind his back. The other two men became impatient. The businessman stepped closer and cleared his throat. "Three days ago," the writer told him, "I went for a two-hour walk with him in the vineyards. Do you know what he talked about? About a trip to Sweden that he had planned for the summer, about a new folder of Rembrandt prints that were just published in London by Watson, and finally about Santos Dumont. He explained all sorts of mathematical and physical details of hot-air balloons, which, to tell the truth, I didn't quite understand. Certainly he wasn't thinking about death. Of course, it's possible that at a certain age one stops thinking about death."

The doctor had gone into the adjoining room. It would be all right to light his cigarette here. It gave him a start, almost scared him, to see a bit of white ash in the bronze ashtray on the desk. Why am I still here? he wondered, as he sat down on the armchair in front of the desk. Of us three I have the most right to leave since evidently I was called only in my capacity as a doctor. We weren't such good friends after all. At my age, he continued thinking, it's probably not really possible to be friends with someone who has no career, who never had a career. If he had not been rich, what would he have done? He would probably have taken up writing, since he was very witty. And he remembered many of the bachelor's hostile witticisms, in particular those about the work of their common friend, the writer.

The writer and the businessman entered. The writer made an injured face when he saw the doctor sitting in the now orphaned desk chair with an unlit cigarette in his hand, and closed the door behind him. Now they found themselves more or less in another world.

"Do you have any inkling?" asked the businessman.

"Of what?" the writer replied distractedly.

"Of what could have motivated him to send for us, the three of us in particular?"

The writer found it superfluous to look for a particular reason. "Our friend," he declared, "felt he was near death, and even though he was living rather reclusively, at least lately—in such an hour, those of a basically sociable character feel the need to have close friends around them."

"But he did have a lover," remarked the businessman.

"A lover?" repeated the writer, lifting his eyebrows contemptuously.

Then the doctor noticed that the middle drawer of the desk stood half open. "I wonder if his will is in here," he said.

"That's none of our business," the businessman said, "at least not now. Anyway, he has a married sister in London."

The servant entered the room. He felt free to ask for advice about the laying out, the funeral arrangements, and the death certificate. As far as he knew, there was a will filed with the master's lawyer, but he doubted that it contained directives about these things. The writer felt the room to be stiflingly muggy. He drew the heavy red drapes away from one of the windows and opened both shutters. A broad, dark-blue strip of spring air streamed in. The doctor asked the servant if he knew why the deceased had sent for the three of them, since, when he really thought about it, he had not been called to this house in his capacity as a doctor for many years. The servant acted as though he had expected this question, pulled a very large portfolio from his jacket pocket, took out a piece of paper, and explained that his master had written down the names of the friends that he wanted to see assembled around his deathbed seven years ago. Therefore, even if his master had no longer been conscious, the servant would have been able to send for them on his own authority.

The doctor took the piece of paper from the servant's hand and found five names written on it: aside from those of the three of them, one was a friend who had died two years ago, and the other was someone unknown to them. The servant explained that the latter was an industrialist with whom the bachelor had kept company nine or ten years ago but whose address was now either lost or forgotten. The men looked at one another self-consciously and filled with emotion. "What do you make of this?" asked the businessman. "Did he intend to make a speech in his last hour?"

"Maybe give his own eulogy," the writer added.

The doctor was looking at the open desk drawer and suddenly three words in large Roman letters jumped out at him from an envelope: "To my friends."

"Oh," he exclaimed, took the envelope, lifted it up, and showed it to the others. "That's for us," he said, and, turning to the servant, he indicated to him with a toss of his head that his further presence would be unnecessary. The servant left. "For us!" said the writer wide-eyed. "There's no doubt," said the doctor, "that we are authorized to open it." "Obligated," said the businessman, and buttoned his overcoat.

The doctor took a letter opener from the glass cup, opened the envelope, put the letter down, and put on his pince-nez. The writer took advantage of the moment to take up the paper and unfold it. "Since it's for all three of us," he remarked apologetically, and leaned on the desk so that the light of the ceiling lamp fell over the paper. The businessman stood next to him. The doctor remained seated. "Read it out loud," said the businessman. The writer began:

"To my friends." He interrupted himself, smiling. "Yes, he's written it here again, gentlemen," and then continued reading without stopping. "A quarter of an hour ago, more or less, I breathed my last. You are assembled around my deathbed and are preparing to read this letter together—if the letter still exists in the hour of my death, I'll add. Because it could happen that a better impulse could move me . . ."

"What?" asked the doctor.

"A better impulse could move me," repeated the writer and continued to read: ". . . and that I would decide to destroy this letter, since it can't do me any good and will cause you at the very least some unpleasant hours, if it doesn't destroy the life of one or the other of you."

"Destroy our lives?" repeated the doctor questioningly, and wiped the lenses of his pince-nez.

"Faster," said the businessman in a hoarse voice.

The writer continued reading:

"And I ask myself what kind of strange mood is now driving me to my desk and pushing me to write down words whose effect on you I will no longer be able to see? And even if I could, the pleasure would be too small to count as an excuse for the monstrous pettiness which I am making myself guilty of right now—and with a feeling of great contentment."

"Ho," cried the doctor in a voice that he didn't recognize himself. The writer cast him a quick and hostile glance and continued reading, more quickly and more tonelessly than before.

"Yes, it's just a whim, nothing more, because at bottom I really have nothing against you. I even like you all, in my way, just as you like me in yours. I don't even think badly of you, and if I have made fun of you at times, I have never sneered at you. Not even, yes, least of all, in those hours that you will soon picture in the most lively and painful way. Where does this mood come from, then? Could it not after all stem from a deep and at bottom noble wish not to leave the world with too many lies? I could make myself believe that, if I had ever felt even once the slightest hint of what men call 'remorse.' "

"For God's sake, read the ending," commanded the doctor in a new voice. The businessman reached over, took the letter from the writer, who was feeling a kind of paralysis creep into his fingers, quickly dropped his eyes down to the end of the letter, and read these words:

"It was fate, my friends, and I can't change it. I have possessed all your women. All."

The businessman suddenly stopped and leafed back through the pages. "What are you doing?" asked the doctor.

"The letter was written nine years ago," said the businessman.

"Read on," commanded the writer. The businessman read:

"They were of course very different kinds of relationships. With one of them I lived almost as though married, for many months. With another it was more like what is called a wild adventure. With the third it went so far that I wanted to die together with her. The fourth I threw down the stairs because she betrayed me with another. And another was my lover just once. Are you all breathing in relief again, my friends? Don't. It was perhaps the most beautiful hour of my . . . and of her life. So, my friends. I don't have any more to say. I am now folding this piece of paper and putting it in my desk, and here may it wait either until I destroy it while in another mood, or until you get it in the hour that I'm lying on my deathbed. Goodbye."

The doctor took the letter out of the businessman's hand and seemed to read it carefully from beginning to end. Then he looked at the businessman, who stood there with his arms crossed, looking down with a scornful smirk. "Even though your wife died last year," the doctor said calmly, "this applies to her also."

The writer paced up and down in the room, occasionally shaking his head back and forth as though he had a cramp; suddenly he hissed between his teeth, "Scoundrel," and followed the word as though it were a thing that dissolved in the air. He tried to recall the image of the young creature that he had once held in his arms as wife. Other images of women appeared, both those often remembered and those believed long forgotten, but the one he desired he could not force into his memory. For his wife's body was now faded and odorless for him, and it had been all too long since she had been his beloved. But she had become something else for him, something more and something nobler: a friend and a companion, proud of his accomplishments, full of sympathy for his disappointments, full of insight into his deepest being. It appeared to him not impossible that the old bachelor in his meanness had attempted nothing less than to rob him, his secretly envied friend, of his companion. Because all the other things—what did they really mean in the end? He remembered certain adventures from recent and from more distant times that he could hardly have avoided in his successful artist's life, adventures that his wife had either smiled or wept away. Where were they all now? They had wilted just as had the distant hour in which his wife had thrown herself into the arms of an unworthy man, perhaps without consideration, without thought; almost as faded as the memory of this same hour was in that dead brain that was resting in the other room on the painfully rumpled pillows. Perhaps in the end it was a lie after all, everything written in the testament? Perhaps a pathetic ordinary man who knew he was condemned to be eternally forgotten had taken his last revenge on the chosen man over whose works death had no power. That could be the case. And even it were true—it still was a petty revenge and one that failed to succeed.

The doctor stared at the piece of paper in front of him, and he thought about the aging, gentle, and yes, kind woman who was now sleeping at home. He also thought about his three children: the eldest, who was just now serving his year of voluntary military service; the oldest daughter, who was engaged to a lawyer; and the youngest daughter, who was so charming and attractive that a famous artist had recently asked to paint her while she was at a ball. He thought about his comfortable home, and everything that was said in the dead man's letter seemed to him not so much untrue as mysteriously, even exaltedly, irrelevant. He hardly felt that he had learned anything new at this moment. He remembered a peculiar episode of his life some fourteen or fifteen years ago, a time in which he had experienced certain problems with his medical career, and when, morose and finally reduced to a state of confusion, he had planned to leave his town, his wife, and his family. At that time he had begun to lead a kind of wild and thoughtless existence in which a peculiar and hysterical woman had played a role, a woman who had later committed suicide over another lover. How his life after that had gradually resumed its regular course he could not remember now at all. But it had to have been in that miserable epoch, which had passed just as it had arrived, like an illness, that his wife had deceived him. Yes, it had to have been then, and it was clear to him that he had really always known it. Wasn't she once near to telling him about it? Didn't she drop hints? Thirteen or fourteen years ago . . . on what occasion . . . ? Wasn't it once in summer, on a vacation trip—late one evening on a hotel terrace? In vain he tried to remember the faded words.

The businessman stood at the window and looked into the gentle, white night. He tried with the best will in the world to remember his dead wife. But as much as he strained his inner senses, at first he only saw himself standing between the frame of an open door, in the light of a grey morning, wearing a black suit, accepting and reciprocating sympathetic handshakes; he remembered the flat odor of carbolic acid and flowers in his nose. Only gradually did he succeed in recalling her image. But at first it was only the image of an image. For he could really see only the large gold-framed portrait that was hanging in the salon over the piano at home, which showed a proud woman of about thirty in ballroom dress. Only then did she herself appear to him as the pale and shy young girl who had accepted his courtship almost twenty-five years ago. Then the image of a blossoming woman appeared before him, enthroned next to him in a box at the theatre, her eyes fixed on the stage and far from him emotionally. Then he remembered an eager woman who had received him with unexpected passion when he had returned from a long trip. Right after that he remembered a nervous, teary person with green, dull eyes, who had spoiled his days with all sorts of bad moods. Then once more he saw an anxious tender mother in a light morning robe, watching over the bed of a sick child who had also had to die. Finally he saw a pale being lying in bed with the corners of her mouth drawn in pain, cold drops of sweat on her forehead, in a room filled with ether, which had filled his soul with painful sympathy. He knew that all these images and a hundred others, which were now racing through his mind at incredible speed, were one and the same person, the person who had been lowered into the grave two years ago, whom he had mourned, and after whose death he had felt liberated. He felt as though he had to choose one of the images in order to arrive at some nameless feeling, because right now free-floating anger and shame were scanning a void. Indecisively he stood there and looked at the houses that were floating yellow and reddish in the moonlight in the gardens opposite, houses that seemed to be pale painted façades behind which there was nothingness.

"Good night," said the physician and stood up. The businessman turned around. "I have nothing more to do here either." The writer had taken the letter, put it unnoticed in his jacket pocket, and now opened the door to the next room. Slowly he went up to the deathbed, and the others saw how he looked silently down at the body, his hands behind his back. Then they left.

In the hallway the businessman said to the servant: "Concerning the funeral—it's possible that the will at the lawyer's will have more detailed instructions after all."

"And don't forget," added the doctor, "to wire your master's sister in London."

"Certainly not," answered the servant as he opened the door for the men.

The writer overtook them while they were still on the steps. "I can take both of you with me," said the doctor, who was awaiting his carriage. "Thanks," said the businessman, "but I prefer to walk." He shook hands with both of them, walked down the street toward the city, and allowed himself to be comforted by the mild and gentle night.

The writer got into the carriage with the doctor. In the gardens all around the birds began to sing. The carriage drove past the businessman, and all three men lifted their hats to one another, politely and ironically, all with the same faces. "Are we going to get to see something of yours in the theatre soon?" the doctor asked the writer in his usual voice. The writer spoke of the extraordinary difficulties connected with the performance of his newest drama, which, he had to admit, did contain attacks on much of what society ostensibly held sacred. The doctor nodded and didn't listen. The writer didn't either, as the oft-reiterated sentences had long fallen as if by rote from his lips.

Both men climbed out in front of the doctor's house, and the carriage drove away.

The doctor rang. Both of them stood there in silence. As they heard the porter's steps approach, the writer said, "Good night, my dear doctor," and then, with a twitch of his nostrils, he added slowly, "By the way, I'm not going to tell mine either." The doctor looked in the air past him and smiled sweetly. The door opened, they shook hands, and the doctor disappeared into the entryway; the door shut. The writer left.

The writer reached into his breast pocket. Yes, the piece of paper was there. His wife should find it well preserved and sealed in his belongings. And with that rare power of imagination with which he was blessed, he could already hear her whisper at his grave: "You noble man . . . you magnanimous soul. . . ."

Dream Story

"TWENTY-FOUR BROWN-SKINNED SLAVES rowed the magnificent galley which was to bring Prince Amgiad to the palace of the caliph. But the prince, wrapped in his purple cloak, lay all alone on the deck beneath the dark blue, starry sky, and his gaze . . ."

Up to this point the little girl had been reading aloud, but now, suddenly, her eyelids fell shut. Her parents looked at each other and smiled. Fridolin bent down, kissed her blonde hair, and closed the book lying on the table that had yet to be cleared. The child looked up as if caught at some mischief.

"It's nine o'clock," the father said. "Time for bed." And as Albertine had also bent down to her, the parent's hands now met on the beloved forehead, and their glances met with a tender smile no longer meant only for the child. The governess entered and asked the little girl to say good night to her parents. She got up obediently, offered her lips for her father and mother to kiss, and without protesting let herself be led away from the room by her governess. But Fridolin and Albertine, now left alone under the reddish glow of the hanging lamp, were suddenly in a hurry to continue the conversation they had begun before supper about their experiences at yesterday's masquerade ball.

It had been the first ball for them this year, and they had decided to attend it just before the end of the carnival season. Fridolin had no sooner entered the ballroom than he had been greeted, like a long lost and now impatiently awaited old friend, by two red dominoes, whom he couldn't for the life of him identify, though they had shown strikingly detailed knowledge of certain episodes of his student and internship days. They had left the loge to which they had eagerly invited him with the promise that they would come back—unmasked—very soon, but had stayed away for so long that he, becoming impatient, had decided to go back down to the ballroom where he hoped to meet the two enigmatic figures again. But however carefully he looked around, they were nowhere to be seen; instead, another woman unexpectedly took his arm. It was his wife, who had just abruptly freed herself from a stranger whose melancholy and blasé manner and foreign, evidently Polish, accent had at first charmed her but who had then offended and even frightened her with a casually dropped, unexpectedly vulgar, and hatefully impertinent remark. And so husband and wife, at bottom glad to have escaped the disappointing and banal masquerade game, soon had sat like two lovers among other lovers, eating oysters, drinking champagne, and chatting animatedly as though they had just met, reenacting the comedy of gallantry, resistance, seduction, and surrender. After a quick ride home through the white winter night, they had sunk into each other's arms in lovemaking more ardent than they had experienced for a long time.

A grey morning had awakened them all too early. The husband's profession called him to the bedside of sick patients at an early hour, and household and motherly duties prevented Albertine from staying in bed much longer than he. So the hours had flown by soberly in predetermined daily routines and work, and the events of the previous night, those at the beginning as well as those at the end, had grown pale. Only now, when the day's work was finished for both of them and no disturbance was likely, the child having gone to bed, did the shadowy forms of the masquerade, the melancholy stranger and the red dominoes, rise into consciousness again. And all at once the insignificant events were magically and painfully imbued with the deceptive glow of neglected opportunities. Harmless but probing questions and sly, ambiguous answers were exchanged. Neither failed to notice that the other was not completely honest, and so both felt themselves justified in taking a mild revenge. They exaggerated the degree of the attraction that their unknown masquerade partners had exerted upon them, made fun of the jealous tendencies of the other, and denied their own. But the light banter about the trivial adventures of the previous night gradually became a more serious conversation about those hidden, scarcely suspected desires that are capable of producing dark and dangerous whirlpools in even the most clearheaded, purest soul. They spoke of those hidden regions that barely attracted them but to which the incomprehensible winds of destiny could still drag them, even if only in a dream. For though they were united to each other in thought and feeling, they knew that yesterday wasn't the first time that the breath of adventure, freedom, and danger had touched them. Uneasy and self-tormenting, each pretended curiosity and sought to draw confessions from the other. Anxiously drawing closer to each other, both searched for an event, however indifferent, for an experience, no matter how trivial, that might count as an expression of the inexpressible and whose honest confession now could perhaps free them from the tension and mistrust that was gradually becoming unbearable. Albertine, whether she was the more impatient, the more honest, or the more kindhearted of the two, first summoned the courage for a frank confession. She asked Fridolin in a rather uncertain tone of voice whether he remembered the young man who, along with two officers, had sat at the table next to theirs at the beach in Denmark where they had vacationed the previous summer. He was the one who had received a telegram one evening at dinner, and had then hastily excused himself and departed.

Fridolin nodded. "What about him?" he asked.

"I had already seen him that morning as he was rushing up the hotel stairs with his yellow briefcase," answered Albertine. "He glanced at me, stopped after he had gone up a few more steps, then turned around and looked at me. Our glances met. He didn't smile; in fact, it seemed to me that his face darkened, and I suppose mine did too, for I was more deeply affected than I had ever been before. That whole day I lay on the beach, lost in dreams. Had he called to me—so I believed—I could not have resisted. I thought I was ready for anything. You, my daughter, my future—I felt ready to give it all up, and at the same time—can you understand this?—you were more precious to me than ever. Just on that very afternoon—surely you remember—it happened that we talked more intimately about a thousand things, about our common future, about our daughter, than we had for a long time. At sunset we were sitting on the balcony, you and I, when he walked by down on the beach. Though he didn't look up, I was overjoyed to see him. But it was you whose forehead I stroked and whose hair I kissed, and in my love for you there was a lot of sorrowful pity at the same time. That evening I looked very beautiful—you told me so yourself—and I wore a white rose. Perhaps it was not an accident that the stranger and his friends sat near us. He didn't look at me, but I played with the thought of standing up, walking over to his table, and saying, 'Here I am, my long awaited one, my beloved—take me!' That was the moment he received the telegram and read it, whereupon he turned pale, whispered a few words to the younger of the two officers, and left, glancing at me with a strange look."

"And?" asked Fridolin drily, when she stopped.

"There isn't any more. I only know that I woke up the next morning with a certain anxiety. I don't know what I feared more—that he had left or that he was still there—and I still don't know. But when he hadn't appeared by noon, I breathed a sigh of relief. Don't ask me to tell you any more, Fridolin. I've told you the whole truth. You had some sort of experience at that seashore, too—I know it."

Fridolin rose, paced up and down the room several times, and then said, "You're right." He was standing at the window, his face in the shadow. "In the mornings," he began in a veiled and slightly hostile voice, "sometimes very early, before you got up, I used to walk along the beach, out beyond the town. No matter how early I went, the sun was always shining bright and strong over the sea. Out on the beach there were small cottages, as you know, each one standing like a world of its own. Some had fenced-in gardens and others were completely surrounded by forest, but they were separated from the beach huts by the road and a section of beach. I hardly ever met anyone at this early hour, and there were never any swimmers around. But one morning I suddenly became aware of a female figure that had been quite hidden only a moment before and was now cautiously walking on the narrow ledge of a beach hut set on piles in the sand, her arms spread out backward against the wooden wall behind her. She was a very young girl, maybe fifteen years old, with loose blonde hair flowing over her shoulders and to one side over her delicate breast. The girl was looking down into the water, and slowly sliding with her back along one wall as she focused on the far side of the wall, and suddenly she was standing immediately opposite me. She reached her arms far back as though she wanted to get a firmer hold. Looking up, she suddenly saw me. A tremor passed through her body, as if she wanted either to sink down into the water or to flee. But since she could only move very slowly along the narrow ledge, she decided to restrain herself and stay where she was—and now she stood there, first with a frightened, then with an angry, and finally with an embarrassed look. All at once, however, she smiled at me, smiled marvelously. There was a greeting, even a wink in her eyes—and at the same time a slight teasing as she very lightly dipped her foot into the water that separated us. Then she stretched her slim young body upward, glad of her beauty, and, as was easy to see, proud and sweetly aroused by the obvious admiration of my gaze. So we stood opposite each other, maybe ten seconds, eyelids half open and eyes misty. Instinctively I stretched my arms out to her. Her eyes expressed surrender and joy. But suddenly she shook her head vigorously, took one arm from the wall, and with a commanding gesture signaled that I should go away. When I couldn't get myself to obey immediately, such a look of pleading and begging came into her childish eyes that there was nothing for me to do but to leave. I went on my way as quickly as I could. I didn't turn around and look at her even once, not really out of consideration, obedience, or chivalry, but because I was so profoundly moved by her last look, moved so far beyond anything I've ever felt, that I felt dangerously close to fainting." And he stopped.

"And how often," asked Albertine, looking down, in an even voice, "did you take the same way after that?"

"What I just told you," answered Fridolin, "by chance happened on the last day of our stay in Denmark. I too don't know what might have happened under other circumstances. Don't ask me to tell you anything else, Albertine."

He was still standing at the window, motionless. Albertine stood up and walked over to him, her eyes moist and dark, a slight frown on her forehead.

"In the future, let's always tell each other these kinds of things at once," she said.

He nodded in silence.

"Promise me."

He pulled her to him. "Don't you know I will?" he asked, but his voice still sounded harsh.

She took his hands, stroked them, and looked up at him with misty eyes in whose depths he could read her thoughts. She was remembering other, more real experiences he had had when he was younger, many of which he had confessed to her in the early years of their marriage, when, too willingly yielding to her jealous curiosity, he had surrendered many secrets that he should have kept to himself. He knew that what he had said inevitably reminded her of these affairs, and he was hardly surprised when she spoke the half-forgotten name of one of his early sweethearts. It sounded to him like an accusation, even like a covert threat.

He raised her hands to his lips.

"In every woman—believe me, even though it sounds trite—in every woman I thought I loved it was always only you that I sought. I know that more surely than you can understand, Albertine."

She smiled at him weakly. "And what if I had searched for you in others before, too?" she said. The look in her eyes changed, became cool and impenetrable. He let her hands slip from his as though he had caught her in a lie or a breach of faith. But she said, "Oh, if you men only knew . . ." And she fell silent again.

"If we only knew—? What are you trying to say?"

In a strangely harsh voice she answered, "Just what you imagine, my dear."

"Albertine—so there is something that you've kept from me?"

She nodded and looked down with a peculiar smile.

Incomprehensible, unreasonable doubts awoke in him.

"I don't quite understand," he said. "You were barely seventeen when we got engaged."

"Older than sixteen, yes, Fridolin. And yet—" she looked him squarely in the eye—"it wasn't thanks to me that I was still a virgin when I became your wife."

"Albertine—!"

But she continued:

"It was at Lake Wörther, just before our engagement, Fridolin. There, one beautiful summer evening, a very handsome young man stood in front of my window that looked out into the large and spacious meadow, and while I talked with him I was thinking—yes, just listen to what I was thinking—What a lovely, charming, young man—he would only have to say the word—the right word, of course—and I would come with him into the meadow and walk with him wherever he wanted to go—maybe into the woods—or, even better, we could take a boat out into the lake—and I would grant him anything that he wanted that night. Yes, that's what I was thinking. But he didn't say the word, that charming young man; he only kissed my hand tenderly—and the next morning he asked me—to be his wife. And I said yes."

Fridolin, annoyed, let her hand drop. "And if," he said, "someone else had by chance stood at your window that night and said the right word, if it had been, for example—" and he pondered what name he should say, but she had already lifted her arms in protest.

"Any other man, no matter who it might have been, whatever he might have said—it wouldn't have helped him. If it hadn't been you standing in front of the window"—she smiled up at him—"then very likely the summer evening wouldn't have been so beautiful!"

His mouth assumed a scornful expression. "So you say now, so you may even believe now. But—"

There was a knock on the door. The maid entered and announced that the housekeeper from Schreyvogel Street was there to fetch the doctor to the councillor, as he was feeling very ill again. Fridolin went out into the hall, learned from the messenger that the councillor had had a heart attack, and promised to come at once.

"You're leaving—?" Albertine asked in an angry tone as he was hastily preparing to leave, as though he were doing her a premeditated injustice.

Fridolin answered, almost in astonishment, "Yes, I have to."

She sighed regretfully.

"I hope it isn't very serious," said Fridolin. "Up to now three centigrams of morphine have always pulled him through."

The maid had brought his fur coat. Fridolin kissed Albertine on her forehead and her mouth, rather absentmindedly, as though the conversation of the last hour had already slipped from his memory, and hurried away.

II

On the street he had to unbutton his fur. It had suddenly begun to thaw; the snow on the sidewalk had almost melted, and there was a hint of spring in the air. It was less than a quarter of an hour from Fridolin's home near the General Hospital in the Josephstadt to Schreyvogel Street, and soon Fridolin was walking up the dimly lit, winding staircase of the old house to the second floor and ringing the doorbell. But before the old-fashioned doorbell even sounded, he noticed the door was ajar. He entered through the unlit foyer into the living room and saw at once that he had come too late. The green-shaded kerosene lamp hanging from the low ceiling cast a dim light on the bedspread under which a lean body lay motionless. The dead man's face was in shadow, but Fridolin knew it so well that he thought he could see it distinctly—the high forehead, the thin and wrinkled cheeks, the white, short beard, and the strikingly ugly ears covered with coarse, white hairs. Marianne, the councillor's daughter, was sitting at the foot of the bed, her arms hanging limply from her shoulders as if in total exhaustion. An odor of old furniture, medicines, petroleum, and cooking permeated the room, along with a trace of cologne and rose-scented soap; yet somehow Fridolin also perceived the sweet, bland odor of the pale girl who was still young but who had been slowly fading for months, even years, under the stress of heavy household and difficult nursing duties and night watches.

She had looked up when the doctor entered, but in the dim light he couldn't quite see whether she had blushed as she usually did when he appeared. She started to rise, but a movement of Fridolin's hand restrained her, and so she greeted him with a nod, her eyes large and sad. He walked over to the head of the bed and mechanically placed his hands first on the dead man's forehead, then on the arms lying on top of the bedspread in loose and open shirtsleeves. He dropped his shoulders with a slight expression of regret, stuck his hands in the pockets of his fur coat, and let his eyes wander about the room until they finally rested on Marianne. Her hair was blonde and thick, but dry; her neck well formed and slender, though no longer wrinkle-free and rather yellowed; and her lips were hard and narrow, as though from holding back many unsaid words.

"Well, my dear Marianne," he said in a slightly embarrassed whisper, "you weren't entirely unprepared for this."

She held out her hand to him. He took it sympathetically and dutifully asked about the particulars of the final, fatal attack. She reported briefly and to the point, and then spoke of her father's last and comparatively easy days, during which Fridolin had not seen him. Fridolin had drawn up a chair and was now sitting opposite her. He tried to console her by saying that her father couldn't have suffered very much in his last hours, and asked if the relatives had been notified. Yes, she said; the housekeeper was already on the way to tell her uncle, and Dr. Roediger would soon come in any case. "My fiancé," she added, and looked at Fridolin's forehead instead of his eyes.

Fridolin only nodded. In the course of the year he had met Dr. Roediger two or three times in the councillor's house. The overthin and pale young man with the short, blonde beard and spectacles, an assistant professor in history at the University of Vienna, had made a good impression on him without, however, arousing any further interest. Marianne would certainly look better if she were his mistress, he thought. Her hair would be less dry; her lips would be fuller and redder. I wonder how old she is? he asked himself. The first time I was called to the councillor, she was twenty-three. At that time her mother was still alive. She was more cheerful when her mother was still living. Didn't she take singing lessons for a time? So she is going to marry this assistant professor. Why, I wonder? Surely she isn't in love with him, and he isn't likely to have a lot of money either. What kind of marriage will that turn out to be? Well, probably a marriage like a thousand others. Why should I care anyway? It's quite possible that I'll never see her again, since there is nothing more for me to do in this house. Oh, how many people have I never seen again, people that I cared for more than I do for her?

While these thoughts were running through his mind, Marianne had begun to speak of the dead man—with a certain fervor, as though he had suddenly become a remarkable person through the simple fact of his death. So he was really only fifty-four years old? Of course, he'd had so many worries and disappointments—his wife always ill—and his son had given him so much grief! What, she had a brother? Certainly. She had once told the doctor about him. Her brother was now living somewhere abroad; a picture he had painted when he was fifteen was hanging over there in Marianne's room. It depicted an officer galloping down a hill. Her father had always pretended not to see the picture at all. But it was a good painting. Her brother would have made something of himself if he'd only had the chance.

How excitedly she speaks, thought Fridolin, and how her eyes are gleaming! A fever? Quite possible. She's grown much thinner lately. Probably has tuberculosis.

She kept on talking, but it seemed to him that she didn't know to whom she was talking, or as if she were talking to herself. It was now twelve years that her brother had been away from home; yes, she had been still a child when he suddenly vanished. They had last heard from him four or five years ago, at Christmastime, from a small town in Italy. Strange to say, she had forgotten the name. She continued a while talking of indifferent, unimportant matters, almost incoherently, until she suddenly stopped and sat there silently, her head resting in her hands. Fridolin was tired and even more bored; he was anxiously waiting for someone to arrive, one of her relatives or her fiancé. The silence in the room was oppressive. It seemed to him that the dead man joined in the silence, not because he couldn't talk anymore but on purpose and with malicious joy.

With a sidelong glance at the body, Fridolin said: "In any case, as things are now, it's good, Fräulein Marianne, that you won't have to stay in this house much longer." And since she raised her head a little, without, however, looking at Fridolin—"Your fiancé will probably get a professorship soon; his chances are better in the Faculty of Philosophy than they are with us in Medicine." He was thinking that years ago he had also aspired to an academic career, but had in the end decided to practice medicine instead because of his wish for a more comfortable lifestyle; and suddenly he felt inferior to this noble Dr. Roediger.

"We're going to move in the fall," said Marianne listlessly, "he has a position at the University of Göttingen."

"Oh," said Fridolin, and was about to offer his congratulations when it seemed to him rather inappropriate in this place at this moment. He glanced at the closed window and, without asking her permission, as though in his capacity as physician, he opened both windowpanes and let the air in, which had in the meantime become still warmer and more springlike and seemed to bring with it the soft odor of the awakening distant woods. When he once more turned toward the room he saw Marianne's eyes fixed questioningly on him. He moved closer to her and remarked, "The fresh air will I hope do you good. It's become quite warm, and last night—he was about to say: we drove home from the masquerade ball in a snowstorm, but he quickly changed the sentence and continued, "last night the snow was still lying half a meter high on the streets."

She scarcely heard what he said. Her eyes moistened and large tears streamed down her cheeks; once more she buried her face in her hands. Instinctively he placed his hand on her hair and stroked her head. He felt her body beginning to tremble as she sobbed, first hardly audible sobs, then gradually louder and louder, and finally completely unrestrained. All at once she slipped down from her chair and lay at Fridolin's feet, clasping his knees with her arms and pressing her face against them. Then she looked at him and with wide-open, suffering, and wild eyes, whispered ardently, "I don't want to leave here. Even if you never return, even if I'm never to see you again, I want to live near you."

He was more touched than surprised, because he had always known that she was in love with him or imagined that she was in love with him.

"Please get up, Marianne," he said softly, bent down to her, and softly raised her head. He thought: of course there is hysteria in this, too.

He cast a sideways glance at her dead father. I wonder if he can hear everything? he wondered. Maybe he isn't really dead. Perhaps every man only seems dead the first few hours after he dies—? He held Marianne in his arms but kept her a little away from him. Almost unthinkingly he planted a kiss on her forehead, an act which seemed a little ridiculous even to him. Fleetingly he remembered a novel he had read years ago in which a very young man, almost a boy, was seduced, in fact, raped, really, at his mother's deathbed, by her best friend. At the same time—he didn't know why—he found himself thinking of his wife. He felt a bitterness against her rise up in him, and a dull animosity against the man in Denmark with the yellow briefcase on the hotel stairs. He pulled Marianne closer to him but didn't feel the slightest arousal; on the contrary, the sight of her lusterless dry hair and the slightly sweet and dull odor of her musty dress gave him a feeling of revulsion. The outside bell rang once more and he felt saved. He quickly kissed Marianne's hand as though in gratitude, and went to open the door. It was Dr. Roediger standing in the doorway, wearing a dark grey topcoat, with overshoes, an umbrella in his hand, and a serious face appropriate to the occasion. The two men greeted each other much more intimately than their actual state of acquaintance merited. Then they walked into the room together. Roediger, after a shy glance at the deceased, offered his sympathy to Marianne; Fridolin went into the adjoining room to write out the official death certificate. As he turned up the gaslight over the desk, his glance fell on the picture of a white-uniformed officer galloping down a hill with a sword drawn against an invisible enemy. It hung in a narrow gilded gold frame and made no better impression than a modest print.

When he had finished filling out the death certificate, Fridolin returned to the room where the engaged couple sat hand in hand by the father's bed.

Again the doorbell rang. Dr. Roediger rose to answer it. When he was gone, Marianne said, almost inaudibly, with her eyes on the floor, "I love you." Fridolin answered only by speaking her name, not without tenderness. Roediger returned with an elderly couple. It was Marianne's uncle and aunt. A few words appropriate to the circumstances were exchanged, with the embarrassment that the presence of a dead person creates around him. The small room suddenly seemed crowded with mourners. Fridolin felt superfluous, made his regrets, and was escorted to the door by Roediger, who felt himself obliged to express a few words of gratitude and the hope that they would see each other again soon.

III

Once outdoors, Fridolin looked up at the window he had opened a short while before; the windowpanes were trembling softly in the early spring wind. The people he had left behind up there, the living as well as the dead, seemed equally unreal and ghostlike. He felt as though he had escaped from something, not so much from an adventure but from a melancholy spell that he must not let overpower him. Its only remnant was a strange unwillingness to go home. The snow in the streets had melted. To the left and right there were small heaps of dirty white piled up; the gas flames in the lanterns flickered and a nearby church bell struck eleven. Fridolin decided that before going to bed he would spend another half-hour in a quiet café near his flat, and he took the path through the courthouse park. Here and there tightly clasped couples were sitting on shady benches, as though spring had already arrived and the deceptive warm air was not pregnant with dangers. A rather tattered-looking man was stretched out full length on one of the benches. What if I woke him up and gave him money for a shelter for the night? Fridolin thought. But what good would that do, he reflected further. Then I would have to get him shelter for tomorrow night too, otherwise there would really be no point, and in the end·I might be suspected of having criminal relations with him. He quickened his steps so as to escape as rapidly as possible from all responsibility and temptation. Why pick just this one? he asked himself. There are thousands of such poor devils in Vienna alone. What if one were to worry about all of them—about the fate of all the poor devils! And he remembered the dead man whom he had just left, and with a shudder, indeed, not without disgust, he thought about how in that lean body stretched out underneath the brown flannel blanket, decay and decomposition had already begun their work, in accordance with the laws of nature. And he was glad that he was still alive, that in all probability he was still far from all these ugly things, that indeed he was still in the prime of youth, had a charming and lovable wife, and could still have another woman or several other women in addition, should he choose to. To be sure, such affairs required more leisure than he had—he remembered that he had to be in the hospital ward tomorrow morning at eight, visit private patients from eleven to one, hold office hours from three to five in the afternoon, and still see a few patients in the evening. Well, he hoped he wouldn't be called out again in the middle of the night, as he had been today.

He crossed Courthouse Square, which gleamed dully like a brownish pond, and turned toward his home in the Josephstadt. In the distance he heard the muffled sound of marching steps and then saw, still quite far away, a small troop of fraternity students, six or eight in number, turning a corner and coming toward him. As the young people came into the light of a streetlamp, he thought he recognized a few members of the Alemannia fraternity, dressed in their blue, among them. He himself had never belonged to a fraternity, but he had fought a few saber duels in his time. The memories of his student days reminded him of the red dominoes who had lured him into the loge at the ball last night and then had so despicably deserted him soon after. The students were quite near now; they were talking and laughing loudly. Perhaps he knew one or two from the hospital? It was impossible to make out their faces accurately in this dim light. He had to stay quite close to the wall in order not to collide with them. Now they had passed by. Only the last one, a tall fellow with an open overcoat and a bandage over his left eye, seemed deliberately to lag behind, and bumped into him with a raised eyebrow. It couldn't have been an accident. What was he thinking? thought Fridolin, and instinctively stopped. The other man took two more steps and also stopped. They looked at each other for a moment with only a short distance separating them. But suddenly Fridolin turned back and went on. He heard a short laugh behind him—he almost turned around again to confront the fellow, but he felt his heart beating strangely—just as it had on a previous occasion, twelve or fourteen years ago, when there had been an unusually loud knock on the door while he was with that charming young creature who was always going on about a distant, probably nonexistent fiancé. But in fact it had been only the postman who had knocked so threateningly. He now felt his heart beat just as it had at that time. What is this? he asked himself angrily, and now noticed that his knees were shaking a little. Coward—? Nonsense! he answered himself. Should I go and confront a drunken student, I, a man of thirty-five, a practicing physician, married, and the father of a child! Formal challenge! Witnesses? Duel! And in the end get a cut on my arm and be unable to work for a few weeks because of such a stupid affair? Or lose an eye? Or even get blood poisoning—? And perhaps in a week end up in the same state as the man in Schreyvogel Street under the brown flannel blanket! Coward—? He had fought three saber duels and had even been ready to fight a duel with pistols; it wasn't his doing that the matter had been called off amicably at the end. And his profession! There were dangers everywhere, anytime—one just usually forgot about them. Why, how long was it since that child with diphtheria had coughed in his face? Only three or four days, no more. That was a much more dangerous thing than a little fencing match with sabers. And he hadn't given it a second thought. Well, if he ever met that fellow again this affair could still be straightened out. He was by no means obligated to react to such a silly student prank at midnight on his way to or from seeing a patient—he could just as well have been going to a patient—no, he was not obligated at all. On the other hand, if now, for example, he should meet that young Dane with whom Albertine—oh, nonsense, what was he thinking? Well—well, really, she might just as well really have been his mistress! It wasn't any different. Even worse. Yes, just let him cross his path now! Oh, what joy it would be to face him and somewhere in a forest clearing aim a pistol at that forehead with the smoothly combed blonde hair!

Suddenly he found himself past his destination, in a narrow street in which only a few pathetic hookers were strolling around in their nightly attempt to bag masculine game. Like specters, he thought. All at once the students with their blue caps also became unreal in his memory, as did Marianne and her fiancé, her uncle and her aunt, all of whom he now pictured standing hand in hand encircling the deathbed of the old councillor. And Albertine, too, whose image, soundly sleeping with her arms folded under her head, now floated up into his mind's eye, began to seem unreal—even his daughter, who was at this moment lying rolled up in a heap in the narrow white brass bed, and the apple-cheeked young governess with the mole on her left temple, too—all of them had now moved into the realm of specters. And although it made him shudder a bit, there was something calming in this feeling, as it appeared to free him from all responsibility, to absolve him from all human connection.

One of the girls wandering about invited him to go with her. She was a delicate, still very young creature, very pale, with red-painted lips. That could also end in death, he thought, only not as fast! Cowardice again? In essence, yes. He first heard her steps and soon after her voice behind him. "Don't you want to go with me, doctor?"

Instinctively he turned around. "How do you know me?" he asked.

"I don't," she said, "but in this district they're all doctors, aren't they?"

He had had nothing to do with women of this sort since his student days in the Gymnasium. Did the fact that he was attracted to this creature mean that he was suddenly regressing to adolescence? He recalled a casual acquaintance, an elegant young man who was rumored to be fabulously successful with women. Once, when he was a student, he had been sitting with Fridolin in a nightclub after a ball. After leaving with one of the regular girls who worked the place, he had answered Fridolin's questioning glance with "Well, it remains the most convenient way after all—and they aren't the worst by any means."

"What's your name?" Fridolin asked her.

"Well, what do you think? Mizzi, of course." She had already turned the key in the door of her house and unlocked it, stepped into the hallway, and waited for Fridolin to follow her.

"Come on!" she urged as he hesitated. Suddenly he was standing next to her, the door closed behind him; she locked it, lit a wax candle, and lit the way for him. Am I crazy? he asked himself. Of course I won't touch her.

In her room an oil lamp was burning. She turned it up. It was a fairly comfortable room, nicely kept, and in any case it smelled a lot better than, for example, Marianne's place. Naturally—there was no old man who had for months been lying sick there. The girl smiled and without seeming forward approached Fridolin, who gently warded her off. Then she pointed to a rocking chair, into which he was happy to drop.

"You must be very tired," she said. He nodded. And while she undressed without haste, she said:

"Well, no wonder, with all the things a man like you has to do all day long. People like us have an easier time of it."

He noticed that her lips were not made up but colored by a natural red, and he complimented her on that.

"But why should I use makeup? How old do you think I am?"

"Twenty," Fridolin guessed.

"Seventeen," she said and sat on his lap, putting her arms around his neck like a child.

Who in the world would suspect that I'm here in this room at this moment? Fridolin thought. Would even I have found it possible even an hour, even ten minutes ago? And—why? Why? She sought his lips with hers; he drew his head back; she looked at him wide-eyed, a little sad, and slipped from his lap. He was almost sorry, for in her embrace there had been much tender comfort.

She took a red dressing gown, which was hanging over the foot of the unmade bed, slipped into it, and crossed her arms over her breasts so that her entire body was wrapped up.

"Is this better now?" she said without mockery, almost shyly, as though she was making an effort to understand him. He hardly knew what to answer.

"You guessed right," he finally said. "I'm really tired, and I find it very pleasant to sit here in the rocking chair and just listen to you. You have such a lovely, gentle voice. Just talk, tell me something."

She sat on the bed and shook her head.

"You're just afraid," she said softly—and then, to herself, so that it was barely audible, "Too bad!"

These last words made a hot wave race through his blood. He walked over to her, wanted to embrace her, explained to her that he trusted her completely and was speaking the truth. He pulled her to him and wooed her like a sweetheart, like a beloved woman. She resisted, and he felt ashamed and finally gave up.

She said, "You can never tell, some time or other it's got to happen. You're completely right to be afraid. And if something were to happen, you would curse me."

She refused his money with such vehemence that he could not insist. She put on a narrow, blue woolen shawl, lit a candle, lit his way, accompanied him down the stairs, and opened the door for him. "I'm going to stay home tonight," she said. He took her hand and instinctively kissed it. She looked up at him in surprise, almost in shock, and then laughed, embarrassed and happy. "Just as though I were a lady," she said.

The door closed behind him, and Fridolin quickly made a mental note of the house number, so as to be able to send the poor sweet thing some wine and a few pastries tomorrow.

IV

Meanwhile it had become even warmer. The warm wind was bringing an odor of wet meadows and intimations of spring from a distant mountain into the narrow street. Now where? wondered Fridolin, as though it wasn't obvious that he should go home and go to bed. But he couldn't decide to do so. He felt homeless, like an outcast, since that repulsive meeting with those students. . . . Or was it since Marianne's confession? No, longer than that—it was ever since this evening's conversation with Albertine that he felt himself moving farther and farther away from his everyday existence into some other strange and alien world.

He wandered about aimlessly through the dark streets, letting the soft breeze caress his forehead, and finally, as though arriving at a long-sought destination, he turned resolutely into a dimly lit, third-rate café which was comfortable in an old-fashioned Viennese sort of way, not very large, and almost empty at this late hour.

In one corner there were three men playing cards. A waiter who had been watching them helped Fridolin take off his fur coat, took his order, and placed illustrated magazines and evening newspapers on his table. Fridolin felt reassured and safe and began to look cursorily through the newspapers. Here and there his eyes were arrested by some news item. In a Bohemian city, street signs with German names had been torn down. In

Constantinople there was a conference about the construction of a railroad in Asia Minor in which Lord Cranford took part. The firm of Benies and Weingruber had gone bankrupt. A prostitute named Anna Tiger had thrown acid on her friend Hermine Drobizky in a fit of jealousy. This evening a fish dinner was to be held in Sophia Hall. A young girl, Marie B, of Schönbrunner Street 28, had poisoned herself with mercuric chloride. In their prosaic ordinariness, all these facts, the insignificant as well as the tragic ones, somehow had a sobering and calming effect on Fridolin. He felt sorry for the young girl, Marie B. Mercuric chloride, how stupid! At this very moment, while he was sitting snugly in the café, while Albertine was sleeping quietly with her head pillowed on her arms, and the councillor had passed beyond all earthly suffering, Marie B., Schönbrunner Street 28, was writhing in meaningless pain.

He looked up from the newspaper and encountered two eyes fixed on him from the opposite table. Was it possible? Nightingale—? The latter had already recognized him, threw up both arms in happy surprise, and came toward Fridolin. He was a tall, rather broad, almost stocky, and still young man with long and blonde, slightly curly hair with a touch of grey in it, and a blonde mustache that drooped down Polish fashion. He was wearing an open grey coat and underneath a somewhat dirty suit, a crumpled shirt with three fake diamond studs, a wrinkled collar, and a dangling white silk tie. His eyelids were red as if from many sleepless nights, but his blue eyes beamed brightly.

"You're here in Vienna, Nightingale?" exclaimed Fridolin.

"Didn't you know?" said Nightingale in a soft Polish accent that had a moderate Jewish twang. "How could you not know? I'm so famous!" He laughed loudly and good-naturedly, and sat down opposite Fridolin.

"What?" asked Fridolin. "Have you been appointed professor of surgery in secret?"

Nightingale laughed still louder. "Didn't you hear me just now? Just this minute?"

"What do you mean—hear you? Why, of course!" And Fridolin realized that he had heard piano music drifting up from the depth of some cellar as he entered; in fact, that he had heard it even earlier, as he was nearing the café. "So that was you?" he exclaimed.

"Who else?" laughed Nightingale.

Fridolin nodded. Why of course—the idiosyncratic vigorous touch and the strange, somewhat arbitrary but wonderfully harmonious left-hand chords had seemed awfully familiar to him. "So you've devoted yourself to it completely?" he asked. He remembered that Nightingale had given up the study of medicine after his second preliminary examination in zoology, which he had successfully passed though he had taken it seven years late. Yet for some time afterward he had hung around the hospital, the dissecting room, the laboratories, and the classrooms. With his blonde artist's head, his ever-rumpled collar, and the dangling tie that had once been white, he had been a striking and, in the humorous sense, a popular figure, much liked not only by his fellow students but also by many of the professors. The son of a Jewish tavern owner in a small Polish town, he had left home early and had come to Vienna in order to study medicine. The trifling subsidies he had received from his parents had from the beginning hardly been worth mentioning and in any case had soon been discontinued, but this did not hinder him from continuing to appear at the table reserved for medical students in the Riedhof, a circle to which Fridolin also belonged. After a certain time, one or another of his more well-to-do fellow students had taken over the payment of his part of the bill. He sometimes was also given clothing, which he also accepted gladly and without false pride. He had already learned the basics of piano in his home town from a pianist stranded there, and had also studied at the Conservatory in Vienna, where he was alleged to be thought a musical talent of great promise, at the same time he was a medical student. But here, too, he was neither serious nor diligent enough to develop his art systematically, and soon he contented himself with musical triumphs within his circle of friends, or rather with the pleasure he gave them by playing the piano. For a time he had a position as a pianist in a suburban dancing school. University student friends and table companions tried to introduce him into fashionable houses in the same capacity, but at such occasions he would play only what he liked and only for as long as he liked. His conversations with the young women there were not always innocent, and he drank more than he could hold. Once, playing for a dance in a bank director's home, he succeeded long before midnight not only in embarrassing the young women who were dancing near him with flattering but improper remarks which offended their male companions, but he also decided to play a wild cancan and sing a risqué song with his powerful bass voice. The bank director scolded him severely. In response, Nightingale, as if filled with a blissful gaiety, arose and embraced him, and the latter, outraged, though himself a Jew, hurled a common insult at him. Nightingale unhesitatingly avenged himself by giving him a powerful slap—an act which appeared to end his career in the more fashionable houses once and for all. He behaved better, on the whole, in more intimate circles, even if it was necessary on some occasions to eject him forcefully from the premises when the hour was late. But usually all such momentary lapses were forgiven and forgotten by all participants the next morning. Then one day, long after his colleagues had all finished their studies, he had suddenly disappeared from the city without a word. For a few months, postcards from various Russian and Polish towns had arrived, and once, without any explanation, Fridolin, who was one of Nightingale's favorites, was reminded of his existence not only by a postcard but by a request for a moderate sum of money. Fridolin had sent the sum at once but had never received a word of thanks or any other sign of life from Nightingale.

At this moment, however, at a quarter to one in the morning, after eight years, Nightingale insisted on paying his debt, and took the exact amount of cash from a rather shabby wallet, which was so well filled that Fridolin was able to accept the repayment in good conscience.

"So things are going well for you?" he asked with a smile, as if he wished to be reassured.

"Can't complain," answered Nightingale. And, placing his hand on Fridolin's arm, he said, "But tell me, what are you doing here in the middle of the night?"

Fridolin explained his presence at such a late hour by his urgent need for a cup of coffee after a nighttime visit to a patient, but he concealed, without quite knowing why, the fact that he had found his patient dead. Then he talked in quite general terms of his medical duties at the General Hospital and of his private practice, and mentioned that he was married, happily married, and the father of a six-year-old girl.

Nightingale took his turn and explained that he had, as Fridolin rightly guessed, spent the time as a pianist in all sorts of Polish, Romanian, Serbian, and Bulgarian cities and towns, that he had a wife and four children in Lemberg—and he laughed heartily, as though it were exceptionally funny to have four children in Lemberg, all by one and the same woman. Since autumn he had been back in Vienna. The vaudeville company that had originally hired him had fallen apart not long afterward, and he was now playing anywhere and everywhere, anything that happened to come along, sometimes in two or three places the same night, as for example, in the cellar of this place—not a very fashionable establishment, as he noted, really a kind of bowling alley, and as far as the patrons were concerned . . . "But if you have to provide for four children and a wife in Lemberg"—and he laughed again, though not quite as merrily as before. "Sometimes I also have private engagements," he added quickly. And, noticing a smile of reminiscence on Fridolin's face, he continued— "not in the houses of bank directors and such, no, but in all kinds of places, larger ones, public and secret."

"Secret?"

Nightingale looked straight ahead with a gloomy and sly air. "I'm going to be picked up very soon."

"What, you're playing somewhere else tonight yet?"

"Yes. Things don't start there until two."

"Must be a pretty chic place," said Fridolin.

"Yes and no," laughed Nightingale, but immediately became serious again.

"Yes and no—?" repeated Fridolin, curious.

Nightingale bent across the table toward him.

"I'm playing in a private house tonight, but I don't know whose it is."

"So you're playing there for the first time tonight?" asked Fridolin with mounting interest.

"No, for the third time. But it will probably be a different house again."

"I don't get it."

"I don't either," laughed Nightingale. "Better you don't ask any more."

"Hm," remarked Fridolin.

"No, you're wrong. It's not what you think. I've seen a lot; it's un-believable what one sees in small towns—especially in Romania. But here. . . ." He drew back the yellow curtain from the window a little, looked out on the street, and said, as though to himself, "Not here yet." Then, turning to Fridolin, he explained, "I mean the carriage. A carriage always comes to get me, and it's always a different one."

"You're making me curious, Nightingale," Fridolin remarked coolly.

"Listen," said Nightingale after a slight hesitation. "If there is any-one in the world that I would like—but how can I do it—" and suddenly he burst out, "Do you have courage?"

"That's a strange question," said Fridolin in the tone of an offended fraternity student.

"I don't mean it that way."

"Well, what do you mean? Why does one need special courage for this affair? What can possibly happen?" And he gave a short and con-temptuous laugh.

"Nothing can happen to me. At the most, tonight might be the last time—but that may be the case anyway." He fell silent and once more looked out between the curtains.

"Well?"

"What did you say?" asked Nightingale as if in a dream.

"For heaven's sake, tell me more. Now that you started. . . . A secret party? An exclusive society? Only invited guests?"

"I don't know. Last time there were thirty people, the first time only sixteen."

"A ball?"

"Of course, a ball." He seemed to regret that he had said anything at all.

"And you're providing the accompaniment for it?"

"What do you mean, for it? I don't know for what. I play, just play—with blindfolded eyes."

"Nightingale, Nightingale, what kind of song are you singing?"

Nightingale sighed softly. "But unfortunately I'm not totally blindfolded. Not so much that I can't see anything. In the mirror opposite me I can see through the black silk handkerchief over my eyes. . . ." And he fell silent again.

"In a word," said Fridolin impatiently and contemptuously, though he felt strangely aroused, ". . . naked females."

"Don't say 'females,' Fridolin," answered Nightingale as though offended. "You've never seen such women."

Fridolin cleared his throat a little. "And how much is the entrance fee?"

"You mean tickets and such? Hey, what are you thinking of?"

"Well, how does one gain admission?" Fridolin asked with compressed lips, and tapped his fingers on the table.

"You have to know the password, and every time it's a different one."

"And what's the one for tonight?"

"Don't know yet. I'll find out from the coachman."

"Take me along, Nightingale."

"Impossible. Too dangerous."

"A minute ago you yourself were about . . . to invite me to come along. I bet you can figure out a way."

Nightingale looked at him critically. "It would be absolutely impossible for you to go as you are right now, for they're all masked, both the men and the women. Do you have a masquerade outfit with you? Impossible. Maybe next time. I'll try to figure out some way." He listened attentively and once more peered again through the opening in the curtains, then said with a sigh of relief, "The carriage is there. Goodbye."

Fridolin held him by the arm. "You're not getting away from me so fast. You've got to take me along."

"But my dear fellow . . ."

"Leave the rest to me. I know it's dangerous—maybe that's exactly what tempts me."

"But I've already told you—without costume and a mask—"

"There are places to rent costumes."

"At one o'clock in the morning—?"

"Look, Nightingale. At the corner of Wickenburg Street there's just such a place. I walk by it several times a day." And he added hastily, in growing excitement, "You stay here for another quarter of an hour, Nightingale. In the meantime I'll try my luck there. The owner of the rental shop presumably lives in the same building. If not—then I'll just give up. We'll let Fate decide. There's a café in the same building; it's called Café Vindobona, I think. You tell the coachman—that you forgot something in the café, walk in, and I'll be waiting near the door. Then you can tell me the password and immediately get back into your carriage. If I manage to get a costume, I'll immediately take another carriage and follow you—the rest will have to take care of itself. I'll assume all the risk, Nightingale. You have my word of honor."

Nightingale had tried several times to interrupt him, without success. Fridolin threw the money for the check on the table with an all too generous tip, which however seemed to him appropriate for this kind of night, and left. Outside stood a closed carriage. A coachman dressed entirely in black, with a high top hat, sat motionless on the box. Looks just like a hearse, thought Fridolin. After jogging for a few minutes, he reached the corner building that he was looking for, rang the bell, asked the caretaker whether the costume shop owner Gibiser lived here, and secretly hoped that he didn't. But Gibiser did actually live here, on the floor beneath the costume shop, and the caretaker didn't even seem surprised at having such a late visitor. Instead, feeling friendly because of Fridolin's generous tip, he remarked that it was not at all unusual during carnival for people to come to rent costumes at such a late hour. He lit the way from below with a candle until Fridolin had rung the doorbell on the second floor. Herr Gibiser opened the door himself, as though he had been waiting there. He was a haggard, bald-headed man, beardless, wearing an old-fashioned flowered dressing gown and a Turkish cap with a tassel, which made him look like the old man in a stage comedy. Fridolin explained what he wanted and said that price was not an issue, whereupon Gibiser remarked, almost disdainfully, "I ask a fair price, no more."

He led Fridolin up a winding staircase into the storeroom. There was an odor of silk, velvet, perfume, dust, and dried flowers, and gleams of silver and red flashed out of the indistinct darkness. A number of little lamps suddenly gleamed from between open cabinets in a narrow, long hallway, the end of which was lost in the darkness. To the left and right hung all sort of costumes—on the one side there were knights, squires, farmers, hunters, scholars, orientals, and jesters; on the other, ladies in waiting, knights' ladies, peasant women, ladies' maids, and queens of the night. On a shelf above the costumes were the corresponding headpieces, and Fridolin felt as though he were walking through a gallery of hanged people who were on the verge of asking one another to dance. Herr Gibiser followed him. "Is there anything special that you want? Louis the 14th? Directoire? Old German?"

"I need a dark monk's cassock and a black mask, that's all."

At that moment the sound of glasses clinking rang out from the end of the hallway, and Fridolin, startled, looked straight at the costume shop owner, as though he owed Fridolin an immediate explanation. But Gibiser himself stood rigidly still and groped for a switch hidden some-where—and all at once a blinding light poured down to the end of the hallway where a small table set with plates, glasses, and bottles was suddenly visible. Two men dressed as inquisitors in red robes arose from the chairs to the left and to the right of the table, while at the same moment a graceful little creature disappeared. Gibiser rushed forward with long strides, reached across the table, and grabbed a white wig in his hand, while at the same time a graceful, very young girl, still almost a child, wearing a Pierrette costume with white silk stockings, wriggled out from under the table and ran to Fridolin, who was forced to catch her in his arms. Gibiser dropped the white wig on the table and was holding the inquisitors, one to the left and one to the right, by the folds of their robes. At the same time he shouted to Fridolin, "Sir, hold on to that girl for me!" The girl pressed herself against Fridolin as though he would protect her. Her small narrow face was dusted with powder and covered with several beauty spots; from her delicate breasts there arose an odor of roses and powder—mischief and desire laughed in her eyes.

"Gentlemen," cried Gibiser, "You'll stay here until I've handed you over to the police."

"What are you thinking of?" they exclaimed, and, as if with one voice, "We're here at the young lady's invitation."

Gibiser released them both, and Fridolin heard him say to them,

"You'll have to explain this later. Didn't you notice immediately that you were dealing with a lunatic?" Then turning to Fridolin, he said, "Forgive this interruption, my dear sir."

"Oh, it doesn't matter," said Fridolin. He would have preferred either to stay here or to take the girl with him—whatever the consequences. She was looking up at him seductively and childlike, as if spellbound. The judges at the end of the hallway were arguing excitedly with each other, and Gibiser turned matter-of-factly to Fridolin and asked, "You wanted a cassock, sir, a pilgrim's hat, and a mask?"

"No," said the Pierrette with gleaming eyes, "you must give this gentleman a cloak lined with ermine and a doublet of red silk."

"Don't you budge from my side," said Gibiser, and pointed to a dark cassock that was hanging between a medieval soldier and a Venetian senator. "This one's your size, and here's the matching hat; take it quick."

The two judges spoke up again. "You'll have to let us out at once, Herr Chibisier"—to Fridolin's surprise, they pronounced the name Gibiser as though it were French.

"That's out of the question," said the rental shop owner contemptuously. "You'll kindly wait here until I return."

Meanwhile Fridolin slipped into the cassock and tied the ends of the hanging white cords into a knot. Gibiser, standing on a narrow ladder, handed him the black, broad-brimmed pilgrim's hat, and Fridolin put it on; but he did all this unwillingly, because more and more he felt it to be his duty to remain and protect the Pierrette from the danger that threatened her. The mask that Gibiser now pressed into his hand, and that he immediately tried on, reeked of a strange and rather disagreeable perfume.

"Walk in front of me," Gibiser said to the girl, and pointed commandingly to the stairs. Pierrette turned around, looked in the direction of the end of the hallway, and waved a wistful yet gay farewell. Fridolin followed her gaze. There were no longer two inquisitors there but two slender young men in coat and tails and white ties, though both had red masks covering their faces. Pierrette floated down the winding staircase, Gibiser followed her, and Fridolin followed the two of them. In the hallway below, Gibiser opened the door that led to the inner rooms, and said to Pierrette: "You're going straight to bed, you depraved creature, you. We'll talk as soon as I've settled with the two upstairs."

She stood in the doorway, white and delicate, and with a glance at Fridolin sadly shook her head. In the large wall mirror to the right, Fridolin caught a glimpse of a haggard pilgrim—and this pilgrim seemed to be him. He wondered how that was possible, even though he knew it could not be anyone else.

Pierrette had disappeared, and the old costume shop owner locked the door behind her. Then he opened the apartment door and pushed Fridolin into the entrance hall.

"Excuse me," said Fridolin, "I owe you . . ."

"Never mind, sir, you can pay when you return the things. I'll trust you."

But Fridolin did not stir from the spot. "You swear that you won't hurt that poor child?"

"What business is it of yours, sir?"

"I heard you describe the girl as mad—and now you called her a 'depraved creature.' Rather a contradiction, don't you think?"

"Well, sir," answered Gibiser in a theatrical tone of voice, "aren't the insane and the depraved the same in the eyes of God?"

Fridolin shuddered in disgust.

"Whatever it is," he finally said, "I'm sure something can be done. I'm a doctor. We'll talk about this more tomorrow."

Gibiser laughed mockingly without uttering a sound. A light suddenly flared up in the entranceway, and the door between Gibiser and Fridolin closed and was immediately bolted. Fridolin took off the hat, the cloak, and the mask while going down the stairs, and put everything under his arm. The caretaker opened the outer door, and Fridolin saw that the hearse with the motionless driver on the box stood opposite. Nightingale was just on the point of leaving the café and didn't seem very pleased that Fridolin had appeared so promptly.

"So you managed to get yourself a costume?"

"As you can see. And the password?"

"So you're determined?"

"Absolutely."

"Well, then—the password is 'Denmark.' "

"Are you crazy, Nightingale?"

"Why crazy?"

"Oh, never mind, never mind. As it happens I was on the Danish coast this summer. Well, get back in your carriage—but not right away, so that I can have time to take one of those carriages over there."

Nightingale nodded and lit a cigarette in leisurely fashion while Fridolin quickly crossed the street, hired a carriage, and, in an innocent voice, as though he were playing a joke, told the driver to follow the hearse that was just starting out in front of them.

They crossed Alser Street and then drove on under a viaduct through dim and deserted side streets toward the outlying district. Fridolin was afraid that the driver of his carriage would lose sight of the carriage ahead, but whenever he stuck his head out of the open window into the unnaturally warm air, he saw the other carriage and the coachman with the tall black silk hat sitting motionless on the box a little distance in front of him. This may end badly, too, thought Fridolin. At the same time he remembered the odor of roses and perfume that had risen from Pierrette's breast. What kind of strange story did I wander into there? he asked himself. I shouldn't have left—maybe I was obliged not to leave. Where am I now, I wonder?

The road rose slowly uphill between modest villas. Fridolin thought he knew where he was. Years ago he had sometimes come here on walks: this had to be the Galitzinberg that he was ascending. Down below on the left he could see the city, indistinct in the mist but glimmering with a thousand lights. He heard the rumble of wheels behind him and looked back from his window. Two carriages were following his, and he was glad of it, for now the driver of the hearse would not be suspicious of him.

Suddenly, with a violent jolt, the carriage turned into a side street and plummeted down as though into an abyss between iron fences, stone walls, and terraces. It occurred to Fridolin that it was high time he put on his costume. He took off his fur coat and slipped into the monk's cassock in the same way he slipped into the sleeves of his surgical coat every morning in the hospital ward, and he was relieved to think that, if every-thing went well, in a few hours he would be walking between the beds of his patients as he did every morning—a doctor ready to offer help.

The carriage stopped. What if I don't get out at all—but go back im-mediately? thought Fridolin. But go where? To little Pierrette? To the girl in Buchfeld Strasse? To Marianne, the daughter of the dead man? Home? And with a slight shudder he realized that he would rather go anywhere but home. Or was that only because home was the farthest away? he asked himself. No, I can't turn back, he thought. I'll go on, even if it means death. And he laughed at the big word but didn't exactly feel cheerful as he did.

A garden gate stood wide open. The hearse in front drove on, deeper into the abyss, or into the darkness that seemed like one. Nightin-gale must already have gotten out. Fridolin quickly jumped out of the carriage and told the driver to wait for his return up at the bend, no matter how long he might be. To make sure he would wait, he paid him well in advance and promised a similar amount for his return trip. The carriages that had followed him arrived. Fridolin saw the veiled figure of a woman climb out of the first one; he went into the garden and put on his mask. A narrow path, lit by lamps from the house, led to the entrance door; two wings opened, and Fridolin found himself in a narrow, white entryway. He heard a harmonium playing, and two servants in dark livery, their faces covered by grey masks, stood to the left and right of him.

"Password?" two voices whispered in unison. And he answered, "Denmark." One of the servants took his fur coat and disappeared with it into an adjoining room; the other opened a door, and Fridolin stepped into a dimly lit, almost dark room with high ceilings, hung on all sides with black silk. Masked people in clerical costume were walking up and down, sixteen to twenty persons all dressed as monks and nuns. The strains of the organ music, an Italian church melody, gently swelled from above. In a corner of the room stood a small group, three nuns and two monks. They had turned to him for a second when he entered, but had turned away again immediately, almost deliberately. Fridolin noticed that he was the only one wearing a hat, took it off, and wandered up and down as nonchalantly as possible. A monk brushed up against him and nodded a greeting, but from behind the mask a searching look, a full second long, bored deep into Fridolin's eyes. A strange and heavy perfume reminiscent of a tropical garden enveloped him. Again an arm brushed up against him. This time it was that of a nun. Like the others she too had a black veil over her face, head, and neck, and under the black silk lace of her mask a blood-red mouth glowed. Where am I? wondered Fridolin. Among lunatics? Or conspirators? Have I gotten into the meeting of some religious sect? Had Nightingale perhaps been ordered and paid to bring some uninitiated stranger to be a target of their pranks? Yet everything seemed far too serious, too intense, too eerie to be just a carnival prank. A woman's voice had joined the strains of the harmonium, and an old sacred Italian aria resounded through the room. Everyone stood still and seemed to listen, and even Fridolin surrendered for a moment to the wonderfully swelling melody. Suddenly a female voice whispered behind him, "Don't turn around to look at me. There's still time for you to leave. You don't belong here. If they discover you it will be very bad for you."

Fridolin started in fright. For a second he considered obeying the warning. But curiosity, desire, and above all pride were stronger than any misgiving. Now that I've gone this far, he thought to himself, I don't care what happens. And he shook his head no, without turning around.

Then the voice behind him whispered, "I would be sorry if something happened to you."

He turned around. He saw the blood-red mouth shimmer through the black lace and felt dark eyes penetrate into his. "I'm staying," he said in a heroic voice that he didn't recognize as his own, and he looked away again. The song now swelled throughout the room, and the harmonium had a new sound that was anything but sacred. It was worldly, voluptuous, and roared like an organ. Looking around, Fridolin noticed that all the nuns had disappeared and only the monks were left in the room. In the meantime, the voice had also changed from dark seriousness to a bright and jubilant tone by way of an artistically rising trill, and in place of the harmonium an earthy brazen piano had begun to play. Fridolin immediately recognized Nightingale's wild and inflammatory pounding, and the previously noble woman's voice had, with a last piercing and voluptuous outcry, risen to the ceiling and lost itself in infinity. Doors to the left and right had opened. On one side Fridolin recognized Nightingale's indistinct outline at the piano, but the room opposite was radiant with a blaze of light. All the women stood there completely motionless, with dark veils around their heads, face, and necks, and black lace masks over their faces, but otherwise completely naked. Fridolin's eyes wandered thirstily from voluptuous bodies to slender ones, from delicate figures to luxuriously developed ones—and the fact that each of these women remained a mystery despite her nakedness, and that the enigma of the large eyes peering at him from under the black masks would remain unresolved, transformed the unutterable delight of gazing into an almost unbearable agony of desire. The other men were probably feeling what he felt. The first delighted gasps had changed into sighs that sounded like deep anguish. Somewhere a cry broke out—and suddenly, as though they were being pursued, all of them, no longer in their cassocks, but now dressed elegantly in white, yellow, blue, and red cavalier costumes, rushed from the dim room to the women who received them with wild, almost wicked laughter. Fridolin was the only one who remained in a monk's gown, and, nervously, he slunk back into the farthest corner near Nightingale, whose back was turned to him. Fridolin saw that Nightingale had a blindfold over his eyes, but thought he could see how from behind it Nightingale's eyes were staring fixedly into the tall mirror opposite him, which reflected the gaily colored cavaliers dancing with their naked partners.

Suddenly a woman stood beside Fridolin and whispered—for no one spoke aloud, as though even the voices had to remain a secret—"Why are you all by yourself? Why aren't you dancing?"

Fridolin saw that two noblemen were watching him sharply from another corner, and he suspected that the figure at his side—she was boyish and slim—had been sent to test him and tempt him. In spite of that he was reaching his arms toward her to pull her close to him when at the same moment one of the other women left her dance partner and quickly walked up to him. He knew immediately that she was the one who had warned him before. She pretended that she was seeing him for the first time, and whispered, yet in a voice loud enough to be heard in the other corner of the room, "You've finally returned!" And, laughing gaily, she added, "All your efforts are useless. I know you." And, turning to the boyish woman, she said, "Let me have him for just two minutes. You can then have him again, if you want, until morning." And then more softly to her, as though she were overjoyed, "It's really him, him!" The other replied in astonishment, "Really?" and floated away to the cavaliers in the corner.

"Don't ask any questions," the woman now cautioned Fridolin, "and don't be surprised at anything. I've tried to mislead them, but I tell you now: it won't succeed for long. Flee now, before it's too late. And it may be too late almost any minute. And be careful that they don't follow you. No one must find out who you are. You'll have no peace or quiet for the rest of your life if they find out. Go."

"Will I see you again?"

"Impossible!"

"Then I'm staying."

A tremor went through her body and shook him too, and almost robbed him of reason.

"Nothing more can be at risk here than my life," he said, "and right now you're worth it to me." He took her hands and tried to draw her to him.

She whispered again, almost despairingly, "Go!"

He laughed and heard himself laughing, as one does in a dream. "I can see where I am. You're not here, all of you, just to drive men crazy with looking at you. You're just playing with me in order to drive me completely mad with desire."

"It'll soon be too late, go!"

He wouldn't listen to her. "Do you mean to tell me there are no out-of-the-way rooms here where couples who have found each other can go? Will all these people here say goodbye with polite hand kisses? Hardly!"

And he pointed to the couples that were dancing in time with the wild tunes of the piano in the too bright, mirrored adjoining room, white bodies pressed against blue, red, and yellow silk. It seemed to him as though no one was concerned with him and the woman next to him now; they were standing alone in the semi-darkness of the middle room.

"Your hopes are in vain," she whispered. "There are no small rooms such as you are dreaming of here. This is your last chance. Flee!"

"Come with me."

She shook her head violently, as though in despair.

He laughed again and didn't recognize his own laughter. "You're making fun of me! Did these men and these women come here only to inflame each other and then go away? Who can forbid you to come away with me if you want to?"

She took a deep breath and dropped her head.

"Ah, now I understand," he said. "That's the punishment you impose on the one who comes uninvited. I couldn't have thought of a more cruel one! Please let me off. Have mercy on me. Impose some other penalty on me. Only not this one, that I have to leave without you!"

"You're mad. I can't go away with you—not with you or anyone else. Whoever tries to follow me would forfeit his—and my—life!"

Fridolin felt as though drunk, not only with her, with her fragrant body and her glowing red mouth, not only with the atmosphere of this room and the voluptuous secrets that surrounded him—he was intoxicated and at the same time parched from all the experiences of this night, none of which had come to a satisfactory conclusion; with himself, with his own boldness, and with the change that he felt in himself. He touched the veil that was wound about her head with his hands, as though he wanted to tear it off.

She seized his hands. "One night one of the men tried to tear the veil from one of us during the dance. They ripped the mask from his face and drove him out with whips."

"And—she?"

"Maybe you read about a beautiful young girl . . . it was only a few weeks ago . . . who took poison the day before her wedding?"

He remembered the incident and even the name. He said it out loud. "Wasn't it an aristocratic girl who was engaged to marry an Italian prince?"

She nodded.

Suddenly one of the cavaliers, the most distinguished-looking of them all, the only one in a white costume, stood in front of him, and with a short, polite, but at the same time imperious bow, asked the woman talking to Fridolin to dance with him. It seemed to Fridolin that she hesitated for a moment. But he had already put his arm around her and danced away with her in the direction of the other couples in the brilliantly lit adjoining room.

Fridolin found himself alone, and this sudden abandonment fell over him like a frost. He looked around. No one seemed to be paying any attention to him at this moment. Perhaps this was his last chance to leave safely. What held him spellbound in his corner despite his feeling that he was at the moment unobserved and unattended—was it his wanting to avoid an inglorious and perhaps ridiculous retreat? the excruciatingly unsatisfied desire for the beautiful female body whose fragrance still enveloped him? or his feeling that everything that had happened so far was perhaps a test of his courage and that the magnificent woman would be his prize after all? He didn't know himself. It was clear to him in any case that he could not bear this tension much longer, and that he would have to end it, no matter what the danger. Whatever he decided, it couldn't cost him his life. Perhaps he was among fools, perhaps among libertines, but certainly not among scoundrels or criminals. He toyed with the idea of going to them, acknowledging himself as an intruder and placing himself at their mercy in a chivalrous fashion. Only in this way—in a noble manner—could this night end if it was to amount to something more than an unreal and chaotic succession of dismal, miserable, scurrilous, and lascivious adventures, not one of which he had been able to bring to a satisfactory conclusion. And so, taking a deep breath, he prepared himself.

At this very moment, however, a voice near him whispered, "Password!" A cavalier in black had come up to him without his noticing it, and since Fridolin didn't answer immediately, he asked a second time. "Denmark," said Fridolin.

"That's right, sir, that's the password for admission. But the password for the house, if you please?"

Fridolin was silent.

"You won't do us the favor of telling us the password of the house?" it sounded like a sharp knife.

Fridolin shrugged his shoulders. The other man stepped into the middle of the room and raised his hand. The piano stopped playing and the dance ceased abruptly. Two other cavaliers, one in yellow and one in red, stepped up to him. "The password, sir," they both said simultaneously.

"I've forgotten it," answered Fridolin with an empty smile, and felt very calm.

"That's a pity," said the man in yellow, "because it doesn't make any difference here whether you forgot it or whether you never knew it."

The other masculine masked figures streamed into the room, and the doors on both sides closed. Fridolin stood alone in his monk's robe in the middle of the colorful cavaliers.

"Off with the mask!" a few demanded simultaneously. Fridolin stretched his arms out in front of him as though for protection. It seemed to him a thousand times worse to be the only unmasked one among so many masks than to be the only one naked among people who were dressed. And with a firm voice, he said, "If one of you is offended by my presence here, I am ready to give him satisfaction in the usual way. But I will take off my mask only if all of you will."

"It's not a question of satisfaction," said the cavalier in red, who until now had not spoken, "but of expiation."

"Take off the mask!" another commanded in a high-pitched, insolent voice, which reminded Fridolin of the tone of an officer giving orders. "We'll tell you what's in store for you to your face, not your mask."

"I won't take it off," said Fridolin in an even sharper tone, "and woe to him who dares touch me."

An arm suddenly reached for his face, as if to tear off his mask, when suddenly a door opened and one of the women—Fridolin had no doubt which one it was—stood there dressed as a nun, as he had first seen her. Behind her in the overbright room the others could be seen, naked with veiled faces, crowded together, silent, a frightened group. But the door closed again immediately.

"Leave him alone," said the nun. "I'm prepared to redeem him."

There was a short, deep silence, as though something monstrous had happened, and then the cavalier in black, the one who had first demanded the password from Fridolin, turned to the nun with the words, "You know what you're taking upon yourself in doing this."

"I know."

There was a general sigh of relief in the room.

"You're free," the cavalier said to Fridolin. "Leave the house immediately, and be careful not to make any further inquiries into the secrets whose vestibule you have slunk into. If you attempt to put anyone on our trail, whether successfully or not—it will be your undoing."

Fridolin stood motionless. "How—is this woman supposed to redeem me?"

No answer. A few arms pointed toward the door, a signal that he should leave at once.

Fridolin shook his head. "Impose whatever punishment you want on me, gentlemen, but I won't tolerate that another person should pay for me."

"You wouldn't be able to change what happens to her in any case," the cavalier in black said very gently. "When a promise is made here, there is no turning back."

The nun nodded slowly, as though in confirmation. "Go!" she said to Fridolin.

"No," he said, raising his voice. "My life means nothing to me if I have to leave here without you. I won't ask who you are or where you come from. What difference can it make to you, gentlemen, whether or not you keep up this masquerade drama, even if it's supposed to have a serious ending? Whoever you may be, gentlemen, you surely have other lives than this one. But I'm not an actor, not here or elsewhere, and if I've been forced to play a part from necessity, I give it up now. I feel I've happened into a fate that no longer has anything to do with this masquerade, and I will tell you my name, take off my mask, and be responsible for all the consequences."

"Don't do it!" cried the nun, "You'll only ruin yourself without saving me! Go!" And turning to the others, she said, "Here I am, take me—all of you!"

The dark nun's habit dropped from her as if by magic, and she stood there in the radiance of her white body. She reached for her veil, which was wrapped around her face, head, and neck, and unwound it. It sank to the floor. A mass of dark hair fell in great profusion over her shoulders, breasts, and hips, but before Fridolin could even glance at her face, he was seized by irresistible arms, torn away, and pushed to the door. A moment later he found himself in the entryway. The door fell shut behind him; a masked servant brought him his fur and helped him put it on, and the outer door opened. As though driven by an invisible force, he hurried out. He stood on the street as the light behind him was extinguished. When he turned around, he saw the house standing there quietly with closed windows from which not a glimmer of light escaped. I must remember everything clearly, was his main thought. I must find the house again—everything else will follow.

Darkness surrounded him. Some distance away, where the carriage was waiting for him, the dull reddish light of a lantern was visible. The hearse drove up from the bottom of the street below as though he had called for it. A servant opened the door.

"I have my own carriage," said Fridolin. The servant shook his head. "If it's gone, I'll walk back to town."

The servant replied with a wave of his hand so little servantlike that any objection was out of the question. The coachman's ridiculously high top hat towered into the night sky. The wind blew gusts; violet clouds flew across the sky. In view of his experience tonight, Fridolin could not fool himself into thinking that he was free to do anything but step into the carriage, which started off the moment he was inside.

Fridolin resolved to clear up the mystery of his adventure, no matter how dangerous it might be. His whole existence, so it seemed to him, no longer had the slightest meaning if he could not find this incomprehensible woman who at this very moment was paying the price for his salvation. It was only too easy to guess the price. But why should she sacrifice herself for him? Sacrifice—was she the kind of woman for whom the things that stood before her, to which she was now submitting, constituted a sacrifice? If she took part in these affairs—and it couldn't be her first time today since she obviously understood the rules so well—what difference could it make to her whether she belonged to one of the cavaliers or to all of them? Indeed, could she possibly be anything other than a prostitute? Could any of these women be anything else? Prostitutes—no doubt about it, even if all of them had a second life, a bourgeois life, aside from this prostitute life. Perhaps everything he had just experienced had been only an outrageous prank played on him. A prank planned, prepared, even rehearsed for the occasion when an outsider should sneak in. And yet, when he thought again about the woman who had warned him from the beginning and was now prepared to pay for him—there had been something in her voice, her bearing, in the royal nobility of her nude body, which could not possibly have been a lie. Or was it perhaps only his, Fridolin's, sudden appearance that miraculously caused a change in her? After everything that had happened to him tonight—and he was not conscious of any self-inflation in this thought—he felt that such a miracle was not impossible. Are there not hours or nights, he thought, in which a strange and irresistible charm emanates even from men who under normal circumstances have no special power over the other sex?

The carriage continued uphill. If all were well, he should have turned onto the main street a long time ago. What did they intend to do with him? Where was the carriage taking him? Did they intend to continue this farce? And what would they do? What would it be? Perhaps an explanation? A happy reunion at another place? A reward for passing the test creditably? Initiation into the secret society? Undisturbed possession of the magnificent nun—? The windows of the carriage were shut and Fridolin tried to look out—but they were opaque. He tried to open the windows, first the one on the right, then the one on the left—but it was impossible. The glass partition between him and the coachman's box was just as opaque, and just as tightly closed, as the windows. He knocked on the glass, he called out, he shouted, but the carriage went on. He tried to open both doors, first the one on the left, then the one on the right, but neither would budge, and his renewed shouting was drowned out by the rattling of the wheels and the whistling of the wind. The carriage began to jostle, going downhill, faster and faster. Fridolin, gripped with anxiety and alarm, was just about to smash one of the opaque windows when the carriage suddenly halted. Both doors opened simultaneously as if through some mechanism, as though Fridolin was sarcastically being given the choice between the right and the left door. He jumped out of the carriage; the doors closed with a bang—and, with the coachman paying not the slightest attention to Fridolin, the carriage drove away across an open field into the night.

Clouds raced across an overcast sky, the wind rustled, and Fridolin stood in the snow which was casting a faint light all round. As he was standing alone with an open fur coat over a monk's robe, the pilgrim hat on his head, an uncanny feeling overcame him. The main street was some distance away, and a row of dimly flickering lamps indicated the direction of the city. But Fridolin ran straight across the sloping, snow-covered field, seeking a shortcut to get to others as quickly as possible. With feet soaked, he came to a narrow, barely lit side street, and at first walked between high fences groaning in the wind. Turning at the next corner, he stumbled into a somewhat broader street where scattered small houses alternated with empty construction sites. Somewhere a clock tower struck three in the morning. Someone in a short jacket, hands in trouser pockets, head down between his shoulders and hat pulled over his forehead, was coming toward Fridolin. Fridolin prepared himself for an attack, but suddenly the vagrant unexpectedly turned around and ran away. What does this mean? Fridolin asked himself. Then he realized that he must present a rather uncanny appearance, took his pilgrim's hat from his head, and buttoned up the coat under which the monk's habit was flapping down to his ankles. Again he turned a corner and came into a suburban main street. A man in peasant dress walked past him and greeted him as one greets a priest. The light of a street lantern fell upon the street sign fastened to a corner house. Liebhartstal—so he wasn't very far from the house he had left less than an hour ago. For a second he was tempted to go back and wait in the vicinity to see what would happen. But he gave up the idea immediately, realizing that he would only expose himself to grave danger without getting any closer to solving the mystery. The image of the events that were probably taking place in the villa at this moment filled him with anger, despair, shame, and fear. This feeling was so unbearable that Fridolin almost regretted that the vagrant he had met had not attacked him; yes, he almost regretted that he wasn't lying against a fence in the deserted street with a knife gash between his ribs. That at least might have given some kind of meaning to this senseless night with its absurd, unfinished adventures. To return home in his present state seemed to him positively ridiculous. On the other hand, nothing was lost yet. Tomorrow was another day. He vowed that he would not rest before he had found the beautiful woman whose dazzling nakedness had so intoxicated him. Only now did he think of Albertine— with the feeling that he would first have to win her too, as though she could not, must not, be his again before he had betrayed her with all the other women of this night, with the naked woman, with Pierrette, with Marianne, and with the hooker on the narrow street. And shouldn't he also try to find the insolent student who had bumped into him deliberately, so that he could challenge him to a duel with sabers, or better yet, with pistols? What did someone else's life, what did his own, matter to him? Should one always stake one's life only out of a sense of duty and self-sacrifice, never out of a whim or a passion, or simply to match oneself against fate?

And once again the thought came to him that even now his body might be carrying the germ of a fatal disease. Wouldn't it be absurd to die because a child with diphtheria had coughed in his face? Maybe he was already ill. Didn't he have a fever? Perhaps at this very moment he was lying in bed at home—and everything that he thought he had experienced tonight was merely delirium?

Fridolin opened his eyes as wide as possible, passed his hand over his forehead and his cheeks, and felt his pulse. Hardly any faster. Everything was all right. He was completely awake.

He continued down the street toward the city. A couple of market wagons came up behind him, rumbled past, and here and there he met shabbily dressed people whose day was just beginning. Behind the window of a café, on a table over which a gas flame flickered, sat a fat man with a scarf around his neck, sleeping with his head in his hands. The houses were still enveloped in darkness; a few windows here and there were illuminated. Fridolin thought he could feel that people were gradually awakening. It seemed to him that he could see them stretch in their beds and arm themselves for their miserable and sour day. A new day faced him too, but for him it was not miserable and gloomy. And with a strange beating of his heart he became happily aware that in only a few hours he would be walking between the beds of his patients in his white hospital coat. At the next corner stood a one-horse carriage, the coachman asleep on the box. Fridolin woke him up, gave him his address, and climbed in.

V

It was four o'clock in the morning when Fridolin walked up the stairs to his flat. Before he did anything else he went into his consulting room and carefully locked the costume in an armoire. As he wished to avoid waking Albertine, he took off his shoes and clothes before going into the bedroom. He carefully turned on the dim light on the little table beside his bed. Albertine was lying there quietly, her arms folded around her neck; her lips were half open, and painful shadows surrounded them. It was a face that Fridolin did not know. He bent down to her forehead, which immediately became lined with furrows, as though he had touched it, and her features distorted themselves strangely. Suddenly, still asleep, she laughed so shrilly that Fridolin became frightened. Instinctively he called her name. She laughed again, as though in answer, in a strange, almost uncanny way. Fridolin called her once more in a louder voice. At that she opened her eyes wide, slowly and with difficulty, and stared at him as though she didn't recognize him.

"Albertine!" he called for the third time. Only then did she seem to come to her senses. An expression of repulsion and fear, even of terror, came into her eyes. With her mouth still open, she raised her arms, senselessly and as if in despair.

"What's wrong?" asked Fridolin with bated breath. And since she continued to stare at him as if horrified, he added, in an attempt to calm her, "It's me, Albertine." She breathed deeply, tried to smile, let her arms fall on the bed covers, and as from a distance asked, "Is it morning already?"

"Not yet, but soon," replied Fridolin. "It's after four. I've just come home." She was silent. He continued, "The councillor is dead. He was already dying when I came—and naturally I couldn't—leave the family alone right away."

She nodded but seemed hardly to have heard or understood him. She stared into space right through him, and he felt—though he knew at the same moment that the idea was ridiculous—that she knew everything that had happened to him that night. He bent over her and touched her forehead. She shuddered slightly.

"What's the matter?" he asked again.

She only shook her head slowly. He stroked her hair. "Albertine, what's the matter?"

"I've been dreaming," she said distantly.

"What did you dream?" he asked mildly.

"Oh, so much. I can't quite remember."

"Maybe if you try?"

"Everything was so confused—and I'm so tired. You must be tired, too."

"Not in the least, Albertine. I won't be able to sleep very much. You know when I come home so late—the best thing would be for me just to go immediately to my desk—it's in just such morning hours that—" He interrupted himself. "But wouldn't it be better if you told me your dream?" He smiled a little unnaturally.

She answered: "You should really lie down and get a little rest."

He hesitated a while, then did as she suggested and stretched himself out at her side. But he was careful not to touch her. A sword between us, he thought, remembering a half-joking remark of that sort that he had once made in similar circumstances. They both lay there silently, with open eyes, and each of them felt the nearness and the distance of the other. After a while he raised his head on his arm and looked at her for a long time, as though he could see much more than just the outline of her face.

"Your dream!" he suddenly said again, and it was as though she had expected this demand. She held out her hand to him; he took it and, as was his custom, held her slender fingers in his hand as if playing a game, more absentmindedly than tenderly. She began:

"Do you remember the room in the small villa on Lake Wörther where I lived with my parents the summer that we got engaged?"

He nodded.

"That's where the dream began. I was entering this room—I don't know where I was coming from—like an actress stepping onto the stage. I only knew that my parents had gone on a trip and had left me alone. That puzzled me, for our wedding was supposed to be the next day. But my wedding dress hadn't arrived yet. Or was I mistaken? I opened the wardrobe to look, and instead of the wedding dress a great many other clothes were hanging there—costumes, actually, like in an opera, splendid, oriental. Which of these should I wear for the wedding? I wondered. At that point the wardrobe suddenly fell shut or disappeared, I can't remember exactly. The room was very bright, but outside the window it was pitch black. . . . All of a sudden you were there—galley slaves had rowed you here—I saw them disappear into the darkness. You were dressed in splendid clothes, in gold and silver, with a dagger in a silver sheath at your side, and you lifted me down out of the window. I too was now gorgeously dressed, like a princess. We both stood outdoors in the twilight, and a fine grey mist reached up to our ankles. It was our familiar countryside: the lake was there, in front of us were the mountains, and I even saw the country houses that looked like the tiny houses out of a toy box. But we two, you and I, we floated, no, we flew, above the mist and I thought: So this is our honeymoon. Soon we were no longer flying but walking on a forest path, the one to the Elisabeth Heights, and suddenly we found ourselves very high up on the mountain in a clearing which was surrounded on three sides by forest, while behind us was a steep towering cliff. Above us was a starry sky more blue and more expansive than ever it is in reality, and that was the cover of our bridal chamber. You took me in your arms and loved me very much."

"I hope you loved me back," remarked Fridolin, with an invisible, malicious smile.

"I think even more than you loved me," Albertine answered seriously. "But how can I explain to you—despite the intimacy of our embrace, our love was very melancholy, as though with a premonition of future sorrow. The meadow was light and covered with flowers, the forest around glistened with dew, and over the rocky wall sunbeams quivered. And now the two of us had to return to the world and to others; in fact, it was high time we left. But then something awful happened. Our clothes had disappeared. I was seized with unspeakable terror and a burning shame that almost consumed me, and at the same time with a rage against you, as though you alone were to blame for the misfortune—and all of that, the horror, the shame, and the rage, too, was more vehement than anything I have ever felt while awake. But you, conscious of your guilt, rushed away naked as you were in order to go down and get us clothes. And when you had disappeared, I became almost gay. I neither felt sorry for you nor was I worried about you—I was just delighted to be alone, and ran happily about the meadow and sang. It was the melody of a dance that we heard at the carnival ball. My voice was beautiful, and I wished that everyone down in the city could hear me. I didn't see this city, but I knew it was there. It was far below and was ringed by a high wall—a really fantastical city that I can't describe. It was neither an oriental city nor an old German one, exactly—rather it was first one and then the other. In any case, it was a city buried long ago. But suddenly I was lying on the meadow, stretched out in the sunshine—far more beautiful than I really am, and while I was lying there a young man dressed in a light, fashionable suit came out of the forest. He looked, I now realize, somewhat like that Dane I told you about yesterday. He went his way, greeted me very politely as he walked by, but otherwise paid no attention to me. He went straight to the cliff and looked at it attentively, as though he were considering how to get over it. At the same time, however, I also saw you. You were rushing from house to house and store to store in the sunken city, sometimes beneath rows of trees, sometimes through a kind of Turkish bazaar, and you bought me the most beautiful things you could find: clothes, linens, shoes, jewelry—and then you put them all in a small handbag of yellow leather, which somehow held everything. But all the time you were being pursued by a mob of people that I couldn't see but whose muffled, threatening shouts I could hear. And now the other man, the Dane who had been standing in front of the cliff, appeared again. He walked toward me again from the forest—and I knew that he had circled the whole planet during this time. He looked different from the way he did before, but he was the same nevertheless. Like the first time, he stood once more in front of the cliff, then disappeared again, then came out of the woods again, disappeared and reappeared. That happened two or three or a hundred times. He was always the same man and yet always different. Every time he walked by me he greeted me, but finally he stood still in front of me and looked at me searchingly. I laughed more seductively than I've ever laughed in my entire life. He stretched his arms out toward me—and now I wanted to flee, but I couldn't—and he sank down beside me on the meadow."

She stopped speaking. Fridolin's throat was dry. In the darkness he could see how Albertine had concealed her face in her hands.

"A strange dream," he said. "Is it finished?" As she said no, he said, "So tell me the rest."

"It's not easy," she began again. "It's hard to express these things in words. Well—it seemed to me that I lived through countless days and nights; there was neither time nor space; and I was no longer in the clearing surrounded by the forest and the cliff, but on a flower-bedecked plain that stretched far into the distance and lost itself at the horizon on all sides. For a long time—strange, this 'long time'—I had no longer been alone with this man on the meadow. But I can't say whether there were three or ten or a thousand other couples besides us or whether I saw them or not, whether I belonged only to that man or also to the others. Just as that earlier feeling of terror and shame was way beyond anything I could ever have imagined while awake, so nothing in our conscious existence can match the feelings of release, freedom, and ecstasy that I felt in this dream. Yet at the same time I didn't forget you for a moment. In fact, I saw you, saw how you were seized by soldiers, I think—a few priests were also among them—someone, a gigantic person, tied your hands together, and I knew that you were going to be executed. I knew it without feeling any sympathy for you, any fear, as though I were far removed. They led you into a courtyard, a kind of castle courtyard. There you stood with your hands behind your back, completely naked. In the same manner that I saw you, though I was somewhere else, so you saw me, too, as well as all the other couples and the man who was holding me in his arms, saw this infinite sea of nakedness which foamed about me, of which I and the man who held me in his embrace were but a wave. Then, while you stood in the courtyard, a young woman with a crown on her head and a purple cloak appeared at one of the high arched windows between red curtains. She was the queen of this country, and she looked down at you with a stern and questioning gaze. You were standing alone; the others, though there were many, stood pressed against the wall, and I heard a malicious and threatening murmuring and whispering. Then the queen bent down over the railing. Everything became quiet, and the queen gave you a sign, as though she were commanding you to come to her, and I knew that she had decided to pardon you. But you either didn't notice her gaze or didn't want to notice it. Suddenly, however, with hands still tied but now wrapped in a black coat, you stood opposite her, not in a room but somehow outdoors, as though floating. She was holding a piece of parchment in her hand—your death sentence, in which both your guilt and the reasons for your conviction were written. She asked you—I didn't hear the words, but I knew it—whether you were prepared to be her lover, in which case your death sentence would be canceled. You shook your head, refusing. I didn't wonder about it, because it seemed natural that you couldn't be other than faithful to me eternally, in the face of all danger. At that point the queen shrugged her shoulders, waved her hand in the air, and suddenly you were in a subterranean cellar, and whips were whizzing down on you without me seeing the people who were swinging the whips. Blood flowed in streams down your back, I saw it, and was aware of my cruelty without questioning it. Then the queen moved toward you. Her hair was loose and flowed over her naked body, and she held out her diadem to you—and I realized that she was the girl from the Danish seashore that you saw one morning naked on the ledge of a bathing hut. She didn't say a word, but the meaning of her presence, yes, of her silence, was to find out whether you would be her husband and the ruler of the country. Since you refused her once more, she suddenly disappeared, and I saw at the same time that they were erecting a cross for you—not down in the courtyard, no, but on the flower-bedecked, infinitely broad meadow where I was resting in the arms of my lover in the middle of all the other lovers. But I saw you, saw how you walked alone through the ancient streets without a guard, yet I knew that your course was marked out and escape was impossible. Then you came up the forest path. I waited for you anxiously but without sympathy. Your body was covered with welts which had stopped bleeding. You climbed higher and higher, the path became wider as the forest receded on both sides, and then you were standing at the edge of the meadow at an enormous, incomprehensible distance from me. But you greeted me with smiling eyes, as a sign that you had fulfilled my wish and had brought me everything I needed: clothing and shoes and jewelry. But I thought your gestures stupid and senseless beyond belief, and I was tempted to make fun of you, to laugh in your face—because you had refused the hand of a queen out of loyalty to me, had endured torture, and now came tottering up here to a horrible death. I ran toward you, and you toward me faster and faster—I began to float in the air, and you did too, but suddenly we lost sight of each other, and I knew: we had flown past each other. Then I hoped that you would at least hear my laughter, just at the moment when they were nailing you to the cross. And so I laughed, as loudly and shrilly as I could. That was the laugh, Fridolin—with which I awoke."

She fell silent and remained motionless. He, too, neither moved nor spoke a word. Any word at this moment would have appeared stupid, false, cowardly. The further she progressed in her story, the more ridiculous and insignificant did his own experiences appear to him, and he vowed that he would bring them all to a conclusion, then faithfully tell her and so revenge himself against this woman who in her dream had revealed herself as that which she was—faithless, cruel, and treacherous, and whom he now believed he hated more than he had ever loved her.

He realized that he was still holding her fingers clasped in his hands and that no matter how much he wanted to hate this woman, he still felt only the same, unchanged tenderness—if anything, a more painfully acute tenderness—for these slender, cool, and so familiar fingers. Instinctively, yes, even against his will—he pressed his lips gently against them before he let the familiar hand drop from his.

Albertine's eyes were still closed, and Fridolin thought he could see how her mouth, her forehead, yes, her entire face radiated a happy, beatific, and innocent smile, and he felt an incomprehensible desire to bend over her and press a kiss on her pale forehead. But he checked himself, realizing that it was only the all too understandable exhaustion of the stirring experiences of the last few hours that was disguising itself as a sensuous tenderness in the deceptive atmosphere of the bedroom.

Whatever his present state of mind—whatever decisions he might reach in the course of the next few hours—the most pressing demand of the moment was to flee into sleep and forgetfulness for a little while at least. He had been able to sleep the night following the death of his mother, had slept deeply and dreamlessly, and should he not be able to sleep now? He stretched himself out beside Albertine, who seemed to have fallen asleep again already. A sword between us, he thought again. And then: we are lying here like mortal enemies. But it was only an expression.

VI

The maid's gentle knocking on the door awakened him at seven o'clock early the next morning. He cast a quick glance at Albertine. Sometimes, not always, this knocking awakened her too. But today she was sleeping soundly, all too soundly. Fridolin dressed himself quickly. Before he left, he wanted to see his little daughter. She was lying quietly in her white bed, her child's hands clenched into little fists. He kissed her on the forehead. Then once more, on tiptoe, he crept up to the door of the bedroom where Albertine was still sleeping, motionless as before. Then he left. With him he carried the cassock and the pilgrim's hat safely hidden in his black doctor's bag. He had drawn up the schedule for the day with great care, even obsessively. First there was a visit to a seriously ill attorney in the neighborhood. Fridolin examined him carefully, found him somewhat improved, expressed his satisfaction in a sincerely happy manner, and ordered an old prescription refilled. Then he went straight to the cellar of the house where Nightingale had played piano the night before. The place was still closed, but the cashier at the counter in the café above knew that Nightingale lived in a small hotel in the Leopoldstadt. A quarter of an hour later Fridolin arrived there in a carriage. It was a miserable place. In the hall there was an odor of musty beds, rancid fat, and chicory coffee. A tough-looking concierge with sly, red-rimmed eyes, ready to give information to the police, willingly gave Fridolin information. Herr Nightingale had driven up around five o'clock in the morning in the company of two other gentlemen who had disguised their faces, perhaps intentionally, with scarves wrapped high around their heads and necks. While Nightingale was in his room, the gentlemen had paid his bill for the last four weeks, and when he didn't appear after half an hour, one of the men had personally brought him down. All three had then driven to the North Train Station. Nightingale had appeared to be very agitated— well, why not tell the whole truth to a man who seemed so trustworthy?—and, yes, had tried to slip the concierge a letter, which however the two men had immediately intercepted. Any letters for Herr Nightingale—so the men had explained—would be picked up by a person properly authorized to do so. Fridolin took his leave and was glad that he had his doctor's bag in his hand as he went out the door, so that anyone seeing him would not take him for a resident of the hotel but would think he was an official. There was nothing to be done about Nightingale for the time being. They had been extremely cautious and probably had good reason for it.

Then he drove to the costume rental shop. Herr Gibiser himself opened the door. "I'm bringing back the costume I rented," said Fridolin, "and would like to pay my bill." Herr Gibiser named a moderate sum, took the money, made an entry in a large ledger, and looked up at Fridolin, evidently surprised when he made no move to leave.

"I am also here," said Fridolin in the tone of a police magistrate, "to have a word with you about your daughter."

Herr Gibiser's nostrils twitched—whether it was out of discomfort, scorn, or annoyance was difficult to tell.

"What do you mean?" he asked Fridolin in a similar tone of voice.

"Yesterday," said Fridolin, with the outstretched fingers of one hand resting on the office desk, "you said that your daughter was not quite normal mentally. The situation in which we found her does seem to indicate that. And since chance made me a participant or at least a spectator of this strange scene, I would very much like to advise you to consult a doctor about her."

Gibiser, twirling an unnaturally long penholder in his hand, surveyed Fridolin with an insolent air.

"I suppose the doctor himself would be so good as to take the treatment upon himself?"

"I beg you not to put words in my mouth that I haven't said," Fridolin answered sharply.

At that moment the door that led to the inner room opened, and a young man with an open coat over an evening suit stepped out. Fridolin knew immediately that it could be none other than one of the inquisitors of the night before. No doubt he came from Pierrette's room. He seemed taken aback when he caught sight of Fridolin, but immediately regained his composure, greeted Gibiser casually with a wave of his hand, lit a cigarette, for which he used a match lying on the desk, and left the flat.

"So that's how it is," remarked Fridolin with a contemptuous twitch of his mouth and a bitter taste on his tongue.

"What do you mean?" asked Gibiser with perfect equanimity.

"So you changed your mind, Herr Gibiser," said Fridolin, letting his eyes wander about significantly from the entrance door to the door from which the judge had come, "changed your mind about notifying the police."

"We came to another agreement, Herr Doctor," remarked Gibiser coldly, and stood up as though an interview had ended. Fridolin started to go. Gibiser obligingly opened the doors, and in an affectless manner he said, "If the Herr Doctor should want anything else . . . it needn't necessarily be a monk's robe."

Fridolin slammed the door behind him. Well, that's finished, he thought with a feeling of anger which even to him seemed inappropriate. He hurried down the stairs, walked to the Polyclinic, and first of all telephoned home to find out whether a patient had sent for him, whether the mail had come, or whether there was any other news. The maid had scarcely answered when Albertine herself came to the phone and greeted Fridolin. She repeated everything that the maid had already said, and then she said casually that she had just gotten up and wanted to have breakfast with their daughter. "Give her a kiss from me," said Fridolin, "and enjoy your breakfast."

Her voice had done him good, and just for that reason he quickly ended the call. Actually, he had wanted to ask Albertine what she was planning to do this morning, but what business was it of his? In the depths of his soul he was through with her, no matter whether their superficial life continued or not. The blonde nurse helped him out of his street coat and handed him his white doctor's coat, smiling at him a little, just as they always smiled at everyone, whether one paid them any attention or not.

A few minutes later he was on the ward. The doctor in charge had sent word that he suddenly had to leave the city because of a conference, and that the assisting doctors should make rounds without him. Fridolin felt almost happy as he walked from bed to bed followed by students, examined patients, wrote prescriptions, and consulted with the other assistant doctors and the nurses. There was a lot of news. The journeyman locksmith Rödel had died during the night; the autopsy would be in the afternoon at half past four. A bed had become free in the women's ward but was already occupied again. The woman in bed seventeen had had to be transferred to the surgical division. In between there was also a lot of personal gossip. The appointment of a man to the ophthalmology division would be decided the day after tomorrow. Hügelmann, now professor at Marburg University, had the best chance, even though only four years ago he had still been a mere second assistant to Stellwag. A rapid promotion, thought Fridolin. I'll never be considered for department head, if only because I don't have the required docent degree. Too late. But why, really? I could begin doing scientific research again, or I could take up more seriously some of the things I've already begun. My private practice still leaves me enough time to do it.

He asked Dr. Fuchstaler to take charge of the outpatient clinic and had to confess to himself that he would rather stay here than drive out to the Galitzinberg. And yet, he had to. He felt obliged—and not only for his own sake—to investigate the matter further, and there were all sorts of other things that also had to be done that day. And so he decided to ask

Dr. Fuchstaler to take charge of the evening rounds too, just in case. The young girl with the suspected tuberculosis over there in the last bed smiled at him. She was the one who had recently used the opportunity of a physical examination to press her breasts trustingly against his cheeks. Fridolin answered her smile coldly and turned away, frowning. They're all alike, he thought with bitterness, and Albertine is just like the rest of them—she's the worst of them all. I'll separate from her. Things can never be the same again.

On the stairs he exchanged a few words with a colleague from the surgical division. How was the woman who had been transferred last night doing? As far as he was concerned, he didn't really think it was necessary to operate. They would, of course, tell him the result of the histological examination?

"Of course, Doctor."

At the corner he took a carriage. He consulted his notebook—a ridiculous charade for the coachman's sake—to make it appear that he was just now making up his mind where to go. "To Ottakring," he then said, "the street along the Galitzinberg. I'll tell you where to stop."

In the carriage he was suddenly overcome by a painful and yearning emotion, almost a feeling of guilt that in the last few hours he had hardly thought of his beautiful savior. Would he now succeed in finding the house? Well, that wouldn't be particularly difficult. The only question was: what then? Notify the police? That might have disastrous consequences for this woman who had sacrificed herself, or was at least prepared to sacrifice herself, for him. Or should he turn to a private detective? That seemed in rather bad taste and not quite dignified enough. But what else could he possibly do? He had neither the time nor the skill to carry out the necessary investigations himself. A secret society? Well, yes, it certainly was secret. But they probably knew one another. Were they aristocrats, perhaps members of the court? He thought of certain archdukes who might easily be capable of such pranks. And the women? Probably . . . recruited from brothels. Well, that was not by any means certain. At any rate, they were very attractive. But what about the woman who had sacrificed herself for him? Sacrificed? Why did he persist in imagining that it was really a sacrifice? It had been an act. Of course, the whole thing had been an act. He should have been grateful to have gotten out of the scrape so lightly. Well, why not? He had preserved his dignity. The cavaliers must have recognized that he was nobody's fool. And she must have realized it in any case. Very likely she had cared more for him than for all these archdukes or whatever they were.

At the end of the Liebhartstal, where the road led more sharply up-hill, he got out and took the precaution of sending the carriage away. The sky was pale blue with white clouds, and the sun shone with the warmth of spring. He looked back—nothing suspicious was to be seen. Not a carriage, not a pedestrian. He walked slowly up the road. His coat became heavy; he took it off and threw it over his shoulder. He came to the spot where he thought he would find the side street where the mysterious house was branching off the road. He couldn't go wrong; the road did go downhill but not nearly as steeply as it had seemed to him when he was driving on it last night. It was a quiet little street. In one front garden there were rose bushes carefully covered with straw; in the one next to it there stood a baby carriage; a boy, dressed from head to foot in a blue wool knit, was romping about and a young woman was looking down from the first-floor window, laughing. Next came an empty lot, then an uncultivated fenced-in garden, then a small villa, next a lawn, and then, no doubt about it—there was the house he was looking for. It didn't look grand or magnificent in the least. It was a one-story villa in modest Empire style and obviously renovated not very long ago. The green blinds were down, and there was nothing to show that anyone lived there. Fridolin looked around. There was no one in the street, except that farther down two boys with books under their arms were walking in the opposite direction. He stood in front of the garden gate. And now what? Should he simply walk away again? That would be too absurd. He looked for the electric bell button. And if someone opened the door, what should he say? Well, that was easy—was the pretty country house available to be rented this summer? But meanwhile the door of the house had already opened, and an old servant in plain morning livery came out and slowly walked up the narrow path that led to the garden gate. He held a letter in his hand and silently pushed it through the iron bars to Fridolin, whose heart was pounding.

"For me?" he asked, catching his breath. The servant nodded, turned around, walked back, and the door to the house fell shut behind him. What does this mean? Fridolin asked himself. Is it perhaps from her? Maybe she's the one who owns the house? Quickly he walked back up the street, and it was only then that he noticed that his name was written on the envelope in tall, dignified letters. At the corner he opened the letter, unfolded a sheet of paper, and read: *"Give up your investigations, which are completely useless, and regard these words as your second warning. We hope, for your own good, that this will be sufficient."* He let the sheet of paper fall.

This message disappointed him in every respect—at any rate it was different from what he had foolishly expected. Still, the tone was peculiarly reserved, completely without sharpness. It suggested that the people who had sent the message by no means felt secure.

Second warning—? How was that? Oh yes, he had received the first one during the night. But why was it the "second" warning—and not the last? Did they want to test his courage again? Was he supposed to pass a test? And how did they know his name? Well, that wasn't so strange; they had probably forced Nightingale to betray him. And besides—he smiled at his absentmindedness—his monogram and his address were sewn into the lining of his fur coat.

But even though he hadn't made any progress, the letter on the whole calmed him, though he wasn't able to say why. At any rate, he was convinced that the woman he was so uneasy about was still alive and that he could find her if he went about it cautiously and cleverly.

When he arrived home, feeling tired but otherwise strangely relieved—though at the same time he felt that his relief was an illusion—Albertine and the little girl had finished eating their lunch but nevertheless kept him company while he ate his. There she sat opposite him, she who last night had calmly let him be nailed to the cross, with an angelic look, the good wife and mother, and to his surprise he didn't hate her. He enjoyed his meal, found himself in a somewhat agitated but on the whole cheerful mood, and, as was his habit, spoke in a lively manner about the little professional incidents of the day, especially the personal gossip, about which he always kept Albertine well informed. He told her that the appointment of Hügelmann was as good as settled and spoke of his own resolution to take up his scientific work again with greater energy. Albertine knew this mood, knew that it usually didn't last very long, and betrayed her doubts through a slight smile. When Fridolin became quite heated on the subject, Albertine gently stroked his hair with a light touch to calm him. But at that he started slightly and turned to the child, so as to remove his forehead from the embarrassing touch. He took the little girl on his lap and was just beginning to bounce her up and down on his knees when the maid announced that several patients were already waiting for him. Fridolin rose with a sigh of relief, mentioned casually that Albertine and the child should use the beautiful sunny afternoon hour to take a walk, and went into his consulting room.

In the course of the next two hours Fridolin had to see six old patients and two new ones. In each case he was fully able to focus his mind, examined, took notes, wrote prescriptions—and was happy that he felt so wonderfully fresh and clearheaded despite having spent the last two nights almost without sleep.

After finishing his consulting hours he stopped to check on his wife and child, as he usually did, and ascertained, not without satisfaction, that Albertine's mother was visiting and that the little girl was having a French lesson with her governess. And only when he was on the stairs again did he realize that all this order, all this regularity, all this security of existence was nothing but an illusion and a deception.

Although he had excused himself from his afternoon duties, he felt irresistibly drawn to his ward. There were two cases of special importance there for the scientific research he was planning, and he busied himself with a more detailed study of them than he had before. Then he still had to make a visit to a patient in the heart of the city, and so it was already seven o'clock in the evening when he stood before the old house in Schreyvogel Street. Only now, when he was looking up at Marianne's window, did her image, which in the meantime had completely faded, come to life in his mind once more, more clearly than that of all the others. Well—here he could not fail. Without any special exertion he could begin his revenge here; here there was little difficulty and no danger. And that which might have deterred others, the betrayal of her fiancé, only made him all the keener to do it. Yes, to betray, to deceive, to lie, to play a part, here and there, with Marianne, with Albertine, with this good Dr. Roediger, with the whole world—to lead a kind of double life, on the one hand the competent, reliable physician with a future, the upright husband and father—and on the other a libertine, a seducer, a cynic who played with people, with men and with women, just as the spirit moved him— that seemed to him delightful at this moment—and the delightful part of it was that at some future time, long after Albertine fancied herself secure in a peaceful marriage and family life, he would confess all his sins to her, coolly, in retribution for all the bitter and humiliating things she had done to him in her dream.

In the entryway he found himself opposite Dr. Roediger, who held out his hand to him innocently and heartily.

"How is Fräulein Marianne?" asked Fridolin. "Is she a little calmer?"

Dr. Roediger shrugged his shoulders. "She's been prepared for the end long enough, Doctor—only when they came around noon to get the body—"

"Ah, that's been done already?"

Dr. Roediger nodded. "The funeral will be tomorrow afternoon at three. . . ."

Fridolin looked down. "I suppose—Fräulein Marianne's relatives are with her?"

"Not any more," answered Dr. Roediger. "She's alone now. She'll be pleased to see you again, Doctor. Tomorrow my mother and I are taking her to Mödling." To answer Fridolin's politely questioning look, he continued, "My parents have a little house out there. Goodbye, Doctor. I have a lot of things to do. It's unbelievable what has to be done in such a—case! I hope I'll find you still upstairs when I return, Doctor." And he was already out the door and in the street.

Fridolin hesitated a moment, then slowly went up the stairs. He rang the bell, and Marianne herself opened the door. She was dressed in black, and around her neck she wore a black jade necklace that he had never seen on her before. Her face became slightly flushed.

"You've made me wait a long time," she said with a feeble smile.

"Forgive me, Fräulein Marianne, but I had a particularly busy day."

He followed her through the death chamber where the bed was now empty into the next room where yesterday he had filled out the death certificate beneath the picture of an officer in a white uniform. A little lamp was already burning on top of the desk, so that the room was half lit. Marianne offered him a seat on the black leather sofa and sat down opposite him at the desk.

"I just ran into Dr. Roediger down in the entryway. So you are going to the country tomorrow?"

Marianne looked at him as though she were surprised at the cool tone of his questions, and her shoulders drooped when he continued in an almost hard voice. "I think that's very sensible." And he explained in a matter-of-fact way what a favorable effect the good air and the new environment would have on her.

She sat motionless, and tears streamed down her cheeks. He saw them without sympathy, more with impatience; and the thought that she might in the next minute perhaps be lying at his feet once more, repeating her confession of yesterday, filled him with fear. And since she said nothing, he stood up brusquely. "Much as I regret it, Fräulein Marianne—" He looked at his watch.

She raised her head, looked at Fridolin, and her tears kept flowing. He would gladly have said a kind word to her, but he couldn't bring himself to do it.

"I suppose you'll stay in the country for a few days," he began in a forced way. "I hope you'll stay in touch. . . . Dr. Roediger, by the way, told me that the wedding is to be soon. Let me offer you my best wishes now."

She didn't move, as though she had heard neither his congratulations nor his farewell. He held out his hand to her, but she did not take it, and he repeated almost in a tone of reproach, "Well, I sincerely hope that you'll keep me posted about your health. Goodbye, Fräulein Marianne."

She sat there as if turned to stone. He left; for a second he stopped in the doorway, as if he were giving her a last opportunity to call him back. But she seemed rather to turn her head away from him, and he closed the door behind him. Out in the hallway he felt something like remorse. For a moment he thought about going back, but he felt that this would have been the most ridiculous thing of all to do.

What now? Go home? Where else! Anyway, there was nothing more he could do today. And tomorrow? What should he do? And how? He felt awkward and helpless; everything he touched failed. Everything seemed unreal, even his home, his wife, his child, his profession, yes, even he himself, walking mechanically through the evening streets with his thoughts roaming far afield.

The clock on the courthouse tower struck half past seven. Not that it mattered what time it was; time lay before him endlessly. Nothing mattered anymore, nobody concerned him. He pitied himself not a little. Suddenly it occurred to him—it wasn't exactly a plan—to go to some train station and take a train somewhere, it didn't matter where, and to disappear, leaving everyone he knew behind, and then to surface somewhere else and begin a new life as another, different person. He recalled certain strange pathological cases of double lives that he knew from psychiatry books. For example, a man living in normal, well-ordered circumstances suddenly disappeared, was missing for a while, returned after several months or years, and didn't remember where he had been all the while. Later someone who had run across him in a foreign country recognized him, but the man himself remembered nothing. True, such cases were rare, nevertheless they were authentic. And others probably experienced similar things to a lesser degree. For instance, when one comes back from dreams. True, one remembers. . . . But there are surely other dreams that one completely forgets, of which nothing remains but a mysterious mood, a curious numbness. Or one remembers the dream only later, much later, and then no longer knows if one has really experienced it or only dreamt it. Only . . . only—!

And as he wandered aimlessly on and yet instinctively in the direction of his home, he came near that dark, rather questionable street in which, less than twenty-four hours ago, he had followed a forlorn creature to her shabby and yet cozy room. "*Forlorn*," was she? And just exactly this street, "*questionable*"? Strange how again and again we are misled by words, how we categorize streets, events, and people and form judgments about them out of lazy habit. Wasn't this young girl really the most charming, yes, the purest of all the people he had come in contact with last night? He felt rather touched when he thought of her. And now he remembered his resolve of yesterday and, deciding quickly, went into the nearest store and bought all sorts of delicacies. Walking along the walls of the houses with his little package, he felt happy knowing that he was doing something that was at least sensible, perhaps even laudable. Nevertheless he turned up the collar of his coat as he stepped into the entryway and went upstairs several steps at a time. The bell of the flat rang with unwelcome shrillness, and when a disreputable-looking woman informed him that Fräulein Mizzi was not at home, he breathed a sigh of relief. But before the woman had the opportunity to receive the package for the absent Mizzi, another woman, still young and not unattractive, wrapped in a kind of bathrobe, came into the hallway and said, "Is the gentleman looking for Fräulein Mizzi? Well, she won't be coming home very soon."

The older woman made a sign for her to keep quiet; but Fridolin, as though he urgently needed to confirm what he himself really already knew, remarked offhandedly, "She's in the hospital, right?"

"Well, since you know anyway. But there's nothing wrong with me, thank God!" she exclaimed gaily, and moved quite close to Fridolin with lips half open, throwing her voluptuous body back boldly in such a way that her bathrobe opened. Fridolin, declining the invitation, said, "I just stopped by in passing to bring Mizzi something," suddenly feeling like a high school student again. And in a new, matter-of-fact tone he asked, "In what ward is she?"

The younger woman mentioned the name of a professor in whose clinic Fridolin had been an assistant doctor a few years ago. And then she added good-naturedly, "Give me the packages, I'll take them to her tomorrow. I promise not to eat any of it. And I'll give her your regards and tell her that you haven't been unfaithful to her."

At the same time, however, she stepped closer to him and laughed invitingly. But when he drew back a little, she gave up immediately and remarked consolingly, "In six, or at most eight weeks, she'll be back home, the doctor said."

When Fridolin stepped out into the street from the entryway, he felt tears choking in his throat, but he knew this was less because he was deeply touched than because his nerves were gradually giving way. Intentionally he struck a faster and more lively pace than he was in the mood for. Was this experience another and final sign that everything he undertook was bound to fail? But why should he think that? He might just as well take it as a sign that he had escaped a great danger. And was that the goal—to avoid danger? Many other dangers still stood before him. He had no intention of giving up the search for last night's marvelous woman. Of course it was too late to do anything about it now. And in any case he had to consider carefully just how to continue the search. If only there were someone with whom he could consult about it! But he didn't know anyone to whom he was willing to confide the adventures of the previous night. For years he had not really been intimate with anyone except his wife, and he could hardly discuss this with her. Neither this nor anything else. For no matter how one looked at it, the night before she had allowed him to be nailed to the cross.

And now he knew why, instead of going home, he was instinctively walking ever farther in the opposite direction. He just wouldn't, he couldn't, face Albertine right now. The most reasonable thing to do was to eat out somewhere, then go to his ward and look after his two cases—and under no circumstances go home—"home!"—until he could be certain of finding Albertine asleep.

He entered one of the more elegant and quieter cafés in the vicinity of the courthouse, telephoned home that they shouldn't expect him for supper, and then hung up quickly so that Albertine wouldn't have a chance to get to the telephone. He sat by a window and drew the curtain. In a distant corner another man had just taken a seat; he was wearing a dark overcoat and was otherwise also rather inconspicuously dressed. Fridolin thought he had seen his face before sometime during the day. But of course it could be just a matter of chance. He picked up a newspaper and read a few lines here and there, just as he had done before in the other café: reports of political events, theatre, art, literature, and minor and major accidents of all sorts. In some American city that he had never heard of, the theatre had burned down. The chimney sweep Peter Korand had thrown himself out of a window. It struck Fridolin somehow as peculiar that even chimney sweeps occasionally committed suicide, and he found himself wondering if the man had first washed himself properly before he had hurled himself down into nothingness, or whether he had jumped black with dirt just as he was. In an elegant hotel in the heart of the city, a woman had poisoned herself, a strikingly beautiful woman who had registered there several days before under the name of Baroness D. Fridolin immediately felt a strange presentiment. The woman had come home at four in the morning in the company of two men who had left her at the door. Four o'clock. That was exactly the same time that he . . . had arrived home. And around noon she had been found unconscious—so the report continued—in her bed with signs of fatal poisoning. . . . A strikingly beautiful woman. . . . Well, of course there were many strikingly beautiful young women. . . . There was no reason to believe that Baroness D., or rather the woman who had registered at the hotel as Baroness D., and a certain other woman were one and the same. And yet—his heart pounded, and the newspaper trembled in his hand. In a fashionable hotel. . . . Which one—? Why so secretive? So discreet? . . .

He lowered the newspaper and saw how the man in the distant corner raised his, a large illustrated magazine, in front of his face like a curtain. Fridolin immediately picked up his paper again and knew at this moment that the Baroness D. had to be the woman he had met last night. . . . In an elegant downtown hotel . . . there were not many that would be considered so—by a Baroness D. . . . And now what would happen would happen—but this was a clue which he had to follow. He called the waiter, paid, and left. At the door he once more turned around to look at the suspicious man in the corner. But, strangely enough, he was already gone. . . .

A fatal poisoning. . . . But she had been found alive. . . . At the moment they had found her she was still alive. There was in the end no reason to assume that she had not been saved. In any case, he would find her—dead or alive. He would see her; no one on earth could stop him from seeing the woman who had died because of him; indeed, who had died for him. He was the cause of her death—he alone—if this was the same woman. Yes, it was she. Returned to the hotel at four o'clock in the morning in the company of two men! Probably the same ones who had brought Nightingale to the train station a few hours later. They didn't have a lot of scruples, those two!

He stood in the large broad square in front of the courthouse and looked around. Only a few people were in sight, and the suspicious man from the café was not among them. And even if—the men had obviously been afraid; he clearly had the upper hand. Fridolin hurried on, took a carriage when he reached the Ring, and asked to be taken first to the Hotel Bristol, where he asked the concierge, as if he had been authorized to do so, whether the Baroness D. who had poisoned herself this morning had stayed at the hotel. The concierge didn't seem particularly surprised—perhaps he took Fridolin for a policeman or some other official. In any case, he answered politely that the sad case had not occurred here, but in the Hotel Archduke Karl. . . .

Fridolin at once drove to the designated hotel and found that Baroness D. had been taken to the General Hospital as soon as she was found. Fridolin asked how they had made the determination that it was a suicide. Why had they at noon already been concerned about a lady who had only come home at four o'clock in the morning? Well, that was quite simple: two men (the two men again!) had asked for her around eleven o'clock in the morning. Since the lady had not answered repeated telephone calls, the maid had knocked on the door. When there had been no answer and the door had remained locked from the inside, there was nothing to be done but to break it open, and when they did, they found the baroness unconscious in bed. They had immediately called the ambulance and notified the police.

"And the two men?" asked Fridolin sharply, feeling like an undercover detective.

Well, the men, yes, that was suspicious, for they had completely disappeared in the meantime. Anyhow, it was certain that the lady was not really Baroness Dubieski, under which name she had registered at the hotel. This was the first time she had stayed at this hotel, and there was no such family with this name, at least no aristocratic one.

Fridolin thanked the concierge for the information and left rather quickly, since one of the hotel managers who had just approached him was eyeing him with unpleasant curiosity. He climbed back into the carriage and asked to be taken to the General Hospital. A few minutes later, in the admissions office, he learned not only that the alleged Baroness Dubieski had been taken to the Second Clinic for Internal Medicine, but that at five o'clock in the afternoon, despite all the doctors' efforts, she had died without regaining consciousness.

Fridolin took a deep breath—so he thought—but it was really an agonized groan that escaped him. The official on duty looked up at him in surprise. Fridolin pulled himself together immediately, politely took his leave, and the next minute was standing outdoors. The hospital park was almost empty. In one of the neighboring avenues under a lantern a nurse in a blue-and-white-striped uniform and white cap was walking. "Dead," said Fridolin to himself. "If it's her. And if it isn't? If she's still alive, how can I find her?"

Fridolin could answer only too easily the question of where the body of the unknown woman was at this moment. Since she had just died a few hours ago, she was undoubtedly in the hospital morgue, only a few hundred steps away. As a doctor he would of course have no difficulty in gaining entrance there, even at such a late hour. But—what did he want to do there? He only knew her body—he had never seen her face, had only been able to catch a hasty glimpse of it at the moment he was leaving the ballroom last night, or rather had been chased out of the ballroom. He realized that he had not thought of this fact before because, up to this moment, in the last few hours since he had read the notice in the newspaper, he had envisaged the suicide, whose face he didn't know, with Albertine's face. In fact, as he now shuddered to realize, it had been his wife that he had imagined as the woman he was seeking. And once more he asked himself what exactly he wanted in the morgue. Yes, if he had found her again alive, today, tomorrow—or years from now, when and wherever—he would have known her unquestionably only by her gait, her bearing, and above all by her voice—of that he was sure. But now he would see only her body, a dead female body, and a face of which he remembered only the eyes—eyes that were now lifeless. Yes—he would know those eyes and the hair that had suddenly become untied and had enveloped her naked body when they had driven him from the room. But would that be enough to tell him unmistakably whether or not it was her?

With slow and uncertain steps he took the way through the familiar courtyards to the Institute of Pathology and Anatomy. He found the door open, so he didn't need to ring the doorbell. The stone floor resounded under his footsteps as he walked through the dimly lit hallway. The familiar, even somewhat homey odor of all sorts of chemicals, which overwhelmed the smell of the building itself, enveloped Fridolin. He knocked on the door of the histological room, where he expected to find an assistant still at work. To the sound of a rather gruff "Come in," Fridolin entered the high-ceilinged, almost festively illuminated room, in the middle of which, just raising his eye from the microscope, stood—as Fridolin had almost expected—his old fellow student, Dr. Adler, the assistant at the institute, now rising from his chair.

"Oh, it's you," Dr. Adler greeted him, still a little annoyed, but at the same time surprised. "To what do I owe the honor of your visit at such an unusual hour?"

"Forgive me for disturbing you," said Fridolin. "You're just in the middle of work?"

"Unfortunately," answered Adler in the sharp tone that he retained from his student days. And a little more softly he added, "What else could one be doing in these sacred halls around midnight? But you're not disturbing me in the least. What can I do for you?"

And since Fridolin didn't immediately answer him, he added, "That Addison case you sent down to us today is still lying upstairs, untouched. Dissection is tomorrow morning at 8:30."

When Fridolin indicated with a gesture that this was not the reason for his visit, he went on, "Oh yes, of course—the pleural tumor. Well— the histological examination has unmistakably shown sarcoma. So you needn't get any grey hairs over that one."

Fridolin shook his head again. "It's not a matter of any—official matter."

"Well, so much the better," said Adler. "I was beginning to think that a bad conscience was driving you here at a time when others are sleeping."

"Well, it does actually have something to do with a bad conscience, or at least with conscience in general," answered Fridolin.

"Oh!"

"Well, to be brief"—he tried for a dry and offhand tone—"I'm trying to get some information about a woman who died tonight of a morphine overdose in the Second Clinic and who is likely to be down here now, a certain Baroness Dubieski." And he quickly added, "I have a feeling that this so-called Baroness Dubieski is someone I knew casually years ago. And I'd like to know if I'm right."

"Suicidium?"

Fridolin nodded. "Yes, suicide," he translated, as though he wished to restore the matter to a personal plane.

Adler jokingly pointed his finger at him. "Unhappily in love with yours truly?"

Fridolin denied it a little angrily. "The suicide of this Baroness Dubieski doesn't have anything to do with me personally."

"Please, please, I don't mean to be indiscreet. We can see for ourselves at once. As far as I know, no request from the coroner has come tonight. At any event—"

A postmortem examination ordered by the court flashed across Fridolin's mind. That might easily be the case. Who knows if the suicide was a voluntary one? He thought again of the two men who had so suddenly disappeared from the hotel after they had found out about the suicide attempt. This affair might well still develop into a criminal case of great importance. And wouldn't he—Fridolin—perhaps be called as a witness—indeed, wasn't it in fact his duty to report to the police?

He followed Dr. Adler across the hallway to the door opposite, which was ajar. The bare, high-ceilinged room was dimly lit by the two open, lowered flames of a two-armed gas fixture. Only a few of the twelve or fourteen morgue tables were occupied. A few bodies lay there naked, and others were covered with linen sheets. Fridolin stepped up to the first table beside the door and carefully drew back the sheet from the head of the corpse. A piercing beam from Dr. Adler's electric flashlight suddenly fell upon it. Fridolin saw the yellow, grey-bearded face of a man and immediately covered it up again with the shroud. On the next table lay the naked, haggard body of a young man. From another table Dr. Adler said, "Here's a woman between sixty and seventy; she can't be the one either."

Fridolin, however, as though irresistibly drawn, had gone to the end of the room, where a woman's body gleamed faintly in the darkness. The head was hanging down on one side; long, dark strands of hair fell almost all the way to the floor. Instinctively Fridolin reached out his hand to put the head in its proper position, but with a dread which, as a doctor, was otherwise foreign to him, he hesitated. Dr. Adler had come up to him and, pointing behind him, said, "All those are out of the question—is this the one?" And he pointed his flashlight at the woman's head which Fridolin, overcoming his dread, had just seized with both hands and lifted up a little. A white face with half-closed eyelids stared at him. The lower jaw hung down limply, the narrow upper lip was drawn up, revealing bluish gums and a row of white teeth. Whether this face had ever, even as recently as yesterday, been beautiful, Fridolin could not have said—it was now a face without expression; empty. A dead face. It could just as easily have belonged to an eighteen-year-old as to a thirty-eight-year-old.

"Is it her?" asked Dr. Adler.

Fridolin bent lower, as though his piercing look could wrest an answer from the rigid features. And he knew immediately that if it were her face, her eyes, the same eyes that had shone at him yesterday with such passion and life, he would not, could not—and in the end he didn't really want to know. And he gently laid the head back on the table and let his eyes roam over the dead body, led by the wandering beam of the electric flashlight. Was it her body—that wonderful, voluptuous body for which only yesterday he had felt such agonizing desire? He saw a yellowed, wrinkled neck; he saw two small and yet already somewhat limp girl's breasts between which—as though the work of decomposition was already beginning—the breastbone already stood out with terrible clarity from the pale skin; he saw the rounding of her brown-tinged abdomen; he saw how the well-formed thighs now opened indifferently from a dark and now secret and meaningless shadow; saw the kneecaps, slightly turned outward, the sharp edges of the calves and the slender feet with the toes turned inward. All of these disappeared one after the other into the darkness, since the light of the flashlight went back the way it had come, swiftly, until finally it remained, trembling slightly, on the pale face. Instinctively, as though compelled by and directed by an invisible power, Fridolin touched the forehead, the cheeks, the shoulders, and the arms of the dead woman with both hands, and then entwined his fingers with those of the corpse as though in love play. Rigid as they were, it seemed to him that the fingers tried to move, to seize his; yes, it seemed to him as though from underneath the half-closed eyelids a vague and distant look was searching for his eyes, and as though pulled by a magic force, he bent over her.

Suddenly he heard a voice whisper behind him, "What on earth are you doing?"

Fridolin came to his senses instantly. He freed his fingers from those of the dead body, clasped the slender wrists, and with great care, even a certain pedantry, he laid the ice-cold arms alongside the trunk. And it seemed to him as though she had just now, just now this moment, died. Then he turned away, directed his footsteps to the door and across the resounding hallway back into the workroom they had just left. Dr. Adler followed him silently and locked up behind them.

Fridolin walked over to the wash basin. "With your permission," he said, and cleaned his hands carefully with Lysol and soap. Meanwhile Dr. Adler seemed anxious to take up his interrupted work without further ceremony. He had switched the necessary lights on again, turned the micrometer screw, and looked into the microscope. As Fridolin walked over to him to say goodbye, he was already completely absorbed in his work.

"Do you want to have a look at this preparation?" he asked.

"Why?" asked Fridolin, absentmindedly.

"Well, to quiet your conscience," said Dr. Adler—as though he assumed that, after all, Fridolin's visit had been only a medical-scientific one.

"Can you make it out?" he asked as Fridolin looked into the microscope. "It's a fairly new staining technique."

Fridolin nodded without lifting his eye from the glass. "Almost ideal," he remarked, "a most colorful picture, one could say."

And he inquired about various details of the new technique.

Dr. Adler gave him the desired explanations, and Fridolin told him that these new methods would probably be useful for the work he was planning for the next few months. He asked permission to come again the next day or the day after to get more information.

"Always at your service," said Dr. Adler. He accompanied Fridolin across the resonating flagstones to the outer door, which had by now been locked, and unlocked it with his key.

"You're staying?" asked Fridolin.

"But of course," answered Dr. Adler, "these are the best hours for work—from about midnight until morning. Then at least one is fairly certain not to be disturbed."

"Well—" said Fridolin, with a slight, almost guilty smile.

Dr. Adler placed his hands on Fridolin's arm reassuringly, and then asked with some reserve, "Well—was she the one?"

Fridolin hesitated a moment, then nodded wordlessly and was hardly aware that his affirmation might in fact be a falsehood. Because whether the woman who was now lying in the morgue was the same one he had held naked in his arms twenty-four hours ago while Nightingale played his wild piano, or whether the dead woman was someone else, a stranger he had never met before, he knew: even if the woman whom he had sought, desired, perhaps loved for an hour, was still alive and no matter how she now lived her life—he knew that what was lying behind him in that arched room, illuminated by the light of flickering gas flames, was a shadow among shadows, dark, without meaning or mystery like all shadows—and meant nothing to him, could mean nothing to him except the pale corpse of the past night, doomed to irrevocable decay.

VII

Fridolin hurried home through the dark and empty streets, and a few minutes later, after undressing in his consultation room as he had done twenty-four hours earlier, entered his bedroom as silently as possible.

He heard Albertine's calm and even breathing and saw the outline of her head pressing into the soft pillow. Unexpectedly, a feeling of tenderness, even of protectiveness, filled his heart. And he decided to tell her the story of the past night soon, perhaps even tomorrow, but to tell it as though everything he experienced had been a dream—and then, only after she had first felt and understood the utter futility of his adventures, he would confess to her that they had been real. Real? he asked himself—and at that moment he noticed, near Albertine's face, on the next— that is, on *his*—pillow something dark and defined, like the shadowy features of a human face. For a moment his heart stopped beating, but an instant later he knew what it was, reached down to the pillow, and picked up the mask he had worn the night before. It must have slipped down without his noticing it when he was making his bundle this morning and found either by the maid or by Albertine herself. He couldn't doubt that Albertine, after finding this, suspected something, and presumably many more and much worse things than had actually happened. But the manner in which she intimated this to him—placing the dark mask next to herself on the pillow, as though it were his face, the face of the husband that now had become an enigma to her—this playful, almost joking manner, in which both a gentle warning and a readiness to forgive seemed to be expressed, gave Fridolin the hope that she, probably remembering her own dream, was inclined to take whatever might have happened not all too seriously. But Fridolin, suddenly at the end of his rope, let the mask drop to the floor, and, letting a loud and painful sob escape him—quite unexpectedly—sank down beside the bed and cried softly into the pillows.

After a few seconds he felt a soft hand stroking his hair. He lifted his head and from the depths of his heart it escaped from him: "I'll tell you everything."

She raised her hand as if to stop him; he took it and held it in his, and looked at her both questioningly and beseechingly; she nodded in agreement, and he began.

A grey dawn was already creeping through the curtains when Fridolin finally finished. Albertine hadn't once interrupted him with a curious or impatient question. She probably felt that he neither would nor could keep anything from her. She lay there calmly, her arms folded under her head, and remained silent long after Fridolin had finished. Finally—he was lying stretched out beside her—he leaned over her, and looking into her immobile face with the large, bright eyes, in which morning also seemed to be dawning, he asked in a voice of both doubt and hope, "So what should we do now, Albertine?"

She smiled, and with a slight hesitation, she answered, "I think that we should be grateful that we have come away from all our adventures unharmed—from the real ones as well as from the dreams."

"Are you sure we have?" he asked.

"Just as sure as I suspect that the reality of one night, even the reality of a whole lifetime, isn't the whole truth."

"And no dream," he said with a soft sigh, "is entirely a dream."

She took his head with both her hands and pressed it warmly to her breast. "But now I suppose we are both awake," she said, "for a long time to come."

Forever, he wanted to add, but before he could say the word she put a finger on his lips and whispered almost as if to herself, "Don't tempt the future."

So they both lay silently, dozing a little dreamlessly, and close to each other—until there was a knock on the door, as there was every morning at seven; and the new day began with familiar noises from the street, a victorious ray of light through the opening in the curtain, and bright childish laughter from the next room.